INVOLVED

INVOLVED

Walther Habers

SOHO

Copyright © 1994 by Walther Habers.
All rights reserved.
Library of Congress Cataloging-in-Publication Data

Habers, Walther, 1926–
Involved / Walther Habers.
p.   cm.
ISBN 0-939149-95-8:
I. Title.
PT5881.18.A28I58   1994
833'.914—dc20   94-12837
CIP

Soho Press Inc.
853 Broadway
New York, NY 10003

Book design and composition by The Sarabande Press
Manufactured in the United States
10   9   8   7   6   5   4   3   2   1

For Heleen

INVOLVED

1

The boy lay on his belly, anxiously waiting for his homemade sailboat to come out of the culvert that ran underneath the country road.

The driver of the Alfa Romeo was looking into the sky, impressed by the Boeing 747 that glided over and in front of him on its way to the landing strip at Schiphol Airport. The driver saw too late the boy's legs, which stuck out into the road. He hit the brakes the very moment the right front wheel touched the youngster. When the boy arrived at the hospital, there was not much left to amputate.

——

The man couldn't work up the courage to visit the boy. He wasn't guilty . . . at least not according to the police. But they didn't know about the 747. LOOK AT THE ROAD AND NOT INTO THE SKY. He had seen that sign often enough. It would have made the difference of two legs. Half legs, they told him later.

He could still see the little white face, the trembling eyelids and the gray eyes. It wasn't his fault, but if he hadn't been watching that plane, it wouldn't have happened. No one knew that.

He hadn't told Francien the complete story, either. So she didn't understand why he didn't go to visit the child right away.

"But Bram, even though it's not your fault, you could show some interest, couldn't you? Or shall I go and see him?"

"I'll go, but what's the hurry?"

"You're right, he won't run away."

"Hey, do me a favor. Stay out of it, will you? I'll go when I have time, all right?"

"Why not do it right away and have it over and done with?"

"What do you mean, 'over and done with'? Did I hit that boy or did *you?*"

"Sorry. Of course, it's your baby."

Without another word he slammed the front door shut and drove to his garage. He *had* to go to the hospital, he knew. He had to bring something for the boy, he knew that, too. Hendrik-Jan Verwal, twelve, born 7 July in Rotterdam, Bakkerstraat 25 at Gouda. He knew the details of the police report. Twelve years old! Probably called Henkie.

Tomorrow it would be three days since it had happened. Tomorrow Henkie might be in a better. . . . My God, what a thought, as if you only had a foul temper for a day or two after somebody crunched your legs into tatters. Maybe he was being operated on again? He had to go, he knew it. It would not undo the damage, but if he didn't, he wasn't only a stupid driver but also a coward.

———

In the toy shop they had everything: roller skates, footballs, tennis rackets, hockey sticks, the lot. He forced himself to accept that it had to be something for a boy in a wheelchair.

"Well, sir, next I have for you a Porsche with remote control. The best there is," the guy in the shop claimed. "Exactly to scale, perfect steering and a hell of an acceleration. It can do at least sixty kilometers per hour."

With enthusiasm the sales clerk demonstrated it on the shop floor. "Nice stuff, sir. Your son will have a lot of fun with it."

Bram thought the box too large and the paper too cheerful, as if it were meant for a birthday party. He put the box in the car trunk. He would put it in his flight bag tomorrow.

That evening Francien paid extra attention to the meal. She was surprised the accident was not bothering him much. It wasn't at all like Bram to be so cool about something like that.

After dinner he sat staring at the television, without his usual comments. About ten-thirty Francien rose. "A whiskey before we go to bed, dear?"

"Uh, what? . . . uh yes, all right."

He got the ice and she the whiskey. With the television switched off, they listened to the silence.

After Francien had emptied her glass, she got up. "Shall we . . . ?"

"You go, I'll come later."

When he entered the bedroom after two more whiskeys, she was still awake. She started to caress him. She had a healthy body. He put his feeling of guilt aside; at least he tried. However, the real fire wasn't there and when he toiled and toiled to spark it, it crossed his mind that if you still had your knees, you could fuck normally. That killed whatever fire he had in him. He gave up, rolled onto his back and stared at the ceiling.

Francien didn't know what to do. After his reaction that morning, she didn't dare bring up the accident again. He moved onto his side, put his arm around her and she snuggled her buttocks in his lap. After she had fallen asleep, he lay imagining how he would open the conversation with the boy: "So my boy . . ." No. "Hello, young man . . ." "Morning, Henkie . . . May I introduce myself? I'm Bram Aardsen, the man who demolished your legs. . . . How is it now, young man, and what did your parents think? . . . Sorry, man, I really regret it very much, but look what I brought for you. A car with a *hand* control."

Would Henkie ever get as far as owning a real car? Most likely Henkie would now get nowhere, and certainly not far. If your knees were still in order, you could at least fuck normally. After a while Bram got up, went to the living room and drank whiskey until he fell asleep on the couch.

———

The surgeon hadn't had much good news to tell. If Bram hadn't braked, then there would have been something to repair, but not now. If Bram had run the patient over, it would have been better. Yes, he had been on duty when they had brought the boy in. The surgeon had asked where the rest of the legs were. According to the ambulance people, they were plastered over a six-yard skid mark. The only good news: the knee joints were undamaged. First a wheelchair, later prostheses.

Room 528.

The little boy said nothing. He stared in silence at the mound that had been built over his legs. A white face on a white pillow. His white blond hair had dried on his head the way it had been combed. Bram didn't say anything, either. He took a chair and sat down with the flight bag between his feet. The conversations around the other three beds lowered to a whisper. Bram moved his chair closer and rested his elbows on its side. The small face continued staring at the mound. Slowly Bram moved his hand over the small one that lay on the blanket. The youngster looked at him— without reproach, just like someone looking into a shop window. Then the eyes went back to the mound.

"Does it hurt?

The small head on the pillow shook no.

After about ten minutes Bram rose. He increased the pressure on the boy's hand a little, bent over and said, "I'll be back tomorrow." He left the flight bag on the floor.

In the hall he lit a cigarette. When he had smoked it, he went looking for a nurse.

"Are you looking for someone, sir?"

"Yes, that boy, Verwal, how is he?"

"Are you his father?"

"No, the accident . . . I couldn't help it."

"I see. Well, it's very sad. Since he came out of the anesthesia he hasn't said a word, neither to us, nor to the other children. According to the police, his mother is in a hospital in Gouda. We don't know the where-abouts of his father. He was staying with an aged aunt in the Haarlemmer-meer who can hardly walk. There hasn't been anybody to visit him as yet."

"I'll be back tomorrow. . . . By the way, I left something on the floor for him."

Not waiting for a reaction, he walked down the corridor and took the stairs to his car, where he sat, his hands on the wheel, staring at nothing.

———

"Have you finally thought to see that child?" Francien asked that evening while she was pouring the coffee.

Bram nodded. "I've been there."

"And? How is he?"

"Jesus, woman, what do you mean, how is he? He was dancing with pleasure, okay?"

"My God, I'm only asking."

He was unfair, she thought, feeling locked out. They could have gone to the hospital together. She knew better how to cheer up people than he. They could have talked about it, anyway.

"Sorry," he said. He knew he was rude. "I'll go again tomorrow."

"C'mon," she insisted. "Didn't he say anything?"

"No."

"And you?"

"I asked him if he was in pain, and he shook his head."

"That's all? Didn't you sit with him?"

"Yes."

"Did you bring him anything? Candy or something?"

"A toy car."

"Well, that'll do him a lot of good! You would've done better buying him a book. A nice book for boys, with adventures. That would take his mind off his problem."

Bram didn't know any heroes in books who were in wheelchairs. There was the pirate with his wooden leg, but that was it. And Ironside, but he was a jerk.

"Were his parents there?"

"No, they don't know where his father is and his mother is in a hospital in Gouda."

"In a hospital, too? What's wrong with her?"

"I don't know, I didn't ask."

"But doesn't she know what happened to her son?"

"Jesus, I don't know!"

Francien gave up. She would go and find out for herself, tomorrow. Bram wasn't handling this properly.

The next day Francien phoned the police.

Her husband wanted to visit the boy from the accident, but he had lost the name of the boy and the hospital and could they help her out. When they told her where the boy was, she asked about the parents and learned that the father was somewhere in America and that the mother was in the Van Dam hospital in Gouda. No, they did not know what was wrong with her.

That afternoon she went to see the boy, but the doctors were busy with him. Could she please come back in the evening? Or another day?

Next she phoned Bram. Would he be late that evening? He thought he would.

Well, that was no problem, because shops were open late Thursday night. She would go shopping with her friend, Marjet.

. . .

The Porsche stood on the mound. The remote control was still in the box under the bed. The face of the boy was as pale as the day before, but now his hair had been combed into loose platinum curls.

When Bram sat down the eyes glanced at him for a moment.

"Super, isn't it?" the boy said.

Bram nodded.

After a while the boy turned his head again. "Did they find my boat?"

"What boat?"

"The police. Did they find my sailboat? I made it myself. I lay waiting for it to come out of the culvert".

"Was that why you had your legs on the road?"

"Yeah, stupid, huh?"

"I'll ask the police tomorrow," Bram promised.

They stared at the Porsche in silence. Bram said, "Does it hurt?"

Again the boy shook his head, and again Bram had nothing more to say.

———

It was only when Francien entered the house at nine-thirty that evening, that she realized she'd better not tell Bram about her visit to the mother of the child in Gouda. He apparently considered the accident his business, and she knew he didn't like her to meddle. Not that the meeting had been such a success, on the contrary. It had been antagonistic from the first moment. The woman was good-looking, even though she had no makeup on.

Yes, she knew what had happened to her son. Yes, it was very sad she couldn't see him.

When Francien asked why she was in the hospital, she answered it was because she had problems with her back.

Francien tried again. "When do you think you will be released?"

"As soon as possible."

"Should I give the child your regards?"

"No, that isn't necessary. He knows I can't come, and I've talked to the surgeon."

The woman didn't volunteer any further information.

After a while Francien left. Once outside she became angry. So much for trying to help. Arrogant bitch. A call girl for sure.

On the way home she decided to leave the matter alone. She hoped Bram would be himself again soon, for when he was like this it made her uncertain.

"Well," said Bram, "you took your time. Did you buy anything?"

"No, I tried on a few things, but nothing fit. I'm too fat. Starting tomorrow I'm going to do something about it. Have you eaten?"

"Yes, I had a sandwich. This afternoon I had lunch with the president of the factory—Signor Lantini," he added superfluously. Francien knew who the big boss was.

Again she had the feeling that something was odd. That she was being kept at arm's length—the same feeling she had had with that woman in Gouda.

When they went to bed Bram tried to fuck without using feet. He managed but it took a long time. Francien was the one who benefited and fell asleep five minutes later.

————

In the morning Bram went to the police station to ask if they had found the toy boat. It would have been nice to bring it along that evening, but the police hadn't found it. He could buy something like it, then at least he wouldn't arrive empty handed, but that wasn't the same.

Maybe it was still somewhere out there?

He drove to the airport and searched the ditches on both sides of the road. He found nothing. It would've been too good anyway.

When he walked back to his car, he realized he hadn't checked the concrete culvert. He looked down the country road in both directions. There were no cars in sight. Flat on his belly, supporting himself with his hands, he lowered his head, and peered in. In the middle something stuck out of the water. A branch and something else . . . That could be it. Craning his head a little more to the left, he saw the silhouette of a small sail. But how to reach it? He needed a fishing rod. He got up and looked around, more for an idea than for a rod.

The shortest distance between two points was a straight line. Just get into the culvert, and bring the thing out. Very simple. But then he would have to take his clothes off. As manager of a car-importing company, swimming in a country ditch was not exactly an everyday event.

Come on, don't be a shit, he told himself. Just go and get the thing.

From far away came the hum of a tractor: a farmer turning hay. Bram had undressed quickly before, although for other purposes. He pulled his tie loose, then unbuttoned his shirt and unbuckled his belt. In one movement he pushed down his pants and drawers, sank his naked bottom onto the grass and shucked the whole lot off in one go, including socks and shoes. Coat and shirt also went together and in a moment he was up to his knees in mud, and up to his groin in water.

He felt the bubbles of the marsh gas climbing up the inside of his thighs. The culvert was smaller than he had thought. Floating and supporting himself on his hands, he moved into it. Every now and again his hair got stuck on the rough concrete ceiling but, walking with his hands on the culvert bottom, he reached the branch and the little sailboat. Moving backward with the boat in one hand was difficult, so he decided to push ahead to the other end with the boat in front of his face the way a water-polo player pushes the ball.

Struggling to get out of the culvert, he passed over a sharp branch underneath the water. It scratched his chest and belly. He did not feel it. Reaching the ditch, his hands lost the firm support of the bottom and sank deep into the mud. His head shot underwater and he started swimming, but his legs were still in the narrow space of the culvert and he grazed his knees on the concrete. It was only when he stood upright in the ditch with the little boat in his hands that he saw the countrywoman, leaning over her bike, attentively studying his manhood. She was a real farmer's wife. Hay arms and a lap that could hold a litter of piglets.

"Where did *you* come from all of a sudden?" he asked in an indignant tone as if he were fully dressed.

"I should ask you. This isn't a place where one goes swimming. Don't you have trunks?"

He saw no way to explain the situation, so he waded to the side of the ditch and pulled himself up by a tussock of grass. However, the pull of his body when it came out of the water, was more than the tussock could bear, and he tumbled back into the ditch. The second time, he managed it. Dripping wet, his legs muddy up to his knees, he still had the full attention of the woman. A couple of yards away the little boat sailed peacefully away on a light breeze.

Angrily he dove back in. His belly, landing flat on the water, gave a loud splash. With two strokes he reached the boat.

Back on the bank, he walked toward his car. The woman followed. "Were you hot?" she said.

He dried himself with an old raincoat from the trunk and put on his shirt and coat in one go. The woman revelled in watching him. His prick, partially hardened by the woman's scrutiny, peeped out between his shirttails. Looking down at it and at his muddy legs, he realized he was quite a sight. He went back to the side of the ditch and cleaned his legs. Once he had hoisted himself into his trousers, he felt better.

"You'll come here again to swim?," she asked, getting on the bike.

"And you'll come again to watch?"

"You bet," she laughed and rode off.

He picked up the toy boat. It had, with enormous patience, been sandpapered into shape from a massive piece of wood. The letters H. V. were delicately burned into the wood on both bows. It had a mainsail, a foresail and a rail. Of course, it was ridiculous what Bram had done, but it was a nice piece of work. He felt pleased with himself. He put the vessel on the backseat, got into the car and drove off. After a while he pulled up his trouser legs a little, because his knees were smarting. A few kilometers farther, he pulled over and examined his knees. A few scratches. From the first-aid box he cut two plasters to size, stuck them on and forgot about it.

He decided to go to the hospital that afternoon instead of in the evening so as not get home late again. He didn't want another interrogation by Francien. She wasn't a bad wife, neither in bed, nor in the kitchen, but . . . "Have it over and done with it," she had said.

———

The boy's face was still ashen, but his eyes followed Bram from the door till he was seated. The Porsche stood atop the mound.

"It can really go fast," Bram said.

"How fast?"

"It easily goes sixty."

The small face expressed disbelief.

"You can run it around the floor if you like." Bram took the remote control from the flight bag, which still sat under the bed, and handed it to the boy. Then he realized that when you are flat on your back you can't see the floor, and the boy probably couldn't sit upright yet. He lifted the Porsche from the mound and held it aloft. "Give it some gas."

The boy looked at him questioningly.

"The handle with the knob—push it forward."

The boy did. The rear wheels spun with a screaming noise, shocking him into releasing the handle. Cautiously he tried again, and soon managed to control the speed of the wheels. His face lit up.

"If you move the handle left or right you can steer it at the same time."

Bram held up the Porsche and the boy mastered it quickly. He discovered by himself that the wheels spun backwards when you pulled the handle towards you.

Bram watched him drive along imaginary roads, overtake imaginary cars. It was fascinating to see. The youngster had colored from excitement. After ten minutes Bram had a stiff arm.

"Let's take a break." He moved to put the Porsche back on the bed.

"We are not allowed to stop here. Wait!" The boy accelerated, steered a few curves, executed parking manuvers and killed the engine. "You can put it down now," he said, and let his head fall back onto the pillow.

"Where did you learn that?"

"I have a dinky toy with a steering wheel."

"What do they call you?" Bram said.

"At school they call me Binkie, but my mother doesn't like that. She calls me Dick."

"My name is Abraham but they call me Bram."

"Did you go to the police?"

"Oh, yes." Bram picked up the plastic bag from the floor, took the boat out and handed it to the boy.

"They *really* did have it?!"

"No, it was still stuck in the culvert."

A fingertip followed the line of the hull. "So that's why it didn't come out. You know, I didn't really notice about my feet. . . . Now you won't come back anymore, will you?"

"I will. When is your mother leaving the hospital?"

Dick shrugged. "She hurt her back."

"Herniated disk?"

Dick nodded.

After a while Bram rose, pressed the small hand and left. The gray eyes followed him to the door.

When Bram arrived home there was a visitor. A stocky woman in coat and skirt. Francien rose from her chair.

"Bram, this is Mrs. Jas of the Adoption Council. Madam, this is my husband."

Jesus Christ, Bram thought as he sank into his chair. Just plain forgot;

glad I didn't go to the hospital tonight. Francien would have phoned and nobody would have known where I was—and that woman sitting there all the time, watching.

"Can I get you a glass of Spa?" Francien asked him.

"Spaaa?! . . . uh . . . yes, that will be fine." He got the message: no whiskey.

When he and Francien were seated behind their glasses of Spa and Mrs. Jas had her second orange juice, he thought he might as well do his bit.

"So, you came to see what kind of people you are dealing with. I mean, it must not be an easy task to judge where a child will find a good home."

"Not always." The eyes were observant. "You operate a garage?"

"Yes," answered Francien, my husband is head dealer for Alfa Romeo for the entire country."

Bram would have preferred to give his own answers. The woman's gaze moved attentively from Francien to him. Francien went on: about how her husband was liked by his staff and that he knew everything about cars and that he was such a safe driver—that, too, *nota bene*—and the nice holidays, and that they often went walking together, and that they loved nature, and on and on. When their perfect marriage, their affluence and their harmony with society were exhausted as topics, Mrs. Jas leaned forward a bit.

"Why do you really want to adopt a child?"

The direct question took Bram by surprise.

Mrs. Jas waited.

Then Francien said, "Well, you see, because I want it, and a child is not a dog, otherwise we would . . . have taken . . ."

She left the sentence unfinished. She felt something more apt should have been said and looked to her husband. Bram found it an odd way to put it, but it covered the crux of the matter.

"And you, sir?"

"Yes, we want a child, not a dog."

That was all he could say. Nothing of the nice sentiments about giving one's life meaning, a task, the warmth, passing on the values and the right of every child to a place it could call its home, and that they were convinced they could supply that and that they hoped Madam would share their opinion. Nothing, nothing of that at all. He had tried the nice phrases out on Francien, thereby convincing himself. Francien had admired him for it.

Mrs. Jas told them about the multitude of applications, explained the procedure, warned them not to set their hopes too high, and left.

When Bram saw Mrs. Jas walking down the garden path, he sighed with relief and went to pour himself a whiskey.

Francien turned back from the window. "For God's sake, where were you?"

"Why, I arrived in time, didn't I?"

"That's not what I mean. The question, why we wanted to adopt a child. You knew it all so well before. *You* had all the words and phrases ready and then all of a sudden you say nothing."

"But you answered the question correctly. A child is not a dog and that is it. Very simple."

"Yeah, yeah, it's me again who's simple," she said.

"Come on, that woman can take an honest answer. Don't worry."

"Don't you think I spoiled it? What must she think?"

"Simply that we want a child. It would have been much worse if she had the idea that it wouldn't make all that much difference to us. But do me a favor next time with your Spa water, will you?"

"If she sees you drinking whiskey, she could easily hold that against you," Francien said.

"Come off it, that woman may not be beautiful but she isn't stupid. I'm not a Spa man. By the way, how long was she here?"

"About half an hour. If only I haven't spoiled it with my silly answer!"

He put his arm around her and pulled her close to him.

"Of course not. Besides, that was no way to put a question like that. You don't ask people why they eat, do you? They eat because they are hungry."

While Francien laid the table, Bram switched on the television. Crossing his legs, he felt the plasters on his knees. Better remove those before going to bed, he thought. With her habit of spotting every pimple, bruise or scratch, and demanding an explanation for each, he knew he couldn't possibly explain. She would loathe the story and most likely not believe it at all. Remembering the ditch, the farmer's wife and his prick, he smiled. The retrieval of the little boat felt good.

"What's so funny?" Francien asked when she entered from the kitchen with the meal on a tray.

"Funny?"

"Yes, you were smiling. What were you thinking of?"

"I don't think I was smiling, and anyway, my thoughts are mine."

"You were laughing about me and my stupid remark."

Bram rose. "Oh, please, come off it. I told you it was a straight answer to a straight question and, come to think of it, much better than the whole bunch of balanced phrases I had in mind."

"You really think so?"

"Listen, I don't tell you all my thoughts, but when I do, they *are* my thoughts. Come on, let's eat."

Apart from the usual, "How do you like it?" and his, "Fine, fine," they ate in silence, Francien wondering what it would be like to have a child to look after. Bram was wondering how long it would take before the boy would be released from the hospital.

Later, on the toilet he flushed the plasters away. Hardly a trace left. Relieved, he entered the bedroom, got into bed and reached over his head to switch off the light.

"What have you got there!?" Francien exclaimed pointing at his chest.

"Where?"

"*There!*" and she pointed from his chest to his groin.

He looked and saw three red lines, like nail scratches, extending from his chest over his belly and disappearing into his pubic hair. The culvert, it dawned on him.

"Gee, I never felt it," he mumbled.

He saw flames come into her eyes. Hurriedly he invented spare parts jumping out of sockets. A spring, a ventilator belt . . .

"*Whoremonger!*" she hissed.

Just in time he saw the claw with the red nails coming. Catching it and bending over her, he forced her powerless onto the mattress.

"You *lie,* I *see* it!"

"You're wrong," he tried to soothe her.

They were both right, but they weren't to get around to that. Her aggression made him hard, inside and outside. She tried to wriggle from under him, but her left arm was stuck under his body, and with his leg over hers, he had her caught and she knew it, and she hated it. The more she fought to free herself, the harder he got. Aggression with sex wasn't new to them. Sex became war, peace came after. He pushed his knee between her thighs, opening up her legs.

"*No! No! I will not!*"

With one push he moved on top of her and planted his other leg inbetween as well. Her left hand, free now, hammered on his ear, the back of his head and his neck. With both hands he grasped her buttocks, pressed her belly against his and pushed into her.

As if she consisted of two women, her nails dug deeper into his back and her legs wrapped around his hips. She had dug her teeth into his shoulder and tasted blood. The pain only stimulated him. Together they reached a violent climax, after which they remained sticky and motionless, stuck together, their panting gradually diminishing.

A minute passed. She drew her nails out of his back and lowered her legs. He slid onto his side and turned onto his back. Francien felt humiliated and satisfied, and he felt satisfied and yet displeased with himself.

Gradually he began to feel the damage the nails had done and that was somewhat justifying. With one finger he smoothed the hair from her forehead and started to stroke her softly.

The second time he came slowly, late and gently, with Francien's arms around his neck.

Exhausted, she nestled her bottom in his lap. He switched off the light, slid a hand around a breast and before he could think up a plausible explanation for the scratches, he too fell asleep.

As Francien awoke at ten o'clock the next morning, Bram was already at 30,000 feet, no doubt observing the movements of the lithe stewardess. The glow of sex always lingered long in him. Memories slowly penetrated the hazes of Francien's sleep. On the pillow and the sheet were blood spots. She had gone mad again. She despised that, acting as if she were a wildcat. She wanted to be sweet and soft, talking gently and intelligently. But when she got jealous, she flew into rages.

Were they nail scratches? How could a woman scratch a man over the front of his body? Only if you rode him as he lay on his back, but Bram didn't like it that way. It would disturb him, as surely the scratching would. No pain for pain's sake. But the story about spare parts flying around, that was bullshit.

She stretched full-length. Her body felt fine and that was strange. She rose, changed the sheets and took a bath. Lying in the hot water, she was sure that Bram loved her. Otherwise, he couldn't have been so nice the second time. Yet he could be so closed, and when she didn't know what was in his mind, she got nervous. It gave her the feeling she didn't really matter. Still, she shouldn't fight like that. But what else could she do? A guy did what pleased him and then forgot about it. If she were stronger than he, it would not have happened, but she wasn't. She was a woman and smaller, so what else could she do? As a matter of fact, it had been pure rape, she thought, but did it feel like that? The second time wouldn't have been possible if the first time had been rape. She shuddered at the thought of something like that being forced upon her by a total stranger. Only Bram could get away with it, she was sure.

The water cooled.

While she dried her body in front of the big mirror, she looked at herself carefully, stretching her arms above her ears so that her breasts came up a little. Not that they were sagging—she could still wear a blouse without a bra. She turned her left side to the mirror and tried to pull in her stomach, but it didn't work. Men could do it. Men were apparently built differently. The telephone rang.

"Marjet here," the voice said. "Coffee?"

"Where? I am stark naked."

"Why? Is Bram still at home?"

"No, he went to Milan for the presentation of a new model."

"Didn't you have to join him?"

"Me? No way. All those petrol groupies make me feel old."

"Okay, coffee at your place then. In ten minutes? See you!"

———

". . . so I don't know. He hasn't been the same since that accident, but these scratches . . ."

"It's possible. How old is Bram now?

"Forty."

"You see, Francien, after all the climbing, men get scared when they reach the upland plain of their life. There's no more mountain to climb, so they climb Mount Venus."

"Why? He's got all he wants."

"That's not important. Once a man is on the upland he realizes for the first time that from there on it's a straight line to the end."

"But what should I do? You can't expect me to—"

"Oh yes, I can. Listen. *If* it's true, the more fuss you make about it, the sooner he'll be gone, because your hollering makes the other woman look like the most understanding, sweetest lady there is. It's not difficult to look up to a man with adoring eyes when you've just fallen in love with him. Suppose he really has a girlfriend, and you keep yelling at him, where do you think he would prefer to be?"

Francien sipped her coffee and lit a cigarette. "So you think . . . ?"

Marjet nodded. "Bram is not a bad guy. He provides food, shelter and satisfaction, doesn't he? They all have something peculiar. Take my advice. Don't make a fuss, don't nag, and most of all don't bully him, and you'll be all right. Have you already made holiday plans?"

"The usual. The visit to the factory in Milan, and then on to Viareggio. You?"

"Yes, and this time it's the two of us. The kids go to a holiday camp. Thijs wanted us to be by ourselves for once."

"Where are you going?"

"Rome."

After they discovered they were to be in Italy at about the same time, Francien suggested they should spend a day or two together in Viareggio. Marjet liked that. They kissed good bye.

When Marjet was gone, Francien sat on the couch for a while. Their talk hadn't been very helpful. Deep down she had always felt inferior to men. They just did things, made passes, made love, made children, airplanes, furniture, wars, perfume—the lot. A woman just had to accept what they cared to make. She liked the protection, of course. Who wouldn't? But she felt inferior. Men mastered subjects faster, jumped easily to conclusions, all without making fools of themselves. And when, for once, *she* was the first to answer a question, she was sure to make a fool of herself.

What did she really do? She washed clothes, cooked meals and made love. If only she had been more than a nurse before they married—a doctor or something—that would have made a difference. She wished she had something of her own. Something she was really good at. If only she had made a career. . . . But ifs and buts didn't help. There he was, being important in Milan, and here she was, washing, cleaning, cooking, having coffee with Marjet, and now waiting for him to come home. *If* he deigned to come home. *If* he *was* in Milan.

Should she phone the garage? No, don't make a fuss. If only she could be sure. If only they had children . . .

After two sherries she felt better. She would wait and see when he came home. Would he bring a present . . . to make up for it? To make up for what? After the fourth sherry she stretched out on the couch and fell into a worried sleep.

When Bram came home at eight, he had no present and she was none the wiser. Either he had nothing to make up for, or he wasn't bothering anymore. She put it out of her head, glad that he was there.

He said, "It took much longer than scheduled. I nearly missed my plane. I missed the duty-free shop. In the plane they do have things for sale, but they had nothing I liked. By the way, have you seen my lighter anywhere?"

"No, but it'll be in one of your suits, as usual."

The next morning he checked all his suits and didn't find it. That thing always made him a little nervous. A Dupont, gold, a present from Francien. She had really been extravagant. He couldn't just lose it. Earlier he had thought that he had, which had given him a sad feeling of something irrevocable. Of course, he could buy a new one—there were thousands of Duponts for sale in the world—but you couldn't just replace it. That would devalue the gift, as if the care of choosing and the decision taken weren't that important. It would be somewhat the same if people who had lost a child would think, Okay, we'll make a new one. That new individual could never be a replacement. He knew that it was silly to compare it that way, just a lighter, but well, he was like that. He got attached to objects. The longer they lasted, the more he loved them until they weren't really replaceable anymore. A new car never meant much to him until they had gone a long way together. The less it let you down, the more intimate it became. Could he have lost it during the swimming excursion, when he had rushed out of his clothes?

The next afternoon he went back to the culvert to look for the lighter. As he squatted in the grass, searching, the same countrywoman came pedaling down on her bike.

"You hot again?"

"No, I didn't come for a swim."

"Are you looking for something?"

"Yes, my lighter. I am rather fond of the thing."

"A square one, of gold."

"Yes, that's it!"

"This?" she said, the Dupont between thumb and forefinger.

2

Dick told Bram they let him ride in a wheelchair one hour every morning. "Later I'll get artificial feet. Do you think I'll be able to walk normally then?"

Although he didn't think so, Bram said he thought Dick would. He didn't like to think about the boy's future.

Bram continued visiting the boy in the afternoons. In that way he avoided a lot of questions from his wife. Unconsciously he assumed Francien would have thought it excessive and pressed him to stop, or she would have insisted on coming along. He wanted neither option.

Dick's mother had been operated on for her back. It had been decided that Dick would stay in the Haarlem hospital till his mother was released.

A couple of days later Dick met Bram in the corridor in a wheelchair, steering the Porsche in front of him.

"Tomorrow Mama is leaving the hospital. She phoned. If you bring me, I can go home tomorrow."

"Well, that's no problem. I'll come and pick you up around two P.M., okay?"

Bram didn't know much about it, but arrangements had to be made when one came home in a wheelchair. Regarding thresholds, for instance, and maybe other things.

That night he drove to the hospital in Gouda and introduced himself.

Blue eyes, straight black hair, a long slender body, Grecian profile, long fingers and long lashes.

"Nice that you visited Dick so often." The voice was soft and clear. "He is apparently very fond of you. He phoned that you will bring him home tomorrow."

Bram nodded.

"He was such an agile boy." She bit her underlip, blinking her eyes against upcoming tears. "How is he really? Does he talk about how it will be later?"

"He only asked me whether he would be able to walk normally on prostheses. I said yes. What else can one say? It'll be hard enough for him later on. He is crazy about cars, I understand."

She nodded. "Yes, from the time he was a toddler. You know what worries me a lot? I can't lift him because of my back and he will have to be lifted some times."

"He'll have to do a lot on his knees. I'll see if I can find kneepads, the kind that roller skaters use and we can cover the thresholds with sheet iron for the time being, so that they slope up and down."

She nodded.

He brought the metal sheets the next day and the kneepads. When he took the blanket off the legs to lift the boy into the car, he saw for the first time the damage he had done and had to force himself to push his arm under the remnants of the legs. The boy weighed so little, even less without feet, he thought.

"Nice car." The small hand stroked the upholstery. "Real leather?"

Bram nodded.

With difficulty he managed to get the empty wheelchair into the back seat. He seated himself behind the wheel. Dick had already fastened his seat belt.

"Okay, yes, here we go," Bram said, without knowing what he was heading for. "I went to see your mother last night. She'll be at home by now, I guess."

"Can she walk all right?"

"Yes, but she must be careful lifting things."

"Then you better come and live with us to lift me on to my wheels. Now I'm a man on wheels. That's not so bad after all, because I always wanted to become a race driver."

Bram put the car in motion. It was all too simple for him. The boy had lost both his feet. Racecar driving was out of the question for him, but what wasn't? Walking, cycling, tennis, soccer, skating.

With a heavy heart he steered out of the parking lot and set out for Gouda. He avoided the Polder, took the A-9 and, after that, the A-4 till Leidschendam. When they were on the provincial road, Dick asked Bram if he thought the Porsche would be able keep up with them.

Bram shrugged. "The man in the shop said it could do about sixty kilometers per hour. But I doubt whether its road contact will be good enough for that speed, though the surface here is nice and even."

"Can't we try?"

"Well, I don't know. How will you steer it?"

"Out the window. I can sit on my knees, they are still okay."

"All right, let's try."

He stopped the car and got the box out of the trunk. Dick had worked himself around on his knees and hung half out the window. Bram put the Porsche in front of the car and handed Dick the remote control. When he got back behind the wheel the little car was already far ahead of them.

"You've got to hurry!" Dick cried. "Otherwise I'll be home long before you!"

Tires shrieking, Bram started the pursuit. The guy in the shop had not exaggerated. Bram was doing ninety before he began to gain on it. He caught up. The Porsche really did go between 60 and 70.

Dick kept the Porsche nicely on the road. Bram was glad that nobody overtook them, because he wasn't sure whether the Porsche would have survived. It would be horrible if the boy, on top of everything, saw his car demolished.

Dick's hair was flattened by the wind. Tears blew out of his eyes. He was fully concentrating on the tiny toy in front of them. As Alphen aan de Rijn approached, Bram tapped him on the shoulder and signaled to reduce speed. He pointed to a parking lot and Dick steered the Porsche into it.

Once Bram had stopped the car, the Porsche ran another lap and came to a standstill at Dick's side. Dick sat back on the pillow, opened the door and reached over to pick it up. Misjudging the height, he toppled out.

Bram had gotten out of the car and was around back, picking up the Porsche. He hadn't seen it happening.

"Damn it, what are you doing now?" he shouted when he saw Dick on his back on the ground, clutching the Porsche.

"Nothing, I just fell. I didn't think I was sitting so high."

Bram bent over to pick him up. Dick held up his hand and put the Porsche on the floor in front of the seat.

"Let me see if I can get back in. He turned on his knees, keeping the stumps off the ground.

"Those little stones hurt."

"Wait, I've got something. Stay where you are."

Bram got the kneepads from the trunk. Dick watched Bram buckle the first one on. He managed the second one by himself.

"Good idea," he said, looking up to Bram with adoration. On his knees, holding up the little stumps in the cutoff stockings, he crawled up against the car, got one knee on the chassis, clawed the front seat for a hold, found the hand brake and hoisted himself in. His face was flushed with excitement and exertion, pearls of sweat glistened on his upper lip. Bram had watched, speechless and very moved.

Back behind the wheel Bram lit a cigarette and realized for the first time what the word *cripple* really meant.

With one hand braced against the dashboard, Dick picked the Porsche up from the floor.

"That did go well, didn't it? We should do that again. At Zandvoort . . . Yeah, that would be great. On the racetrack they have such nice curves. If I had a racecar with a handle like this, then I could easily drive it."

"What about the shifting?"

"Well, that wouldn't be a problem. I've still got my two hands!"

One didn't win races with an automatic transmission, Bram thought, or did one? Anyway, not without brakes.

They reached Bakkerstraat 25.

Since Dick now knew that getting out of the car was more difficult than getting in, he willingly let himself be put in the wheelchair. While Bram got the metal sheets from the trunk, Dick wheeled towards the entrance. He could just reach the button of the intercom.

"It's me, Mama, the man on wheels!"

With the sheets tucked under his arms, Bram followed Dick into the hallway. Dick was already waiting in the elevator. On the gangway to his front door Dick increased his speed. Bram slowed. He saw the boy stop, turn 90 degrees and get stuck against the threshold. Two slender arms reached out to help him and then he bolted out of sight. Bram paused, then approached. He entered and closed the door behind him.

They were on the couch, holding each other. Dick had his eyes closed: a

23

white face and platinum curls against her black dress. She had tears in her eyes. The wheelchair had been overturned in their meeting.

How can a mother like her have such a white blond child?

He felt he had entered too early. He put the wheelchair upright and went to fit the metal plates over the thresholds. Only the one over the front-door entrance didn't fit.

"And this is Bram," said Dick, who had forgotten that Bram had already met his mother. She rose slowly, long and slender.

"My name is Pauline. I didn't even introduce myself yesterday. You understand . . ."

He nodded.

"I go faster than him," said Dick. "He had to go up to a hundred before he could catch up with me."

Pauline looked questioningly from one to the other.

Bram pointed at the Porsche, which sat on the floor. She didn't understand, but since it was apparently something between the two of them, she would hear all about it later. On the couch, Dick turned himself on his belly, slid onto the floor and crawled on hands and knees to the wheelchair. He tried to get in by putting one knee on a foot support and the other on the seat, but he failed. The seat was too high. Pauline's heart was in her mouth and she looked at Bram, who watched intently.

"You should have an in-between support," Bram suggested.

"If I can get into it by myself, nobody has to lift me," Dick said. "If the other foot support could be higher on the bar, I could use it as a kind of step-up, and when you have no feet, you don't need foot supports, anyway."

"That can be fixed. In the workshop at the garage it'll be fixed in no time."

I can do it myself, Bram thought. The welding gun and the blow torch had no secrets from him. During the weekend, because it was nobody else's business.

Dick hobbled over the threshold into his room. Pauline rose and slowly straightened her back, supporting it with the palms of her hands.

"Anything I can do for you," Bram volunteered.

"I think I better look in and see what he's up to."

"*Bram!*" Dick called from his room.

"It's you he wants," Pauline said. "Go ahead."

Bram went. Dick had maneuvered the wheelchair to the ladder at the foot of his high bed. He looked sideways at Bram. "That won't be easy."

"No, certainly not." The ladder stood rather steep. Dick moved the chair against it, pulled the brake and tried to hoist himself onto the rungs. It didn't work. The ladder came to him instead of he to the ladder.

"Can't we fix it? A rope?"

They both looked around. No rope in sight. Bram went back to the living room. "Do you have some rope?" he said.

"In the kitchen drawer, maybe. Does it have to be strong?"

"Yes, rather."

"What I have is only good enough for small packages. A belt maybe? In the bedroom on the inside of the closet door. The door over there."

The bedroom had the same strange fragrance as her perfume. Women's clothes were always so colorful. There was a lot of silk among the items. He picked two belts with solid clasps. With a waistline like hers, one belt would surely be too short.

When the ladder was fixed, Dick climbed it on his knees and stretched out with a deep sigh.

"Tired?" Bram said.

"Yeah, my legs are throbbing."

"That's not surprising after all the hassles today. Stay there for a while, then the pulsing of the blood will diminish."

"And? Did it work?" Pauline asked when Bram came back into the living room.

"He's in bed. His legs are palpitating. He did have an exciting day."

"Would you like a drink. . . . Bram, if that's all right with you?"

"Sure, and I would like to have a beer, if you got it. Shall I? And can I bring something for you, too?"

"A glass of hot water. I'm a model, my waistline is my equipment." Her eyes were even bluer than his.

"Shall I pick Dick up the day after tomorrow, that is Sunday? Then I can change his chair in such a way that he can get in and out by himself. About two o'clock?"

"That'll be fine."

He told her a bit about what he did for a living and when he had finished his beer, he gave her his card in case she might need him.

When he shook her hand, she kissed him on the cheek. "Thank you for looking after him, Bram."

Dick had fallen asleep.

. . .

As he drove he could hear her voice: "Thank you for looking after him."
Thank you for demolishing his legs?

Back in the garage he snapped at his people, grumbled about what had
and hadn't been done, and didn't wish them a good weekend. After they
had left, he sat in his office and stared out the window, unable to sort out
his feelings. Toward seven he sighed, shrugged, and left.

When he came home Francien asked where he had been. She had
phoned to find out whether it was all right for Thijs and Marjet to come
that night. "You weren't in and normally you tell them where you can be
reached."

"Maybe I forgot. What have you arranged?"

"They are coming, so let's eat quickly. Don't you notice anything
special?"

He looked around.

"No, at me!"

She looked fine. Her dress fit tightly, but he'd seen that before. "You look
fine. New makeup?"

"I spent two hours in the beauty parlor. You *do* see it."

He went up to her. She did look well. She was thirty-eight. The white of
her eyes was still really white. With both his arms around her waist, he
pulled her stomach against him and kissed her on the lips.

"See you later, alligator," she said, and disengaged herself from his arms.
"It's already seven-thirty."

———

The evening was pleasant, the way it should be for the well-to-do middle
class. Marjet asked Francien if she had bought herself something new of
late, and they talked about fashion. About the magnificent things they had
seen, but regretfully couldn't wear anymore. About moisturizing emul-
sions, foundations and other remedies the cosmetics industry produced to
make a woman believe that the effects of forty years of wind and weather,
of the burning sun and the saltwater of the Mediterranean, of car fumes
and emissions of the chimneys of that same chemical industry, could be
undone with a splotch from a jar.

Bram was listening with one ear. The buttocks remained nicely white,
he thought. One should be able to move one's skin from one part of one's
body to another. At least women should.

"What do you think about the situation in Iran?" Thijs asked. "Haven't those people there fallen years behind?"

"Sure, but what do you expect, when religion gets the upper hand." Bram retorted.

"What do you mean? I happen to be religious, too."

"If you need religion," said Bram, while he poured himself a fourth whiskey, "then you want to exist even after you are dead. That's just ordinary cupidity. You can't accept that you are only allowed a short interval down here, and then have to knock off because it's somebody else's turn."

Thijs put his glass down and bent forward in his chair. "It's religion, man, that keeps the world together. Otherwise, no conscience, no law and no order. The world would be populated with nothing but gangs of thieves and killers, all standards gone, everybody motivated only by his own greed. But of course, it has to be the true religion."

"Then what about wars like the one between Iran and Iraq? Fifteen- and sixteen-year-olds flying straight to heaven, with automatic rifles blazing, taking others along with them, but not to the same heaven. If that were the case, wouldn't they be surprised? They all think *they* have the true religion, don't they?"

"Obviously, but they have a wrong idea of God. God is love."

Bram saw the stumps again. "Yeah. God is love. With the blood spilled in the name of God, one could color all the seas of the world dark red. Real greed is not a bigger car, a stereo system, a video camera or what have you. No. It's heaven, because that's forever and completely happy. Those guys who sell religion, they are very clever. If you promise everybody a Rolls Royce, you wouldn't find a dog who believed you. Everybody knows what it costs. And they would immediately worry about its petrol consumption, the road tax, and the insurance premium for such a car. No, sir, much too practical. Heaven, that is far away, somewhere over the clouds and there you don't eat, don't shit. Nobody has yet expressed an opinion regarding fucking, but the little angels on the ceiling all have little prickies, so girls are apparently not among them. That again would be too practical, for what would a guy do then, finding his three girlfriends and his own wife there. No, they keep it vague but marvelous and the more unbelievable, the more believers."

"Boy, Bram, why are you so steamed? Is something bothering you?"

Bram decided he disliked Thijs's mustache, especially the ends sticking straight out. Those surely should serve to compensate for the narrow shoulders, he thought venomously.

Francien had also noticed the hostility in Bram's voice. But please, she thought, not at Thijs. Thijs was a darling, with his perky mustache, his undulating blond hair, and he was always very caring with Marjet. Bram would do better to take him as an example. Thijs was not coming and going as he pleased.

"Yes, Bram," she said, "you always get worked up when you talk about religion. You better get us another drink, will you?"

As Bram went to the kitchen to fetch more ice, he heard Francien say to Thijs, "He's like that sometimes. Don't let it bother you."

Bram drank a glass of water and got mad at the ice tray. The blasted thing! The ice always stuck. He cut his finger. He did not feel it because of the cold and whisky, but he saw it.

He returned to the living room with a bottle of sherry, the ice bucket and his handkerchief around his finger. He said, "By the way, Thijs, what about a new car? I'll pay you fair value for your old one. The new model would fit you perfectly."

Later at the front door Thijs said, "Till Sunday, old boy," and patted Bram understandingly on the shoulder.

"Old boy," Bram repeated, as he closed the door and leaned against it. "Old boy, my ass."

When he entered the room Francien had already removed the glasses. *Abrupt* was the word for it. His glass hadn't been empty.

"Pleasant, wasn't it," Francien said.

———

Sunday afternoon, at one o'clock, Bram rose from his chair and took his golf clubs out to the car.

"You are early. You only have to be there at two. Don't you want any more coffee?"

"Yes, please." And sitting down again he pushed his cup toward her.

"Say, Bram," Francien began after she had poured the coffee, "I have been thinking about Friday night. I think it's not good to be so adamant. You'll rebuff your friends. And Thijs is your friend, isn't he? He *did* arrange the building permit when you wanted to expand the garage?"

"Well, it's better to get excited about religion than about a moisturizing emulsion."

Francien didn't understand. What did that have to do with it? She had thought that this would be the right moment to talk reasonably.

"Bram, what's the matter with you? You are being so difficult lately. Is the business not going well? The sales of new cars are down, I read that."

"*That* has nothing to do with it. This year down, next year up. I won't lose any sleep over that." Bram noticed he had stressed the word *that*. However, Francien had missed it and so she went on: "I only mean that you . . . like with Thijs, he comes here for company."

"Maybe you're right. It makes no sense anyway." Bram finished his coffee, rose, patted her shoulder.

Dick, wearing the kneepads, met him in the hallway. When they reached Bram's garage in Haarlem, the youngster was impressed. "Is this all yours?"

Bram nodded, put him on a workbench and gave him welding glasses. "Don't look into the light, you'll spoil your eyes."

He cut one foot support loose with the blowtorch, sawed an oversized pipe in two lengthwise, welded one half to the footrest and then the footrest halfway up to the bar of the wheelchair. After having filed away all the raw spots and polished them with sandpaper, he got a silver-color paint spray from the storeroom and sprayed the welded spots in the same color as the aluminum of the chair.

That's easy, Dick thought, having looked on closely.

"Now let's see if it works." Bram lifted the boy from the bench and put him on his hands and knees in front of the chair. Dick grasped the seat, leaned his upper body on it, put one knee on the lowest support, then the other on the higher one, and got himself into the chair without much trouble. He looked radiantly at Bram.

"You know, I really do hate being carried. Now I can get in it by myself. Don't need anyone anymore."

Bram fetched a Coke from the machine and they went into his office.

"Are you in here the whole day—the boss?"

"Yes, something like that, but I'm not here the whole day."

"And those cars, they are shipped from Italy?"

"Yes, from Milan"—and pointing at the wall—"that's an aerial picture of the factory." He pulled open a drawer, got some leaflets out of it and after searching through them, gave one to Dick: "That is our top model, Road Star Grand Tourissimo. It goes two hundred, eighty kilometers per hour."

Dick tried to look through the window into the hall. "Have you got it here?"

"No, they sell better at the Riviera."

Dick opened the folder and his eyes shone like the gloss on the color picture of the Road Star.

All together it had taken more time than Bram had thought it would to modify the. One hour in the workshop, twice up and down to Gouda, and a long chat with Pauline. She was fascinating. White became her as well as black. At the door they had shaken hands.

"Dick will miss you, Bram."

It made no sense anymore to go to the golf course. On the way home he thought about it: "Dick will miss you." Would he? And so what? How long did you care afterward? He didn't know. Nor did he know what should be done next. He hadn't said farewell. He shrugged. We'll see.

When he walked up the garden path the front door opened. He started to parody a royal bow, but stopped when he saw Francien's face. "What's the matter, lass?"

"Where *were* you?"

"Why?"

"Thijs just phoned to see if there was something wrong with you, since you hadn't shown up at the country club."

Bram passed through the foyer and put his clubs under the stairs. "Just a moment," he said, and went to the toilet. While he sat there watching his feet, he noticed little burn holes in his trouser legs; there was also some paint on his fingers. When he came out, Francien was standing there, waiting for him.

"Have you got acetone? I've got some paint on my fingers."

"How do you get paint on your fingers?" Francien asked, walking to the dressing table in the bedroom.

"At the garage. And I also have a few holes in my trousers from the blowtorch."

"At the garage?"

"Yes. I have an appointment with the dealer in Leiden on Monday, and I had left his file in the office. Since I was early anyway, I went to pick it up."

"And then found you had forgotten the key of the safe, and you cut it open with the blowtorch, is that it?"

Bram grinned while putting on another pair of trousers.

"Well, it's not exactly like that, but when I wanted to drive through the gate, there was a guy in front of it, stuck in a broken-down wheelchair. He couldn't move either way."

Bram put his arm around Francien's shoulder. "Come along and I will tell you the rest. A sherry?"

Getting the drinks, Bram continued: "The guy came from IJmuiden and was training for the marathon. He asked if I would phone a cab for him, but when I saw it was just a broken axle I suggested I weld it. That really was a weight off his shoulders, because he hadn't known how to pay for the taxi and the repair of the chair on top of it.

"When the thing was fixed, it was too late to go to the club, so we talked a while about his chances in the marathon and what the trick really is, apart from the fact that you need strong arms. The problem for him was that both arms had to be equally strong, otherwise you pulled the chair a little bit out of line with every push, and it costs energy to correct that. He had been paralyzed from birth, had no job. Had had one for sometime, but his wife could earn more than he, so he ran the house and looked after their child."

Relieved, Francien refilled their glasses. "You have to call Thijs back. A good thing that he phoned me only just before you arrived, otherwise I would have been sweating all this time."

Damn it, Bram thought as he picked up the telephone.

———

The whole of August he hadn't been in touch with her or the boy. However, somewhere in his head it had been decided that he would go and see Dick before he went on holiday.

Tuesday was best. Francien would have her bridge evening then and wouldn't be home before midnight. He phoned ahead but nobody answered. He had bought a miniature of the Grand Tourissimo and decided he could always put that in the mailbox if nobody was there.

He had lingered at the flower shop. He did not want a common or garden bouquet and he didn't see anything that expressed his feelings. A crossbreed between a daisy and a baccarat might, but they didn't have that.

When he walked to the flat at seven-thirty that evening, he saw Dick coming the other way. When Dick saw him, he came speeding up so fast that he couldn't stop the wheelchair in time. He hit Bram's shins. Bram tumbled forward and clutched the back of the chair for support, while

Dick threw both arms around his neck. About to topple, chair and all, Bram sank quickly to his knees. And there he was, on his knees in the street and a boy around his neck.

"Mama was right!"

"Right?"

"Yes. She said you would come back and see me. Come on, I'll show you something."

In the living room Dick pointed at the couch. "You sit there and close your eyes and when I say *open,* you look. Got it?"

Dick rolled out of the room and Bram closed his eyes. He smelled Pauline, faint but clear.

"Open!"

A fifty-centimeter-long model of the Grand Tourissimo slowly rolled towards him and stopped at his feet.

"Where did you get *that?!*"

"Surprises you, doesn't it?"

It did indeed and Bram's face showed it. Dick was enjoying himself.

"I don't understand. How did you get this model? At the factory they are really misers about this. You get one only if you buy the real thing. Tell me, how did you get it?"

"Mastermind, man!" said Dick, proud as a peacock. "I had that folder from you, and in it was the address of the factory. I wrote to them that you drove my feet to pieces, because I had them out on the road, and that I wished to be a race-car driver later, but that I didn't yet know how, without feet, and wondered whether they had a model of that car. And then the parcel came yesterday."

"But did you write to them yourself, in Dutch?"

"No. Mama asked that, too. The Bosom, she translated it for me, and then I rewrote it myself."

"The Bosom?"

"Yeah, the geography teacher. She's not bad."

Shaking his head in astonishment, Bram sat looking at the boy.

"What are you shaking your head for now? You think I shouldn't have asked? Mama didn't think it such a splendid idea, either."

"It's all right with me. I am only surprised. You are a go-getter, aren't you."

Dick smiled happily.

"Isn't your mother home?"

"No, she had a show this afternoon. She'll be here any moment."

Bram picked up the model from the floor. It was a beauty.

"A pity it doesn't have an engine, otherwise it could race the Porsche," said Dick.

"Then you'd need your left hand for one of the two and that one would always lose."

Searching for his cigarettes, he felt the dinky toy in his pocket but left it there.

Dick told about how he went to school, and that he had a separate desk now. They had taken away a few thresholds, and he was allowed to use the teachers' toilet because that one was big enough for the wheelchair. He had a kind of step-up for his knees, though when he had to shit it was quite a maneuver.

Bram forced himself to ask it, because he had to know: "Are you serious about wanting to become a racecar driver?"

Dick looked him square in the face and after a few moments said, "Do you think it's still possible?"

As Bram took his time to frame an answer to this straightforward question from that open face, Dick continued: "If I have a handle to control the power and the steering with one hand, and I can shift with the other . . . only the brake . . . I don't know, but I must be able to do *something* with what I've got left?"

He looked at Bram inquiringly, but Bram didn't know about the brake either, nor about the clutch, although what with all the electronics in the future . . .

"I don't know, Dick. Given all the ongoing technical developments . . . Let me think about it during my holiday."

"When are you going?"

"Next week."

"Oh . . . long?"

"Three weeks."

"And will you come back then . . . here I mean?"

The front door opened and Pauline entered.

"Hello, Bram, you're here. That's a surprise!"

She settled near Dick, kissed him and brushed away the curls from his forehead. Then she shook hands with Bram. "I'm working again."

Underneath a black, ankle-length cape, she wore blue silk and a handwide sash of black leather.

Later that evening, after Dick had gone to bed, Bram asked Pauline how he had managed in the past weeks.

"He is very busy trying to solve all his problems and finding all kinds of solutions. He's a referee on the school soccer team, but that's very tiring and they run over him once in a while since he can't get out of the way quickly enough. He refuses to join in sports for the handicapped. He doesn't want to be an invalid, so he just doesn't admit he is one."

"He says he wants to be a racer," said Bram, "but God knows how."

"You know what his latest game is? Sitting on his bed, driving the Porsche through the corridor, into the living room, round the table and then back to his room, where he's laid out a track, and then back into the living room. He wants me to clock his laps."

"But from his bed he can't see where he is going, can he?"

"That's right, so I have to tell him to go right or left. In his opinion one should be able to drive a track blindfolded as well."

Bram shook his head. "That stupid accident."

"It could have been worse, Bram. His head is still intact and he's handling it marvelously. But I must admit I do worry a lot, too, about all that he'll have to face. But he fancies you, you know."

Bram sighed.

"Where are you going on holiday?" she said.

"Italy. First I call at the automobile factory and then to Viareggio. An apartment—years already—sunshine, nice beach, reading, shopping, a trip here, a trip there. You know."

Pauline had been to Sweden the last two years with Dick, who liked to go camping.

"Camping, *you?*"

"No, not really, but he's fond of it and Sweden is so quiet. Not for any price will I ever go on holiday to Italy again. Did it once. But with a figure like mine you don't have a moment's peace during the entire holiday. Italians think they are irresistible, but they're insufferable for a woman alone."

Bram was wondering about her husband, but asked about her work instead. At the door Bram felt like holding her in his arms, but only held her hand a little longer.

3

They arrived in Milan later than Bram had planned. They reached the factory only in the afternoon and the president, Lantini, had insisted on their having dinner with him. The apartment in Viareggio had been booked in advance as usual, but Bram had still asked Lantini to phone that they would arrive late. It was now after ten and dark. Coming from the Strada del Sol to the coast, they had just passed La Spezia and were heading south when the steering wheel started pulling to the left.

Bram wondered if it was crosswind or a flat. In a parking lot along the highway it appeared to be the left front tire. He was glad that he hadn't left the spare underneath all the luggage this time but had put it upright in the trunk. After taking one suitcase out, he got the spare and rolled it forward. As the nuts squeaked loose, a large old American cabriolet with three unsavory types in it rolled slowly into the parking lot. In passing, the characters in the coupe looked at Bram and Francien. About forty meters farther down they stopped. Cigarettes were lit. Francien saw their faces light up red when they drew on the fags.

"I think we better hurry up, Bram."

"That's what I'm doing."

He asked Francien to wind down the jack, while he rolled the flat tire to the back of the car. As he lifted it into the trunk, he heard car doors slam and saw the three men walking toward them.

The tallest, one step ahead of the other two, shot his cigarette butt away with a long glowing arc. Bram went to get the jack, but Francien didn't have it down yet.

"Mit das Weib koennen wir uns schön amusieren."

Francien felt cold fear running down her spine as she realized they were talking about amusing themselves with her.

Bram turned his back to Francien and waited for them, the blood draining from his face.

The tall one, apparently the leader, halted in front of Bram: slender, wiry, broad leather jacket, long narrow legs, thumbs in the waistband, balancing on the balls of his feet.

"Nice car, hey."

The other two positioned themselves on either side of Bram. Bram had imagined situations like this many times before in nightmares and had figured out all possibilities of escape, but waking up had so far been his only salvation, and his stiletto was at home in the drawer of the nightstand. It would not have helped anyway, even if it had been a one-to-one fight. These guys would be far faster with a knife than he. The eyes would possibly be the only thing they were not prepared for. Supremacy neglects its defense. He had read that somewhere. When the guy at his left moved behind him, he knew that his time was up.

His left punch to the face of the tall one was knocked aside as if the guy were chasing away a fly, but his simultaneous right with two fingers spread was not expected and hit both eyes with full force. For a second the leader remained paralyzed, then he bowed his face into his hands.

"My eyes. you dirty bastard!"

Before Bram had recovered from the astonishment of his success, the guy behind him jumped on his back, pinning both his arms. The third one in front of him swung a full blow. Bram managed to save his nose but not his eye. Unable to use his arms, Bram tried to kick the man in the groin, but the guy pulled back. Bram saw the shoe coming. With his right leg lifted he protected his groin and caught the kick on the outside of his thigh. And then—he was loose, so suddenly that he half fell toward his opponent. Bram rammed his head into the face. The guy stumbled backward and fell over the leader, still on his knees. Before the attacker could scramble up, Bram was at him and kicked him hard in the nose. He drew back for an other kick but the fellow lay motionless.

Jesus Christ! Get the hell out of here!

He jumped back, snatched the jack out of Francien's hands, flung it into the trunk and slammed it closed.

"Come on, don't stand there staring—scram!"

Francien hadn't yet closed the door when he lifted the clutch and the 192-horsepower flung the car forward with screaming tires.

"The suitcase!!" Francien screamed over the roar of the engine. She hadn't yet fastened her seat belt. Her head hit the windshield hard when Bram slammed on the brakes, threw the car gnashing into reverse and shot back full throttle. Braking near the suitcase threw Francien back in her seat.

Bram jumped out of the car, tossed the suitcase on the back seat and shot off, passing the three guys again, two of whom lay motionless. The tall one was still on his knees with his face in his hands.

On the autostrada, going well over 200 kilometers an hour, Francien recovered. She saw Bram, bent over the wheel, pale in the reflected light, peering tensely ahead. The car radio was on but was drowned by the whine of the engine and the wind.

"Bram!"

No reaction.

"My God, Bra-am! If the police . . ."

That hit home. He stretched his arms and released the throttle . . . 190 . . . 180 . . . 170 . . . 160 . . . 150 . . . At 120 the engine hummed with friendly confidence. Francien passed him a lit cigarette. His hand was shaking. He took it and inhaled deeply.

The sign VIAREGGIO emerged from the darkness. Still 25 kilometers. Slowly the adrenalin eased off.

"Are you all right?" they asked at the same time. It was only then that Bram felt that his right leg really hurt. Francien carefully touched the growing bump on her forehead.

When they turned off the freeway and entered Viareggio, Bram stopped at the side of the road and killed the engine. Then there was silence in the car. The terror of the attack and the elation of the escape neutralized each other. They sat staring through the windshield for a while.

"What a scum," Bram muttered, but there wasn't much venom in his voice. His leg was hurting pretty bad. He got out of the car. Broken? No. Air sucked through his teeth when he tried to stand. With one hand leaning on the car he tried a few steps. It hurt a lot. He got back in the car.

"I want a drink and I've got to pee," Francien said, as they pulled away.

Five minutes later Bram stopped in front of the apartment. It was nearly midnight, but the caretaker was still there.

"Signor Aardsen, signora, buona sera. You late, telephone from Milano."

Getting the suitcases out of the boot, Bram saw the jack. There was blond hair on it. He closed the trunk and stared at Francien, who stood beside the car, her face in the shadow of the street lamp.

The man attacking from behind had turned him loose all of a sudden. Francien? He felt a warmth inside.

The caretaker picked up the suitcases and led the way. The fight with the Germans along the freeway was nobody's business, Bram thought. To hide his limp he put his arm on Francien's shoulder for support, and together they walked into the building like a loving couple.

Bram sat on the edge of the bed, his trousers at his ankles, examining his thigh. It was scratched, the bruising not yet visible. Francien got a bottle of whisky out of a suitcase. She always took one along for you-never-know. After two glasses, the heat, the quietness and the safety spread through their bodies. In the meantime Bram had taken off his shoes, trousers and socks.

"That guy behind me, you knocked his brains out?"

"Yeah, he collapsed like a pudding," she said. Francien knocked back the rest of her drink, rose and stretched herself like a stalking panther. "I want to go to bed." The skirt floated down, the panties had stayed behind in the bathroom. The silk blouse slipped off her shoulders, along her buttocks and onto the floor. Looking at the ceiling, she unhooked her bra.

Then she took Bram by the shoulders. Kissing him, she pushed him backward onto the bed.

On top of him Francien climaxed with a cry of triumph, her arms straight up, her fists clenched.

———

Bram sat on the beach under an umbrella. He wore Bermuda shorts to hide the big blue spot on his thigh and sunglasses to hide his black eye.

He saw two plainclothes policemen approaching. What a profession, he thought. In that heat with a trilby hat, raincoat with belt, and black shoes in the white sand. They halted in front of him, exactly far enough apart that he could fit between them.

He knew what was coming. He had started the fight. Those three guys had only wanted to have a chat with him, maybe see if they could be of any help. And, then, you didn't just stab somebody's eyes out.

He rose and, between them, he walked toward the ice cream stalls.

They had missed Francien. That was good. She had just gone for a swim and would surely be smart enough to swim straight on, through the Straits of Gibraltar and then turn to the right to Holland. Or did Italy have a navy? Never heard of it. Her Majesty's Ravioli? He grinned, but no, he shouldn't do that. If these two knew he was laughing at the Italian navy, it would surely make things worse.

Would they like an ice cream?

No, they did not want an ice cream.

The guy at his right (they really did look like twins) watched Bram's leg. He limped, he knew that, and the guy had seen it and glanced knowingly at his partner, who had seen it, too, and nodded, barely noticeably, but all the more threatening. They were convinced they had got the right guy.

Bram thought it very unfair: That leader had gotten some dirt in his eye, and now they blame me for it. But after they'd grabbed him, it had been self-defense, and they can't arrest me for that. I hit his eye by accident. Intended to pat the guy on the shoulder but the guy had made an unexpected move, that's what had happened. Anyway they won't get Francien, or would Holland extradite her own people? He wished he had cleaned the hair off the carjack.

Behind a camping table, sat the boss of these two. He looked at Bram from beneath very heavy eyebrows. There were dogs with hair that hung in front of their eyes, too, and you thought they couldn't see very much, but apparently they did.

Bram was allowed to sit down. He felt the iron legs of the chair sink deep into the sand.

Would Bram like a cigarette?

Yeah, yeah, he knew about that too. First put you at ease and then, once you've relaxed . . . bang, your front teeth down your throat. Should he go along with it? Maybe better . . . wouldn't make any difference. He would have to eat his front teeth anyway.

On the table was a glass of red wine. Would Bram also like a glass of wine or perhaps a Heineken? He was very much tempted to choose the Heineken, but that might be considered insulting to Italian wine.

"Wine, please."

From over his shoulder came a bottle, long fingers and a slender arm. As the woman poured him a glass he felt a bare breast on his shoulder. A pity he couldn't turn around, but if he did they would have him for sure.

When the man took a sip, Bram did the same, but he did not have the nerve to touch glasses.

Then the man put his glass down in the sand beside his chair. The sunlight sparkled beautifully in the red wine against the white of the sand. The man leaned forward on his elbows.

"Signore, terminato!"

That was quick,' Bram thought, he hadn't even finished his wine. He wondered whether he could still catch up with Francien. With his sore leg, he doubted it. Maybe with a speedbo—

"Signor violenza! Si, si, signor, always violence." Then at the top of his voice: "Signor *Violenza*."

Apparently the situation was different from what Bram had thought, but if there was somebody who didn't like violence, it was he.

The man arched his eyebrows and looked straight at him with black eyes.

Well, if those eyes are the mirror of his soul, Bram thought, then that guy can forget about heaven all together.

Bram looked back with his innocent blue eyes, but he had his sunglasses on and dared not take them off because of his black eye. Shit, wasn't this unfair. He had only come for a vacation.

With a bang the man slammed his open hand on the little table.

Yeah, yeah, Bram got it—of course he shouldn't be thinking cheeky thoughts. A guy like that knew right away. He had been in the police business a long time. You saw that immediately.

They shone a searchlight in his face. The third degree, he realized. A hand on his shoulder forced him to look at it. He tried to lift his glass from the table to throw the wine into the lamp, but the glass seemed rooted. With an enormous effort he lifted it. It was more pushing than throwing. When he fell toward the lamp, table and all, somebody pulled him back. He felt nails in his shoulder.

Francien shook him until Bram opened his eyes and looked at her. Recognition slowly dawned.

"Say, you dream deeply. Can you fix the window? It's creaking. I tried to slam it shut but that didn't work. Can you have a look at it, otherwise it'll go on all night."

"Please switch off that light."

Francien pulled the string of the overhead fixture and switched on a bed lamp.

Carefully he got out of bed, sparing his sore leg as much as possible. After working the mechanism back and forth he managed to close the window tightly.

When he came back to bed, Francien crawled toward him.

Of course he had dreamed the harsh light and the blow, but he *had* started the fight. That was a fact. If all three of them would testify to that—nice boys, never hurt a fly, mothers there, plus a lawyer—then he wouldn't stand a ghost of chance. Blind for life, plus the blow with the jack. Francien wasn't exactly an Amazon, but in panic one can hit hard and the jack was heavy. What should he do now? Pack up and flee? That would surely draw attention and show guilt. If one was dead and one of the others had the number or the make or even only the nationality of his car . . . his arrival time would fit the incident perfectly.

It took quite a while before he fell asleep again.

———

Francien woke first. It was nine o'clock, the sun shone and the colors of his eye ran from yellow to green to nearly black.

She must have struck really hard, Francien thought. She sat up, arms around her knees, and experienced again how the jack had hit the skull. The hood had collapsed. Men were not as invincible as they had you believe. One good blow and that was all there was to it. Could Bram be felled that easily, too? She studied his head, the graying hair. Why had she always been so afraid of men, or not really afraid but impressed by their strength?

She got out of bed. Under the shower she studied her arms, her belly, her legs. She did look good, well muscled. Humming, she rubbed herself dry, and when she came back into the bedroom Bram was awake and worried.

"Hello there, awake? How are you?"

Bram cautiously got up from the bed and tried his right leg. He could stand on it, but the bruise was blue-black now, about the size of a hand.

"That leg and that black eye will get you a lot of attention on the beach."

"And that's exactly what we don't need. If you killed that guy, there'll be a police investigation. Maybe we better go to the police ourselves and tell them the story," he said.

"What?! Go to the police?! Don't be silly. We have given these hoodlums a good hiding. They got their lesson. So, it hasn't anything to do with us anymore. We are definitely not going to sit in a police office and surely not in an Italian one. It would be mad. Furthermore, I'm hungry and I want to go to the beach."

"But I can't go to the beach like this, and not to the breakfast room, either."

Francien looked at him, surprised. "Don't be silly. It's only a black eye."

"No, together with a dead guy along the autostrada, *and* someone with his eyes stabbed out *and* an unconscious guy on top of it, it's not just a black eye."

"You are kidding yourself. Those thugs got out of there as fast as they could, afraid that we'd send the police after them. That's what I think. You don't really believe that they stayed there waiting for a patrol car to pass by? They'd have to wait all night, anyway, because the police are never there when you want them, as we found out again this time. Moreover, how do you know for sure that one is dead or that the other one is . . . injured? There wasn't too much light and you really did have something else on your mind than examining what was wrong with them. Come on, Bram, you're just tired. You needed a holiday long ago. The accident with that child and now this. But it ended well, didn't it? You know what I'll do? I'll go and have breakfast and bring something for you, and after that you can go to the beach with your sunglasses on. I'll also buy you Bermuda shorts, if that'll make you feel better. You can keep them on in the sea. That leg, it's not a pretty sight."

He sank back on the bed and sighed.

Francien stepped into her panties, fished a dress from a suitcase, slipped it over her head and combed her hair with her fingers.

"I'm back in a jiffy. Come on, don't be so difficult, please?" She patted him encouragingly on the shoulder and walked, hips swinging, to the door.

"Francien!"

"Yes?"

"Bring a newspaper, will you?"

"De Telegraaf?"

"No, Italian, preferably local."

"But darling, how do I know which is a local newspaper? You can't read Italian anyway."

"Please try. As long as it doesn't have Roma or Milano in the name."

"You think we'll have made the headlines: WOMAN SLAYS AUTO-STRADA ROBBER!"

Bram looked up at the ceiling in despair.

"Okay, I'm off. By the way, are you hungry?"

"No."

"I am," With a superior smile she turned around and left the room, leaving Bram behind, astonished. He heard her confident heels on the corridor marble fade away.

Francien with self-confidence, with an air of recklessness?

He took a step in the direction of the bathroom. Pain—his leg. With that much pain he wouldn't even reach the beach. Slowly he tried again. He should work the stiffness out of it.

After ten minutes limping up and down the room, he was soaking with sweat, but at least he could walk. Herniated disk, that's what he could say if anyone asked him. He needed warmth—that's what he came to Italy for—and it would be well after a week, to Italy's credit.

He filled the bath, hot. Looking in the mirror he was shocked by his eye. He did look awful. The heat of the bath helped. Maybe Francien was right in that he saw ghosts.

When he had finished sweating out his fear in the hot bath, he heard her footfalls again. She had coffee, rolls, a newspaper and a parcel. She dropped the paper and the parcel on the bed and put the breakfast on the small table between the easy chairs. The headline: ASSASSINIO LUNGO LA AUTOSTRADA

With one blow the nightmare was back. *Assassin* was murderer in French and together with the word *autostrada* he knew it was their case the article was referring to. It was also clear that the police hadn't assumed the guys they had found were the culprits. He tried to read the story. "Un morto . . . un cieco? . . ." One death, anyway, and it had happened somewhere along the autostrada, north of Marina di Massa, but that was all he could figure out. He tried to learn whether the police had a clue, or if they knew the nationality of the suspects, but he didn't see anything that looked like it.

"Well," Francien asked, "are we in it?"

"Not us, but the case is."

"Fine, now don't let your coffee get cold. I want to catch some sun."

Bram gave up. It made no sense—done is done and *if* he had wished to do so, he should have told the police his story last night. Now it was too late. He forced himself to eat a roll, washing it down with the coffee.

"Look, what do you think of these?" Francien proudly held up a pair of Bermuda shorts. "I hope they fit."

They did. A quarter of an hour later they were on the beach. Francien lay on a towel in the sun. Bram was already sweating, so he sat under the umbrella. He had brought the newspaper with him and tried to figure out more about the story. In the end he gave up and put the paper beside his chair on the sand. Every now and again he looked toward the ice cream stalls, but no one came on the beach looking like the plainclothes policemen from his nightmare.

When they had swum in the sea, they walked back to their chairs. An Italian stood reading his newspaper. He and his wife had taken the chairs next to theirs and he threw Bram an apologetic look. "Scuzi, il suo giornale?"

Since it was his paper, Bram nodded, whereupon the man produced a melodious stream of Italian sounds, none of which Bram understood. The man looked at him questioningly.

"Parla italiano?"

Bram shook his head.

"Inglese?"

"Yes."

"I read terrible. Two German tourist, one dead, one blind. Very bad for Italy, for tourist business."

"Yes, I understand." Bram saw his chance. "Do they know who did it?"

The man went on reading, his lips moving with the text.

"No, police do not know yet, but happens many times now. Police thinks same criminals all the time."

Bram lowered himself slowly into his chair.

"You bad leg?"

"No, bad back," Bram said, pointing at the small of his back. "Herniated disk." He was glad of his sunglasses and the Bermuda shorts.

The man offered him his newspaper back, but Bram waved it away.

"See, they know nothing," whispered Francien. "Come into the sun, that will do you good."

Bram spread his towel in the sand, lay down on his stomach and was asleep in minutes. He was tired, exhausted to the marrow of his bones.

After half an hour, Francien woke him with an ice-cold can of beer on his back. He was sweating like hell and had great difficulty in returning to consciousness.

"You've got to turn over, otherwise you'll burn."

The cool beer did a lot of good.

After lunch they went to their room and had a nap. By four o'clock they were back at the beach. From one of the stalls Francien brought back two double whiskeys on the rocks.

Sitting in the deck chairs, sipping their drinks, their feet in the soft sand, the light breeze from the Mediterranean making the heat agreeable, they looked at the people on the beach and in the sea.

"Bram, you really think I killed that guy?"

"It's very possible."

"Serves him right. Good riddance. The three of them were attacking you. But I can tell you this, it's a great experience to see a guy like a tree tumble down like a rag doll."

Bram looked at Francien. "If it hadn't been for you we wouldn't be sitting here."

"If it hadn't been for you we would not be sitting here, either."

"Cheers."

"Cheers."

After they finished their drinks, Francien went for another swim. Watching her well-shaped, well-kept body walk through the shifting sand with powerful pushing steps, Bram shook his head. How could it be? He felt like a criminal and she felt like she deserved a medal.

That evening Francien wanted to go out for dinner. They found a decent restaurant with waiters in black, white tablecloths and a candle on each table. The menu was international and the waiter lit the candle while they chose dishes. There were a few other couples, conversing in low voices. It was very quiet till the pianist filled the space with a medley.

Over soup Francien watched Bram closely. His eyes moved uneasily from table to table, back to her eyes, on to the waiters and back to her eyes again. He didn't like to be scrutinized.

"What do you want?" He just managed to swallow *from me.*

"I want you to look at *me* instead of all over. Looking for something sexier?"

"If I wanted that, we should have gone someplace else."

"I wouldn't mind," she said.

"Don't forget, this is your choice."

"Yes, because *you* don't like Italian food. I would rather eat pizza under fishnets with dripping candles and a sentimental tenor to match, but I can't get you to set foot in a place like that. As a matter of fact I would also like to vacation somewhere else for a change. For years we have been coming to Italy. If only for once we went some other place in Italy, but, no—to Viareggio. Year after year. And always the same apartment. When we go home, we can just as well leave our things here, we'll be back anyway."

Bram let the spoon sink back into his plate. Speechless he sat staring at her.

"But . . . but you're the one who is always bragging about Italy. How clean the beach is, how lovely the weather and how pleasant it is that they know us. Jesus, girl, what's the matter with you? Is it about last night?"

"That has nothing to do with it. I can want something else, can't I? But you always have to go to the factory, to see that sticky Lantini with his clammy hands."

"And *you* found that man so charming, not such a Dutch clodhopper!!"

"Puh."

Francien finished the soup and so did he. The waiter brought their dinners. Bram watched Francien pensively. Her solid red-brown hair, the roundish face with matching nose, the small shoulders, the breasts, visible in the gloss of the silk. He knew her from crown to crotch, from top to toe. Her feet, her calves, the thighs and the buttocks she sat on. In scent and color he knew her. At least he'd thought so.

He said, "Of course we can go somewhere else, why not? But I never knew you didn't like it here."

"I didn't say that, but now I'm fed up with it. My God, another few years and I can forget it."

"Forget what?"

"You know what I mean."

"You're still young and you want something, is that it?"

"Maybe. But I'm not all that old yet. Am I?" she said.

"Shall we leave tomorrow? We can go to France or Yugoslavia or we can stay in a hotel in Switzerland." She shook her head. "That would be nice, but we can't. We've already paid for three weeks, and Thijs and Marjet will be here tomorrow on their way to Rome. I arranged with Marjet for them to stop over for a day, remember?" She scrutinized his face.

"You *do* want to go, don't you? You are still worried about yesterday. I don't understand it. We just let that bunch of scum have it and—"

"Oh no," Bram interrupted. "All of a sudden I visualized how you would like to go waterskiing on the lake at Geneva or riding on horseback in the Languedoc. Have your picture painted in Montmartre. Go sailing on the Mediterranean or drink sherry with a bullfighter in a small bar in Toledo."

"Oh yes, if that were possible!"

"Then you better watch out. Men who regularly look death in the eyes develop insatiable desires."

"I can handle that, don't you worry."

Bram was surprised by her self-confidence. He didn't know her to be like that. He said, "Las Vegas, or Hollywood would be nice, too, or a safari in Africa."

The caretaker stood in front of the apartment, talking with a man. When they passed him with a "buona sera," he called after them: "Signor Aardsen! Un momento per favore!"

They halted. Bram took his arm from Francien's shoulder. He started to take off his sunglasses, but just in time remembered his black eye. The man with whom the caretaker had been talking was definitely not a tourist. Dark suit, light shirt, dark tie.

"Mister here wants to talk to you," the caretaker said, pointing. The man approached and showed a card with a small picture on it. "Battoni."

"Police," the caretaker added.

"You, from Holland?"

Bram nodded.

"Your car, please."

Bram pointed it out parked near the entrance of the small lot. The man beckoned Bram to come with him and walked in the direction of the car. Bram followed, doing his utmost to hide his limp. Dammit, why hadn't he cleaned the jack, stupid ass that he was. He'd had the whole day to do it. Instead he had brooded all day.

Francien caught up with them. "What does this fellow want?"

"I think it's about yesterday."

"Oh yes? Then leave it to me." And with a few steps she was beside the man.

"Hey, maestro, we have no business with you at all. We are on vacation—vacanza, signore—and now we go to bed. Dormire and you get lost, will you?" Then she turned around and put her arm through Bram's.

"Come on, we go to bed. We have no business with this Baritoni, or whatever the jerk's name is."

Battoni refused to put up with that and showed Francien his identity card. "Polizia!"

"Yes, young man, nice picture. Bella photo, bambino," and pushing his arm aside, they went into the building, leaving the officer behind. The fact that they didn't look like autostrada robbers made him hesitate.

In their room Bram leaned back against the door, his arms limp along side his body, shaking his head.

"What's it this time? Didn't I handle this nicely?"

"Your act was terrific, but it solves nothing. The jack."

"What about the jack? You mean my fingerprints are on it? So what. Can't I change a wheel once in a while? Emancipation, my boy. You should have a drink. You look awful and your eye looks even blacker."

Bram put his sunglasses on the small table, sat down and invited Francien to do the same.

"The jack has hair on it from that guy you conked."

"So what? Then he has a bald spot on his head. Serves him right. As a souvenir. Now he might think twice next time."

"But since he's dead, the police will want to know how it happened. And it was me who started the fight."

"Oh Christ, man, what else could you do? All right, if it's so important, I will go and clean the jack. But first let's have that drink."

Five minutes later Bram saw Francien walking outside toward their car. Before she reached it, a police car stopped at the entrance. Battoni walked up to it and pointed Francien out to the descending cops. Francien was standing near the trunk, watching the cops getting out of the police car. Two cops quickly walked up to her, each taking an arm, but she pulled herself loose and kicked at one of them. Bram turned from the window and made for the door as fast as he could.

This was madness. Arresting Francien!

He met Battoni, already in the corridor with one of his mates. They seized him without wasting words and a few moments later he was sitting next to Francien in the police car. It drove off immediately.

"You shouldn't have kicked" he said.

"Only his shins," she said, miffed.

"Will you please stop resisting! It gets us nowhere, only makes things worse."

"They should keep their hands off me. Bunch of paparazzi."

"Paparazzi are journalists. Francien, please!"

Within five minutes they were at the police station, planted on a wooden bench. A loud "Silenzio!" made clear to them they were to remain silent.

"Car keys!"

Bram took the car keys from his pocket and handed them to Battoni, who in turn handed them over to one of the cops with a flow of Italian words. The cop left.

After messing about for a long time with Battoni's poor English, they understood that they were suspected of murder, maltreatment and car theft.

They looked at each other. "Car theft?"

Their talking together in a language that the officer couldn't understand started to annoy Detective Battoni very much. They didn't look like what they were suspected of, otherwise he would have made it clear, in a way not open to misunderstanding, who pulled the strings here. The autostrada robberies had been a thorn in the flesh of his superiors and everybody was put under pressure to catch the culprits, who had become more and more reckless of late. Now, for the first time, someone was dead.

When Bram and Francien continued talking together in Dutch he snapped his fingers and pointed at Bram: "Lui in cella!"

Francien was already on her feet before the officers had gotten up. The one whom Francien had kicked in the shins eagerly approached her. Bram pulled Francien down, himself up and turned his back to the officer.

"Did you see the eagerness in his eyes to get his hands on you? He hopes you give him a reason. Sit and smile for God's sake, otherwise you're on your own."

"Okay."

For the first time Bram thought, I've never been in a cell before.

A plank bed, stool, toilet, door, four walls and a lamp on the ceiling behind an iron grill. After the door was bolted it became quiet.

Car theft? Of course. One of them had cleared out with the car. That one wasn't dead anyway. Now that he thought about it, Battoni had talked only about two victims. Hence the story that Francien and he had stolen their car. It would be best if he brought up the third man himself. Moreover, Francien would not leave the third man out of her story, because that weakened the threat the three had imposed upon them. Of course, they could not be convicted for murder, but being arrested for it and held for a couple of weeks or maybe months would be disaster enough.

It was already past midnight when they came to fetch Bram. There was another man in plainclothes, older than Battoni. Francien sat on the bench and the jack lay on the table.

"I told them everything, Bram."

"One more word from you and you go into the cell," the new man warned Francien. Then he turned to Bram.

"My name is Garzo, Chief Inspector of the Italian C.I.D. You speak English?"

He told Bram what they were charged with. A patrol car had found the victims. One dead, and the other one with his eyes stabbed out. That one had told the cops the culprits drove a car of an Italian make and that they spoke Dutch, he believed.

After Bram told his side of the story, Garzo remained silent for a while.

"Your story is the same as your wife's. She is your wife?"

"For thirteen years. Could you please phone Signor Lantini of the Alpha Romeo factory in Milan? The number is 4378252."

The call wasn't answered.

Garzo had a problem. They did not look like autostrada robbers, and the caretaker had told Battoni that they came every year and that he had received a call from Milan that night that they would be late. But the woman had killed a man and the husband had jabbed another man's eyes out. He couldn't let either of them go. It was too hot an item higher up in Rome. Yet there was only one cell. To keep the man in jail and let her go while she was a murder suspect, or at least suspected of manslaughter, was impossible. To let him go and keep her here was equally impossible. Even according to their own version, he was the one who had started the violence. If there really was a third man, why had he not come forward with his story? *If* he existed?

The blind man had said he didn't know the number of the stolen car, nor did he know the identity of the dead man. He had hitchhiked. His passport and the papers of the dead man should be in the stolen car.

If this Dutch couple had told the truth, the shoe was on the other foot. Then the victims might appear in the police records.

Garzo decided to try Interpol and to give them the description of the two surviving victims. It was a shot in the dark, but it couldn't do any harm.

He explained to Bram that he could not let either of them go and that they could decide between them who would spend the night in the cell and who on the bench.

"I suggest, Francien, you go and sleep in the cell and I stay here. There's a bed and a toilet and you can sleep."

Francien agreed and went with one of the officers. Garzo talked for a while with Battoni. Bram couldn't understand what they said. He only understood "domani" and "Genova"; so, there wouldn't be much happening that night anymore. Maybe they would phone Milan tomorrow or bring them to Genoa.

On his way to the door Garzo turned around. "Why didn't you go to police with your story when you come, or next morning?"

"Don't forget, *we* are the victims and not them."

"In that case more reason you help us make an end to robberies. Also, you leave injured people behind with no medical help. I don't knows whether is permitted in Hollanda, but is criminal offense in this country."

"In our circumstances you can't reasonably expect us, having escaped scum like them, to turn back and check whether they felt all right. As a matter of fact it was more up to the third man to do that."

Garzo nodded. "*If* there is third man."

———

At six o'clock the next morning the telephone rang. After a lot of "Si, si," Battoni put down the receiver, and Francien was brought from the cell. She had slept, but was wrinkled and felt dirty. There wasn't much to say. It had come home to her, as well, that everything depended on whether that third man would be found.

In Genoa they were brought to the police headquarters, where they were locked away separately. They each got a cup of coffee and a roll. Bram asked them to try Lantini again and they said they would do that. He also asked them to summon a lawyer and they said they would do that, too. Nothing happened.

At noon they got some more coffee and a sandwich. At three o'clock they came for Bram and brought him to a room, where Garzo was seated behind a desk with Francien in front of it. Garzo waved him into the other chair.

"Signor Aardsen and signora. I am sorry, terrible. By mistake we think you had done the crimes at the autostrada. We have talked with Signor Lantini. You are respectable direttore representation Alfa Romeo in Hollanda. Interpol did find the third man. He and his friends committed many robberies earlier. The German police search for them, too. They took the third man from his bed this morning in Munich. The car was parked in front of the house and the nose was broken. The blind man, who is in hospital in Massa, is the owner—of the car. The third man confessed the plan to take your automobile with everything in it. His story is like your story. You kick him in the face, he was unconscious. When he comes round, he flee. Signor Lantini is on his way here. Information from the German police came in later, Signor Lantini was already on his way. You are free to go, but I like you available to sign statements, and for in the case we have further questions. Will you stay in Italy another week on the same address?"

"That is possible, although we are not exactly in a holiday mood after all that has happened. What I would like to know is, how did you find us so soon?"

Garzo smiled. "Very simple. We think you are on the way south. We check all hotel and tourist registrations, because the blind man tells us Italian car and maybe from Holland. From La Spezia you were the only couple without children. Simple. I apologize for our mistake. However, you would have much less troubles and save us lot of work, if you come to the police immediately."

"Sorry, but you know, in a foreign country and feeling innocent as we did and coming for a vacation, one likes to dodge it." Bram couldn't possibly say that he didn't trust the Italian police.

A police officer came in and gave them their things back. Then Garzo left them to see whether Lantini had arrived and to arrange transport back to Viareggio.

After a while Garzo came back with Lantini, who laved them with apologies and concern. He kissed Francien, held Bram's hand with his and nearly kissed him, too. "Bastards, should kill them all. You are free to go. Will you come with me, to be my guests? Plenty room in my house."

Bram liked the idea. He had never been invited to Lantini's house before, but Francien wouldn't hear of it. She felt wrinkled and sticky and her makeup had worn off.

After satisfying Lantini's curiosity a bit and promising that they would come and see him on the way back home, a police car was ready to bring them back to Viareggio.

At the Viareggio police station Bram was given back his car keys by Battoni, who in turn offered his apologies. Would they please come back the next day or so to sign the statements?

It was six-thirty in the evening when they pulled into the parking lot of the apartment.

"A drink and a shower and . . . wait a minute, Thijs and Marjet should be here by now." Francien looked around but their camper was not there.

Bram said, "Come on, maybe they're delayed. Let's get cleaned up and have that drink." Bram limped ahead. In the hall the caretaker jumped up.

"Signor Aardsen! You back from police. I never believe you bad man. Stupid Italian police!"

"Yes, fine, but we want to wash and change, thank you," and they walked to the stairs.

"Signor! Momento. Man and woman come here and ask you. From Holland."

"Where did they go, did they say?"

"I told them police come for you and they asked where police was, so I explained. Then they go, say nothing."

"Come on, Bram, let's go back to the police station to see if they're there."

"Not me. Battoni will tell them we are back, but they may just as well have gone to find a place at one of the campgrounds, or maybe for dinner."

Francien had the bathroom first. When she had finished, Bram took his time, soaking, with his whisky within reach. When he came out of the bathroom, he was stunned by the way Francien had dressed: golden high-heeled slippers, black velvet pants sharp as a knife, a bare waist, a gold-bronze blouse knotted under her breasts, large wooden earrings, and a headband made of the same material as the blouse tied together at the back of her head, the two ends dangling.

With her right hand on her hip, holding a cigarette and waving the fingernails of her left hand dry, she arched her breasts up and looked at him expectantly, her eye shadow perfectly matching the green eyes.

It took him a moment or two before he found his voice. Standing naked in the door opening, hair uncombed, his dirty clothes in one hand, his

empty whiskey glass in the other, leaning over a bit to spare his right leg, he
was aware of the contrast.

"Well?"

"It's smashing! Really, it's very good! I suppose we are not in for a quiet
evening in our room."

"You bet we're not. You really like it?"

"I do, and I presume it's fishnets and dripping candles tonight."

There was a knock on the door as it was thrown open, and Thijs and
Marjet came in.

"Thank God, you're here. We were really worried."

Thijs kissed Francien several times, and Marjet looked Bram over.

"Sorry for barging in," she said.

"Well, if you will excuse me for a second, I will be dressed in no time."
He went to the cupboard, slipped on underwear and rummaged through
the hangers for trousers and a matching shirt.

"What is that?!" Marjet asked, pointing at the large blue area on his
right leg.

"That's part of the story. Sit down, please, and help yourself to a drink."
He chose white slacks and a white shirt. When he turned around he saw
Thijs staring at Francien as if he had never seen her before.

The story was more or less told, and Bram suggested they all go for
dinner.

The place, the caretaker had advised them, was always crowded, poorly
lit, and had a noisy band playing teenybopper music. Francien and Thijs
sat opposite Marjet and Bram. They were barely seated when Thijs asked
Francien to dance, which she eagerly accepted.

"Are you all right, Bram? You look tired," said Marjet.

"No wonder. I've been worried stiff. I—"

The flashgun blinded them both. They stared at the photographer, who
snapped on from various angles.

"Signore Aardsen?"

"Yes."

"Autostrada attaco?!"

"Yes, but what do you want?"

"Viareggio newspaper, tomorrow morning, you and your wife big heros.
Help solve crime. Pictures for the paper. Must hurry."

"How did you know about us?" Bram shouted over the music.

"Battoni my father. Ciao!" He dashed off, young, eager and happy with his *primeur.*

Perplexed, Bram stared at Marjet, who slowly smiled. "I'll be your wife tomorrow," she said.

Bram smiled. "You think they will be our witnesses?" he said, looking at Francien and Thijs as they returned from the dance floor. Francien was looking up at his face and apparently enjoying what he had said.

"We can ask. From the look of it, they won't mind very much."

When they were seated Marjet asked, "Did you see the photographer?"

Francien had. "You should have brought your camera, too, Bram."

"No need to, my dear. We have a private photographer."

"A private photographer?"

"The son of Battoni. He heard our story from his father and came here to take our picture."

"Where is he?" Francien wanted to know, checking her hair at the same time.

"Gone. He took Marjet and me, because he thought she was you. So tomorrow you will see your husband and his new wife in the *Viareggio Star* or something. Marjet and I were just wondering whether you two would be our witnesses," he added, grinning.

The wineglass sailed over his head into the fishnets that hung from the ceiling.

"Francien!" Marjet shouted, seizing her arm and holding it.

Bram and Thijs each lit a cigarette and started studying the menu. Pizza, pizza and pizza. When the waiter came, Marjet let go of Francien's arm and chose a pizza from the menu. The men ordered and then they waited for Francien, who sat staring at the menu without really seeing it.

"The same for me," she said after a while, not looking at the waiter.

"The same what, signora?"

"Like hers." She pointed at Marjet.

Thijs poured the wine, and Bram told them they had decided to go somewhere else on holiday next year. "No, it has nothing to do with our experience with the highwaymen—that could have happened in any country, even in Holland. No, we just want a change and go, for instance, to . . ." and he started summing up the possibilities they had thought up the night before.

Thijs and Marjet saw to it that the subject, safe as it was, wasn't exhausted.

Francien listlessly picked at her food. A thing she shared with Bram was that anger and food didn't mix. And she was angry, because she had missed the photo opportunity.

She drank more wine than usual, as Marjet kept her glass filled, but it didn't affect her much. She was a hard-liquor lady. Before the coffee Marjet got up, held out her hand to Francien and together they walked off, taking their handbags with them.

Finished with their coffee, Bram and Thijs realized that the girls had gone farther than the toilet, so they drank the girls' coffee, too, ordered double brandies and gradually ran out of subjects of mutual interest. They waited for the women to come back.

In the end Bram got fed up with the noise, having to repeat every question and shout the answers.

"Come on, let's get out of here. They must have gone. Let's get some fresh air."

On the beach they sat in the sand, looking at the black sea. "That was a bad joke, Bram. She was so nice before, happy, shining—I never saw her like that—and then you come up with this lousy story."

"Who cares about a shitty picture in a shitty newspaper? In my opinion, the girls are having a drink somewhere. It's just the aftermath of the tension. Come on, let's go and see if they have gone to the apartment."

In silence they walked back to the apartment, where they found the women chatting and the bed covered with all of Francien's latest clothes.

"Francien, where did you get that marvelous outfit you are wearing?" Bram asked as a gesture of peace.

"Small shop in The Hague in the beginning of the summer. Kept it for the holidays. I got more, you'll see them later."

After Thijs and Marjet had left, Francien kicked off her slippers, threw her clothes on a chair and stretched out on the bed. She fell asleep almost immediately, cigarette still between her fingers.

Bram took it and put it out.

4

The telephone rang. Bram picked it up.

"Aardsen here . . . Yes . . . Yes . . . Yes, that's us. . . . No, not now. . . . Uhuh . . . uhuh . . . What time is it? . . . Half past ten? . . . No, she is still asleep."

"Who is it, Bram?" Francien said, awake.

"Somebody from the television or something. Wants to see you."

"From the television?"

"Shh! Hang on. Hello, what did you say? . . . Lunch? What time? . . . All right, we'll be ready. Good-bye."

Francien was sitting up, wide awake now.

"Who was it? What did he want?"

"Some guy from the television who wants to interview you about your part in the fight. He's going to pick us up for lunch."

"Oh dear, what shall I wear? I have nothing to put on and my hair is a mess. I must go and buy something. What time is he coming?"

"One o'clock."

Francien shot out of bed. "Come on, hurry, you know shops close at lunchtime and I have to find a hairdresser as well."

"Hey, hold your horses, please. Let's first wait and see what this guy has to say. Most likely, it's just an interview like we've seen so often. You sit there, a jerk of a newscaster asks you whether you weren't scared, the camera goes back to him and he tells the viewers that he is glad that there are brave women like you. And then it's the weather report. We are not going to spend a couple of hundred guilders for a split second on the screen."

"But maybe it's for a program. I mean, a longer program. Something like "Behind the News" or something. They have that over here, too, don't they?"

Bram shrugged. "Maybe, but we are not going to buy anything before we know more about it."

Bram had to cajole to get her to the beach for an hour, and it was only the argument that a bit more tan would do her good that made her give in.

Toward one o'clock they were waiting in their room, Francien all dressed up, made up and worked up.

At one sharp there was a knock on their door and a handsome man in his early thirties, dressed in fast clothes, introduced himself as Signor Lanjoni. He looked from one to the other and then he produced the *Viareggio Star* from his pocket. He looked at the picture on the front page and then back to Francien.

After they had explained to him how that had happened, they took off in Lanjoni's open Lancia. With Francien beside him and Bram squeezed into the back seat, he drove away from the beach, up the road to Camaiore, where they stopped at a roadside inn and had lunch on the terrace.

Lanjoni told them he was the producer of a program called *La Donna Questa Settimana,* "The Woman This Week," covering the important happenings of the week concerning women. From the *Viareggio Star* they had learned about what had happened and they wished to interview Francien for her role in the fight. He explained to Bram that it was nothing special if a man was involved in a fight and won or lost it. Happens every day. That a woman took part in a man's fight and had a decisive influence on the outcome, that really was something special. He was sure the viewers were interested in knowing what a woman under those circumstances felt and what such a woman was like. He suggested taking Francien along with him to the Livorno studio a couple of hours before going on the air so that she could get the feel of it: a kind of rehearsal to make her familiar with the procedure, and put her at ease in order to bring out her real personality. Very few people could just walk in and act normal.

Francien was hanging on his words but Bram didn't like it very much. He felt a bit left out.

"I'll see to it that she is safely brought back after the program." It was clear he did not want Bram to come along.

"Can't he come with us?" she said.

"Battoni told me that you have been married for thirteen years. For a woman it is very difficult after such a time to speak her own mind. Male dominance. It's much better for the show when you do this on your own, than at the side of your husband."

He had a point there, so they went back to drop Bram at the apartment.

"Can you stop a moment at the police station?" Bram asked when they entered Viareggio.

"Why is that?" Francien asked in Dutch.

"Nothing special, I just want to see whether they have their reports ready for us to sign."

"But don't I have to come along to sign, too?"

"No, that won't be necessary, I don't think."

When Lanjoni halted in front of the police post, Bram got out of the car. "I'll be back in a minute."

Thank heaven Battoni was there.

"Mr. Battoni, do you know who the producer of *La Donna Questa Settimana* is?"

"Yes. Mr. Lanjoni. Here this morning. He ask about your case. Why you ask?"

Bram couldn't very well explain that he did not trust Italians all that much, and that he suspected Mister Lanjoni of intending to kidnap his wife from under his nose in broad daylight.

"Oh, nothing, just curious. Thanks a lot. Ciao." And before Battoni could phrase another question in English, Bram was outside and hopping into the car. "Not yet ready. You can drop me at the apartment."

The drive along the coastal road, the sea, the beach, the sky, the convertible, the wind blowing in her hair, circling through the car and blowing up her dress once in a while, his long eyelashes, tanned hands on the wheel and long legs in the tight slacks, and the prospect that she would appear on television, were all very exciting.

Shortly before they arrived at Livorno, Lanjoni turned slowly right, nosed onto the beach and killed the engine.

Francien looked at him questioningly.

Lanjoni turned to her, one arm on the wheel and one on the back of her seat. "You want to buy some clothes, you said?"

"Yes, and I would like to go to the hairdresser."

"No need for that, because makeup and hair is done at the studio. Let's see, it's four o'clock now. We have to be in the studio at seven. So let's find a boutique first and then take it from there. One never knows how long it takes a woman to find the dress that's just *it*."

He stroked her hair. His hand lingered on her neck for a second and then, moving lightly over her shoulder, went back to the ignition key and started the engine. Putting his hand on the gearshift his outstretched fingers lightly touched her leg.

After Lanjoni and Francien had left, Bram went to Thijs and Marjet to tell them about the television interview. They decided to stay another day and come to his apartment later on to watch it. Bram then bought picture postcards. He sent one to Dick with *I am thinking* on it and one to Pauline with *See you*. Glancing over the newspapers, he saw the *Viareggio Star* with Marjet and him on the front page. He bought one. The picture wasn't bad, but the reporter wouldn't have much of a career after his boss saw Francien on television.

On his way back to the apartment he mailed the two postcards and kept the rest for Francien to decide who got which. Then he tried to figure out what to do with the boy's dream to become a racing driver. A go-cart? The idea appealed to him. He wondered what Pauline would say about it. He also wondered what Pauline would look like when he came back. He looked forward to it.

Arriving at Livorno, and on their way to a boutique, Francien tried to figure out what she wanted. A sporty touch? Or chic matron-like? Or chic softly feminine? Or wild, like she felt when she remembered the fight.

When they entered the boutique she saw that *chic* would be no problem. The saleslady, however, seeing her roundish face, hips and strong legs, thought *chic* would be a problem.

"Mr. Lanjoni, how nice to see you again. How are you?" She nodded to Francien.

"Madam here should like to see a new dress. She speaks English and she will be on my program tonight."

"Oh, let me see what I can do for you, sir. Did you have anything in mind, madam?"

The assuredness of the saleslady, and the cool style of the shop, left no room for something "wild." That's certainly not appropriate, Francien thought.

"I think," Lanjoni said, "something with a somewhat loose style. Scandinavian? Sophisticated primitive."

Francien didn't like what she heard but felt too awkward to say anything. She waited to see what they might come up with.

"Okay, let me see," said the saleswoman, and walked toward one of the racks. "A skirt and a blouse, I think."

She looked Francien over for size and color. Rummaging through a rack, she dug up something that looked like it was made of a jute bag, although that was surely not the case. It was very wide, with stitched-on pockets and a belt of the same material. She handed the skirt to Francien and turned to another rack. Francien looked at the price tag: 60.000—lira. Expensive, yes, but not out of the question.

The woman reappeared with a pastel green silk blouse with wide sleeves and turtleneck. Francien held it up in front of her. She liked what she saw. Trying it on, it felt good. The skirt might look like it was made of jute, but it felt soft as velvet and the silk lining was cool around her legs. Lanjoni nodded approvingly.

The lady tucked the fabric of the blouse into the waistline so that the breasts were accentuated. As Francien walked toward a mirror the skirt swung with grace. Only the dark brown shoes didn't match. When she returned, she heard Lanjoni say to the lady, "We'll match the makeup with the blouse at the studio." He turned to Francien. "Well, how do you like it?"

"I need other shoes, I think."

"That won't be a problem. There's a shop just around the corner. I know the owner."

Francien wondered whether knowing the owner made things cheaper or more expensive.

The shoe shop was small and the owner was nice. It took quite some time before the choice was made. High-heeled, light-green suede with an ankle strap. Back in the car Lanjoni suggested that she could do with a shower and a quiet place to change into the new outfit. "I have a flat here."

Without waiting for an answer, he started the engine and moved into traffic.

The flat had a view of the Mediterranean and its main color was white, interrupted only by a couple of colorful abstract paintings.

Over a glass of wine, Lanjoni asked about her youth, where she lived, did she have children, a job, how long had she been married, was Bram her first man?

Francien shook her head.

"Is he your only man?"

"Of course!" The indignation she heard in her own voice, the way Lanjoni looked at her and the superior smile at the corners of his mouth made her feel like a schoolgirl.

Lanjoni suggested she take a shower and change while he made a sandwich.

Francien locked the bathroom door, showered, changed and reappeared. They ate. Lanjoni wanted to know what she thought about women's lib, emancipation and women being equal to men.

Francien wasn't very outspoken about it. She didn't really care. Of course, she didn't like being considered inferior, and there was no reason for it. She had proven that, hadn't she? Lanjoni smiled, but kept his counsel.

He explained to her that the interview would be live and, of course, have to be translated. That had never caused any problem for the guests. "You just wait till the next question."

When they left for the studio, Lanjoni told her to leave her dress and shoes. In the studio they so they could easily get lost. They would pick them up on the way back.

The makeup was heavy. Her hair was brushed back behind her ears, which, short as it was, gave her a slightly manly appearance. She was seated behind a microphone at a table. With the hot lights, her nerves and the poor air-conditioning, she felt sweat itching on her head and the silk lining of the skirt sticking to her legs.

Lanjoni was making a long introduction. she picked up only her name, Olandesa and autostrada. She wasn't sure where to look because she had no idea which camera was on.

"Mrs. Aardsen, I may call you Francien, may I not? What did you think when those three men approached you and your husband?"

"I was scared. I saw straight away they were thugs, so I said to Bram to hurry, because—"

Lanjoni held up his hand to translate.

"What made you so sure they had evil intentions? They could just as well have come to help your husband change the tire, couldn't they?"

Francien was taken aback. She pondered whether that could have been the case, but lacking time to work it out, and sensing that cameras were zooming in on her, she said, "Scum like them don't help people!"

"So, apparently they weren't going to help your husband," Lanjoni continued with a pleasant smile, "otherwise you wouldn't have gotten off scot-free, after the interference of one highly placed gentleman of the Alfa Romeo factory in Milano."

"But Mr. Lantini—"

Lanjoni's hand went up for translation.

"Since it is not every day that you knock a man's brains out, I should like to know, what made you decide to strike this man, from behind?"

"I don't know. I just did it. I think because they attacked my husband."

"Do you mean to say that, if it had been somebody else's husband, you wouldn't have done it?"

Francien thought that wasn't what she meant to say at all. How would she know?

Lanjoni didn't wait for an answer. "Would you say of yourself that you are a possessive type?"

"Oh, well, maybe . . . but you see—"

Lanjoni's hand went up again. Francien wondered what he was telling the audience.

"Now let us get to the point where you hit that man and he crumbles under the blow and falls dead on the ground. Did you have a kind of 'well done' feeling?"

"Yes, of course." She felt relieved that he understood her now.

"And afterwards, now that you know that this young man died from the blow you gave him, what do you feel? Still satisfaction?"

She hesitated. Of course, she still felt satisfaction, but she smelled a trap without knowing where it was.

"Well?" Lanjoni was waiting. "Are you still satisfied about what you did?"

She felt cornered. That always made her angry and stubborn. She refused to water down her own victory, which she had come to be honored for.

"Yes, I do and rightly so. Why should men always get away with things because they are stronger? That's unfair and they are not so superior after all, as you see." She smiled.

Lanjoni looked at her till her smile faded away, knowing that the camera was on *her*. After the translation he went on: "So you don't have any compassion for the man you killed, not even when you think of the young life lost and of his mother?"

"No." Francien dug in her heels. Lanjoni had not misjudged her. On the contrary.

"But, Francien," he went on in a relaxed tone, "if you think about it—this young male, once a baby loved by his mother who is now grieving over his death. Cannot we all go astray at one time in our lives? Don't you think it's very sad that one meets a kind of death penalty for possibly only intending to get away with a small part of somebody else's money?"

Francien hated this kind of sentimental crap. Her anger flared up. They were always talking to her till she eventually found something wrong with herself, but not this time, no way. She jumped up, hitting the side of the table with her upper legs, tipping over a glass of water and the mike. Leaning with her hands on the table she said, "Now you listen, Lanjoni, this guy was a rotter, like most men, and it serves him right. Going around, knocking decent people down and stealing their money. And don't give me the bullshit about poor fellow this and poor fellow that." And then, turning to the camera that was looking her in the face: "And *you stop that!*"

The cameraman thought he was getting a great shot, so he didn't shift his position. Angrily she grabbed the mike from the table and threw it at the camera. The wire, however, was too short to let it fly that far. Then she stamped away from the table, hooked a foot in one of the cables and fell full length on the floor.

Lanjoni jumped up, knelt at her side, helped her up from the floor, and took her in his arms, shielding her from the stares of the cameramen and the audience.

"Now, there, easy, easy, my dear. You can't just walk away. We haven't given you your award yet."

Francien looked up, eyes brimming with tears from powerless anger and a growing feeling of humiliation.

"Did I forget to tell you that we award a prize every week to a heroic woman who, with her courage has, done something good for the people?"

Francien was flabbergasted. The switch was too fast for her. She let herself be led back to the table, where the microphone was back in its place and somebody put down a fresh glass of water.

When she sat down, Lanjoni waved the camera away from her and started talking Italian again, ending with ". . . donna coraggiosa."

"Dear Francien, I would like to present you with the prize for this week's most courageous woman, who cleared the autostrada of Italy of a group of criminals who had made our freeways unsafe for a long time. We are all very grateful to you and it is my privilege to offer you this little bronze statuette of Pax, the Roman goddess of peace, placed on a pedestal of Carrara marble, together with a check for one million lira, which I believe is in your money about five thousand guilders."

Francien just sat and stared at him, while Lanjoni explained to her that the prize was not always so high, but it depended on the value of the act for society. She, Francien, had played a major role in solving a string of crimes that would, without her help, have cost the police a tremendous amount of time to solve, if they would have ever solved it at all.

He handed her the statue and the envelope, kissed both her cheeks, and said good-bye to the viewers.

Then the main lights went out, the cameras rolled away and nobody paid attention to them anymore as they sat at the table.

"You were marvelous, Francien."

"Me? Marvelous?"

"Yes, you are a natural. You speak your mind, not caring whether you are on the screen or not. It was a good show—never had such action before."

"Because I made a fool of myself."

"Nonsense, you were great. You know what we'll do? We'll have something to eat before you go back to Viareggio. It's eight o'clock now. Dinner will take an hour and a half, so you'll be back at eleven. Is that all right with you?"

She nodded, still confused.

After her makeup was restored to normal, they left the studio and walked a block to the restaurant. The cool evening air dried her skin and made her feel all right again, though still a bit dazed.

Bram, Thijs and Marjet had been watching the show in the dining room with most of the other guests who had been informed by the caretaker. When the glass of water went over the table and the microphone was flung straight at the camera and hit the floor with a terrible bang, Bram got up.

"Where are you going?" Thijs wanted to know.

"Gonna get her, before she demolishes the whole studio! I know that girl!"

"I'll come with you."

Off they went, leaving Marjet to be stared at by the other guests.

When they reached the studio, neither Francien nor Lanjoni were there. Yes, they had left. No, they didn't know where they had gone. Maybe to Lanjoni's flat or maybe to his house in Lucca. They gave Bram the address of the flat, but they didn't know the address in Lucca. That shouldn't be a problem, however, because everybody knew him down there.

Nobody answered the bell at the flat.

"Of course, he's taken her to his house in Lucca," said Bram. "Come on, let's go there." When the taillights of Bram's car disappeared around the corner of the street, Lanjoni's headlights lit up the other end.

After dinner Lanjoni had suggested returning to his flat to pick up her clothes. When they entered his flat, Francien put her dress over her arm, picked up her shoes from the floor and looked around for the shopping bag.

"You are in a hurry?"

She was, for she wanted to tell Bram about the million liras she had earned, but it looked too greedy to say so, as if that were the price for killing somebody.

"No, not really."

"You like a glass of wine?"

She hesitated, then shrugged. "No, whiskey."

"Ice?"

She nodded, feeling somewhat ill at ease. She would rather be with Bram and Thijs and Marjet and show them her prize and hear what they thought about her interview. She put her dress and the box with her old shoes in the shopping bag beside the door and sat on a stool at the bar in the living room. He poured a double whiskey on the rocks, took a glass of wine himself, walked around and stood behind her.

His hand touched her side and then moved forward, cupping her breast. With his free hand he took his glass from the counter and held it up for a toast. Francien picked up her glass and turned towards him in order to free her breast. Looking up to him, she lifted her glass and touched his. Before she could bring it to her lips, he kissed her, put his glass down and had his hand under her skirt, starting to pull her panties down as far as they would go.

Taken by surprise, she was paralyzed for a second, which he used to take the glass from her hand and put it on the counter. Bending her backward, his left arm around her back, his right arm under her legs, he lifted her from the stool and carried her towards the bedroom.

She tried to push him away: "Nee, dat wil ik niet! *Verdomme!*" she yelled in Dutch.

He held her tightly, pushed the bedroom door open and plopped them both down on the bed. Catching his weight on one arm, his other hand tore her panties down to her knees and then down to her ankles. She tried to kick his hand away. One foot slipped out of the panties and that was all he needed. His breast on hers, his head against hers, his face down in the bedspread, her legs kicking uselessly in the air, his pants unzipped. He always fucked his female guests after the show and this clodhopper would be no exception to the rule. Knocking a man's brains out. That should be nipped in the bud. He would teach her who knocked up whom. Moreover, the primitiveness of this bitch excited him very much. He moved to get his leg between hers but she anticipated that, crossed her legs and pulled them up. She grabbed his hair with both hands, pulled his head up with a jerk and spat in his face before he could push his head back down in spite of the pain. Both of them were furious. He rolled himself over and tried to enter her from below. She felt him coming and stretched out, squeezing his prick between her thighs and the bed cover. That was all that was needed for him to come.

When he relaxed his grip, shaking from the orgasm like a wounded rabbit, she pushed him aside, got off the bed, rushed into the living room and grabbed her things. On the way to the door, she halted, went to the bar, took her whisky glass, emptied it in one gulp, flung it into the direction of the bedroom, and not waiting to see where it landed, she made for the door and closed it behind her with a bang.

Once in the street, quieting down somewhat from the stress of the struggle, she became really infuriated. Men, damn them all. Always after that. Damn, damn, damn them all!

Walking without direction, she wondered where she was going and realized this way she wasn't going anywhere. She had to get back to Viareggio, but how? A taxi slowed down at her side. "Taxi, signora?" Why not, she had money enough, hadn't she?

She got in. "Viareggio."

"Viareggio, iez bery farr, you pagare money?"

Francien got out the envelope, took out a couple of bank notes and showed them to the driver. Satisfied, he turned around and, from the signs he followed, Francien could see that he was heading for Pisa, on the way to Viareggio.

He was an elderly man, she noticed, and felt at ease at last. Touching her skirt she felt a wet spot. Damn it, the bastard had soiled her new skirt. Well, anyway, he hadn't gotten her. Fighting with Bram had its advantages, she thought wryly. The humming of the car, the whiskey and the excitement of the interview began to take effect. After a while she dozed off and woke up only when the streetlights of Viareggio pushed the darkness from the car.

"Signora, address?"

"Via Graziani, sixty-seven."

That, however, did not help much. She tried to guide him with movements of her hand, but he had to look back at her so often, that he nearly hit other cars.

"You stop, halt, momentito. Stop here!"

Slowly the man understood and stopped. Francien got out and went to sit next to him.

Under her guidance they arrived safely at the apartment. She paid him the 30,000 lira he asked, not caring one bit whether he overcharged her, and went into the apartment. She found Marjet sitting in their room reading a book.

After Marjet had explained to her that Bram and Thijs had rushed off to find her, it took Francien half an hour and two whiskeys to tell her friend the truth and nothing but the truth. Marjet couldn't help smiling.

"What's so funny? It's always me that things like this happen to. The bastard, making me angry in front of the cameras and, on top of it, grabbing me like I'm a cheap Italian whore. Why me?"

"Yes," Marjet said, "why not me?"

Francien looked at her questioningly. "What do you mean?"

"Just what I said. I wouldn't have minded having a go at a famous Italian television producer, good-looking as he is."

"You mean I should have let him have his way?"

"No, of course not, but in the first place you should've changed in the shop, and in the second place you should not have left your things in his flat, unless you wouldn't mind coming back there with him. He is handsome, isn't he. But I must say, I admire you. You didn't see his face when all the water ran off the table onto his trousers. And imagine what he thinks about women now. *He,* the big star, being shoved aside by a Dutch country girl—because that is what he thinks with his wounded ego, cleaning the spit off his face and his semen off the bedspread. I bet you he is in a far fouler mood than you."

"Good for him. Grabby, arrogant bastard. You know, Marjet, what I sometimes wish? I know it's silly, but as revenge I would like to grab *them* one time."

"Well, that's not so silly. You should do that, but not the way they do. You are a woman, you have your own ways. When it comes to sex, men are such assholes. You can see them coming from miles away and then *you* decide what goes or what doesn't. You are a little naive at times, but not about buying clothes. What a marvelous skirt and blouse, and where did you find the shoes? Perfect. Bram was very impressed when he saw you on the screen. And now he's racing all over Italy to save his poor helpless little wife from the claws of a sex maniac. And Thijs with him, because that one is always fond of shabby stories. I wouldn't be surprised if they go to the Livorno police and get them searching for you. Imagine their faces when they come home and find you safe and sound."

Francien chuckled at the thought. "I wonder what Bram will do about Lanjoni when he hears about it?"

"You'll never know."

Francien looked at Marjet. "Why not?"

"Because you won't tell him. Men don't like their wives to be grabbed. When they are present, they see to it that it doesn't happen, and when they are not present, *you* see to it that it doesn't happen."

"But—"

"There are no *buts* in this case. Don't tell. It makes a man feel powerless, so it makes them angry, and in the end they blame you for it. Lanjoni brought you back. Understood?!"

Francien thought about it. "At times I have the feeling you are my elder sister."

By twelve Francien couldn't keep her eyes open anymore. Marjet didn't want to go back to the camper on her own. She suggested that Francien go to bed. She would wait till the men came back from their rescue operation. After a feeble objection, Francien gave in and was fast asleep minutes later, in spite of the light of the bed lamp that enabled Marjet to read.

Bram and Thijs had found Lanjoni's place in Lucca, but nobody was in. The police refused to search for Francien. They knew Lanjoni, a gentleman—yes, he liked women and women liked him. No job for the police. They wrote everything down and asked where Bram could be reached, just in case. Taking down the caretaker's number, the officer asked Bram whether he had phoned yet to find out if she had returned home in the meantime. Thijs went back to the car while Bram phoned. The caretaker told him Francien had come home.

"And?" Thijs said when Bram got in the car.

"Back at the apartment."

"You're kidding."

"No. The caretaker saw her come in." Bram, his arms resting on the wheel, was shaking his head. "Women!" he said. "You never know. When you worry about them, you make a fool of yourself, and when you don't, they make fools of themselves."

"I don't know what you mean," Thijs replied, "but surely this time we made fools of ourselves, trying to save an innocent woman from the clutches of a predator."

"Maybe it was the other way round."

"I know you're joking, but there may be some truth in it."

Bram shrugged. "I don't know whether I am joking or not, but I know that she is not the fragile little creature that we have been raised to defend."

"That may be so, Bram, but when I see Marjet and Francien together it strikes me sometimes as a mother-daughter relationship."

"I wouldn't know about that," said Bram, starting the engine. "Let's get back, shall we?"

They left town and sped north through the moonlit landscape. Thijs asked Bram what his real reason had been for the rescue attempt.

"I don't know. To keep her out of mischief, maybe. To prevent damage, I think."

"Suffered or caused?"

"What do you mean, and why are you asking? She's in a foreign country, doesn't speak the language, and was apparently in trouble. So what do you do?"

Thijs was silent for a while. "Weren't you afraid that they would go to bed together?"

"Who?"

"Well, Francien and this guy from the TV, what's his name?"

"Lanjoni?"

"Yes. He is good-looking. A charmer. You can't deny that."

"Why should I?"

"So you were not rushing off like you did to get her away from that fellow?"

"Like I said, to prevent damage."

"And them going to bed together doesn't come under the heading 'damage' in your opinion?"

"I wouldn't know. Should it? Anyway, she wouldn't do it, so there's no sense in asking whether or why."

"How can you be so sure?"

"I don't know. I just am. Aren't you?"

"No, I'm not. Marjet is a great lady, but independent as hell. If she felt like sleeping with somebody else, she would make no bones about it. That's the only thing I am sure of."

"Why should she? It doesn't make the world fall apart, does it? Or are you afraid that she would damage your career by it?"

"No, that's not it, and the world won't fall apart either. I know that. I only wish I had your certainty."

"So you have married the wrong girl. Did your parents pick her for you or did you choose her yourself?"

Thijs chuckled. "That's funny. I picked her myself, but I'm sure my parents would have picked her for me, too, if it had been up to them."

"Why fuss about *ifs?* I need a drink, that's what I'm sure of."

It was after midnight when they arrived at the apartment. Marjet heard the car doors slam. She closed the book, took her handbag and waited for them in the corridor.

"How is she?" Bram asked in a low voice.

"Fast asleep. She was exhausted."

"Of course, it hasn't exactly been a holiday so far. Anyway, the bugger had the decency to bring her back."

"That's right," Marjet lied. "We'll see you tomorrow. Come on Thijs, let's go." She kissed Bram good night, and took Thijs by the arm.

Thijs and Marjet came by the next morning at eight-thirty to say they were moving on to Rome. They shook hands, kissed good-bye, and went off.

The stares of people at the beach, around the apartment house and in the town, spoiled their holiday mood. After a couple of days Bram suggested they go home—a slow journey back, with a night spent in Milan, one in Switzerland and maybe one in southern Germany. And he would still have a couple of days off when they were back home. He still hadn't found a way for Dick to drive a racecar. But carting would come first. He thought a lot about the two people in Gouda.

Francien didn't put up much of a fight against their early departure, although the idea of going home didn't appeal to her like it did to Bram. She had an uneasy feeling that things wouldn't be the same again anymore.

Bram phoned Lantini at the autoworks, telling him they'd decided to go home. Lantini insisted that they visit him on their way back.

"When are you leaving?"

"Tomorrow."

"Well, make it the day after and then you are my guests for the night, so don't worry about a hotel. You stay with us. My wife would also like to meet you both."

CHAPTER

5

It was around five in the afternoon when Bram turned the car through the gate and up the drive to the large white-plastered house with three steps leading up to a wide porch. They were impressed.

Before they had gotten out of the car, a black-haired, middle-aged woman in an expensive, silk dress opened the door and approached them with outstretched hands and a big smile.

"You must be Mr. Aardsen, from Holland, yes?"

"Yes, madam, and this is my wife, Francien."

"What a pleasure to meet you. Do come in. I will show you to your room." She linked arms with Francien. "We'll have dinner at seven, and after dinner we'll have a few guests: something very informal, nothing to worry about, my dear." She patted Francien on the arm, and led her into the house. Bram followed. The hall, the paintings, the antique furniture, the marble and the space—he was awed.

Mrs. Lantini showed them into a large room with a sideboard, easy chairs, a fridge, a double bed and a connecting bathroom.

"If you give me the car keys, I'll have the valetto bring up the luggage. You have plenty of time to refresh yourself. Please feel at home. Mr. Lantini is on his way from the factory."

She left them in a cloud of heavy perfume. They felt somewhat small in these surroundings.

"Don't smoke in here," Francien said when Bram got the cigarettes out of his breast pocket.

"Why not, there's an ashtray over there." He lit his cigarette and opened the fridge.

"What are you doing?"

"I'm thirsty. I am looking for a beer."

"Don't be so uncivilized. You don't enter people's houses, tearing open fridges looking for a *beer.*"

"What's wrong with beer? Would it look better if I was looking for a glass of wine?"

"Don't be so stupid. You know quite well what I mean. What will Mr. Valetto, or what's his name, think when he comes in with the luggage and finds you plundering the icebox within minutes after you came in?"

"His name is not Valetto, he is a valet, and why do you think they've put the fridge here? For us to use, I would say." Bram took a beer and opened it.

A knock on the door stopped their conversation. The servant put the luggage down, wanted to know if there was anything else he could do for them, and when they said no, he gave Bram back his car keys and left.

The problem of what to wear claimed Francien's attention. Bram took a shower. Francien hung up some of her clothes, took a bath, and half an hour later they were shining and ready. Francien had, upon Bram's suggestion, put on the same ensemble she had worn on television.

Lantini came to fetch them with well-meant kisses for Francien, hand-shakes and back-pats for Bram.

Dinner was served in a big dining room upon an oval table with a hidden bell to the kitchen. The courses were light, as was the conversation. Mrs. Lantini, apparently from a very well-to-do family, had studied literature in the United States, hence her mastery of English. Of course, they touched on the autostrada attack but concentrated on the happy ending. When they were having the main course, Bram and Lantini discussed criminality and what to do about it.

Mrs. Lantini asked Francien what she thought about Antonio.

"Antonio?"

"Antonio Lanjoni, the one who hosted the program, *The Woman This Week.*

Francien felt color creep into her face and hoped she had tanned enough not to show the blush. The sordid affair was nobody's business.

"Oh yes, a nice gentleman. He wasn't angry at all when I messed up his program. He invited me for dinner afterwards."

"I am pleased to hear that. I have invited some people tonight, and I have also invited Antonio. He wasn't sure whether he could make it, but he'll try. I think it is always nice to have the time for a little chat without cameras. Knowing the cameras are on you creates tension, doesn't it? Sometimes it's difficult for Antonio to put people at ease."

Francien just sat looking at the brown eyes, the superb makeup, the stylish hair and listened to the quiet voice that had told her that she would meet Lanjoni again that evening.

She hadn't fooled Mrs. Lantini, who had noticed the blush and wasn't the least surprised.

After the meal they retired to an adjoining room where coffee was served. When the first guests arrived they moved again to another room, which had a bar.

Introductions were made, more necessary for Bram than for Francien, since most of them had seen her on the screen. After a while it seemed everybody had arrived, apart from Lanjoni. Bram sought out Francien to ask whether she was enjoying herself. "You're looking great. Are you nervous?"

"Yes."

"Why? They are nice people and nobody is pushy or putting words in your mouth, like that Lanjoni." Bram chuckled. "I assume he understands better than to make you angry."

"He's a friend of the family. So you and I better be nice to him—but maybe he won't come after all."

Mrs. Lantini spotted them. Francien's look was clearly a bit too serious for her liking, so she engineered an interdiction. She had Bernardo offer to get Francien a fresh drink, and take her along with him to the bar, while she took Bram's arm and together joined a group of her lady friends.

At the bar the guys around Francien awkwardly asked questions. They did not really feel at ease with her. They knew the story, so they complimented her on her courage. Their macho Italian made them sound very formal. Soon they changed the subject and asked about the town in Holland that she came from. Then they told her where they had been in Holland, that it was a lovely country, that everybody spoke English.

After a couple of drinks she began to relax. The silk of her blouse felt good next to her skin, and she said she liked Italy very much, had spent the holidays there for the last ten years. hadn't seen Rome yet, nor Florence, but had decided that they would go further south next year.

In the mirror behind the bar she could see Bram laughing with three Italian women, their black hair sparkling in the light, faces lifted in expectation, their dark brown eyes reading his lips. He loved their attention, she could see that.

"How does it feel having killed a man?"

She turned from the mirror. Bernardo had asked the question.

"Uh . . . sorry, what did you say?"

"How did it feel to kill a man?"

"Good."

"Sorry, what did you say?"

"Good, I said good." She glanced back into the mirror. Bram had apparently told another joke: the three heads were bobbing anew. Bram had his hand on the bare shoulder of the tallest, holding his glass with the other.

"Francien," Bernardo persisted, "I mean, it's known that men, after killing another human, feel a strong sexual desire, which usually comes with all victories. If you don't mind me asking, I should like to know whether you experienced the same feeling."

"I am really sorry, but what were you saying?" She laid her hand on Bernardo's arm and looked in his eyes. Bernardo thought that she might find it embarrassing to answer such a touchy question with the other two around. Behind her back he waved away Pietro and Marcelli, who were just thinking that the conversation had taken an interesting turn. Francien remained silent.

"I'm a psychologist and practice here in Milan. From a professional point of view it would interest me to know whether a woman reacts the same way to killing as a man. You said it felt good, but did it also stimulate you— sexually?"

Remembering the feeling and the sex she had had with Bram afterwards, she smiled. "It sure does."

Bernardo was surprised by her candid answer.

"But, forgive me for asking, do you consider yourself a very womanly woman, or a not so womanly woman?"

Her smile disappeared. Another jerk with another soul-searching question. She looked again into the mirror. Bram was walking through the doors leading to the porch with the tall one, his arm around her. They disappeared into the darkness. He wouldn't dare, would he? Jealousy shot up inside her.

Bernardo noticed the tightening of her face, which he put down to his questioning. He regretted having been too direct and carefully rephrased the question. Francien heard his voice but not his words. Her hands around the bar rail, knuckles taut, she kept staring into the darkness into which Bram had disappeared. A hand was on her shoulder.

"Well, well, my heroic friend, what an unexpected pleasure to meet you again."

The tone of Lanjoni's voice was gentle. He asked what she was drinking. "Whiskey."

"Have you ever drunk Amaretto di Saronno?"

"No."

"You must try that, darling. It's a legendary Italian liqueur from 1525. Created by a poor, beautiful widow, as a gift to the artist Bernardino Luini, a member of the da Vinci School, out of gratitude because Luini immortalized her in a renowned fresco in a sanctuary in Saronno."

A waiter served her.

Lanjoni continued: "You see, the color of the liqueur matches the chestnut of your hair, like the green of your blouse and your emerald eyes."

Francien was looking at him, remembering how she had left him last. Would he remember her, kicking in the air, her panties fluttering around her ankles?

Lanjoni slid closer. "Geraldini tells me you are leaving earlier than you intended."

"Who?"

"Mrs. Lantini. You're not leaving because of our vehement encounter, I hope?"

The son of a bitch, Francien thought, irritated by the flippant way he referred to his rape attempt. She remained silent and looked into her glass.

Lanjoni did not fancy to have Amaretto all over him. The bitch was capable of it, even in a room full of guests.

"I apologize," he hurried on, "for being so rude last time, but you looked so beautiful and your appearance on the program aroused me very much. I was terribly rude and I hope that you will forgive me for that."

He seemed serious. She shrugged. "Taught you a lesson, I hope."

"You sure did, and to make amends I would like to offer you this as a token of my esteem for a very exceptional lady."

He took a small package from his pocket and handed it to Francien, who had listened to him with astonishment and now looked at the small parcel wrapped in matt black paper, covered with tiny gold stars and bound with a shining black ribbon.

Lanjoni folded her fingers over it. Bending forward, he kissed her on the lips and put his hand between her legs, where it remained for a second. Then he turned around, walked up to Mrs. Lantini and apologized for already having to leave. He waved broadly to the other guests and on his way out threw a last glance at Francien, who now sat alone at the bar, her heart beating, color rising in her face, the parcel in her hand, and not daring to look around for shame that somebody had seen Lanjoni's hand.

Glancing up into the mirror, she saw Bram reappearing from the darkness with the woman. She was leaning against him, her arm linked through his and her other hand holding on to his bicep. As if she owns him! Francien put the parcel in the pocket of her skirt, finished off her Amaretto and rose from the barstool to see to it that the slut would know who owned whom.

Turning, she stood face to face with Mrs. Lantini. Was Francien feeling sad at his sudden departure and needing some sisterly advice to see Lanjoni in his true light?

"You look a bit tired, my dear. You must have had a long day, with all the packing and the long drive. If I may be so free as to give you some advice, woman to woman: a good night's rest cures almost everything, from a cold to a broken heart, and at our age the heart doesn't crack so easily anymore, does it? Maybe just a hairline fracture. You know how men are and Lanjoni is the worst. Come along to your room for a moment. It will do you good to relax, and then we would like to have you back among us."

Francien didn't know how to object. Together they walked the long corridor, and when they reached the guest room Francien urged Mrs. Lantini to go back to her guests. She would be fine and would rejoin them in a while.

She entered, she walked to the bed and sank into the very soft mattress. She took Lanjoni's parcel from her pocket and stared at it, not knowing what to expect. Slowly she pulled the ribbon and unwrapped the paper. When she lifted the lid, textile swelled out of the tiny box. Taking it between thumb and forefinger, she slowly pulled it out of its narrow enclosure and held it up in front of her and stared at it. Then it dawned upon her. My own panties?

They had been left behind after the battle in his apartment. When the realization sank in, tears welled into her eyes. She felt so deeply humiliated that she sat there crying, wiping the tears off her cheeks with one hand, holding the garment with the other. It hurt. Anger would not come. Anger had so far saved her from suffering too deeply, but now there was no anger. The humiliation was too deep.

After a long time, when her tears were finished, she rose and dropped the panties into the pedal bin. Then she poured half a tumbler of whiskey, drank it down in one go, undressed, threw her clothes on a chair, cleaned her makeup away somewhat, switched off the light and went to bed, not wanting to be part of the world anymore.

———

She couldn't tell Bram and Marjet was in Rome. She had only one desire, to clear out and forget the whole thing.

After breakfast and a bath, they packed their suitcases and went to say good-bye to the Lantinis. Mrs. Lantini patted Francien's hand when they were leaving.

"Are you all right now? Forget about Lanjoni, he is one of those men."

Francien nodded, not knowing what to say. When Bram started the engine, Mr. Lantini came up to his window.

"I forgot to ask, but did that child you hit with the car get the model?"

"He sure did and he was ever so pleased with it. He is a car freak, wants to be a racecar driver. God knows how he can make it. He said he would write to you."

"Oh, well, never mind, I just wanted to know. Give him my regards and wish him luck, will you?"

"Sure, and thanks for sending it."

Lantini patted Bram on the shoulder. "Have a good trip." He walked back to Geraldini and they both waved them off.

While Bram weaved through the heavy traffic, sorting out the direction of Lugano, Francien considered the last-minute conversation between Bram and Lantini.

"Say, did you tell Lantini about the accident with the boy?"

"No, I didn't."

"How come he knows about it?"

"Dick wrote him a letter and asked him for a scale model of the Grand Tourissimo, and Lantini sent him one. Amazing—usually you get one only when you buy the real thing."

"How do you know he wrote that letter and that he got that model?"

"The boy told me."

"That means that you have been visiting him."

Bram remained silent, concentrating on the traffic.

"You have been visiting him. Why wasn't I to know about it?"

Bram kept his attention on the road, going as fast as the traffic allowed. He did not answer.

"Well?! What's so secret about it that I shouldn't know?!" Her voice grew louder as her anger rose.

"There's nothing clandestine about it."

"Oh, no?! It's her, that's what so secret! That mother. Visiting her? *Screwing* the slut. *That's* why you cheated on me behind my back. What a fucking, double-crossing bastard you are! No, Mr. Aardsen did not care to go to the hospital. Mr. Aardsen couldn't care less. Ah ha! And that's where the scratches came from! You lied through your teeth, you *filthy fucking swine!*

Bram realized that there would be no slow and easy journey back home. With last night's party still hanging over them and 1500 kilometers ahead of him, he could not handle the car *and* Francien. So he got off the road into the first available rest area.

"Now you listen. It's not what you think. So get off my back while I am driving. We're going straight home and we'll talk about this when we get there, but not now."

"Yeah, yeah! Mr. Aardsen needs time to think up another pack of lies. You are such a—"

Bram did not let her finish the sentence. He turned toward her, grabbed her shoulder and made her face him.

"We will drive straight home, but you shut up till we get there, otherwise I'll kick you out of the car here and now and go home alone! Is that understood? And I mean really *kick* you out of the car, like I would a man!"

The engine roared and the tires screamed as he pulled out back onto the road, full throttle till the speedometer went over 200 kilometers per hour. It worked. Francien kept silent.

Her shoulder hurt, but the fact that she had provoked him into violence and shouting gave her at least some satisfaction.

The dashboard clock showed 5:08 the next morning when Bram, green with fatigue, shut off the engine in front of their house.

They had not exchanged one word during the entire trip. In the roadside restaurants they had helped themselves at the self-service counter, Bram paying for both of them. The grim silence in the car had made Bram an alert driver.

Unloading the luggage, they walked up the garden path. Bram unlocked the front door, put the suitcases in the hall and went into the living room, vaguely lit by the oncoming dawn.

Bram moved his arms to loosen his shoulder muscles and went to the bar.

"Bring some ice, will you?"

Francien went to the kitchen, opened the icebox, broke loose the ice onto the drainboard, gathered the lumps into the ice pail and returned to the living room. Bram sat in his chair, bottle in hand, two glasses in front of him. He grabbed a handful of ice out of the pail, divided it evenly between the two glasses and poured the whiskey, as he had done countless times before.

Francien hesitated, but then sat down in her rocking chair. For a while they sat there smoking and sipping their whiskey, not knowing how to break the silence.

When the melting ice weakened the flavor too much, Bram added some more liqour and did the same to Francien's glass. He didn't want to go to bed. The tension from the long drive was too high. Also, he had promised that the matter would be discussed once they were home. His going to bed would not stop her from bringing it up anyway, and he preferred to face whatever would come in the living room rather than in bed.

Francien was worn out by the emotion and the long trip. As always, being away from home and coming back, made the house look new and yet familiar. As if it had been decorated by a friend who had done it exactly to her taste. The familiarity and the newness gave it greater value. The feeling of having established something of worth made her feel safe and it also made her worries about Bram's loyalty seem unreal and mildly dangerous. The entire holiday had been turmoil, a nightmare. If only he had told her about visiting that boy, but of course if it had only been the boy, he would have told her. It was that woman. Had she had a fat body and terrible hair, he would have told her, she was sure, or he wouldn't have gone at all.

"You are not going to visit her anymore!"

"What d'you say?"

"You are not going to visit her anymore!"

"How do you know?"

"I don't want it. I won't have you screwing around behind my back."

"I didn't go to bed with her."

"Ah, tell that to the cat," Francien snorted. "I saw you last night with that tall Italian you gamboled into the garden. Of course you went to bed with her."

Bram remained silent, unwilling to repeat himself.

"So from now on, no more visits. Understood?"

Bram said nothing. Just stared. Would he promise? He wouldn't, as long as he remained motionless. Francien couldn't have believed it would be so easy.

During the long ride home, she had considered, reconsidered, thought and rethought, and her end conclusion had been that she would forgive him having fucked the slut, but he would have to promise to stop seeing her. The expression "made love to" did not even enter her head, because her primitive instinct sensed a very big problem if he was really making love to that woman.

"I will forgive you for cheating on me. Men, apparently, are like that, fucking animals, but now it has to be over. So no more fooling around with that call girl. Is that understood?"

"She's a model."

"*Ha!* Model?! You believe that? You need your brains examined," she said, tapping her forehead with her index finger. "Anyway, model or no, you are *not* going to see her anymore."

Bram remained motionless.

"Is that understood?"

Bram kept silent.

"Do you hear me?"

"I heard you."

"What do you mean, 'I heard you'? Of course you heard me, you are not deaf, so what do you mean, 'I heard you'?"

"I mean, I have understood every word you said."

Bram felt resistance boiling up inside. Taking orders from her? No way. Against all odds he hoped that, if he sat still and made no move at all, the whole thing would go away. To call Pauline a slut! If ever a woman had class it was Pauline. The way she walked, the way she talked, the way she had reacted to Dick's accident, a boy whom she was raising singlehandedly. In spite of the energy from the whiskey he felt a tiredness in his hands and an emptiness inside his arms. He wanted to embrace, rejoice at the escape from the autostrada killers, the safe passage of 1500 kilometers—anything.

"So that is understood then." Francien finished her glass and rose, picking up her own glass and the ashtray. "You better go to bed, too. You must be tired."

Still Bram didn't move, as if moving were signing a contract he didn't want to execute.

"*Are* you coming to bed with me, or am I not good enough for you anymore? What has she got that I haven't? Maybe you like 'em bony, is that it? Or does it fascinate you that she fucks 'round the clock with every Tom, Dick and Harry, if not with all three of them at the same time, her cunt a kind of club, a meeting place for men. Is that it? A feeling that you are all members? I will send Lanjoni over to her when he comes to Holland, also such a sperm-scattered brain, just like you!"

"What has Lanjoni got to do with it?"

"Well, I taught him a lesson, too, trying to fuck me in his apartment after the show."

"*What* did he do?"

"Tried to fuck me. But I taught him a lesson."

"He was at the Lantini's last night, our last evening?"

"Yes, he was, the swine, bringing me my own panties back, wrapped up in a parcel like a Christmas present."

Glad about the change of subject, Bram asked, "But what happened then between you? You looked all right to me when the program started, and he did bring you back to the apartment after the show, didn't he?"

"Bring me back?! Don't make me laugh!" Francien sat down, concentrating now on her own unsorted emotions. She told Bram what had happened in Lanjoni's apartment and how, for her, Lantini's party had ended with sitting on the edge of the bed, crying her eyes out.

Bram watched her face, childlike as a teenager who has never been told what the world is like. He poured some whiskey into her glass and added ice.

"But it was obvious that he thought you were up for it when you agreed to leave your things in his apartment until after the show. He could have put them in his car."

"Marjet said the same thing, as if it is always *my* fault that you studs can think of nothing else but sex! You are all the same. You are not a hair better than Lanjoni, or those bastards on the highway for that matter, sneaking off to that call girl in Gouda all the time. What must that boy think? First you make him an invalid and then you fuck around with his mother."

"I did not go to bed with Pauline."

"Aha, it's already 'Pauline'! And yet you want me to believe that you didn't go to bed with her. I may be naive, but not so naive that I would believe a lie like that. If you were not sleeping with her, you would have told me you were seeing that boy. I would have found that very understandable. But no, you were not visiting that boy, you were visiting his mother. You like them long and skinny, I presume, or is it the black hair and the blue eyes that you fell for? But I tell you, you are not seeing her anymore and I want your word on that, *now!*"

"How do you know that she has black hair and blue eyes? Do you know her?"

Francien blushed. "No . . . uh . . . well . . . you may just as well know. I have nothing to hide. I looked her up in the hospital to see whether I could be of any help, because you didn't want to go and visit the boy. But of course she didn't want my help. Oh no! She wanted *you.* The whore! I'll be damned if I am not the only decent woman around. Even that Mrs. Lantini is no good, having Lanjoni as a houseguest. Of course, she sleeps with him, too. That must be it."

Every time she called Pauline a name, the gap between them widened and his irritation grew.

"She is not like that and I didn't make love to her."

"The first time I ever find out that you've been in Gouda, you will find your suitcase on the doorstep and out you go!" She emptied her glass and put it on the table with a bang like a chairman closing a meeting. Then she rose and marched off to the bedroom.

She is drunk, Bram thought, looking at the whiskey bottle that was nearly empty. He poured the rest in his glass and listened to the sounds of the awakening neighborhood. The sun's rays moved into the room. Half an hour passed. He stubbed out his cigarette, and trusting that she would be fast asleep by now, he rose and went to the bedroom. The door was locked.

For a moment he was so tired and surprised that he didn't get it. He pressed the knob down again and pushed against the door. It was locked indeed. Then anger soared. Damn it, in my *own* house, being locked out of my *own* bedroom, by my *own* wife. Never!

He strode through the kitchen into the backyard and went into the shed, snatched the ax from the shelf, and rushed back in. He positioned himself in front of the bedroom door, and as securely as the alcohol would let him, landed the ax with a thundering crash on the door somewhere near the lock. Nothing much happened apart from the wood being dented. The resistance of such a simple door made him even angrier. After four blows the wood gave in, the lock lost its hold and the door swung open, revealing Francien in her nightgown staring at him with panic in her eyes. They stood there a couple seconds, staring at each other: his face drawn from fatigue and grim with anger; her face puffy with sleep, hair sticking out, the suntan paled into a dirty sheen by exhaustion and fear.

"There's no need for panic. You're not *that* good."

He spun around, stalked through the kitchen, threw the axe in the shed, walked around the house, got into the car and drove off.

Driving the car always had a quieting effect on him. He found himself heading for Gouda. After a while he realized he couldn't possibly go to see Pauline and Dick at this hour of the day and in this state of mind. He checked into the motel at Leiderdorp, took a shower and went to bed.

6

Two weeks passed. At four o'clock in the afternoon of the second Thursday, Francien woke up from the doorbell's constant ringing. The cigarette had fallen from the overloaded ashtray into a pool of sherry, which had prevented it from burning a mark into the table's surface. The sherry glass had toppled over, a piece of the rim was broken off. With a splitting headache, she got up from the couch, stumbled over an empty sherry bottle and nearly fell onto the television set. Looking ashen and feeling sick, she gathered her morning gown around her and knotted the belt. Then she staggered into the hall and opened the front door, in spite of the fact that she had sworn to herself she wouldn't ever see anybody anymore.

"My God!" Marjet stared at Francien's face, which clearly showed the traces of a fortnight of boozing, smoking and negligence. "What's happened to you? Are you ill? I phoned you several times since we came back from Italy, but you were busy all the time. What's going on with you?"

Without waiting for an answer she stepped inside and closed the door behind her. Francien walked ahead into the living room, took a bottle from the low table, sat down on the couch, put the broken glass upright and sloshed sherry into it. She pushed the bottle over to the side where Marjet sat. Before Francien could put the broken glass to her mouth, Marjet reached over the table and seized her arm.

"Don't do that. You'll cut your lip. That glass is broken."

Francien let the glass be taken from her hand and looked at Marjet. The familiar, well-made-up face, the shining hair and the nicely fitting dress made her aware of her own shabbiness. Tears welled into her eyes and, covering her face with her hands, she started crying. Marjet circled the table and slid down next to her on the couch, taking her friend into her arms. She stroked Francien's sticky hair and patted her shoulder.

After a while Francien became quiet.

"Why don't you wash your face, comb your hair and put some clothes on? Nothing can be so bad that a woman should neglect her appearance. I'll make a cup of tea, and then you tell me all about it. But one question first: Is Bram dead or going to die?"

Francien shook her head.

"Okay, then make yourself a bit presentable." She pulled Francien up from the couch and led her into the bathroom.

In the kitchen another shock awaited Marjet. Francien had never been a compulsive housewife, but dirty dishes were piled high in the sink and pans sat on the range caked with stale-smelling food.

She found the kettle, put it on, fished two cups out of the pile, cleaned them and brought them into the living room. While waiting for the water to boil, she cleared and cleaned the low table, emptied a vase with withered flowers and put crockery into the dishwasher. When she came into the living room with the teapot, Francien was coming out of the bedroom, dressed, her hair combed and lipstick on.

Sitting at the table, Francien spilled out the whole story, erratically at first, but gradually making more and more sense. After an hour, Marjet had a fair idea of what had happened.

"Where is Bram now?"

"I don't know. At work I think. He comes in late, some nights not at all. Then he comes home early in the morning to put on another suit. He spends all his time with that hussy, I think."

"Did he say so?"

"He doesn't say anything. I asked him several times, but he doesn't answer. I did phone the garage and ask for him, but he tells his secretary he'll call me back, which he doesn't. One day I heard that girl say, 'It's *her* again.' After that I stopped phoning."

They were quiet for a while, just sitting there, smoking and drinking tea.

"Marjet, I don't know what to do anymore."

"That's not surprising, but let's get a few things straightened out. First, you can never call her—what's her name?"

"Pauline."

"Right. You can never call Pauline a slut anymore. If she is one, Bram has poor taste. But he married you. If she isn't, you accuse her of being something she isn't, which he will hate you for. Suppose he loves her, then he won't even accept reasonable criticism, let alone unjustified accusations."

Francien nodded reluctantly.

"Secondly, do you want to get rid of him?"

"No, but he has humiliated me so! I . . . don't know anymore."

"Before you do anything else, you have to decide whether you want to get rid of him or not. Realize what you are heading for. You will join the band of divorced women trying to find another man. Can you imagine yourself dating again?"

"Oh, Christ, no!"

"You know what we'll do? You start cleaning up the house. If Bram sees you falling apart like this, he will think you are worthless after all, and if he finds you in the shape I found you this afternoon, he'll lose whatever he feels for you. Call it love, care or protection—whatever—but remember how he raced over half of Italy that night because he thought you were in trouble. So you clean up the house tonight and do a good job. Then go to bed. If Bram comes home, whether in the middle of the night or tomorrow morning, say nothing if he says nothing. If he speaks to you, be as polite as if he were a stranger. Promise?"

"Okay, I promise, but do you think things will ever be as they were?"

"How do I know? I'm not God. Tomorrow morning, at ten, I'll pick you up, and then we'll go to the beauty parlor and restore the damage you've been doing to your face. We'll have lunch somewhere. Tomorrow I want to know whether you wish to get rid of him or not. I have to go now. The kids will be home any minute, and I still have to cook."

When Marjet had left, Francien sank back onto the couch. Gradually, the impact of Marjet's visit made itself felt. It broke the isolation into which she had fled.

She rose and wandered through the house, not knowing where to start, and ended up in front of the bar staring at the whiskey bottle. She shut the small doors, went to the bathroom and took a shower. Slowly turning off the warm water, she gasped for air. After she had rubbed herself dry, she hesitated. Usually, when cleaning and scrubbing, she wore one of Bram's old shirts. The material felt good on her skin. They were practical to work in, and wearing one gave her a feeling of connection. Her tactile need won. Buttoning the shirt, she went to work. By ten-thirty she was exhausted but satisfied. She took a bath and was in bed by eleven.

Bram never came home that night, nor the next morning.

———

The beauty parlor did a good job. Afterward Marjet and Francien went to the Heineken's Corner for a glass of white wine.

"I have been thinking about your situation and talked it over with Thijs last night," Marjet began. "The funny thing is that, like you read in crime novels, there is not a spot of evidence for what you suspect. Is it so bad that he visits the boy he hit with his car? Can he help it that the boy has a mother whose husband is in the States? Maybe she's just a stupid cow, nothing to be afraid of. God knows what she looks like."

"I do."

"Have you seen her?"

"Three days after the accident. I told Bram I went shopping but actually I visited her in the hospital in Gouda. A cool bitch, a call girl, I think. I went there to see if I could be of any help."

"What's she look like? Is she beautiful?"

With difficulty Francien told the truth: "Yes." She paused. "If only he would promise that he will never go to Gouda anymore, everything would be fine."

"You thought you could force a promise like that out of Bram? What about the boy?"

"What boy . . . oh, the boy! What about him?"

"Could it be possible that he really goes there for the boy and that you have put him in a fix because you ordered him to stay away?"

"I never said anything about the boy. I like children. You know we are trying to adopt."

Marjet sighed. "Oh, Francien, don't be such a rotten, spoiled child and don't do this to me. I'm trying to help you out of the mess you've created for yourself."

The barkeeper came and they ordered.

Marjet said, "Where were we? Oh, yes, about you wanting his promise that he wouldn't go anymore. Apparently you forgot about the kid."

"I don't mind the boy. He isn't important, is he?"

"He could be, more than you think."

"What do you mean?"

"Let's suppose that Bram feels responsible for having made him an invalid. Don't you think he might want to compensate for the damage done?"

"But it was not his fault, the stupid kid sticking his legs onto the roadway, lying flat on the ground—anybody can overlook that."

"That's not the point. If Bram feels guilty, he can do two things: Turn away from it and forget it, or go back and try to make up for it in one way or another. He apparently has chosen the latter."

"What must I do then, let him spend all his time with her, that . . . and the boy?"

"I don't know. You have to work that out with Bram. By the way, did he say anything when he came home last night?"

"He did not come home at all. I cleaned up the mess, I did everything to make it nice for him again and *he,* he doesn't even bother to come home anymore. Crap. Where do you think he spent the night?"

"I wouldn't know."

"Ah, Marjet, come on! I may be naive, and you may know more about men than I do, but he was in bed with her, and that is what I can't stand. That makes me furious, absolutely mad. Like a stab in the back by your best friend. I can never, never live with that."

"Then what *can* you live with?"

Francien didn't know. She felt cornered by life, trapped.

"I asked you yesterday to make up your mind whether you wished to keep him. If you want to get rid of him, you go to a solicitor and in a fortnight Bram gets a court order to pack up and go. No need to prove adultery or anything. You just say you can't live with him any longer. Being kicked out of his own house will hurt him so deeply that you'll have definitely seen the last of him, and you know where he will go then. But do you know where *you* will go?"

"I don't want to get rid of him, I want to get rid of *her.*"

"Then you have to outshine her. At least you have to take care she doesn't outshine you."

"What can I do?"

Marjet stared at Francien. "Let me tell you something, girl. Something that maybe you won't like. If you lose Bram it will also be the end of our friendship. I have seen that before, lots. A divorced woman can't socialize with a married couple. The husband either wants to go to bed with her or thinks her a bore. If he doesn't want to go to bed with her and she is not a bore, his wife thinks he will jump in the sack with her the moment he gets a chance, so she'll see that the relationship peters out. No more evening visits, no more lunches like we are having, and lack of common interest will do the rest.

"Now, what I wanted to say is this. You have a strong tendency to jealousy. You are possessive and clumsy with men. You lost your father early, which, in my opinion, is the reason you lack confidence in handling males. You want him to be your father in some way. You can be brave as you proved in Italy. Bram admired you a lot for that and for the way you handled the interview. He likes to live with you, but he will never accept your ordering him around. If you want him, I think I can tell you how to keep him, or rather get him back, because I think you have already done a lot of damage. Maybe more than you and I can imagine at this moment. You leave the bottle alone, do exactly what you have always done and be patient. Let's have a game of tennis tomorrow. That will be good to get the anger out of your system. Waiter!"

Marjet left and Francien did some shopping. She needed to replenish the larder: sugar, bread, onions, vegetables, soft drinks . . . hard drinks? She paused. What if Bram came home and he couldn't have his drink? He liked his whiskey. He was a whiskey man. She passed the rack and then went back. A "welcome back" is a "welcome back." She took a bottle.

Pushing her shopping cart onward, she wondered how one could make a man feel at home with what you put on the table.

"Anything I can do for you, madam?"

Francien woke from her reveries. Life was too complicated for her, or was it complicated for everybody? Surely not for Marjet, for she had Thijs, such an understanding, nice fellow. Why hadn't she married somebody like him? Had she ever met anybody like Thijs? Maybe not or maybe she had. Hadn't Jimmy been like Thijs? He had really wanted her. Why hadn't she married him? He was nice, he was true, but he was such a boy, looking at her as if she were the Queen Mother herself. Jimmy had admired her, taken everything she said seriously. Why, for heaven's sake, had she turned him down? If she had married him, she could have told him what to do and where to go and what to wear. *She* would have been the one who ruled the relationship. Why hadn't she? Afraid of the responsibility? Was that the problem?

She arrived home shortly after four. Opening the front door, she heard voices and her heart beat faster. Bram back? Good thing she had cleaned the house, and bought all the things he liked. In the hallway she saw a workman painting the bedroom door, while another was cleaning up the floor.

"What are you doing in my house?"

"I am painting this door and my buddy here is cleaning the floor."

"Who told you to do that, and who let you in?"

"Mr. Aardsen let us in. We repaired this door and I'm painting it in the same color as the others. You are Mrs. Aardsen?"

"Yes, I am Mrs. Aardsen," Francien replied, putting the shopping bags on the floor, "but I didn't know you were coming this afternoon."

"Your husband said to. He told us just to close the door behind us once the job was done. Terrible thing with all these burglars nowadays, isn't it? Lucky you disturbed them, coming back from holiday, so that nothing is missing, but maybe next time you better not lock the doors inside the house. Once they are in they'll get anywhere they like and do a lot of damage in the meantime if they're impeded. We'll have it finished in five minutes, so don't worry about us, madam."

Five minutes later they were gone.

Unpacking and storing the groceries, Francien tried to reason her disappointment away.

Of course it was silly to expect that Bram would all of a sudden come home as usual, as if nothing had happened. Although, thinking about it, what was it really that had happened? Okay, she had shouted at him, but it hadn't been the first time that they had had a shouting match, and then for no reason at all the brute had demolished the bedroom door with the ax. She smiled at the thought that he hadn't dared to enter once he saw her. What if the ax had been in her hands? She stopped putting away her groceries, remembering that night along the autostrada and the feel of the jack smacking the skull. *That* had solved a lot of problems in one blow.

She opened the kitchen door that led to the back garden and walked the path to the shed. The door stood ajar, the ax lay on the shelf. She shuddered, looked at her hands and then fled back to the kitchen. There she hurriedly put the groceries away, undid the cap of the whiskey bottle, and poured a big shot into a cup.

She gulped it and sat down on the kitchen stool, shocked by her own imaginings. After two more cups she started to relax.

She decided that before her thinking became incoherent, she'd better take the TV along with her into the bedroom, so that she would fall asleep before she drank herself stupid. She was playing tennis the next morning. Marjet would come and fetch her if she didn't show up. She knew what she would look like after a drunken night and feared Marjet's anger. She took a tray and put crackers, snacks and sweets on it. She should eat and not drink. But she added a jar of ice water and the whiskey bottle to the tray. Picking it up and walking to the bedroom, she turned at the door and pushed it farther open with her behind. Placing the tray on the bedstand, she went back into the living room and gathered up the portable TV. It wasn't one of the smallest but she managed not to scratch it or the doorpost.

Tossing her skirt on the chair, she discovered the cream-colored paint on it—a large stain, a print of her apple-shaped buttocks. A flaring anger soared up inside her and she looked around for a target to unload it on. Hands balled into fists, she roared and had the feeling that she wasn't far from turning green with rage and envy. The skirt she had bought with Lanjoni. Damn it, damn it, damn it!! *Why* did it always have to be her? She poured another cup of whiskey; at least that was better than demolishing the TV or the mirror. Although . . . This might well mean demolishing herself. After her anger subsided, she picked up the skirt, emptied a jar of turpentine into a basin, pushed the skirt under the liquid and left it on the drainboard in the kitchen.

Why doesn't Bram come home? Where is he? Well that's a stupid question, she sneered. But how long is it since we had that row? Anyway, long enough for him to have his fling with that sl—okay, Marjet—with . . . I'll be damned if I can call that woman by her name. What did Bram say she did for a living? Model? That's where he is, with his model. Bram and his model. Better than Bram and his slut. Nor was it so threatening as "Bram and Pauline."

She switched on the television but didn't find anything of interest on the three Dutch stations. She moved on to the two Belgian channels, checked the German and Luxemburg programs, and found one politician, a vicar and a pop group. Not having enough mastery of the languages, she skipped the BBC and TV-5 from France and settled for a quiz on Nederland 2. It was followed by "Der Alte," a German police thriller, subtitled. Eating snacks and sipping whiskey-and-water, she relaxed into the pillows and was adrift before the credits were finished.

Bram came home shortly after midnight. He quietly took the tray away, switched off the television and the light, and closed the bedroom door. In the kitchen he found the basin with the garment. He wrung the turpentine out of it, checked it for spots and hung it outside to dry. Going through the cupboards he noticed they had been restocked. He poured himself some Scotch, switched off the kitchen light and sat in the living room in the dark.

He contemplated joining her, but could not get himself to do it. Too much wounded pride. She had locked him out of his bedroom; he couldn't possibly sneak back in. He wondered whether he would sleep in the guestroom for the rest of his life, pride preventing either of them from making the first move. He would have to be begged.

He had to catch the 7:30 plane tomorrow to the Automobile Exhibition in Geneva, which meant rising at six o'clock. Anyway, there was not the faintest chance he could just get into bed and fall asleep. He brought the tumbler back to the kitchen and slept in the guestroom. He left the house at dawn. Francien was still unconscious.

—

A week passed. Bram sat at his desk overlooking the workshop where repairs and preparations for delivery of new cars were in full swing. He saw Marjet enter through the wide doors and look around before she headed for his office. Watching the way she walked, he noticed her elegance, the blond hair dancing with every step. Although she did not really look like the Goddess of Revenge, Bram was sure she hadn't come to talk about the weather, either. Most likely she was sent by Francien, but God knows what good she could do. She smiled at him through the glass door of his office and opened it.

"Good morning, Bram," she said, and, walking around his desk, she put a hand on his shoulder and kissed him on the cheek. Bram inhaled her perfume.

Marjet walked back to the front of his desk, sat down, fished a package of cigarettes out of her bag, lit one and blew the smoke toward him, smiling.

"How are you, skirt chaser?"

Bram grinned sheepishly. True or not, a man considers it a compliment to be called a skirt chaser. Thinking whether he really was one, he nodded a couple of times. "Fine, fine. You care for a cup of coffee?"

Marjet nodded. "Yes, please. Don't you agree?"

Bram's hand, picking up the telephone to order the coffee, stopped in midair. "Agree?"

"Yes, that you are a skirt chaser. That was what you were asking yourself, wasn't it?"

"Well, let me order the coffee first."

While he talked into the telephone, Marjet looked around, wondering what it meant to you if you owned a company, having started with nothing.

Bram told his secretary to hold calls and turned to Marjet. "What accounts for the honor of having your fascinating self in these humble surroundings?"

"Am I to believe that your lordship hasn't the faintest idea why we are here?"

"We?" Bram looked searchingly into the workshop.

"Majestatus pluralis, milord."

"Oh, I see." He heaved a sigh of relief. The last thing he wanted was a shouting match for all his staff to hear.

When the secretary brought in the coffee Marjet watched her closely and came to the conclusion that Francien had nothing to fear from that side. The secretary left and closed the door. She turned to Bram.

"Is she good?"

"How do I know?"

"As a secretary, you fool! See, you *are* a dallier. First thing you thought of when I asked the question."

"That's unfair. The way you looked her over was clearly to judge whether she was or wasn't . . ."

Marjet nodded. "You're right, but that doesn't mean that you are not a philanderer. Like all men. But let me get to the point . . . are you busy?"

"That depends. If you are here to buy a new car, I have time. If you are here to discuss my domestic problems, I'm busy."

"So you're busy. Let me ask you another question. Are you prepared to discuss the problems between you and Francien with me?"

"If I agree to discuss this with you, I'll have to answer your questions. I don't know whether I am prepared to do that. So far you only know Francien's side of the story. What will you do if I tell you my side? How much will you pass on to Francien and, come to think of it, to Thijs?"

Marjet thought about that for a few seconds. "You have a point there. I won't say that I came here for your own good only. I like you *and* Francien both, and I know that I will lose you both as friends if you two break up. I wouldn't like to lose either of you."

Bram sat looking into her gray eyes. Marjet made sense.

"Do Francien and Thijs know that you undertook this mission?"

"No. Listen, can we sit down together sometime in the near future and have a chat?"

"Tomorrow?"

"Are you sure you don't want Thijs to know about this?"

Bram lit a cigarette. "Yes. I don't want to talk about this knowing you'll report back to him. He is an inquisitive type."

"I can't deny that. Politicians—always eager to know other people's problems, preferably those of their opponents. Tomorrow is Wednesday. The kids will be free from school in the afternoon. Let me see what I can arrange. I'll let you know tomorrow morning."

"Fine. Four o'clock at the Motel Leiderdorp. We can have a drink and dinner afterward. But it'll only be between you and me. Promise?"

"Okay," said Marjet, and rose. Bram got up and walked with her through the workshop, where she distracted the mechanics.

Putting out his hand, he said, "Let's not kiss, I fear that there is already enough gossip circulating after the numerous calls Francien has made."

They shook hands.

At ten to four Marjet sat in the restaurant of the motel, watching the entrance to the parking lot.

"Good afternoon, Marjet." Bram's low voice came from so close to her ear that it startled her.

"Oh, hello. Where did you come from? I've been watching the entrance, but I didn't see you come in."

"That's right, I got here at three. I had some business in Utrecht that finished earlier than I had thought, so I came back to my room to work on some papers."

"You have a room here?"

"Yes, the owner is a friend of mine and he gives me a special rate. Like I give him a special rate when he buys a new car. That's what friends are for, isn't it?"

"Have you been staying here since you came back from Italy?"

"More or less," said Bram. "I suggest we go to my room. It won't do if some do-gooder hurries to Thijs to tell him he has seen us together."

"Lead the way."

When they were seated opposite each other in his room, and Bram had poured drinks for both of them, he held out his hand, palm up. "You wanted this, so you can start."

"All right. To begin with, I cannot not guarantee that I won't tell anything of what I might learn here to Francien."

"That might be a problem.

"Listen, Bram. You must understand that I'm here to see whether I can be of any help to Francien, not to you, because you are not a man who needs help, at least not from me. However, don't forget when Francien is in trouble, you are, too."

Bram sighed, but didn't answer. Marjet continued.

"Francien doesn't really *know* anything. She *thinks* that you sleep with the mother of that boy. You never told her you were visiting that boy. Why, Bram? Why did you continue seeing him, without telling her?"

Bram waved his hand in a helpless gesture. "Why didn't I tell her? It just happened, like why she didn't tell me she had visited Pauline in the hospital in Gouda three days after the accident? Have you asked *her* that?"

"No, I haven't."

Bram was thinking what it had been like at the time. It already seemed so long ago.

"She gave me an ultimatum about what I had to do about the boy, and that I had to do it right away. Then it would be over and done with. Mind you, 'over and done with.' I felt so lousy about the whole affair. I had done something irreparable to that kid. The way we sat there in the hospital, holding hands and not saying a word throughout the whole visit . . . I don't know. You read sometimes about a father backing the car out of the garage and overlooking his own toddler. I felt, I think, maybe something like that. Anyway, I knew that it was impossible to get it over and done with. The more so after that first visit. Yet . . . what could I tell Francien? That I was hooked by that boy? While she wanted it finished? That would only have led to constant quarrels I couldn't face. So I kept going. His father was not around, his mother was in the hospital. What could I do? The boy and I got to talking. And then, there comes a time when it's too late, when you can't very well bring it up anymore. Had she realized about Pauline, she would surely have put her foot down and insisted that I stop seeing the boy."

"Maybe. At best she would dislike it, fearing she would have to share the little attention she got from you, with somebody else."

"And at worst?"

"At worst you would have arrived at the same point where you are now."

"And which point is that, Marjet? I can't just tell Dick to go to hell."

"Dick?"

"Yes, the boy. But tell me, where do I stand? We are not on speaking terms anymore. We are not on sleeping terms, either. And all this because I refuse to obey orders based on brutal, vulgar and unjustified accusations."

Marjet shook her head and smiled. "You don't strike me as taking orders easily, let alone from a woman, even if they were nicely formulated and justified."

Bram shrugged. "Maybe."

"At the moment," Marjet said, "your whole problem focuses on the mother, which in my opinion doesn't do justice to the situation. It's hardly ever a passing bird that causes marital problems. When are you bringing Dick home?"

"Home? What do you mean, home?"

"Home. To introduce him to Francien."

"You must be joking! And have him cold-shouldered? Never!"

Marjet shook her head. "You're underestimating Francien. She wouldn't do that."

"Of late I have discovered more things than I have ever dreamed she would do. No, thank you."

"Wouldn't you like to take Dick home?"

"Of course, and maybe it could have come to that, but now that door is closed. The door of my own house, closed to a child I like, by my own wife because of her sick jealousy."

"I'm not so sure whether you are right there. Anyway, if I were Francien, I would see to it that you brought the boy home. However, as the situation stands, maybe it's more up to you. Shall we eat something? I don't want to get back too late."

As they waited for room service to bring the meal, Marjet told Bram how she had found Francien after they had returned from the holiday, and what Francien had told her. After the meal arrived, she picked up the threads of the conversation. "About the door being closed. Why don't you open it?"

"With a child on my hands?"

"It's not simple, I admit. But it would surely reduce the size of the problem. Now, what about the mother?"

"What about the mother?"

"You tell me."

"Why are you asking? What is it you want to know? Blue eyes, black hair, is that it?"

"You are dodging the issue."

"Me, no way. It's you who's dodging the issue, if you ask me."

Marjet hesitated, then braced herself. "Okay. Did you go to bed with her?"

"Is that important?"

"Yes."

"Then I presume it's also important for you to know whether I *shall* go to bed with her?"

"Yes, that's important, too."

"Why is it so important for you to know? Does it make her feel better when she knows that I did or didn't? Or whether I will or won't, or whether I will or won't next year or whether I will or won't with somebody else sometime in the future? I am getting the feeling that it's Francien who sent you to ask this and that disturbs me."

"Come on, Bram. I told you, Francien is unaware of this meeting. It's a reasonable question under the circumstances and there is a simple answer. I would ask the same question if I was your wife. I would want to know if you had slept with her. That is not too difficult a question and you are not too shy to answer it, are you?"

"No. It's much easier for me to answer it, than for you to explain to me why it is important to you. I don't answer questions if I don't understand why somebody is asking them."

"You know damned well why I am asking."

"The only reason I can figure is curiosity. Tell me I'm wrong."

"If I were your wife I would have a right to know where I stood—my future would be involved."

"Damn it, don't give me that legalistic crap. You can't expect your wife to go on living happily while you're in love with somebody! For a woman, it's important to know whether you have or haven't. It's not the same with men. For men it's a question of whether you have another scalp or not. Isn't that right?"

Bram shrugged.

"All right, I will try and to explain why it is important. Let's talk about divorcées, and not about women who want a divorce. Nor are we talking about divorcées who have a money-making profession. They can fail as wives and be very successful in their other professions. But a woman whose only job is to cook meals, wash underwear, do dishes, do shopping, have herself laid, bear children, change diapers, clean noses and the house . . . looking after a future generation is the most important profession in the world and at the same time the most undervalued, and not only by men. Saying that you're a *housewife* doesn't command any respect or admiration. Maybe it was better in the old days when a woman had twelve children. Anyway, it's worse when you have no children—like Francien. Her profession as a housewife doesn't make her irreplaceable. What makes a woman in her situation irreplaceable is whether her husband goes on liking her— the way she walks, her voice, what she says and when she says it. For saying something or doing something that makes him feel happy when he is feeling low. In short, making him feel like a *man* at home, even if he isn't much of a man in the outer world. If she creates a place like that, he will go on sharing his checkbook with her. If the other woman makes him feel *more* like a man, the wife will lose him. If he leaves, the wife is the loser, the one who fails, the one who is rejected.

"Her lady friends will gloat over her failure, because it proves that they are doing better than she. That's the one reason why a divorced woman loses all contact with her married friends. Apart from the fact that her pals don't like to have a woman around who's up for sale, the divorcée doesn't like to sit and see other women being successful where she failed. It's the same, I think, when your car dealer next-door goes broke. It pleases you that *you* are doing well where *he* lost out, and he will never come and see you anymore. Being a married woman is a profession and divorce means bankruptcy, or at least that you are fired. Is it so surprising then that a wife wants to know what her husband is doing with the competition?"

Bram sipped his wine and remained silent. He refused to admit she had a point there, because he didn't want to discuss Pauline with Marjet and thus with Francien. "I'm sorry but I still don't see the sense of it."

Marjet sighed. "You have a thick skull. Let's forget about the mother, but you better do something to get Francien back on her feet. I'm playing two hours of hard tennis with her every day in order to keep her from the booze and the bad dreams, but I won't keep that up much longer. I will phone Francien tomorrow and invite you both for Friday night. Is that all right with you?"

Bram hesitated.

"Well, I'll do it anyway, and then it's up to you whether you come or not."

"I'll think about it. We can't go on like this. Thanks for the invitation. Just a cozy evening, I presume?"

"As far as I'm concerned, yes."

Bram walked with her to the car. They kissed good-bye.

"Thanks for coming," he said.

"That's all right, but consider what I said about bringing the boy home."

"I'll see," said Bram.

Marjet phoned the next morning and Francien was flabbergasted by the invitation. She was sure Bram would not turn up. She said, "I don't want to phone him at the garage anymore."

"No need to. I invited him already."

"*And?* Did he say he would be coming?"

"No, he did not."

"You see what he's like. Never get a straight answer. Always beating around the bush."

"Well, I don't know. One thing I know for sure: you better not force answers out of him, because you may not like them. As to Friday night, just make yourself look like the hottest dame in town and start getting used to the idea that you'll be on your own tomorrow night. However, *don't let me down.* We don't want guys pitying us as a bunch of snivelling, prickless, brainless idiots, who start crying for help when threatened by a mouse and whose only defense is shedding tears. See you tomorrow night. Around eight?"

On Friday morning Francien was rummaging through the closet, contemplating what to wear. The black velvet slacks with the bronze blouse? Too cold for a bare waist. The television outfit was not a pleasant remembrance, either. She went to the living room sideboard and pulled open the drawer where they kept their cash. Counting it, she was surprised that the last note was a thousand-guilder bill. She had not counted more than six hundred guilders a week ago. Looking at the notes in her hand, she pictured Bram taking the bill from his wallet and putting it there. As with having the door repaired, he still cared. Why shouldn't she go and buy something completely new?

At two o'clock she was back home, thrilled by her own daring, and at the same time worried that she had made a fool of herself. She put the parcels on the dinner table and was hanging up her coat when the phone rang.

"Mrs. Aardsen speaking."

"Francien, it's me."

Bram. Her heart skipped.

"Francien?" he repeated.

"Yes."

"About tonight. You know the Fyke, the fish restaurant?"

"Yes."

"I reserved a table. Thijs and Marjet will be there at eight. Will you take a taxi?"

"But I thought Marjet wanted us to come to their house."

"That's correct, but it occurred to me that we have not had our after-holiday dinner this year and that it was my turn to host. So I phoned Thijs."

"I see, but why aren't you coming home first? Haven't you done enough overtime lately?"

"I have to deliver a 164-V6 to a new customer in Den Helder. He's here now, waiting till we have mounted the extras. He will pay cash on delivery in Den Helder. I can't send one of the others to collect a hundred thousand guilders on a Friday afternoon. I think I'll be there at eight, but if not, I'd like you to do the honors."

"But will you come?"

"Sure, I will come. I've organized it, haven't I?"

"But . . ."

"Okay, see you then. Bye."

Pensively Francien put the phone down. Would they be coming home together? Did that also mean bed together? She took a deep breath and felt little butterflies in her stomach.

7

The white cotton dress had a tight-fitting bodice that was styled after a military tunic—collar, epaulets and breast pockets. The broad maroon leather belt had a golden clasp, matching the long row of golden buttons that ran from her throat to the hem. The skirt was wide, reaching mid-calf.

It took her two hours, plus a double scotch, to get washed, dressed and painted. The result was such that she felt like humming when she walked the garden path to the cab, the leather coat loosely over her shoulders, the matching evening bag held under her arm, like an army officer his baton, the skirt swinging around her legs in rhythm with her steps.

She had just seated herself at the reserved table when Thijs and Marjet came in. After the kisses and the compliments about the dress, Thijs suggested they sit at the bar to wait for Bram. Marjet decided that she and Francien would have a mineral water and Francien's mood began to sag as ten minutes passed. When he gave her a light, the bartender smiled. "Are you waiting for somebody?"

"Yes, my husband." Francien looked at her watch.

"Is he always late?"

Francien shook her head. She didn't want to talk about Bram.

"Why is this place called the Fyke?"

"Because we catch hungry customers in it."

"What does it mean? What is a *fyke?*"

"A *fyke* is a long conical fishnet. It has several chambers, each ending with a bottleneck into the next. Once a fish swims into it, it tries to get out by searching for an opening along the inside of the net till it finds the bottleneck, only to enter the next chamber. It never finds its way back out. It is used mostly for—"

"Ah, there he is." Thijs saw Bram enter and walked toward him. Shaking hands he said, "I hear from Francien you had a good day. What kind of money do you make on a sale like that? Ten percent? Twenty or more?"

"Something like that," Bram muttered and faced Francien.

Not knowing the situation, Thijs chatted on: "She looks smashing. I think so, too. What would you like to drink, Bram? Whiskey?"

Bram didn't hear him. The white dress with the martial touches accentuated her suntan as well as her sporty figure. With green eyes and chestnut-colored hair, she really looked exotic, from somewhere like the Ural Mountains. He nodded approvingly and squeezed her shoulders, barely touched her lips, and softly said, "Well done."

After the meal they moved on to Thijs's place, the guys in Bram's car and the girls in Thijs's car. Francien had suggested going straight home, supported by Marjet, but Thijs wouldn't hear of it, because their after-the-holiday dinners traditionally ended at dawn. Bram was glad of the postponement.

Thijs poured stiff drinks, and played records too loudly. He wanted to dance with Francien, but she wasn't in the mood, and he ended up attacking Bram for the fact that he was a religion hater.

Bram tried to dodge the issue, but Thijs wouldn't let him. Moving closer on the couch, he patted Bram on the knee. "You can admit it to your friend. I may say *your best friend*. True or not? Am I your best friend? Now, speak up man, I'm your best friend, yeah, yeah. You can't deny that, and so, since we agree on that, you can also admit that you are a heretic. Come on, Bram, admit it. Be a man!"

"I wouldn't mind admitting it if it were true, but it's not."

"But"—Thijs continued waving his right hand with the glass and pointing a forefinger in Bram's face—"last time, before we went to Italy, I clearly remember you telling me that religion was poison for the people, and you don't like poison, do you? Apart from a smoke and a drink, I mean. Now do you like poison or not? You can tell your best friend. What good are best friends if you can't tell them the truth? Right or not?"

He added some more whiskey to Bram's glass and painstakingly lowered ice cubes into it. He looked up, very pleased with himself.

"Right," said Bram.

"Now we can talk. You are against religion, be honest!"

Bram was getting irritated. "Are you in favor of all the religions in the world?"

"What d'ya mean? That's not fair! You try to put the shoe on my foot, but I was the first to ask, so you are the first to answer, my friend, and don't try to beat a politician in a debate. I am alderman, don't forget that." He smiled benevolently.

"Religion is for the believers, Thijs. Let's drink to that."

Thijs banged his glass against Bram's. "Now you are my best friend, Bram, speaking wise words."

Bram had had enough of that. He got up and, glass in hand, waited for Thijs to do the same. When Thijs saw Francien and Marjet rising, too, he smiled and stood up as well.

Bram raised his glass to the other three. "Here's to a vacation at the Riviera next year, or whichever place we will choose, but not Italy anymore."

The dashboard clock showed 2:25. Bram drove carefully through the night. Francien felt nervous as a teenager on her first date. Get into bed with him? But how? How could she make him if he didn't want to?

Bram was too tired to imagine how it would be as they arrived home. Switching off the engine, he still didn't know how to handle the situation. When they entered the house, Francien disappeared into the bedroom, and Bram hung his jacket and tie over the back of a chair and fetched some ice. They had another drink, smoked another cigarette and commented on the meal and the restaurant. It was the seventh time they had had an after-holiday dinner.

"The lucky number," Francien said, and then they were silent for a while.

"We can't sit here forever," said Bram. He stood up, walked to the hall door and switched off the light. Francien felt her stomach shrink. For a moment, when Bram walked to the door, she dreaded he would leave or go to the guestroom. She sat in the darkness and closed her eyes when she heard him coming toward her. In the vague glow of the streetlamps he took her hand, pulled her out of her chair and led her to the middle of the room. Moving behind her he slowly unfastened the clasp of her belt and let it drop on the floor. His hands moved softly up over her body and his careful fingers started unbuttoning her dress all the way from the collar downward.

The hands of a technician, Francien thought, fighting the weakness in her knees and feeling him harden against her behind. Turning her around Bram slipped the dress off her shoulders. It slid quietly down to become a white circle around her ankles. When Bram unhooked the bra, Francien moved the upper part of her body a bit backward, making space for her hands to unbutton his shirt, and at the same time pressed her stomach forward and tilted her face upward. Their lips clung for a long time. Then Bram scooped her up and walked into the bedroom, where he lowered her on the bed. There was no further foreplay whatsoever. Nor was it needed.

When Francien felt Bram enter, she took a deep breath and threw her legs around him, hooking them together as if never to unclasp him. She came before he did.

Afterward, they lay on their backs with the solitude between them. They did not fit like spoons in a box, as usual. Francien got up and went into the bathroom to clean off her makeup. Bram took a leak and went to the kitchen. He cut himself some cheese and took a can of beer from the fridge. In the living room he left the lights out and sat down in his chair, naked. His body was barely visible in the light from the street.

After having cleansed her face, Francien hurried back to the bedroom, but the bed was empty. She put on her robe and went to look for him. "Are you hungry?"

"Yes"—and waving to the cheese—"help yourself. Can I get you something to drink?"

"No. I have a whiskey here."

He lifted his beer can. "Cheers."

"Yeah, cheers."

Francien didn't like him drinking his beer straight from the can. Would the other one mind? Of course she wouldn't mind. And of course he wouldn't drink beer straight from the can when he was with her. Most likely he drank no beer at all over there. She didn't like the way her thoughts were going, but watching him sitting there naked and drinking beer from the can, she couldn't help seeing him as a primitive male, or rather a primitive ape. The hair on his chest, his belly, and his prick hanging down in the shadows between his legs, as if clothes really didn't matter much. Not at all a gentleman, like Thijs. She only waited for him to burp, which would complete the picture. He just sat there, said nothing, took a piece of cheese every now and then, and washed it down with a swig of beer. The longer it lasted, the more it irritated her. She had to do something.

"What shall we do now?"

"Why don't you go back to bed; you must be tired."

"Why don't you come back to bed; you must be tired, too."

"I'll come, but I'd just like to sit and think for a while."

"Think of *her!* Don't you think you've had your fun? Screwing her all the time and only popping in for a change of clothes and a couple of nights in the guestroom when she has her period? Why are you demolishing everything we have for a roll in the hay with that slut?"

Oh, damn it, she had said it again. Damn it.

"I have been adjusting a go-cart for the boy so he can drive it in spite of his legs. I had to do that in the evenings, and at times I slept at the office. Lazy Willem and I finished it the day before yesterday, and I'm going to pick up the boy tomorrow for a tryout, and on Sunday I'll take him to the races in Zandvoort."

"Liar!" she screamed, snatching up the heavy earthen ashtray and flinging it right at his face.

He managed to deflect it at the cost of cutting open the back of the hand that held the beer can. It all happened so fast and the light was so feeble, neither of them realized very well what exactly had happened, but their fuses had blown. They glared at each other, both on edge.

Bram, flexing his upper body, blowing up his shoulders and pulling back his stomach, hands on his knees, feet wide apart, looked like a displaced Tarzan. His hand was bleeding and it dripped onto the floor, but he didn't feel it.

Francien met his anger head-on. "You are sleeping with that shrew, you lousy liar! *Answer me,* are you screwing her?"

"I'm not, but I wouldn't tell you if I was."

"Why not? Why not? Because you are a stinking coward! Look at yourself, man—a primitive, beer-drinking, fucking ape, who can only mutilate small kids and let himself be saved by his wife when he gets into trouble with a bunch of teenagers. You hypocrite. You should see your pharisaic face. '*I would not tell you if I was,*'" she mimicked. "No, of course, you wouldn't, because you have no balls, *man!* And why, why wouldn't you tell me? Hey! *Now!* Tell me, why wouldn't you tell me? To spare my tender soul? I bet! As if I would care if you fucked that cunt. *Man!* I couldn't care less. For my part you can stick it into a molehill and fuck the whole world in one go. I couldn't care less. It's your lying that drives me mad. Why can't you just admit it? When will you leave me? Tell me! When will you leave?!" She slammed her forehead with her open hand. "Stupid! Of course you wouldn't tell me if you were, would you, my little hero? You would just sneak away to your invalid and his mom. Now that you have mutilated her son, she needs you. You believe for *one* moment that she would have ever deigned to look at you, if you hadn't mangled her son? Mr. Stallion!"

She bent forward, grabbed the bottle and sloshed a big shot of whiskey into her tumbler, gulping it down in three swigs, while Bram sat looking on, perplexed by the venom in her voice, paralyzed by the outrageousness of the accusations. This was the same woman he had admired in the Fyke only a couple of hours ago? The daring creature with her own unorthodox beauty? The daring was still there, but the beauty was gone.

He put the can on the table and rose, while Francien helped herself to a refill. Walking to the hall he heard Francien's voice bordering on panic. "Where are you going?!"

"I'm not going anywhere."

"Of course you are not going anywhere. You are staying here and this whole sordid affair is over and out. Basta!"

"I have told you what my plans are for the weekend and I'm not going to change them because you open your mouth like a stinking sewer."

He caught the tumbler in time, but the whiskey flew out of it and landed in his eyes. It stung terribly. He covered his eyes with his hands. Francien hadn't seen clearly what had happened. She feared that he had glass in his eyes. She jumped up and rushed toward him, just in time to receive Bram's straight punch on the chin and drop cold onto the carpet. He stood there, tears streaming down his cheeks. Gradually his vision came back.

He looked down at Francien. He would be damned if he would let her scratch open his face. Then he realized he might have killed her. Suppose he had hit her too hard. Damn! Don't suppose, do something! he told himself. He put the glass on the floor, picked Francien up, carried her to the bedroom and put her on the bed. He listened at her mouth, and to his relief her breath came regularly. Hesitantly he looked around the bedroom but couldn't find anything more to do. He thought about an ambulance. He listened again. Her breath came as if she were sleeping. He listened to her heartbeat. Soft but regular. Then he shrugged, and went to the guestroom.

When he looked into the mirror he was shocked. There was blood all over his face. Touching it carefully to find the wound, he noticed the back of his hand, which was still bleeding. He had wiped his tears away with the back of his bleeding hand.

A stinging pain in her jaw woke Francien after two hours. She had rolled over in her sleep and touched the pillow with her cheek. She sat up. Bram wasn't in bed with her. They had had a fight. She hadn't kept her mouth shut but it had been his fault.

Slowly she got out of bed and went to the toilet. Then she walked into the living room. The grey dawn fought the streetlights in the drizzle. She went back to the bedroom to fetch her robe. When she came back, she saw the bottle on the table, but didn't see her glass. Looking around the room she spotted it on the floor. She hadn't drunk all that much, she figured. One or two when they had come home and most of the last one had ended up in Bram's face. That was as far as her memory would go. Sipping carefully and smoking a foul-tasting cigarette, she looked around the room and saw Bram's jacket over the back of the chair. She looked at it. His jacket. Men had no handbags. She kept looking at it.

Why not? Hadn't somebody said that in war and in love every thing was permitted? She looked again. Why not? He had no fine character, either.

She rose and walked to the chair. Lifting the jacket, it felt kind of heavy. She shook it but didn't hear a sound. She put her hand in an inside pocket and pulled out his wallet and an envelope. It had been opened. She pulled the letter from the envelope and unfolded it. She walked with it to the window for more light.

Dear Bram. Thank you very much for your letter. I'm sure that Dick will be happy with the surprise you are preparing for him. My back is doing fine and I have a lot of shows. Sorry I missed you last week, but the flowers still hold. I am very grateful for the attention you pay to Dick. He thinks and talks a lot about you. I have told him that you will pick him up on Saturday, around noon. He is counting the days.

Her hands were shaking. I was right, they are having something, the bastards. Only her painful jaw kept her from storming into the guestroom. She searched the other pocket and found a brown envelope. Opening it she didn't realize at first what she was seeing: bills . . . thousand-guilder notes. Good gracious. She started counting, After fifty she lost track. Her mind wasn't working that well. Then she smiled a sardonic smile. They were married. Communal property: so half of it was hers. She started recounting but lost track again when she reached forty. Hell, he was not exactly a fussbudget, either, so she took about half and put the rest in the envelope and the envelope back in the jacket.

Fifty thousand guilders. She was rich. That was cause for celebration, so she poured some more whiskey and took the glass with her to the bedroom. Where could she put it that he wouldn't find it? Her fuzzy brain thought about it for a while. Between the sheets? Under the mattress? In her vanity case? All too obvious. She had to think. Think clearly. She giggled, imagining him finding fifty thousand guilders missing. Better even when he handed the envelope to his bookkeeper, who would then check its contents and find half of the amount missing. That would teach him a lesson. She lay down on the bed, holding the glass in one hand and the bills in the other. She did not notice the glass slipping out of her hand, nor the whiskey disappearing between her legs.

Bram woke up late. His head was spinning and he felt his pulse in his forehead. Cold water and an aspirin cleared his head in the ten minutes it took him to get dressed. He put on his jacket, and felt for his wallet, his lighter and his cigarettes. Looking at his watch, he saw he could just make it. The traffic would be light on a Saturday morning and it was.

At two minutes to noon he turned into the Bakkerstraat. It had stopped raining and the clouds were breaking. Dick was out on the pavement waiting for him. He waved enthusiastically and rolled toward Bram.

"Are you ready?" Bram smiled.

"Yes, sir!"

Bram looked up along the windows and saw Pauline watching them. He saluted in a kind of military fashion, a broad grin on his face. The sight of her was medicine after the night before.

"We don't need the chair. Come on." He held out his arms and Dick did the same. Bram put him into the car. Next, he went to bring the wheelchair back. Getting out of the elevator he pushed the chair along the hallway.

Pauline opened the door. "I couldn't tell him that he didn't need the chair, for then he would have pestered me all day, guessing that I knew what you were up to. How was last night? Did it go as you hoped?"

"Not exactly. As well as it started, it ended badly. But to hell with that now. Let's see if we can make the young man happy. We'll eat somewhere before I drop him off, so don't worry about dinner."

On impulse he took hold of her shoulders, pulled her toward him and kissed her on the cheek. When he let her go, she got hold of his hand, looked at the bandage and then questioningly at him.

"It's nothing. Had an argument . . . with a wrench." He brought her hand to his lips, bowed slightly and was off.

"Where are we going?"

"You'll see."

"You can tell me now. The surprise has now begun, so you can tell me, can't you?"

"Listen, young man. You don't *tell* surprises. People have a lot of imagination and when you tell them beforehand, they imagine something more beautiful than the real thing can possibly be and the surprise turns into a disappointment at the *moment suprème*. You follow me?"

"I follow that you won't tell."

"I'm sorry. You'll have to wait."

"How long does it take to get where we are going?"

"Let me see. About forty-five minutes."

"At what speed did you reckon?"

"Average about fifty-five kilometers an hour."

"If you go faster, say sixty-five, that would shorten the time by roughly twenty percent, which means that it takes about thirty-five minutes only. Let's race. You never showed me what an Alfa can do. I'll buy one later, if you can convince me."

He grinned sideways at Bram.

"Ever heard of speed limits?"

"There's no police around and I'll look out for them."

What the heck, Bram thought, someone who had to go so slow of late is entitled to some extra speed once in a while. He slowly pushed the throttle down and the needle of the speedometer started rising. On the first straight leg of the provincial road it came up to 180. Dick was fascinated, occasionally looking back to make sure there was no patrol car following them.

When they approached the curve, he braced himself. At the very last moment the car braked with force, shifted into third gear and rounded the curve full throttle with engine roaring and tires screeching at 100 kilometers an hour. If it hadn't been for his safety belt, Dick would have been sitting on Bram's lap. Out of the curve, Bram shifted up into fourth. The next curve was nearer, but the procedure was the same. Dick was thrilled, pushed into the back of his seat, thrown forward and at times really hanging on to the handgrip over the door. Not having any foot-support, he was more a plaything for the kinetic energy than he would have been otherwise. Bram realized it, but the boy had asked for it, so he would get what he asked for.

In Alphen aan de Rijn he took the road to Leimuiden. There he took the freeway and once they were on it, he slowed down to the 120 kilometers per hour limit.

Bram said, "Here it's no fun. You have to do over two hundred on a road like this before you get a kick out of it. I would lose my driving license if they caught me. So we'll behave. But what about it? Are you buying?"

Dick grinned. "I don't know yet. I have to hold the wheel myself before I'm absolutely sure. It's a lot of money," the boy added seriously, but then could not help laughing. "Are we going to the garage," Dick probed again when they approached Haarlem, "or are we going to your house?"

"First guess is right."

Dick wondered what they could do at the garage that was fun and that he hadn't seen before.

"You have a Road Star Grand Tourissimo?!" he supposed when they turned into the drive.

Bram smiled. "Maybe something like it, who knows?"

He rolled up the big door of the workshop, drove in and rolled the door down again. Then he went to Dick's side. "Hang on."

Dick put his arms around Bram's neck and had himself lifted from the car. With his arms around the skinny body, Bram walked to the back of the workshop. Something lumpy was hidden under a tarpaulin. With one hand he pulled the cloth away.

It took Dick a few seconds. He was transfixed by the sight of it. The four wheels, the tub seat, the small engine on the back and the leather-covered steering wheel. He tried to wriggle himself free, impatient to get to the ground, forgetting completely his missing feet.

"Easy, easy. What do you think?"

He pulled loose from the vehicle, faced Bram, kissed him hard and then, thin arms clinging around Bram's neck, he fought his tears.

"Well, let's see whether it works and whether you can handle it." He lowered the boy slowly into the tub seat and carefully fitted the legs into the padded holders that had been mounted on the clutch and the throttle.

Then he stood up. "I'll be back in a minute." In the toilet he blew his nose, lit a cigarette and took a couple of deep breaths. He waited a few minutes to give them both time to relax a bit.

Returning to the workshop, he saw Dick's hands touching the machine like a man touching his lover's body.

"Does it work? Have you tried it?" Dick asked and, before Bram could answer, he shook his head. "No, you couldn't. For a normal boy, his feet would be in the way."

"We tried the engine on the roller bench, but the rest is up to you. How do your legs fit?"

"Fine. How did you know the measurements?"

"No need to, you can move the bucket seat back and forth. It had to be like that, because you are growing every day."

"Did you make this all by yourself?"

"No, Lazy Willem and I did it together. Now let's get going."

"Yeah, let's go outside on the road, then I can try it out."

Bram shook his head. "Legally it's considered an automobile, and you have no licence plates, no driver's license and this vehicle has not been approved by the Department of Transport, so you'll be in the wrong in all ways."

Dick's face sagged.

"You know what we'll do. I talked with the guy at the cart track. There are no races today, but he promised to be there at two o'clock, and then you can have the whole track to yourself."

"How will we get there when I can't drive on the streets?"

"We'll get there." Bram went outside and backed in a minibus. The backseats had been taken out. He lifted Dick from the tub seat and put him on the front seat of the minibus. Then he opened the back doors, put two planks from the bus floor onto the garage floor and pushed the cart aboard. Putting two wood blocks behind the wheels, he closed the doors and hopped into the driver's seat. Dick was holding an imaginary steering wheel. "Vroom, vroom, *vroom!*"

Completely nuts, Bram thought, and started the engine.

. . .

At the cart track, Mr. van den Bosch was waiting for them at the open gate.

"Here is the key, Bram. I've got to go, so you two enjoy yourselves. Drop the key in my letter box when you leave."

"No problem, and thanks very much for letting us have the track, Kees."

Kees van den Bosch looked into the cab of the bus. "Is that scrag your race driver to be?"

"He sure is. You wait and see."

"I've got to go now, but next time I'll come and watch. Would you mind, young man?"

Dick shook his head. "No, sir, not at all. I'll have to get used to onlookers anyway."

Van den Bosch raised his eyebrows. "Arrogance enough, now we'll have to see about skill." He raised his hand to Dick. "Good luck, anyway, young man."

"Sir?"

"Yes?"

"How long is the track?"

"Four hundred and eighty meters. Why are you asking?"

"If we don't know, we'll never know how fast I'm going."

Van den Bosch smiled at Bram. "Who knows? I wonder. Don't forget to drop the key, and phone me more in advance next time."

"I will, thank you. Good-bye."

The first circuit didn't go too well. He got around, but the bumpiness of the track surface was troubling his handling of the throttle. It was easy if you could rest your heel on the floorboard, but if you had no heel . . .

Dick tried some more laps and then halted where Bram stood timing the rounds with a stopwatch.

"You know, Bram, this is no good. I have to regulate the gas pedal with the muscles of my hips, where other people do it with their calf muscles. I think it'll be better if I can move my 'gas foot' backward and forward. That's easier than moving my knee up and down. The bumping of the car is also up and down and then I make a mess of it."

Bram thought about it: He has a point. Funny how difficult it is to anticipate his problems when you have complete availability of your limbs.

Looking into the boy's eager face, he said, "It might work if we firmly support your upper leg." He looked at his watch. Two forty-five. They had plenty of time. What the hell, why not.

"Okay. We still got the key, so we can lock up the place, go back to the garage and see whether we can work out your idea. If we are lucky, we will still have time to come back and try it out. But tell me, don't your legs hurt?"

Dick reached up for Bram's hand and pulled him down to his level. "No, it only feels a bit strange. Since then I've just dragged my legs along. Now I am doing something with my legs again. That feels great—" The boy swallowed, and hurried on. "It's marvelous, but it's so different from what I thought it would feel like. I always figured one would glide over the road, smoothly and speedily, something like flying, but this is rough, as if there were no springs and tires."

"There are no springs and racing will shake your bones till they get unhinged. Come on, let's move."

In the workshop Dick sat on the tarpaulin, closely watching Bram screw loose the stump holder. "Now let's see what we need. A fixed upper leg. This," Bram said, pointing at the stumpholder, "tied onto your leg and connected with a rod to the top of the throttle. That's what you had in mind?"

Dick nodded. "How long will it take?"

"Easy my boy. Learn one thing. Construction is a slow job and racing is a fast one. Never push your mechanics, if you ever get there."

"I will."

"Push them?"

"No, get there."

After Bram had gotten them Cokes from the machine, he went to the store. With all the car spare parts available, it wasn't difficult to find what he needed. Returning with an iron rod and a handful of gadgets, he gave Dick a pair of dark glasses. Welding a screw eye to the throttle and bolting the rod to it wasn't difficult. On to the stump holder. The welding glasses were shoved up into their hair; they were thinking hard.

"Can't you just weld it on?"

"We would spoil the foam-rubber coating. Moreover, it won't turn with the position of your leg. You would get blisters in half an hour. We need a fork in between which we can bolt this 'shoe,'" said Bram, holding up the stumpholder.

"If you drill two holes in it and pass a bolt right through, the holder will be flexible."

"Then we'd only need a strap from one side of the shoe over the knee to the other to prevent it slipping off."

"Right."

It was nearly four o'clock when the "shoe" had been reconnected with the throttle and the upper leg could be securely fastened to a rest welded to the floor of the cart. Eating a Snickers bar from the vending machine, they rushed back to the track.

His lap times gradually came down to 39 seconds by the ninth lap. From then on it was 39.5, 41, 41.3, and after a round of 42.4, Bram waved him down.

"You're getting tired. It's enough for today."

"One more round," Dick begged, revving the engine.

"Nope. You may have already caught a cold, and your leg muscles will hurt like hell tomorrow. Come on, untie your leg."

———

Francien woke up well after noon. She had great difficulty in returning to reality. Her brain refused to function, apart from registering a splitting headache. When she swallowed to get the filthy taste out of her mouth, her jaw hurt like hell. She touched it carefully. Must have bumped into something with it, she thought. She rolled onto her back. The sheet under her felt cold.

"Wet? Oh, my God. My period on top of it!" With a shock she sat up. A wave of nausea and dizziness made her close her eyes. After a while it passed. She looked at the sheet. Nothing. She touched the wet sheet and smelled it. Whiskey. Relieved, she sighed and sat with her arms around her knees and her head resting on her arms.

My God, what a mess. Why can't I keep my mouth shut, if only just for once? Why do I always shout like a fishwife? I'm no better than Bram, drinking his beer from the can.

Sad, sick and sorry, an enormous feeling of loneliness took hold of her. A weekend that had started full of expectation. Deep self-pity brought tears. She wanted to flee, away from life, back home. But there was no home anymore. Her mother was dead and her father had not returned from the sea. Bram wouldn't have had the nerve to stay away from home night after night if her father was still alive. But her father had died long,

long ago. Left her alone, when she was still a little girl. Everybody left her. Always. All the boys she had known. Her teenage boyfriend had exchanged her for another after six years of a miserable engagement. Others, too, had turned away sooner or later. Only Jimmy. She still had his letters. Pleading letters. He thought the world of her, would do whatever she liked, she only had to snap her fingers.

And then, when she was twenty-six, Bram had come. A bear of a fellow. Unbelievably, he fell for her. He made her feel secure, satisfied, proud. He was good-humored and capable. She had been thrillingly happy. Every day with him was a joy. His size, his voice, his career—it had been heaven to show him off to her friends. *Her catch.* Okay, he had his own opinion about manners, but he could be very thoughtful *and* he *was* somebody. He was respected and he was a good provider.

And now he was trading her in for another. Except she was nearly forty and everything was senseless defeat and loneliness. Back to work as a nurse? Holidays with another old maid? The empty room when you came home from the hospital. Eating alone, sleeping alone. Applying makeup, for whom? Buying clothes? It was over.

Only two months since Italy. The car jack, that fellow, Bram's admiration; the fight with that Italian journalist, the humiliation. Always ending up holding the wrong end of the stick. Except for that murderous bandit. The only time she had the right end of the stick. Yet what good had it done her? He was dead. She didn't feel the thrill anymore. She didn't feel anything but self-pity. It had been a hollow victory. Nothing to be proud of. She felt she had been considered a good monster. That's what Lanjoni had achieved with his loaded questions. Rape and murder, that's what they had had in mind, but they hadn't done it. One was dead. What if she hadn't killed him? Would she be dead now, or only raped? Dead would be better. She shuddered. From glory into the deepest misery, in two months.

The plans they had made for other holidays—Spain, the Riviera, Greece? She couldn't fathom it. *How? Why?* Tears welled into her eyes. She sat there for twenty minutes, motionless, feeling a deep, sad pity for herself. She got cold and started to shiver. I do have to get up, to clean up, she thought. Suppose Bram comes into the bedroom? No, he wouldn't. What had he said? Something about going somewhere with that boy. He wouldn't be in this bedroom anymore at all. Why should he? To get things thrown at him? Why couldn't I for once have kept my mouth shut?

She swung her legs out of bed and stood up. The world spun and her stomach turned. Staggering, she walked to the bathroom and turned on the taps for a hot bath. Waiting for it to fill, she looked into the mirror. My God, what a mess! Black circles around red eyes, hair sticking out, skin green under the leftover suntan, smudges of makeup.

When she wanted to examine her tongue, she couldn't open her mouth far enough. The pain in her jaw was intense. Leaning on the washstand with both hands, she closed her eyes and listened to the water tumbling into the tub.

I need an aspirin badly. Two.

She fumbled with the box and then shook it. Two encased strips of tablets fell onto the floor. She picked them up.

What if I take them all? Then Bram could have his honey and the boy, and I would be out of my misery.

She pushed one tablet out of the strip. Then a second. A third. She stopped.

It would be *the* solution. No more degradation, no more humiliation. Bram would be happy . . . would he? Would he really be happy if I were dead? Bram wouldn't want that. No, why should he? He would just walk away, like all the others. And I'll be better off, not having to face the humiliation.

The hot water, running over the side of the tub, reached her bare feet. She closed the taps and pulled at the chain to lift the plug. While she waited for the water level to come down, she quickly took the three tablets she had freed from the strip.

Pushing the plug back into the drain, she nearly burned her arm. The water was scalding hot. Routine took over. She added cold water, took the shampoo from the cupboard. Slowly, she lowered herself into the hot water. She adjusted the plastic cushion behind her head. The warmth of the water and the effect of the painkillers relaxed her muscles. Her body enjoyed the warmth. She stayed there fifteen minutes, dozing off every now and again, feeling the benevolent water taking the weight off her body. She was instinctive and tactile, not cerebral.

When the water cooled she washed her hair, got out and dried herself with a rough towel. The routine kept her going and her body appreciated the comfort. Pleasant sensations always improved her spirits. Mulling never did.

After drying her hair, she went to change the bed. When she pulled away the blankets, the whiskey glass rolled toward her. She bent to pick it up and stopped short. Puzzled, she stared at the bed, not believing her eyes. Bills. Thousand-guilder bills. She picked one up and turned it around, examining it closely. A thousand-guilder note. A number of them. From where?

She sat on the side of the bed and it gradually dawned on her: Bram's jacket. My God! What have I done? The money from the car he delivered. The bills. It must be 50,000 guilders. She should put them back before he missed them. That would be absolutely the end of everything.

She scrunched them together, hastily trying to push them into a neat pile. They had been slept on. Nervously, she tried to flatten them with her hand. When she had shuffled them into a bundle, she hurried to the living room to put them back.

The chair was empty, the jacket gone.

It was as if the floor sank away under her feet. She groaned. Stealing his money? But it was worse. It wasn't even *his* money, it was his business's money. Damnit. If only he had stayed in bed. They could have made it some more and gone to sleep. Why did he always have to drink so much, pressing her to follow suit. Surely he was an alcoholic.

She looked again at the bundle of bills. It was Saturday. He wouldn't need them before Monday. Tonight, when he was asleep, she would put them back.

Not knowing where to hide them for the time being, she looked around. She walked to the bookcase and stashed them away behind a row of novels. Uncertain, she looked around again, and then took the bills back out. This isn't good enough, they have to be in something closeable, she thought.

She took the bills to the kitchen. From the shelf she removed a canister with COFFEE on it. Taking out the measuring spoon, she shook the ground coffee onto a plate, then put the notes into the canister and poured the coffee over them, spilling a lot in the process. Edges of some bills stuck out. Nervously she opened a fresh packet and poured more coffee in until the money disappeared.

The spoon would not fit anymore, so she put it on top, and replaced the canister on the shelf, sweeping the spilled coffee into the sink.

She had to eat something, but the thought of eating was not appealing. After she had changed the bed and dried the moist spot on the mattress with the hair dryer, she dressed, made up her face and settled down on the couch. The aspirins had worked. It was ten to five, she noticed.

When will he come back? Where had he said that he was going with the boy? The races at Zandvoort? Were there races at Zandvoort on Saturday? She didn't know.

She picked up *Televizier*. It was not mentioned in the sports review. On Sunday, yes. It would be transmitted the whole afternoon. Maybe it was a training session he was attending. Anyway, that should be finished by six. He could be home by seven, eight at the latest if he had to drive the boy home.

She went to the kitchen, emptied a can of soup into a pan, heated it, poured it into a bowl, took a slice of bread from the bin and settled back on the couch. Her jaw ached with every spoonful. She managed to eat the soup, but the bread was impossible.

She tried watching television. Sports, more sports, a choir, a lecture. The rest was talking animals and cartoons for kids. Stupid, talking animals.

She switched off the television and looked out. There were dark clouds with patches of pale blue. Most of the trees had already lost their leaves, their branches black against the smudged clouds. The garden needed to be cleaned. A few chrysanthemums and autumn asters provided the last vestiges of color to the dying summer. She sank back on the couch, listening to the mantel clock. The clock went way back in her family. Bram had had it repaired and wound it regularly.

Her eyes wandered over the furniture. Inherited, bought, given. Bram's chair was his present from her mother on their wedding day. Francien had gotten the rocking chair. A sentimental hodgepodge—some good pieces, some not. No style to any of it. It was just accumulated.

I wish Bram would come, then we could have a drink together. The thought lingered. No, she could wait. He was the addict, not she.

8

He had to carry Dick into the snack bar. From the tenseness of his body, Bram knew Dick loathed it but had to put up with it under the circumstances.

Stupid, he thought, I could just as well have taken the wheelchair along and have left it in the car. How thoughtless. But it's too late now. I'll have to carry him out and into the flat as well. Must never forget that.

They ordered French fries and sausages. Bram noticed Dick had real color in his cheeks and was eating unselfconsciously with his fingers and enjoying it. His blond-white curls were more wavy than ever.

"What are you thinking?" Dick asked.

"Nothing much."

"What was it?"

"To be frank, I just figured we could have taken the wheelchair along just as well. That would have saved you from being trundled into this place like a baby."

"Don't worry. I hate it, but as long as it's you who does the carrying, it's not so bad. You know, I have been thinking that we have to have a name for the cart. Do you have any ideas?"

"Not really. I have been concerned more about the improvements it needs than about a name. What have you got in mind?"

Dick's half-eaten sausage paused in midair. "What about *Jiffy?*"

"Sounds good. Listen, I'm not sure you can brake well enough. Speed on a track is not only a matter of horsepower. It is also about brakes. When you approach a curve, the trick is to brake at the absolutely last moment, to keep your speed high as long as possible. You remember that first curve this afternoon in my car? I bet you were scared stiff when we neared that curve, fearing we would fly over the shoulder and land in the meadow."

"That's right. How did you know?"

"Simply because many times I have the same feeling myself, sitting next to other drivers. I don't know whether they can handle their cars or whether the cars can take the curve. If they brake too late, they brake too long, that means *in* the curve, and then the wheels lose their grip and the whole caboodle slips onto the shoulder at best, if there are no trees, or into an oncoming car, at worst."

"You think you can improve the brakes?"

"I don't, but on a Wednesday afternoon, when you have no school, I'll introduce you to Lazy Willem. Maybe the two of you can think up something."

"Who is Lazy Willem?"

"My top mechanic."

"Why do you call him Lazy?"

"Because he's lazy. If he drops a screw he takes a pair of tongs to pick it up, that saves him twenty centimeters bending over. Moreover he arrives late at work practically every day."

"And you don't fire him?"

"No. Any problem with a car he solves twice as fast as any other mechanic. You want something more to eat?"

"They've got ice cream here. Italian. May I have one?"

"Sure, what flavor?"

"Just vanilla."

Bram went to the counter and ordered two king-size cups. He himself preferred pistachio. While they were scooped, he observed Dick. From where he stood, the boy looked just like any other kid, the way he sat there with his legs underneath the table. In the cart that afternoon he'd also looked like any other boy. Thank God Lazy Willem had talked him out of mounting a small auxiliary engine on the wheelchair. But a race car later? Wasn't it irresponsible to push the boy into something he was bound to fail at? Bram collected the ice cream and went back to Dick.

"Here you are."

Dick looked up and noticed that Bram had also chosen Italian ice. "You like Italian better too? They have gourmet."

"I saw it, but not for me. Too vague a taste, hardly any flavor. Say, what were you drawing there?"

Dick grinned. "I was wondering if we could make a mechanism to lift the seat, so I could use it as a motorized wheelchair."

"I don't think that'll make much sense, because you can't enter shops and houses with what's-its name?"

"The *Jiffy!*"

"Right, *Jiffy.* But don't you agree?"

Reluctantly Dick nodded.

Bram said, "You know, my original idea was to mount a small engine on your wheelchair, but Lazy Willem suggested adjusting a go-cart for you."

"Much better. Anyway, the wheelchair is only temporary. I'll walk in six months. I'll have my feet then, like everybody else. Only I'll never have cold feet and no corns and nobody can step on my toes, and nobody will want to be in my shoes."

Dick grinned about his own sick humor, but Bram couldn't appreciate it.

"When will you get the prostheses?"

"Next year, they are fully booked till then."

"When next year?"

"They couldn't say. March or sometime. But meanwhile we can practice with *Jiffy.* I can become a member of that club, can't I?"

"I don't know why not, but we'll have to see about racing."

"Why? Because of my legs?!"

"Maybe. You never know. People do react oddly."

"But—"

"Hold it, don't cry before you're beaten. Let's move, it's after seven. Your mother might get worried that you have had an accident with your *Jiffy.*"

"Did she know?"

"Sure, she did."

Bram walked around the table, sat next to Dick, and turned his back to the boy. "Get on. I can't carry you like a baby."

Dick worked himself around on his knees, put his arms about Bram's neck and was lifted off the chair as Bram bent forward to bring the boy's weight over his center of gravity. Standing up, he linked his hands behind his back under the boy's bottom and felt the body nestle against his back.

It was after eight when they arrived at Gouda.

While Pauline was making coffee, Dick followed her, chattering on about the *Jiffy:* its speed, its acceleration, how he handled the throttle in the curves. On and on.

From the living room Bram watched Pauline's graceful movements. He enjoyed the happiness Dick showed. He wondered, Was it the fun of driving a motorized vehicle or was it the possibility of realizing his dream of becoming a racecar driver? Was it wrong to encourage him if he was bound to fail? Or could Dick really make it come about?

The road would be very, very long. Would he be able to support Dick all the way? Bram had enough problems of his own as it was. Yet what else could he do? He couldn't possibly call it off. Dick was his responsibility, despite Francien being mad as she was and his marriage a mess.

After they had finished their coffee and Dick his cola, Pauline told Dick he had better go to bed.

"It's still early, Mama, and tomorrow is Sunday. I can sleep late."

"You never sleep late, and with all the excitement today, you will be in no mood tomorrow if you go to bed late."

Before Dick could protest any further Bram said, "Tomorrow we are going to the races in Zandvoort, so you better get a good night's sleep, my boy."

It took a second for the news to sink in, and then Dick raised his arms high. "Yippee!" His face shone and his eyes sparkled.

"All right, all right. I hope it'll be fun, but you'll only be watching. Don't forget that."

After Dick had gone to bed, Bram and Pauline sat in the living room, not speaking, yet very much aware of each other.

"How are you doing?" Pauline asked.

"Fine, business is not bad. I can't complain."

"That's not what I meant. How are you personally? You look kind of lonely to me. Did something go wrong during your holidays?"

"One could say that."

"I know, the fight and the police, but is that still bothering you? Feeling guilty?"

"No, that's not it. If it hadn't been for Francien, we could have both been killed. However, so much has happened since then, I barely think about Italy anymore."

Pauline waited.

"On the last night, or rather the last morning in Italy, my boss asked me whether Dick had received that model of the Grand Tourissimo. When I told him he had, my wife figured out that I'd been seeing Dick, and consequently you—something I had never told her."

"Oh!"

"We had a row at five in the morning. I knocked the bedroom door to pieces and I've hardly been home since then."

Pauline raised her eyebrows. "Where have you stayed in the meantime?"

"Mostly I sleep in the Leiderdorp Motel. The manager is a friend. I have to keep my business running, and I can't do that having shouting matches every night into the early hours."

"I'm sorry to hear that. So, your wife is jealous."

"Jealous, yes. She loses all perspective. I've always known she had quite a temper. Actually it fascinated me. The challenge of conquering it, maybe. But now that primitive temperament of hers is directed at me, and that's quite different. Normally she's a good sport. I don't think many women could have done what she did in Italy, but if she thinks she can order me around, she's mistaken. I have great difficulty taking orders from a guy, let alone a woman. That's out of the question. Regardless of whether she has a reason to be jealous or not."

"Was that the cause of the damage to your hand, too?"

Bram nodded.

"Does she know you were taking Dick out today?"

"Yeah, I told her. She didn't believe that it was Dick I was going with, so she flung an ashtray at my head. I saw it coming, thank God."

"And you told her about tomorrow?"

"Yes, but let's forget it for the moment. I'll sort that out later. I'm worried about Dick. Aren't *you* afraid that I'm giving him false hopes with this cart?"

"I wouldn't say *false*. You give him hope, yes, and I can't see what's wrong with that."

"I'm afraid he will collapse when it turns out to be an impossible goal."

"That may be, but what is he without hope? Isn't it wanting that keeps us going?

"True. Still, I should like to spare him the disappointment."

"But, Bram, how would you do that? By crushing his dream and disappointing him now? Do you know, Dick never tells anybody that he met you as a result of the accident. He talks a lot about you with his friends. The other day he had a classmate here. I heard the boy asking whether you were his uncle or something. Dick told him that he met you in the hospital in Haarlem where you were for some vague reason or other."

Bram was astonished. "Does that mean he can't live with the idea that I did it to him?"

Pauline shook her head. "He wants you to like him for himself and not because of his tragic stupidity. It was quite a blow when his father went to America. He is convinced his father doesn't like him, otherwise he wouldn't have gone away. He blames himself. Now that you have come into his life, however unfortunate the circumstance that linked you, he wants you to want to know him and he takes great pains to look good in your eyes."

"Do you think I am fond of Dick for what he really is?"

Pauline smiled. "Aren't you?"

"How can I know for sure? Of course I feel guilty. Even more so because he's such a great kid. I've always loved cars, from the time I was a boy. To watch Dick when he first sat in the cart . . . it, was fascinating. And you should have seen his seriousness when he told me this afternoon that his control of the throttle wasn't good enough. As if I were his hired mechanic. Pretty assertive, that son of yours."

"I hope so. He'll need a lot of that in years to come. If he's not arrogant, the world will only offer him pity. By the way, I applied for his prostheses. He may be called in some time early next year. He's expecting miracles. What can you do but hope?"

For a while they talked about Dick's school, Bram's business and Pauline's job. It was late. Bram asked to use the telephone and called the hotel.

"I take it that you don't intend to go home tonight?"

"That's right. I don't know how to handle it just yet. Another row would do neither of us any good." He finished dialing.

"Bram Aardsen here. Is my regular room available for tonight? . . . Fully booked? . . . The races. I see. Well, never mind. Thanks, anyway."

He cradled the receiver and sat down, trying to figure out what he should do. Pauline left the room. After a few minutes she came back.

"Would you prefer a solid pillow or a soft one?"

Bram didn't answer. He took a deep breath.

She continued: "Since you have the blame already, you might as well stay here for the night. So, which do you prefer, a solid one?"

Bram nodded. "Thank you."

She said, "Shall we have a drink and toast to the future of our young racer? He's ever so pleased with his *Jiffy*."

Bram followed her into the kitchen to help with the ice. She reached for the glasses in the high cupboard. He softly laid his hands on her hips. Pauline froze, palms resting on the shelf overhead. Slowly his hands moved up: along the shoulders, along the upper arms, back to the waist. When she lowered her hands, a glass in each, his went to her breasts. The nipples were hard against his palms.

Pauline turned around in the circle of his arms. "You think I don't have a guestroom?"

She was smiling with teasing little stars twinkling in her eyes. Bram, gasping for breath, tightened his embrace. Pauline's arms went over his shoulders, the glasses she held touched loudly behind his head.

Bram lost himself in the deep blue of her eyes, the curve of her lashes. Her breasts against his chest, he kissed an earlobe, an eyelid, her nose. Their half-open lips touched and they inhaled each other. She took both glasses in her left hand. The feather-light touch of her fingertips, caressed his neck and hair. Pauline's lips brushed his cheek, his ear.

"Bram," she whispered.

Bram did not respond. He just stood there, holding her, intoxicated by her fragrance.

"Bram." The whisper of her voice and her warm breath filled him with a strong desire to sink into this woman, body and soul.

"Bram?"

"Mmm?"

"What did we come to the kitchen for?"

He remembered: To touch glasses to Dick's racing. Slowly he straightened up to look into Pauline's face. She had her eyes closed and a fragile smile around her lips. Their foreheads touched; their noses rubbed. They looked into each other's eyes, completely out of focus—blue seas with vague coastlines and white beaches.

"You want ice in your whiskey?" Bram's voice was an octave lower. Pauline felt it rumbling in her stomach, unsettling her knees.

"Yes, I do." She tried to imitate his low voice but failed and that made them laugh.

They slowly disentangled. Bram loosened the ice from the tray, put a handful in each glass, and followed her into the living room. Pauline took a bottle of Dimple from the sideboard and handed it to him.

Seated on the couch opposite him, Pauline held up her glass. She said, "Here's to your son, the racer." They touched glasses.

"My son?" Bram asked, surprised, his glass stopped in mid-air.

Pauline smiled. "You two behave like father and son. If he will ever make it, it will be only with your support." She touched his glass again. "Thank you for liking my kid. To his future."

They drank, raised their glasses again and then put them on the low table between them.

"Do you really think he can overcome his handicap when he has prostheses?" she asked.

Bram explained that he knew very little about what ability Dick could develop. He would have to talk with a specialist, but as far as he could figure out, it didn't seem totally impossible. Then he went on for a long time explaining to Pauline about gears, clutches and the physical strain of racing—the temperatures, the stiff suspension, the conditioning, the alertness, the will to win, as well as the intelligence and the discipline needed. Compared with all that, the feet were only a technical problem. The drive came from the brain and not from the calf muscles.

Around midnight she stood up, walked around the table and stretched out her hands.

"Come."

To his surprise, instead of the guest room, they entered her bedroom, and in the soft light of the bed lamps he saw extra pillows on the double bed. Not bothering about anything else, they threw off their clothes and met between the sheets—strong, supple, smooth. Hungry. They locked together in a wild passion, short-lived, exhausting and satisfying.

They remained joined for a long time, Bram taking the weight of his upper body on his arms, Pauline moving her hands slowly and softly over his back, their heads touching. His manhood refused to give in. It grew hard again from the hands stoking his buttocks, their passionate kissing and the soft warmth of their tongues.

After the second climax they lay side by side, sweating and panting, their hands clasped. The newness made it impossible for them to fall asleep.

"Pauline?"

"Yes."

"I've got to go."

"Do you?"

"Yes. I was thinking. I don't remember exactly when, but somewhere in the beginning Dick suggested that I should come and live here. I've already given him the illusion he can become a racecar driver. If I stayed and he found out tomorrow that I spent the night with you, it could give him the idea that I would come and live here and that would be irresponsible of me at this moment." He fell silent, praying that he had not hurt her feelings. Women didn't like a guy leaving after he had made love.

"I really do have a guest room."

"It would make no difference for Dick. A man staying overnight under these circumstances is a threat if the child hates him and a promise if he likes him."

Pauline was silent for a long time, then she sighed, turning on her side facing him. "You've answered your earlier question."

"What question?"

"You asked if I thought if you were fond of him for himself, remember?"

Bram nodded.

He slowly rose, tucked the blankets around Pauline's shoulders, switched off one bed lamp and put his clothes on. Sitting on the edge of the bed, he bent over and kissed her, expressing the soft warmth he felt inside.

Pauline put her arm around his neck and pulled him closer. Then she released him and smiled.

"I'll be back at noon," said Bram, and quietly left the apartment.

———

It was terribly late when Thijs switched off the television.

"Shall we?"

Marjet yawned. "Yes, let's go." She got out of her chair. "I wonder how Bram and Francien got on after the dinner last night?"

"Got on? Got on with what?"

Oh dear, Marjet thought. For a moment she had forgotten that Thijs didn't know anything.

"What do you mean? Are they up to something that I don't know about?"

"No, nothing special, but from talking with Francien I got the impression that things between them are not as smooth as they look."

"That's strange. She looked smashing to me and Bram's business seems to be running well, so what could be wrong?"

"They have no children, you know. Maybe that's it."

"Saves them a lot of hassle and money. They have much more freedom than we have. They—"

The telephone interrupted him. Surprised, he looked at Marjet. "At this hour?"

"I'll take it." Marjet said, and walked to the desk. "Hello."

"I'm goooiiing te die . . . I wanna saaay gebye . . . te you."

"Who is this? Who are you?"

"Meee . . . Francieien!! I . . . wanna . . . saay . . . good-bye. I . . . don . . . wanna . . . live . . . anymore."

"My God. Thijs, it's Francien. *Francien don't be a fool, I'll be there in a minute! Hang on, you hear me!!*"

"'Tiz tooo . . . laaate. . . . I . . . cut . . . my . . . wrists."

Marjet put the receiver beside the telephone instead of cradling it.

"She's cut her wrists. C'mon, hurry!"

Marjet ran through the hall, grabbing her handbag in passing, flung open the front door and hurried to the car. The engine roared to life as Thijs closed the front door, and the car shot forward the moment Thijs sank into the seat, his ankle caught between the door and the body of the car.

"Are you *crazy?!* For heaven's sake, what's the matter?"

"Francien has cut her wrists," Marjet snapped, approaching the first corner with a speed that made Thijs close his eyes. When she had rounded it, he opened them again. "Why didn't we phone for an ambulance?"

"At best they'd get there the same time as we, more likely much later, and cut wrists can be held closed. When they phone they are usually half-hearted about it. We'll be there in two minutes."

"Why would she do a thing like that? Was that why you were—"

"Shut up and let me drive!"

Thijs did shut up.

Screeching to a halt in front of Bram's house, Marjet was out of the car before Thijs had opened his door. Not bothering to ring, she smashed the small pane in the front door with her elbow, reached in and released the lock.

In the living room Francien was upright on the couch, the telephone still at her ear, talking gibberish and looking at the bleeding wrist of her left arm, tears streaming over her cheeks. Before she realized what was happening, Marjet slapped her on the side of her face so hard that the telephone flew out of her hand and landed in the plants next to the couch.

Francien stopped weeping and stared at Marjet, then at the receiver that hung in the plants, and again back at Marjet, not understanding what was happening. "I was talking . . . how can you . . ."

Marjet saw the empty bottle on the table and the ashtray filled with butts. She took Francien's arm. "Come on, *up!*" she snapped, and pulled her off the couch. "Come on, to the bathroom!" In spite of Marjet steering her, Francien zigzagged.

Exiting the living room, they bumped into Thijs, who had expected something else.

"What's going—"

"Get out of the way! She's more drunk than dying."

In the bathroom Marjet held the wrist under the tap. When the blood was washed away, there appeared a few crosscuts that were still bleeding. From the medicine cupboard she took a roll of sterilized gauze and bandaged the wrist. Clouds of alcohol from Francien's breath enveloped her. Francien stood, swaying on her feet, a stupid expression on her face. Occasionally, she looked up at Marjet with fear in her eyes.

Marjet said, "You know, you might have gotten *us* killed, trying to get here in time." She pushed Francien back into the living room, and into Bram's chair.

"Where is he?" Marjet said.

Francien drew back a little.

"Where is Bram!"

"I don't know . . . he's gone . . . he . . . he'll never come back."

"Don't give me that crap. *Where is he!*"

Francien bowed her face into her hands, and her shoulders started shaking.

Thijs stood waiting by the dinner table. He knew Marjet too well to intrude. Marjet would not hesitate to enlist him in with a snap of her fingers if she needed him.

Marjet stood straight up, looking down on Francien, and considered the situation. "Right," she said, and turning to Thijs: "I know what we'll do. You go home and I'll stay here till Bram comes back. He can drop me off. If he doesn't come home, you pick me up on your way to church tomorrow morning."

"Do you need to?" Thijs had had plans other than spending the night alone, and he was also very curious to know what was going on. He was sure Marjet knew more, but he couldn't ask her in front of Francien, although she appeared not very aware of what was going on around her.

Marjet said, "Yes, I need to. Please go. The kids are alone and God knows what we have left on or open, rushing out like we did."

"Marjet," Thijs pleaded.

She held up a soothing hand. "Come on. I broke the pane in the front door, so everybody can come in now." Putting a hand on his shoulder, she walked him to the door. "Nothing serious, just a few scratches and a lot of booze. When the pain penetrated her drunken brain she apparently stopped sawing herself. Seeing the blood, she thought she was going to die. So she called us."

"Why isn't Bram home?"

"I don't know, but I'll find that out and tell you tomorrow. What's the matter, are you limping?"

"Caught my leg in the car door because you drove off before I could get in properly. You could have gotten us killed, the way you drove."

"Should have had a siren." Marjet smiled. "Now get moving before one of the kids wakes up."

She closed the front door and heard the glass grate underfoot. Well, that's the least of it, she thought, and walked back to the living room. Francien sat with her face in her hands.

Watching Francien huddled in misery, she felt sorry for her and regretted the blow she had delivered. Was it only twenty-four hours ago that this girl had looked robust? How fragile a person could be.

Better start pouring coffee into that girl.

"I'll go and make some coffee."

"No coffee, I don't wan' coffee!"

"Nonsense. You are going to drink a strong coffee and then we'll do some talking before Bram comes home," Marjet went to the kitchen.

"Bram is gone . . . for good," Francien wailed. "I want to *die*. Why didn't you let me die?!"

"There's time enough for that. No need to hurry!" Marjet shouted from the kitchen, where she was pouring water into the coffee machine.

Francien heard the noise. It faintly rang a bell.

"I don't want coffee!" She got out of the chair and sailed to the kitchen where Marjet was just carefully taking the coffee canister from the shelf, trying to prevent the spoon that was on top of it from falling off. Francien tried to snatch the tin from her hand. The canister slipped from Marjet's grasp and fell on the edge of the drainboard. Ground coffee cascaded onto the kitchen floor along with the thousand guilder notes. Both women stood staring at them.

Marjet was the first to recover from her surprise. "My God, haven't you ever heard what banks are for? Is that why you didn't want coffee?"

Francien nodded, and squatted to pick up the bills, but that was too much for her drowned equilibrium. She sprawled. Marjet pulled her up and knocked the coffee from her clothes. She led Francien back to the living room, then returned to the kitchen. She swept up the coffee, saving most of it, filled the machine, switched it on and then started counting the money while waiting for the coffee to filter.

Forty-seven thousand guilders. How could a businessman like Bram stash money in a coffee canister in the kitchen. Why not bury it in the garden? She supposed that Francien hadn't eaten for a long time, so she put a handful of crackers on a tray together with sugar, milk and the pile of money.

Noticing the bills, Francien started whimpering again. "Now you see, he'll never come back. And if he does, he'll *kill* me!"

Marjet was flabbergasted. "What do you mean, kill you? What's the matter with that money? Is it illegal? You don't think *I'll* call the tax people?"

Francien shook her head and whimpered on. Marjet poured more coffee and sat sipping it, staring at Francien, who avoided her gaze. Marjet poured her another cup and loaded it with sugar. When the coffee had cooled, Marjet reached over, pushed Francien against the back of the chair and handed her a cup.

"Now, be good. Stay quiet for a moment, drink it and eat some biscuits."

Francien couldn't help but obey. It didn't matter much anyway, now that Marjet knew. She slowly munched a cookie and washed it down with the coffee.

"Yuck." Francien made a face.

"Drink it!"

The clock ticked away. After their second cup, Marjet went into the kitchen and came back with a glass of milk.

"Please, must I?"

"Yes, you must, and the quicker, the better."

While Francien struggled with the milk, Marjet lit her a cigarette and held it ready, waiting for Francien to empty the glass.

"Thank you, you are my only—"

"Stop it! You have sniveled enough for one day. I'll put you to bed in five minutes, but answer some questions first. Why would Bram kill you?"

"Because of the money."

"Why the money? Did you steal it?"

Francien nodded.

"You *stole* that money?!"

"Yes."

"From whom?"

"Bram." Francien said, barely audible.

"When?"

"Last night."

"Where was it when you took it?"

"In his jacket."

"Then it was you who put the money in the canister and not Bram. Is Bram always running around with forty-seven thousand guilders in his pocket?"

"It was half of the money from the car he delivered. You know, that's why he was late for dinner last night. Was it last night?"

"Yes, it was last night. Why did you take only half of it?"

"I am entitled to half of everything when he divorces me."

"Let's keep it at *if,* shall we? Damn, Francien, you are too jealous, too stupid, too childish and too much an alcoholic to make far-reaching decisions like divorce. Did you have a fight?"

"Yes."

"Why didn't you make love?"

"We did."

"I don't follow you. You made love *and* you had a fight? In what order?"

"We had a fight afterward."

"Why? Did he hurt you making love?"

"*No,* of course not. It happened . . . I don't know. It just happened. When I think of *her,* I feel it hurting all inside of me. It's a pain—not a pain, but it hurts all the same and I can't bear it. I have to do something."

"Ever heard of jealousy? Ever heard of *crime passionelle?* Didn't you read in the newspaper about that guy from Turkey who killed his ex-fiancée because he couldn't stand that she had another? You thought all the time that was a privilege reserved for Mediterranean people? It's not. It's a pain—an irresistible pain that cries out for doing something about it. Did Bram say anything about his plans for the weekend?"

"He would go to the races in Zandvoort, and he said he was going to try out something with that boy, but I can't remember which was when."

"The races are tomorrow. Now, any idea what you are going to do with the money?"

"I wanted to put it back tonight, while he slept. But if he doesn't come back I can't. Where is he? If he's not coming home, where is he sleeping?"

"That's irrelevant at the moment. Get yourself undressed and in bed while I clean up things. If he doesn't pop up before Monday morning, you be at the garage at nine o'clock and hand him the money in a closed envelope. Tell him that you thought it was no good to have so much in one place over the weekend and you kept half of it for him. Where are you putting your housekeeping money?"

Francien pointed at the desk. "In there."

Marjet took the money from the tray, put it into the drawer and sat back with Francien.

A glimmer of hope had returned to Francien's eyes. "I'm stupid."

"We all are once in a while. Let's move."

They both got up. Marjet shoved Francien to the bathroom door and picked up the coffee things. She went to the bedroom and found Francien in bed as instructed. Marjet sat on the edge and stroked Francien's hair. It felt washed. The dope, she must have tried to look good in case Bram would come back that evening, and then with the hours passing, the waiting must have become unbearable. Why hadn't the bastard phoned? He had married her, for better or for worse. Okay, this was worse, so what? She took Francien in her arms and hugged her.

"I'll come and pick you up sometime tomorrow and try to sort out a few things. Now off to sleep."

She kissed Francien on the forehead, she switched off the light and softly closed the door behind her. She waited with her back against it and her hand on the knob, expecting Francien to call after her like her kids did. When no sound came, she went into the living room and lit a cigarette.

If Bram did not come soon, she would go and sleep in the guestroom. She would stick a note on the outside, suggesting that he go and sleep somewhere else. It would be better if he stayed away. Francien needed time to recuperate. Was Francien mentally disturbed? Unfaithful husbands didn't necessarily lead to suicides. Did she need psychiatric help? It sounded so gloomy. She needed to get off booze and improve her condition.

The invalid boy made the whole thing very complicated. She sighed. She rose and walked to the desk to write the note, then retreated to the guest room. The fresh sheets were as she liked them, cool and crisp.

9

'Isn't Uncle Bram there?" his son asked.

Thijs hesitated. How could Thijs know what Marjet would tell the kids later on?

Jeroen sat up on the edge of his bed, the pajama legs wrinkled around his skinny legs. "What's wrong with Aunt Francien?"

"I don't know. You will have to ask your mother when we pick her up. Please hurry. I have to make some breakfast."

In the kitchen Thijs met another problem: Where is what? He decided that a slice of bread and peanut butter with a glass of milk should do. He laid out four slices of bread and got the butter from the fridge. He should have put the butter dish outside the fridge the night before. With great effort he managed to scrape some butter onto the knife, but trying to spread it over the bread pulled the bread apart. Helplessly, he opened a drawer. Seeing the cheese slicer gave him an idea. He took a full package of butter from the fridge, cut off slices with the cheese slicer, covered the bread with them and then spread the peanut butter.

He put the plates and glasses of milk on the dinner table, then went upstairs again to get dressed himself. Passing his daughter's room he looked in and found the floor strewn with clothes. Wanda was trying desperately to get into a pair of stark red shorts she had outgrown.

She had already put on a yellow sweater with a black rabbit covering the front.

"Wanda, for Pete's sake, what are you doing? You can't go to church in that! Look what a mess you made. Mama will not like that."

"Why not?"

"You know why. You never wear something like that to church. Nobody does."

Wanda looked at him with her deep blue eyes, swiping a string of golden hair out of her face. "In camp we did."

"That's different. You're home now and not at camp."

Thijs bent down, searched the floor for something more suitable and fished up a light blue dress with a large white knot on the front. It was a summer dress, he knew, but pressed for time, he held it out to Wanda. "Put this on, please, and hurry."

Wanda pouted. "I don't like that stupid dress."

"Never mind, and come along to the bathroom so I can wash your face."

"I can do that myself."

"Yes, I know, but today Daddy is doing it, otherwise we will be too late to pick up Mama. Come on, be a good girl."

He walked her to the bathroom and washed her face. She didn't need much. Wanda always looked fresh and washed, even when she woke up in the middle of the night.

"Why didn't Mama wait for us?"

"What do you mean?"

"We could have gone and seen Aunt Francien together."

Thijs said nothing. He turned Wanda around and untangled the long flaxen hair, carefully smoothing it backwards.

"Why didn't Mama wait for us, Daddy?"

"Well, she was in a bit of a hurry and it always takes so long before you both get dressed and finish your breakfast."

"Not me. Jeroen is always late."

He pulled the dress over her head and buttoned it up.

"Okay, you are ready, now go downstairs and eat your breakfast. I've put it on the table. Jeroen! Are you ready?"

Pulling up before Bram's house he said, "You two wait in the car." He walked up the garden path. Since Marjet hadn't come home, it meant that

Bram hadn't, either. There was no need to ring the doorbell. He reached through the broken window and opened the front door.

The house was quiet. He knew his way around and went to the guestroom. Marjet was still asleep. He touched her shoulder, she woke up.

"Hello. What time is it?"

"Ten to nine."

"Come and pick me up after the service. I'll be ready by then. Tell the kids Francien hurt her arm and I have to help her get dressed, or something. You better hurry."

"Okay."

Why didn't people behave? No religion, nothing to hang on to but their own sentiments. One could see what came of it.

Back in the car the questions came simultaneously: "Where is Mama?" He told them that she was helping Aunt Francien get dressed, and enlarged on all the problems one had if one couldn't use one's arm and suggested they try to take their coats off with one arm only. By the time they had managed that, he had reached the church. Getting out of the car Jeroen looked at his daddy. "How come you put your arm through their door?"

"Because the little window was open."

Wanda, barely reaching up to his trouser pocket, had to go in a half trot to keep up. She rapidly blinked her eyes to withhold oncoming tears. Thijs wasn't happy, either. The suicide attempt and the breach of his Sunday peace, disturbed him. That's what happens to people who don't believe, he thought, when he sat down in the pew.

After the service, he drove the car back to Bram's house. Marjet came down the garden path and came around to his window.

"I made breakfast here for all of us. Bram had to go and see an important customer whose car broke down. So Bram had to lend him his. He'll be back later in the day."

"Is she . . ." Thijs said.

Marjet nodded. "Yes. She is. Don't worry." And pulling the rear door open, "Come on, kids, we are all going to have breakfast with Aunt Francien."

Happily, the kids frolicked up the path and into the apartment.

Francien had her left arm in a sling, which made her really look like the victim of an accident. Makeup covered whatever needed hiding. Thijs was surprised. If he hadn't seen Francien the night before, he wouldn't have noticed a thing.

Halfway through breakfast, Francien spotted Bram's car pulling up in front of the house and froze. Bram got out, looked at Thijs's car and then at the house. Smoothing his hair and after a moment's hesitation, he walked around the automobile toward the entry.

"Bram," Francien whispered.

Marjet got up at once. "I'll make some more tea."

In the hall, Marjet waited for Bram to enter. When he took too much time studying the broken pane, she opened the door from the inside.

"Marjet, what are you doing here?"

"Having breakfast, the lot of us. Listen, listen well." She lowered her voice. "You have been to a good customer, whose car broke down just as he set off on holiday. You intended to give him your car, but instead you managed to fix his. That's why you're back earlier than expected. Now go in and make believers out of them. No questions. You do exactly that. My kids are there. Understood?"

"But—"

"No *buts*. Go and be nice. I'll make some more tea."

Bram slipped past her into the house. "Well, well, Francien, how nice of you to organize such a large reception committee. . . . What's the matter with your arm? You didn't break it, I hope?"

"No, I only sprained my wrist. Marjet had to help me with a few things, so we all had breakfast together."

"Does it hurt?" he said.

"Not anymore," she said.

Bram bent over her, put a hand on her shoulder and kissed her forehead. "So no tennis for two weeks. Too bad. And you young folks? Breakfast all right?"

The children nodded, both munching on slices of currant bread covered with butter and brown sugar.

"Hi, Thijs. Disrupted your Sunday routine, I presume, but thanks for the support, anyway. It didn't interfere with church services, I hope."

"Not with mine, but Marjet missed it."

"Shouldn't worry about that, she'll go to heaven anyway."

Thijs shook his head. "That's not the prime reason to go to church. It keeps you in line with the society you belong to and makes you adhere to God's rules."

"I believe you," Bram replied, pulling an extra chair between Francien and Wanda. Thijs sat across.

Wanda put her little hand on Bram's sleeve.

"Yes, what is it, bluebird?"

Wanda smiled a moment and then her face became earnest again.

"Uncle Bram, do you still have that box where you keep all the presents you don't want and don't know anybody to give them to?"

"Wanda!" Thijs exclaimed.

Wanda let go of Bram's arm and humbly looked at her empty plate. Bram was reluctant to defy Thijs and let the little girl have her way. Francien, however, simply turned to Bram and said, "Will you get the box? Let them pick out one each."

Wanda and Jeroen exchanged triumphant glances. He had thought it up and had dared Wanda to ask.

Thijs objected. "Francien, you shouldn't have given in. But since you have, would you mind if I check what they pick? As I remember, there are objects suitable for a wide age range.

The respectful approach did Francien good. "Of course not, they are your children," she said.

The kids sat on the floor and, with a kind of Christmas glee, opened up wrappings and turned over in their hands candles, letter openers, paper-weights, spoons, photo frames. The four grown-ups had a last cup of tea and made small talk.

Marjet said, "Francien, there's an exhibition of children's toys in town. It covers everything from the Middle Ages till today. I would like to see it, but I don't want to go alone. Would you mind coming?"

"I would like that. Where is it?"

"At the municipal museum."

"That means I look after the kids for the rest of the day." Thijs voice had a plaintive ring.

"Not at all. We'll take Wanda with us. And, Francien, didn't you mention Bram was going to the races at Zandvoort? Thijs, why don't you go along with Bram and take Jeroen?"

The two men were flabbergasted.

"To *car races,* you mean? On a Sunday?" Thijs was shocked.

"Why not? The church works on Sundays, too, and lots of people go. Isn't that right, Bram?"

Thijs glared at her and noted the barely perceptible nod. "Well, if it's all right with you, Bram? You don't mind?"

Marjet said, "Of course, you don't mind, do you Bram, and neither will your little friend, what's his name again?"

"Dick," Bram said.

"Well, that's all settled then." Marjet clapped her hands. "Francien, let's clear the table and make coffee. The men can work out a plan to pick up Dick."

Francien got up and helped with her one good hand. Bram and Thijs settled in easy chairs.

Wanda cried, "Look, Jeroen, balloons, a whole bagful."

"Can I have one of these, Daddy?"

Thijs looked again at Bram. Although he had insisted on being the one to give permission, he still found it a bit difficult to give away somebody else's property.

"Take five each," said Bram generously, "and beware of that cactus over there by the window."

The children pressed Thijs and Bram to blow up the balloons and screeched and ran after those that escaped and shot about the room.

"Shouldn't be smoking so much," said Bram, a bit dizzy from the strain and huffing.

"Golf doesn't really do much for one's conditioning," replied Thijs.

"You care for an early-morning brandy with the coffee, Thijs?"

"Isn't it a bit early?"

"We have to endure a lot of noise this afternoon, so let's start off on the right foot. Besides, this is a rare occasion: you and I going to car races, at the suggestion of your wife."

"A very rare occasion, indeed."

"So, what do you say?"

"Okay, why not."

Bram brought four glasses and the brandy bottle from the bar and started pouring.

Thijs frowned. "Do you think it's wise to include the girls?"

Bram looked at Thijs in surprise. "What do I hear, Thijs? Old-fashioned discrimination?"

"No, of course not, but—"

He couldn't talk about Francien's behavior of the night before. Marjet had apparently decided it should be swept under the carpet, at least for the time being. He couldn't agree more. This was not the time.

"Don't you worry, Thijs. Francien can drink me under the table and Marjet won't get drunk from a swig of brandy, either. My pouring it doesn't oblige them to drink and only pouring for the two of us could be considered very self-centered. Exclusionary."

"That's true," said Thijs.

When the women came in with the coffee, they were surprised to find drinks on the table. Thijs explained. Marjet took up her glass and saluted Francien. "Cheers".

Francien hesitated, picked up her glass, managed a halfhearted, "Cheers," and sipped.

"You know what, Thijs?" said Bram. "Dick is in a wheelchair and I presume you would like to change into some more casual clothes. So let's go to your house first. We can pick up the minibus, and then pick up Dick. It's past eleven. We better get moving."

At Thijs's, Bram phoned Dick and told him that he was bringing some friends. He contemplated asking Pauline to stay out of sight, but decided against it. Such a request would only insult her and the cat was out of the bag anyway.

When they arrived at the Bakkerstraat, Dick and his mother were just leaving the apartment building. Bram got out of the bus and walked around to open the tailgate door. After hugging Dick, he lifted him into the bus, chair and all.

"Dick, this is Jeroen. Jeroen, this is Dick."

"Hello."

"Hi."

After closing the door, Bram turned to Pauline. She was wearing black high-heeled shoes, black trousers, a black tight-fitting coat and a high-collared blue blouse. The wind buffeted her black hair. He had to control himself not to embrace her.

"Hello."

"Hello. I was on the verge of leaving. I have an appointment with a friend."

A stab of jealousy shot through Bram's chest.

"What time do you expect to bring Dick back?"

"Let me see. Six, or maybe we'll eat out somewhere, if that's all right."

"Oh sure. He's in good hands. I'll be home this evening, so I'll leave it to you. Don't make yourself problems."

"At the moment I don't even know the size of my problems, but I'll sort them out one of these days. Can I offer you a lift?"

"No, she lives just around the corner. Take care." She waved good-bye to the three in the bus and walked off.

Bram pulled himself together and got in. "Here we go, boys! Off to the races!"

Thijs didn't know what to say. What a smasher. So that's why Bram hadn't come home. When was it that accident took place?

The boys were exchanging credentials in the back: age, grade, favorite sport.

"Where is your father?" asked Thijs' son.

"In America. I have a go-cart!"

"Really?"

Bram drove. Thijs didn't know how to bring up the subject uppermost in his mind and remained silent. They arrived in Zandvoort just in time. Thijs tried to buy the tickets, Bram would not hear of it.

"I don't know what's going on, Thijs, but you are here because of me, so the least I can do is pick up the tab."

By the time they found their seats and folded the wheelchair, the Formula One racers were revving their engines. At the green light from the starter, they roared off. At the Tarzan Corner car number five was in the lead. Then they disappeared and a hush descended over the crowd. Dick, cheeks red with excitement, was in another world. Jeroen nudged him with his elbow, "Where are they going now?"

Dick did not speak. He was watching the activity in the pits, so Jeroen pulled his sleeve.

"Hey, Dick, where are they?"

"They'll be back here in less than a minute and a half. They'll come from there," Dick said, pointing.

"You think number five will be first and win?"

"Don't be silly. They're doing seventy-two laps in nearly two hours, so it's still a long time before we'll know who will win." Then, feeling himself responsible, he started to explain to Jeroen everything he knew about Formula One races.

Always interested in sexual relations between other people, Thijs couldn't contain himself any longer. "Are you . . . you know?"

"What should I know?" asked Bram, playing innocent.

"Well . . . you know. Can't blame you. A woman like *that*."

The announcer came on at maximum volume: "And here they come, ladies and gentlemen! It looks like the Brabham driven by Nelson Piquet is in the lead. Yes, it—" He was drowned out by the roar of the engines of the twenty-six cars as they passed the grandstand in one long file.

As the spaces between cars grew wider during the race, there was always one or more passing the grandstand. The announcer filled in the gaps with information about the fastest laps, average speeds, the top speed on the straightaway, the age of the drivers, their records. So Thijs never got a chance to satisfy his curiosity, and Bram was saved the embarrassment of evading, which he surely would have. Bram never discussed sex with other men. You didn't talk about it, you did it. He always felt embarrassed when other guys bragged, and even more so when he knew the woman involved.

Nigel Mansell crashed at the Tarzan Corner and Nicky Lauda came walking back to the pits after he had moved up from eighteenth to twelfth place. All the while the tension grew as numbers five and fifteen, Piquet and Prost, took turns leading the pack. Then René Arnoux in his Ferrari started a terrific march from the tenth to third place, and everybody was wild to see whether he would also take on Piquet and Prost in the fight for the lead. It all ended when Piquet and Prost spun off the tarmac so that Arnoux got the victory thrown into his lap.

Even Thijs toward the end of the race joined the enthusiastic crowd that cheered the Ferrari on as if they could be heard by its driver.

As they walked toward the minibus—Dick and Jeroen in front of them, Jeroen sitting on an armrest since Dick had refused to let him push the chair—Thijs wondered where they would go from there, and how Marjet was getting on.

Bram shielded his eyes. "What do you think, Thijs: shall we have a beer first and let the crowd dissolve before we go back?"

"Good idea."

Along the boulevard in a restaurant overlooking the North Sea, they found a window table.

"You know what?" said Bram, "Why don't we go and pick up the girls and eat out somewhere? Chinese maybe."

"Yeah!" cried the boys, and the three of them looked at Thijs.

"Well, that's fine with me, but then I better phone before Marjet starts cooking something herself." Thijs got up. "I'll be back in a minute."

At the payphone he dialed quickly.

"Marjet, it's me. Are you alone? Can we talk?"

"I'm in the bedroom and Francien is playing Scrabble with Wanda."

"Scrabble with Wanda?"

"Yes, and Wanda likes it."

"Listen, Bram suggests we all go have Chinese together. What do you think?"

Marjet said, "Not a bad idea. What's the boy like?"

"A nice enough chap. He and Jeroen hit it off well. But aren't you afraid Francien will be upset by him? Can't you sound her out while I wait?"

"No. You don't ask shaky people. That only makes them more shaky. What kind of mood is Bram in?"

"He figures something has happened but I had no opportunity to tell him."

"All right, don't. But what kind of mood is he in?"

Thijs shrugged. "He proposed it in a way like, let's all go and have fun."

"Fine, that's good enough. What time will you pick us up?"

"Say six-thirty. By the way, I've seen the mother—worth the sin."

"Don't get carried away, Thijs. So, she's an eyeful. Be here at six-thirty. See to it you wind up driving that bus with Francien. I'll take Bram in our car. Then I can tell him a few things, so we won't have to rush out to rescue her again tonight. I have to go. See you."

She hung up and went downstairs. She found Wanda gleefully telling Francien that *hassole* was a correct and real word, although she couldn't explain to Francien what it meant.

"I am sure I heard Franky call Jeroen 'hassole' when he stepped on Franky's kite. Who was on the phone, Mama?"

"Your father. They are coming to pick us up and then we're going to eat Chinese, the seven of us."

"Seven?" On her stubby fingers Wanda started counting. "Jeroen, Uncle Bram, Daddy and us—that's only six."

"Dick is also coming."

"Who is Dick?"

"A young friend of Uncle Bram's. He's had an accident and he's lost both his feet."

"How does he walk?"

"He can't. He's in a wheelchair, and Uncle Bram has taken him to the races."

Francien paled.

"They'll be here in half an hour, so we still have time for a drink," Marjet said. "Bram may just be the type to get very attached to a boy like that. Don't you think so?"

Francien had trouble keeping herself together, now that the conversation was nearing the crux of her difficulty.

"Don't you think so?" Marjet persisted.

"I guess, and I wouldn't mind that at all . . ."

"Well, then. Drink your sherry and move your worries over to tomorrow." Marjet reached over the table and took her hand. "Don't worry. Just watch. Anyway, you wanted Bram to let you in on it. That's what he's doing now."

Marjet saw Bram exit the minibus and walk toward the house. She looked at Francien. "Don't worry. It'll be all right. Wanda, come on, we're going. Wanda! Where are you! *Wanda!*"

"Coming!" Her voice came from far away in the house.

"You let them in while I see what my little bird is up to."

With butterflies in her stomach Francien opened the front door.

Bram actually managed a smile. "Hi. How's your arm? Let me help you with your coat. By the way, is it all right with you if I introduce you as Francien? He calls me Bram. It would be a bit odd to call me Bram and you Mrs. Aardsen, wouldn't it?"

"That's fine," she said.

With his arm around her shoulders, they walked to the bus. Wanda bolted out of the house, coat flying, hair bobbing, running straight to Bram. "Uncle Bram! Where is your friend without feet?"

"You mean Dick! He's in the van with Jeroen."

Jeroen introduced Wanda as his "silly sister, Wanda." The girl was taken aback by the wheelchair. She had seen a wheelchair before, but it was different when a wheelchair was part of her group.

Just a boy in a wheelchair, Francien thought as she was introduced and slid in next to Thijs. She had seen many as a nurse.

Bram said, "The Green Garden, Thijs. You know where it is?"

Thijs nodded and pulled out. Bram got into the car's passenger seat with Marjet.

"Okay, let me have it," he said.

"Your own doing," Marjet retorted. "Staying away whole nights doesn't do Francien a lot of good. Your marriage is heading straight for the rocks, if you haven't already hit a couple. I'm not even sure whether you can still keep it afloat. But at the moment we have no time to expand on that. What I wanted to say is that after dinner, you bring the boy back to Gouda and come pick up Francien. We'll take her with us after dinner, so I figure that you can be at our place by ten. No, Bram, don't argue. Take it from me— this is necessary. Thijs thinks Dick's mother is worth the damage, but you have to make up your mind. Is she worth your marriage? You may be head over heels in love with her, that's human. That can happen to anybody, but that's not a good enough reason to destroy what has been a satisfying marriage so far. I know Francien hasn't reacted to the developments in the most sensible way. Neither have you. You know what she's like. Anyway, you're due back at ten and not a minute later. Understood?"

Bram sighed.

"Bram, don't be a jerk. You messed up our entire day. The least you can do is to concede me this one thing. Or do you want Francien to accompany you when you bring back the boy?"

"All right, I'll be there."

"Thanks. Now let's make it a pleasant meal, for all of us. Otherwise, Dick might get the impression that he doesn't fit and blame himself for it."

Marjet smiled at him as she parked and pulled on the hand break. She patted his knee. "You know, falling in love at your age is not a sin, but messing everything up is."

She got out of the car and walked up to the bus. Francien, Thijs, Jeroen and Wanda were already out. Dick insisted on waiting for Bram to get him, which was fine with Thijs, who was intimidated by the boy's condition.

During the ride Wanda had quietly studied Dick's face, his chair and legs. Bram lifted him from the bus, chair and all. Wanda suddenly stepped forward in front of Dick and held out a closed little fist to him. "For you. For your feet."

The sudden action, the resoluteness of the gesture and the seriousness in the blue eyes took Dick so much by surprise that he held out his hand before he had even started to feel embarrassed. Wanda dropped a big glass marble into it.

"It's my favorite. It's for you."

Wanda waited, looking at his face expectantly. Dick stared at the marble in his hand. It was a beauty. Then he looked up into her face. He blushed a bit.

Bram, standing behind the chair, bent forward. "That is most likely the last time that a lady gives *you* a present first."

Dick turned his head, looked Bram in the face and noted the slight nod. Then he turned back, took Wanda's arm, pulled her nearer to the chair and onto his lap.

"Ride with me."

Bram eased the chair toward the door of the restaurant, and was followed by the others. Francien was touched, Marjet was smiling. Thijs was frowning, and Jeroen was sulking because Wanda had won over *his* newfound friend.

In the restaurant Bram plucked Wanda from Dick's lap and carried her in his arms. "You are a character, my dear. Now let's see where we would like to sit."

Wanda pointed at a table in the middle.

"Not at the window?"

"No, there."

They all sat: Jeroen at the head of the table, Dick and Wanda on either side, Bram and Francien opposite Marjet and Thijs. They ordered: Nasi goreng, tjap tjoy, mihoen goreng, kroepoek, saté, beer and, for the children, french fries, applesauce and a fricandel.

Thijs started telling what he thought about the race, the first one of his life. Remarkable how he had loathed the din in the beginning and how he hadn't minded in the end.

Bram said, "I'm not absolutely sure, but I thought I heard Dad shouting, 'Get them!' when the Ferrari passed the grandstand in third place, and I'm rather positive I heard him call, 'Oh, dammit,' when Prost and Piquet spun out and Arnoux got the victory for free."

"No, Bram, that can't be true," Thijs protested.

"Well, I'm not absolutely sure, with the din of the engines and the crowd, but I definitely saw you stamping your feet angrily when the leaders lost out."

"Yes, Daddy, that's true. I saw that, too," came Jeroen from the end of the table.

They all laughed, including Thijs.

"Well, maybe I got carried away a little, but anyway it was fun."

—

Dick had been exhausted by all the excitement and was put straight to bed after saying good-bye to Bram with a clinging hug. Bram sat with Pauline for a while and told her how the day had gone. Pauline listened attentively but did not comment.

"I don't know whether it was right to introduce Dick to Francien, but I . . . well . . . it's done."

"There is no reason whatsoever to hide your friendship with Dick from your wife or your friends. Let's keep one thing straight—what's between you and him has nothing to do with what's between you and me."

Bram was relieved. Of course, there was nothing wrong about what he felt for Dick, apart from the fact he'd kept Francien isolated.

When Bram arrived at Thijs's, Marjet opened the door. "You had me sweating, guy. Francien has been on pins and needles the last half hour."

"I promised, didn't I?"

"Yes, but men in love aren't the most reliable. Keep the conversation light when you get home. Don't to try to talk things out tonight. A cup of coffee before you go?"

Bram declined and took Francien away.

In the car, Francien said, "He seems to be a nice boy, Bram."

"You think so?"

"Yes, and I think he likes you a lot."

At home Bram approached the television set to switch it on.

"Bram, wait a moment. Half of the money you collected for the car last Friday is in the money drawer of the desk. I thought splitting . . . Otherwise, you could lose it all. . . ."

Bram froze. He got the brown envelope out of his pocket and went quickly through the pack of bills. Francien stood by paralyzed, a child awaiting punishment. Bram saw the fear in her eyes. It stemmed his rising fury. He walked to the drawer, counted the money and put it with the other bills in the envelope.

He said, "Come on, sit down. It's all there. Everything is all right. I should have put it in the vault before I left work."

Francien sat on the couch, not knowing what to say. She knew she had been a poor liar, but she couldn't tell the truth either.

"How is your arm? Does it hurt?"

"No. Marjet thought it wise to give it a rest for a while."

"That's good, but can you manage with the house and everything?"

"That's no problem. Marjet has promised to help me out if necessary."

Bram picked up the TV listings and switched on the set. After glancing over the page, he sacrificed the sports for *Dynasty,* knowing Francien would like that.

10

They roared through the curve, the rear wheels screeching. Bram needed all his skill to keep the Alpha from going over the shoulder into the gorge. It was a straight drop.

The sky was blue, the sun blinding. The Alpha's engine screamed.

"Fourth gear . . . third . . . second . . . flat out! *Step on it, man.*"

The co-driver was shouting in his ear. Dick's voice, but lower than he'd ever heard it before.

It's madness, he thought. They couldn't win. They hadn't the power. They needed fuel injection. They needed an extra carburetor. But Dick was screaming at the top of his lungs. *"On the floor! . . . Now!"*

They were in second place. The Maserati of De La Haye was 1 minute 17 seconds in front. You couldn't make up 1 minute and 17 seconds in 12 kilometers, and that was all there was left until the finish line.

The next curve was approaching with enormous speed. Which gear? Dick, for fuck's sake. *Dick! which gear?!* He glanced at the helmet next to him. He couldn't see through the visor. He hit the brakes hard, but when the road started curving to the right he *had* to release to keep the wheels rolling.

The mountain was nearly vertical. His heart skipped as he skirted the gorge, sawing loose stones, grass and sand with the power of the tires. He felt the car clawing back onto the hard surface of the road.

"On the floor! Now!"

He was sweating. This was madness. The roadside passed in a blur of green and yellow. The yellow was rock.

"Dick! The curve, give it to me for God's sake!!!"

"Left, forty-five degrees. Third gear, full throttle! Not yet . . . *Now!"*

His hand on the gearshift, the yellow rocks seemed to reach out for the car.

Not third. Impossible. In second, full throttle he avoided the yellows, pinged them with the back fender and launched down a straight leg of asphalt, shimmering in the naked sun.

The colored speck ahead must be the Maserati.

"You can do it, Bram! You can do it! Get him!!" Francien. She was yelling with all her might.

Bram wanted to turn his head, but could not possibly take his eyes of the road. She couldn't be in the backseat. There was no backseat. Who was his navigator? To put an end to this madness he took his foot off the throttle. The speedometer climbed. The distance to the Maserati diminished. He stared at the dashboard. He was approaching the maximum 9,000 revolutions the engine could take. He was gaining on the Maserati without touching the throttle! Pauline was on the side of the road, hitchhiking, her fingernails azure. Thank heaven.

He jammed the brake down. No resistance. Nothing.

"Come on, Braaaam! Hang on! Get him!"

Their voices were mixed now. The headphones distorted them. The roar of the engine had become a piercing scream like a band saw. The revolution meter climbed way over the red mark.

The engine will blow up any moment. With this speed, it will blow us all up.

In the rear mirror he saw Pauline step onto the road, her skirt flapping in the air turbulence he had caused.

She spoke his name. He saw it. He tried the brake again, but it only made the car go faster. Had he hit the throttle? He shifted his foot to the throttle. Nothing. The clutch? He couldn't. That would surely blow up the engine and kill them.

He was gaining rapidly on the Maserati. In the mirror, Pauline was smaller and smaller, frail and black in the middle of the road. Behind her . . . Dick's Jaguar.

He hammered on the horn. No sound. He jerked the steering wheel sharply and threw the car into a four-wheel spin.

When he came to, he saw lights, a room. The nurse was naked. His head hurt. "Nurse, where is—"

"Oh, thank God, Bram. For a second I thought you were dead."

"Francien? What are you doing here?"—and seeing the bandage on her wrist—"Are you hurt? Why are you naked? Is Dick all right?"

"Bram, you must have had a night terror. You swore, you screamed, you stamped your feet. I couldn't wake you up. It was frightening. You banged your head against the bedstand. Here, drink."

His body glistening with sweat, his head still fuzzy, he leaned on his elbow and took the glass. The cool water cleared his brain. He carefully felt the spot where he had hit his head.

"Let's try to get some sleep."

They lay back. "What were you dreaming?" she said.

"Horrible. I was second in the Mille Miglia. The car was completely out of control." It was horrible. Let's try to sleep again."

He switched off the light and turned on his side. Francien molded to his back, her hand slowly descending: his shoulder, over his back, his hip, down to his knee, then back up along his thigh.

———

As soon as he arrived at his office, he phoned Pauline, relieved to hear her voice.

"*This* is early," she said.

"Listen, Pauline, what's the color of your nails?"

He could hear her chuckle. "You'll laugh. Sky-blue. Why do you ask? . . . Bram? Are you still there? Is there something wrong?"

"Yes, I'm here. Yes, uh, no. There's nothing wrong. I had a dream. I was in a car and you were hitchhiking, and your nails were blue."

"How nice of you."

"What d'you mean?"

"That you dream of me. I like to be dreamt of."

"But the fingernails—I have never seen them blue. How come you have them blue and I saw them like that in my dream?"

"Bram, something is worrying you. I hear it in your voice. I saw a friend of mine yesterday. She is color mad and she suggested I do my nails blue. That's all there is to it."

"Yes, but how could I see them in my dream, when I didn't know anything about it?"

"Bram, you are a darling, but things like that do happen . . . sometimes . . ."

She chuckled again from deep in her throat. Bells tinkling, he thought. He felt a strong urge to crawl to her through the line.

"Pauline, are you all right?"

"Yes, Bram. I'm fine. But how about you? You sound worried. Something wrong at home?"

"No. Yes, maybe. Francien has a sprained wrist. Are you free?"

"I have to be at the hairdresser's in an hour."

"And after that?"

"After that I have other things to do."

"Like what?"

"Like protecting myself against a loving male who is dying to possess me."

Again Bram heard the chuckle and the bells. He heaved a deep sigh. "If you laugh like that once more, I'll hang up, hop in the car and be with you in thirty minutes. I bet you are still in bed."

"That's right. But you have work to do. Your staff will be coming in any moment is my guess. Customers waiting to buy cars or make complaints. Your secretary making your first cup of coffee. You can't run away from all that. Not to mention your other ties. You only like to rush out to pull me in. I feel your possessive urge and I can see your invading eyes."

"Pauline! I protest! I am not possessive. I'm a modest, freedom-loving voyeur."

Pauline laughed out loud now, her voice charging all his male hormones. His secretary came in with a stack of mail and his first cup of coffee.

"Belinda has just now brought in the mail and the coffee, but I will be in touch with you later. Bye." He hung up.

"Belinda, will you please enroll Dick—that is, Hendrik Verwal, Bakkerstraat twenty-five, Gouda—as a member of Gonzales? It's a go-cart club. Phone Mr. van den Bosch and tell him it's the boy he met last Saturday at the track. And to bill me here at this address. Then ask Lazy Willem to see me as soon as he comes in."

In the mail was an invitation from the Bugatti Club for the annual meeting in Antwerp. Hotel Bourinage. Years ago he had decided to be a member of every automobile club he knew of. That's where the fans were, and fans bought fancy cars. Twenty-fifth of October. He looked at the calender. A Friday. Reception and a dinner afterward. He pressed the intercom. "Belinda, will you book a double in Hotel Bourinage in Antwerp for the twenty-fifth of this month and accept the invitation for the Bugatti Club dinner?"

Humming, he went through the rest of the mail, and since Lazy Willem wasn't in yet, he drove to the AMRO-bank and deposited the 98,000 guilders.

He arrived back at the garage at the same time as Lazy Willem, the arrogant bastard. It was nearly ten. Bram suppressed his irritation.

"Willem, I've got something for you. Dick tried the cart on the track, but we had to make changes. He couldn't control the throttle properly. I had to improvise. Have a look at the cart and give it a finishing touch, will you?"

"What speed?"

"He started off with thirty-five kilometers an hour, and after the adjustments he made forty-four and a half."

"He liked it?"

"Absolutely nuts for it."

"Good. I'll have a look."

In high spirits Bram made his rounds, talked to his mechanics and then went back to his desk. Friday week—only twelve days to go.

Francien did not feel all that bad. Strong body, she thought. She wished she had an equally strong mind. Seeing the water glass on Bram's bedstand, she remembered his dream. He had been dreaming about *her*. He had been screaming *her* name, loud and clear: '*Pauline, watch out!*'

She was surprised she could remember it without getting furious. He had looked so confused. She had never seen him lost like that before. He'd also asked for the boy. She remembered the boy's mercurial movements, the alert gray eyes and the white hair. He had been nice to Wanda.

She had told Bram she liked the boy, but Bram had been somewhat cool. Maybe he didn't like her to like the boy. She shook her head. That made no sense. If he had wanted to keep the boy for himself, he wouldn't have suggested the dinner together.

Looking at her watch, she saw the bandage instead. It made her feel miserable again. The agony of being forced to part from life voluntarily, and by your own hand. She shuddered, got quickly out of the bed and hurried to the bathroom.

When she was dressed, she picked up the phoned and dialed Marjet. After it had rung several times, she hung up. Why isn't she home on Monday morning? Maybe shopping. No, can't be, all shops were closed on Monday mornings. Twenty past ten. She tried again. And at eleven-thirty, at twelve-fifteen, at one o'clock.

Mustering all her discipline, she waited until two-thirty, the panic increasing every time she heard the telephone ring in the empty house. At three o'clock she couldn't stand it any longer and took the bike and rode to Marjet's house.

Before she could ring the doorbell, Marjet opened it.

"Where were you? Why didn't you answer the phone?"

"Come on in," Marjet said, turning around and leading the way into the living room. "I was convinced it was you who was ringing."

Francien was speechless for a moment. "But why? I don't understand."

"Well, I didn't feel like it. You sure are having a difficult time, but after monopolizing us Saturday night and all day Sunday, I felt like having some time off for myself. Do you think that's unreasonable?"

Francien was taken aback. She hadn't thought of it that way. "But if you had told me—"

"No, Francien, it doesn't work that way. Then we will end up with me asking your permission to be unavailable. You know you leaned on me in your misery. I have two loveable brats and a husband who lean on me, and I don't need another indulged child on my hands. Especially not one my own age. I want you as a friend. All right, in times of crisis we lend an ear, give a hand and supply an objective opinion but for the rest, I like to laugh with you about how we grumble about how we fail, but I'm not a psychiatrist. Moreover, I don't think you need a psychiatrist. What you need is a good spanking. Accept the facts, girl! Scrape your guts together and fight—at least if you are the kind of woman who will only hand over her man to another woman over her dead body.

"Girl, you shocked the hell out of me Saturday night, and now I'm angry. Here is the toughest, bravest woman in town. Hits highwaymen over the head and no sooner some bitch pops up, she takes to the bottle and hands over everything to the interloper without the foggiest idea whether that is what the other woman wants, let alone Bram. To you it's apparently none of his business. I am indeed mad at you, because you are letting me down. Do you understand now why I let the telephone ring?"

Dumfounded, Francien sank into a hardback chair at the table.

"I'll make a cup of tea," said Marjet, and disappeared into the kitchen.

A couple of minutes later she came back and, placing one cup in front of Francien, she said, "Here you are. Careful, it's hot."

Sipping the tea, elbows on the table, Marjet watched Francien, who sat brooding over her teacup. "Drink your tea, girl. Or are you reading the leaves?"

Francien looked up. "I'm sorry."

"That's good," said Marjet, and slowly held out her hand.

Hesitantly, Francien took it. "Friends?"

Marjet nodded.

"You are right. It was very stupid. I don't know what got into me."

"What about the booze that got into you?" Marjet smiled when she said it and then changed the subject. "A nice kid, this Dick, don't you think?"

"Yes. Do you suppose I'll see more of him in the future?"

"I would see to that if I were you. How did it go last night? Don't you think I was curious? Took me a lot of self-control not to phone *you* this morning and even more not to pick it up when it rang. What did he say about the money?"

"Nothing. I just told him the story. He counted it and said he should have put it in the vault."

"He damn well should have, walking around with a hundred thousand guilders. In bed, did you touch?"

"Afterward, yes."

"Afterward? Afterward most men go home."

Francien told Marjet about the nightmare. "He was really shouting at the top of his voice 'Pauline, watch out.'"

"So, the poor girl was in danger. Did he tell you why she had to watch out?"

"No. I didn't ask, either."

Marjet looked at her approvingly. "Why not? That's very unlike you."

"I don't know. I saw him tumble out of bed, and when he came to he looked forlorn, as if he had lost something very important."

"Pauline?"

Francien shrugged. "Who else? Anyway, he sleeps with her. Of that I'm sure. But sleeping with her and making love with me, don't you think he should feel guilty for betraying at least one of us?"

"Him? Feel guilty? I don't think so. Actually, I've always wondered whether men are less loyal in this respect than women. In his lifetime the average male has sexual relations with eight females. On the other hand, I read a magazine piece recently that said half the married American females have had sex with another man in the first five years of marriage."

"Half?"

"Yes. I could hardly believe that, too. In America, mind you, not Sweden. Then the question arises, Are women so much different from men?"

"But then what's left of marital fidelity?"

"I don't know. But there are more ways a man can be disloyal than in bed."

"Like what?"

"Like allowing the kids to do things you have forbidden. Or the other way round."

"I have no kids."

"What about correcting you in public when you tell a story at a party and he thinks you're babbling? Or joining the crowd, laughing the loudest when you've made a stupid slip of the tongue? Sometimes I think that sex and loyalty have very little to do with one another. But that's not your problem, or maybe it's exactly that."

Francien nodded. "But, Marjet, what should I do now?"

"Can't you figure that out yourself? If I tell you, it'll only be what I would do, but can *you* do that? You're not me."

"You can say that again. I hate him. I make love to him. Shit. I'm all mixed up."

"Mixed up or not, you're not an imbecile, are you?

"Well, a bit dumb maybe, but an imbecile? No, I don't think so."

"And when you're dumb, it's only because you are not prepared to fight for what you want. You want it given to you and when that isn't done, you start screaming like a spoiled child. Have a look at men. They meet competition every day, win sometimes and lose at others. They swallow their losses and cherish their victories. Now, after years of protection you are all of a sudden meeting competition. You are out of practice, so you blunder. No harm done. Unless you blunder too long. You know perfectly well that the whole female game is to see to it that you are wanted. And like men bending over backward to win a customer or an order, it's now up to you to bend over backward to wipe out the competitor."

Francien nodded. "You know, I've really thought about going to Gouda and scratching her eyes out."

Marjet shook her head. "You are not the only one who would feel like that in your circumstances, but it doesn't work that way. There are tribes where that is common practice and the woman who wins has the man, but in our tribe the woman who wins loses the man. You have to fight another way."

"But how?"

Marjet hesitated. "No, I'm not going to tell you. You can only successfully use the tactics you find yourself. Your father and mother should have taught you."

"I've hardly known my father, and my mother did what *I* told her."

"Well, so much for upbringing. However, there are a few rules that you have to adhere to. One, if your husband is in love with another woman, don't fight him. Fight the other woman. Be nicer. Two, if you don't know what to say, say nothing. Three, be nice to the young boy whenever you get the chance. As a nurse you know everything about the treatment he is in for. Bram could do with some help there. Four, be at your best. What's better than to have a reason to improve your muscles, your skin, your face? Let the wind blow the smoke from your hair and the alcohol from your breath. Find an outdoor sport that you can do on your own. For instance, the bike. Ride fifty kilometers a day, as fast as you can. You'll lose your shakiness, feel better, walk better and fear less. It transforms aggression into confidence and steels not only your muscles but also your nerves."

"You think it's as simple as that?"

"Yes, as simple as that, but *every day*. You'll find that out. And what about your wardrobe? You have a good feeling for color and you dress well. Reshuffle your wardrobe. Buy a few things. Change a few colors. If you let yourself down, you make it easy for Bram to let you down as well."

"You think it'll work?"

"Come on, Francien. Who do you think I am, God? I only know that you have to do it. If you don't get control over yourself, you'll be at his mercy. You'll lose his respect for good, and without respect every love is doomed. And now I have to fetch the children from school, so beat it. And don't call me, I'll call you. You were alone before you met Bram. You can stand it, and if you can't be alone, you can't have a proper marriage, either."

Reluctantly, Francien rose, sighed deeply, then pulled her shoulders back, stuck out her chest and pulled her stomach in. "That better?"

Marjet nodded and smiled.

When they reached the door, Marjet suppressed the urge to hug her friend. She had to go this road alone. Affection would soften the resolve she had just begun to nurture.

When she opened the front door, the pouring rain surprised them. Francien hesitated, but then thought, Alone is alone. Rain makes no difference anymore. So she refused to be brought home by car and refused to stay till the shower had drifted past. When she had turned the bike around, with one foot on the pedal, she looked back at Marjet. "I won't call then."

"That's right, you won't have time. And don't forget—every day!"

The strong wind blew the rain under her coat and into her collar. She felt the cold rainwater trickle down between her breasts. Okay, wet is wet and I won't melt. I'll dump the clothes, anyway. But why haven't I got my own car? Stupid, I'm married to a garage owner *nota bene.*

When she came home she parked her bike in the shed, dropped the wet clothes in the dustbin and sank into a warm bath. She wondered if she could ask Bram for a car of her own. What would Marjet think about it? Oh, shit . . . no more phoning. She had to make the decision alone.

Through the window of his office, Bram stared out at the rooftops. Gray, low clouds were pouring down loads of rain on soaked meadows. A couple of black crows were the only living creatures in sight. Dick was at the cart track with Lazy Willem, getting wet and experienced. Bram had arranged with van den Bosch that he could train there on the Wednesday afternoons when he had no school. Pauline had not turned down his invitation to come with him to Antwerp, but neither had she accepted it. And Thijs had phoned him to see if he could spare an evening this week. Bram had no clue what for, but he couldn't very well refuse. So why not Friday night? And Francien wanted a car of her own.

Stupid, not having thought about it before. Of course the other women had laughed behind her back when their husbands pointed out to them that this garage business of his apparently did not pay so well, because he evidently couldn't afford to give his wife a car of her own, as they had. What a jackass he had been.

The silly way he'd found out she wanted a car, too. After dinner he had joined her bringing the dishes into the kitchen and had seen the wet clothes in the dustbin. When Francien explained why they were there, he had become irritated. She should have taken a taxi with that weather and her arm like it was. They could afford taxis if she wanted to go somewhere. That was cheaper than throwing away expensive clothes.

"I don't like going by taxi. It's too—how can I put it?—too dignified, too stately, and you have to ask your friends if you can phone for one when you want to go home, and then you have to wait and turn down their offer to bring you back. No, going around in taxis is not for me. I have a better idea."

"And what's that, then?"

"A Suzuki, the small one. It's cute."

"What? A Jap?! No way. The wife of the Alpha dealer driving around in a Jap? That would make me the laughing stock of the trade."

"But it's cheap and gets very good mileage."

"No way. If you want a car of your own I'll get you one, but no Jap, no Korean, and no Eastern European, either."

"Well, it was just an idea."

"I'll see if I can work out something."

Francien hadn't pursued the subject any further.

He could still feel now the indignation at imagining a Suzuki in front of his house for everybody to see. Stupid that he hadn't realized before this how he had made a fool of himself by letting her pedal about on her old bike.

A car was like a suit or a dress and the main contact point was your butt. If it held your butt properly, you felt safe, and feeling safe was halfway to smooth driving and to being safe. What kind of car was Francien's car? A girl who thinks that going about in taxis is too stately could be well looked after with an Alfa reasonably priced. In the old days they had wiped Bugattis and Mercedes off the racetrack. The temperament of an Alfa would surely enable Francien to express her emotions through the throttle.

He suddenly liked the *cart blanche* he gave himself in choosing a car for Francien. But which type? He didn't believe in the nonsense of "*he* picks the brand, the type, the engine, and *she* the color." Gold, white or spring green, because red, black, blue, silver and brown were out. A 33 could be the right type, but the standard model wasn't striking enough. The station wagon was better. Attractively priced under 30,000 guilders. But she was not a mother with kids, so why drive around in a station wagon. To show you wanted them? No.

He and Francien belonged to the well-to-do middle class, he thought, although, Francien? Not in the middle of the class. Rather close to the border of it. The Italian holiday, the bedroom door hacked open, the ashtray, the whiskey in his eyes, knocking her out cold—they flashed through his mind. The varnish of Establishment was extremely thin. It definitely stopped at the front door.

Anyway, something flashy, so the people would notice the make, and also something that would give her the feeling she belonged to the smart set of the poets' quarter of Haarlem East. But 60,000 guilders—it was a lot of money for the Sprint 1.7 Quadrifoglio Verde, a two-seater convertible, no automatic. He tapped the desk with his fingertips. The clouds were hurrying on now, taking the rain somewhere else. It wasn't "convertible" weather, but the more he thought about it, the more convinced he became that was *the* car for Francien. Gold, white or spring green. A convertible.

He pushed the intercom. "Belinda, will you give me the details of the Sprints we have sold over the last five years?"

A few minutes later Belinda told him: "A black one four years ago. A silver one two years ago. Two red ones last year, and a green one three years ago to a Professor Hildebrink in Leiden, for his wife. The professor didn't have a driver's license, and his wife didn't want more than one person at a time with her in the car. You remember?"

"Yes. Get me Professor Hildebrink or Mrs. Hildebrink on the phone, please."

After he had finished his conversation with Mrs. Hildebrink, he rubbed his hands with satisfaction. They might be interested in a newer version, provided he had a buyer who would pay a fair price for her old car.

When he turned to the internal window overlooking the workshop, he saw Lazy Willem switching on the door lifter. When it was a yard high, Dick drove the *Jiffy* in and parked it next to his wheelchair.

The bastard—he surely has been driving the thing from the track to the garage and Lazy Willem has let him, of course. The boy is damaged enough as it is.

Willem looked up and Bram beckoned him to come to the office. The look on his face made it clear that he wanted Willem there at once. Lazy Willem nodded in acknowledgment, but then went to Dick, plucked him from the cart, put him into his chair and together they disappeared into the canteen.

Damn it, who do they think is in charge here? He stormed out of his office past a startled Belinda, across the workshop, and tore open the canteen door. Nobody there. Crossing the room, he went through the door that led to the corridor and the washroom.

Through the door he heard Lazy Willem's voice. "You do that once more, you rotter, and I take a sledgehammer and knock the whole vehicle to scrap iron and I'll have you watching it!"

"You won't. You love it too much yourself!"

"You try me out. He warned me that he wouldn't have any of that nonsense. Don't like to lose my job, because *you* have such a desperate need to show off. In addition to the fact that you need a license and a checkup before you are allowed to drive around in traffic. It's very tricky because the other cars might easily overlook your small ass. And you are damaged enough as you are, aren't you?"

Silence, then: "Well, we better not tell him," the boy said.

"That won't help very much, with you driving off into the street while I'm talking with van den Bosch, and him asking me whether Aardsen thinks it's okay that you go on the road with it? No, man, you tell him before somebody else does, otherwise you'll look sneaky."

Bram turned around, closed the door softly and went back to his office, wondering how the two of them would handle it from there.

When nobody came in, he glanced into the workshop and saw Willem squatting next to the *Jiffy* and Dick bending forward, gesticulating impatiently with his hands.

Ah well, let them. He has survived it and it's understandable. I'll bring it up if they don't, but give them time.

The anger left him.

After a while Dick rolled into his office. "Hello."

"Hi there, how did it go?"

"I drove back here in the *Jiffy*."

"I know, I heard you talking about it when I passed the washroom." Dick sat silent.

"Well, how did it go?"

"Aren't you mad about it?"

"Sure. I am. So you will skip next week's training, and the next time your Jiffy will be gone *in* a jiffy, never to come back. We are dealing with risks that need to be calculated and reduced. We don't need cowboys. Now, how did it go?"

Dick hesitated a moment and then told about the skidding in the rain, the fastest round and the further improvements. Willem had improved controls so that he could better handle the pedals from the knees out. The feeding of the fuel was much more accurate now: he could save fractions of seconds in the curves, and he came around even faster than last time he drove on a dry surface.

"You know, Bram, I was surprised. I thought driving in the rain would be very difficult. Slippery, you know. But once you are used to it, it's not bad."

"That's right. The water between the tires and the road surface smoothes out the moment you go from rolling into sliding, so you have the feeling that you are moving around more elegantly and you are more in control. Quite opposite to what you would expect, isn't it? Come on, let me drop you off, it's nearly six."

Willem was washing up when Bram entered the washroom.

"He told ya?"

"Yes, and I warned him. He's skipping next week."

"He won't like that."

"Sure, he won't, but if he wants to get somewhere, he needs discipline and he must obey. I told him that next time his *Jiffy* goes, never to come back."

Willem grinned. "I told him more or less the same. That I would take it apart with a sledgehammer and have him watch it."

"Isn't that a bit cruel, for both of you? But you better watch out that it doesn't happen again. The boy needs some protection from himself. Gets carried away at times. How's he handling things?"

"A couple of more afternoons and there won't be much left to tell him. I had a few words with van den Bosch because I wanted to know what the usual lap times are. By the way, that was when he cleared off."

"What did van den Bosch say?"

"The record is thirty-seven point four seconds, around forty-seven kilometers per hour. I don't know whether our engine has it, but it's standard so it should be able to do it. Maybe it's the newness and it will take some time before it's completely broken in."

"That's fine with me," said Bram. "We don't want the kid to win the first race or his head will be in the clouds and he won't listen to us anymore."

"We'll have to see first how he'll do in competition with others. Will it slow him down or will it speed him up? Now he's more like a test pilot and not like a race driver."

"Yes, and that's exactly what worries me, Willem. He's a cocky kid, that one. Might easily take too many risks or try and push the others aside. I want him to make friends with them and that will be difficult enough with his handicap. It hurts twice as much to lose to someone with a handicap. So, if need be, slow down the machine a little until he's accepted by the other boys."

"Okay. And I'll have a chat with van den Bosch next week and see if he can arrange something with a couple of other guys."

"There's no next week on the track for Dick, remember?"

Willem raised his eyebrows. "For sure?"

"Yes. See you."

It was already dark when Bram and Dick left for Gouda. The traffic was heavy until they crossed the A-4 and passed Schiphol Airport. Dick was quiet and Bram was listening to the news on the radio. When they were on the provincial road, the one where they had run the Porsche when he was first released from the hospital, Dick couldn't stay quiet any longer.

"Bram, you didn't mean it? About next week, I mean?"

"I meant it."

"But it wasn't dangerous. There was hardly any traffic. I had noticed that when we drove up."

"I told you, it's punishable, so you can't drive around in it. It's much too dangerous."

"I can't lose my feet anymore."

Bram froze. The remark left him speechless. He switched off the radio. The engine and the sizzling sound of the tires on the wet road were the only sounds. Shocked and at a loss for what to say, Bram drove on.

When they approached Waddinxveen, Dick touched his elbow. "Hey, what about next week?"

"No track next week. You can come to the garage by yourself and take the *Jiffy* apart."

"Take it *apart?*"

Bram heard the shock in Dick's voice. "Yes, and put it back together again."

"Oh!" A sigh of relief.

"But what d'you mean, come by myself?"

"By public transportation? The train, for instance."

Dick fell silent.

In Gouda, Bram helped Dick into his chair, got back in the car and drove off without saying a word.

The rush hour being over, the traffic was light. Dick's accusation still nagged. But was it an accusation? Dick had never shown a trace of laying blame. He'd always assumed the blame himself for being stupid enough to put his legs out on the road. But why did Bram still think it was a lousy remark? Dick had wanted to get away without consequences for what he had done and tried to trivialize the transgression, and when that didn't work, he threw in his handicap to finesse a pardon—not abnormal.

Bram came to the conclusion it was his own feelings of guilt that made him touchy. He regretted having left the boy cold shouldered because *he* felt responsible for the accident.

On Friday afternoon he went to see Mrs. Hildebrink and her car. They were both still in good shape. The car needed an overhaul, but with some extra trim it would be the showpiece he wanted for Francien to drive around in.

He had phoned the factory to ascertain when he could get delivery of a new one and found to his disappointment that it would take six weeks. They slowed down the production of convertibles in winter, when half the market was covered with clouds, rain, hail or snow.

Mrs. Hildebrink was not in a hurry, so that was not problematic and the price for her car wasn't either. After signing the purchase contract, they drank a glass of wine. When he got up to go, she offered him another glass but he said he had an appointment.

She smiled. "Okay, then we'll have it next time, when you're not in such a hurry."

He stopped at the nearest phone booth and called Thijs back.

"What about tonight, Mr. Alderman?"

"Is that you, Bram?"

"Entirely." Bram was always in good spirits when he had a sales contract in his pocket. He was wondering what that mustache had on his mind.

"When do you close up?"

"Well, I'm in Leiden at the moment. I could pick you up at the town hall in half an hour—say, quarter to six. How's that?"

"A bit early. You businessmen always maintain that you work twice as long as a civil servant. But let me see . . . What about a quarter past in the Gastronome? You know where it is?"

"I'll be there."

Bram was already sitting at the bar when Thijs came in.

"Hi, man," Bram said.

"Hello. How come you're so early? I thought you never got home before seven."

"Sold a car in Leiden but I have to take back the old one so I went to see it."

When the bartender came up Bram ordered a whiskey on the rocks.

"What are you drinking, martini?"

"Campari, sec. Picked up the habit in Italy. A good appetizer."

"Filthy weather, isn't it."

"You could say that again, but it's October. In this country we're lucky if we have some decent weather in the summer. September can be nice at times, but October . . . I hate the stretch from summer vacation till Christmas. No fun, no parties, your suntan fading away. Your nose back to the grindstone till Christmas and New Year. Then it's the grindstone again till Easter, Ascension Day, Whitsunday and the promise of the summer holidays."

"In short, Thijs, you don't like the winters, do you?"

"Too dull. But that, of course, is different for you with that fabulous girl you have in Gouda and with a good reason to see her because of the boy."

"Thijs, you make it sound as if I use that boy just to meet his mother. What's the matter? Jealous or something?"

"Would there be something wrong with me if I was?"

"Maybe not, but I presume that you didn't invite me for dinner to ask me to introduce you to her, because if so, I better pick up the bill. So tell me what's on your mind?"

"That boy is a nice kid, and obviously he likes you a lot. You know that he didn't want me to lift him from the bus? He insisted upon waiting for you to do it. I had the feeling he would have hit me if I forced the issue."

Bram was pleased to hear that. He shrugged. "What can you do under circumstances like that? There was nobody around to visit him. What would you have done?"

"I don't know. I'm not a hero with invalids. I might have taken the easy way out, but in this case apparently there was no easy way out. I might have done the same. Who knows? Is his mother still married to his father?"

"I don't know. I didn't interrogate her . . . yet," Bram said.

Thijs smiled. "Dick told me he wants to become a racecar driver and that you are going to help him. Is that true?"

"He sure wants it. Whether I am going to help him, I don't know. It's not as simple as Dick sees it. I arranged a go-cart for him and made him a member of a carting club, but now that you ask me, it's more like what you do when one of your kids has had a nasty experience. You spoil him a bit, don't you?"

"I think so, but to me it sounded like . . . how shall I say it? . . . Dick talked about it like someone who has concluded a contract with a sponsor, and you are the sponsor and coach. Something like that."

"Don't you think you are exaggerating a bit?"

"You can be the judge of that, not me."

"I don't know. I like the boy and he likes me. What's wrong with that?"

"Nothing. I only wonder whether you realize that you might be stuck with him for years."

"What do you mean 'stuck with him'?"

"Sorry. That does sound negative, but kids cling. This young fellow can easily claim you for the next five or ten years. You are both car crazy and if he wants to become a racecar driver, I can't see you turning your back on him."

"Why should I?"

"I didn't say you should. But I think you can't go on like this, either."

"And I think that is none of your business."

Thijs finished his drink and rose from his stool. "Come on, let's go to the restaurant and eat. Drinking on an empty stomach can lead to bad tempers."

After they had ordered and tried the wine, Bram lit a cigarette and looked at Thijs through the smoke. "I don't know what you're up to, Thijs, but discussing my private affairs with other people is not my style."

"And you think going to car races on a Sunday is my style?"

"Not exactly. Tell me, what *was* all that about?"

"We were phoned Saturday night by a drunken Francien, who told Marjet that she was going to commit suicide."

"Suicide?"

"Yes. So we rushed out and Marjet handled the situation in a way that had me stunned. Really a no-nonsense method and I must admit it worked."

"How serious?"

"Just a few scratches."

"But, my God, why?"

"According to Marjet, Francien thinks you are going to leave her."

"*Leave* her?"

"Yes, she thinks that you are going to leave her for the mother of that boy."

The waiter approached with the dishes. After he'd put them on the table and wished them a good appetite, Bram started cutting his meat. He took a bite and a sip from his wineglass and looked at Thijs. "Why do I hear about this suicide business only now?"

"Where were you Saturday night, so that we could tell you? Marjet waited at your place to tell you, but you didn't come home until the next morning. You did spend the night with her, didn't you?"

"I slept in the Posthoorn that night."

"With her, I presume."

"She has a flat of her own, so there's no need for her to go to a hotel if she wants to sleep with me. Look, what do you want from me? A solemn promise that I won't ever sleep with Pauline, or with any other woman in the world, for that matter? Is that the errand you've been sent on?"

"Hold your horses, man. I was sent by nobody. Be fair. Now that you know what happened Saturday night, don't you think we acted like friends? We created the opportunity for you to introduce Dick to Francien and you seized it, I must say."

Bram swallowed his irritation. "All right, you did. Thanks."

"You're welcome."

"Listen, Thijs. I have known you long enough to know that you are dying to hear all the details of what's up between me and Pauline, but I also know that wouldn't be a good enough reason for you to invite me out for dinner. And you know me well enough to know that I'm not going to talk about such things. If it's just a roll in the hay, it's not worthwhile bragging about. And if it's serious, you shouldn't talk about it unless there are announcements to make, and I have no announcements." He exhaled smoke in a long stream.

"Francien should stop calling Pauline a whore and me a whoremonger. She shouldn't drink herself to pieces and shout at me like a dirty-mouthed fishwife. Now she has turned to faking suicide. If she thinks she can order me around, then she's in for a big surprise."

"All women aren't the same, Bram. Francien has a character of her own and this may be her way—"

"There's nothing I loath more than being bullied."

"Still, you have a problem."

Bram nodded. "Maybe things would have been different if she hadn't been so pushy in the beginning."

Thijs looked at Bram questioningly.

"After the accident. Francien wanted me to go and see the boy, bring him a present and forget about it. 'Get it over and done with,' she said. I couldn't. Neither did I want to be crossexamined after every visit. So I didn't tell her I continued visiting Dick. Maybe I should have. On the other hand, she's jealous by nature. Hey, I can't just dump the boy because my wife is jealous."

"She is jealous of the mother, not the boy, I would say."

"I can't dump the mother. How can I?"

Thijs looked helpless.

"Can I?"

"Will you dump Francien, that's the question."

"It hasn't yet crossed my mind, but if she carries on like this? Suppose . . . suppose I've fallen in love with Pauline, which Francien believes, and I knuckle under? What will happen then?"

"I wouldn't know," said Thijs, wondering whether his invitation to talk candidly had been such a good idea. "Maybe you are right there. Anyway, I thought you needed to know what was going on. Marjet thinks you shouldn't know about the half-assed suicide attempt. So I don't want you to let Francien know that you know."

Bram finished his dish, sipped his wine, lit another cigarette and followed the rising smoke on its way to the mirrored ceiling.

"Give me one good reason why not and I'm your man."

Thijs took his time. This was a difficult one and a long story wouldn't do. "You said that a man could not help his wife in a case like this, right?"

Bram nodded, tipped the ash off his cigarette and poured the rest of the bottle of wine into their glasses. "Go on."

"This attempt is her problem. She has not told you about it, although she has had five days to do so. Thereby she has made it clear that she considers it *her* problem. If you go home and bring it up, you interfere with her problem. She has decided to keep you out of it, so you have to respect that. Is that a good enough reason not to let her know that you know?"

"It is, but then why were you so desperate to tell me, when Francien didn't?"

Thijs closed his eyes and decided to let the word *desperate* pass. "There are things that do their work from the back of our mind better than from the tip of our tongue. Marjet has convinced me that it would be embarrassing for Francien to know that you know. Now, she still has the possibility to carry on as if she has never done it or embarrassed herself. I, from my side, thought that you are a responsible party in this and that I had to keep you posted about how the land lies. Suppose she really does it one day in the future and you complain to me, 'Why so all of a sudden? It's so unlike her.' And I tell you that she had tried it several times before. *Then* you would be mad at me for not telling you, wouldn't you?"

"I would think so, but now what should I do? Nothing? Just act as if it never happened?"

"If Francien never tells you, you would both be on the same wavelength if you act as if it never happened, and what is more, I *don't* think it was a real attempt. When the first drop of blood appeared, she picked up the telephone and called us."

Bram imagined how Francien had hacked at her wrist. Never mind whether you were drunk or whether you did it as a summons for help, there were more pleasant things in life than poking at your own wrist with a knife.

"I always say to Marjet," Thijs continued, "'That's what happens if people have no religion. You have nothing else to hang on to other than another human being, and that's a very shaky proposition.' Don't you think so? Bram?"

"What was it you said?"

"That things like that happen when one's only mainstay in life is another person. One should have more to hold on to."

"Like what?" The moment he asked, he could have bitten his tongue off. Of course, he knew the answer he would be getting.

"Like religion, for instance."

"Listen, let's not bring religion into this. You believe, I don't. You can't help believing, neither can I help not believing. Discussing it, we'll always arrive at the point where you'll say, 'That's precisely what you must believe,' which is exactly where my problem is. Knowing this beforehand, why waste time and energy to go through all that and hurt each other in the process. Let's have coffee, okay?"

"Please. But what do you really think about religious people?"

"You really want to know?"

"Yes, otherwise I wouldn't ask."

"Okay. They are poor sods who can't live without being barked at once a week and being told what they should or shouldn't do. Dependant souls, if you ask me, which you did."

"So much for arrogance. So you are the sinner and I am the sod. I can live with that."

After Thijs had paid the bill, he followed Bram into the toilet. Standing side by side, Bram was silent. He had never gotten used to talking while peeing. Thijs had no such scruples.

"You know, Bram, I am glad we had dinner. I thought you had to know, in spite of what Marjet thinks about it. But if she finds out because you tell Francien, I'll be in deep trouble."

Bram finished, zipped up and walked to the washstand. When he was soaping his hands, Thijs walked up to him, zipping up in the process. Opening a tap and letting the water run over his hands, he looked at Bram in the mirror. "I have your word that you won't tell Francien?"

"You don't. But I won't."

On the street they buttoned up their coats against the strong, cold wind. When they got to Bram's car, Bram saw that the door was wide open and, by the light of the street lamp, he saw two feet sticking out.

My radio, damn!

The irritation had grown in him steadily from his warrantee customers' coming in with broken windows, twisted door locks and damaged doors caused by addicts pinching an 800-guilder radio to resell for a lousy 25 guilders. He threw his full weight against the open door, slamming it shut on the legs of whoever was inside. A scream erupted. He couldn't care less.

"Thijs, phone the police. I'll hold him here."

While waiting, he held the door firmly under pressure. The person inside had stopped disconnecting the radio and tried to sit up, but the steering wheel was in the way. With one hand on the wheel, he tried to push the door open, but he was no match for Bram's weight pressed against the door.

At any rate, he thought, this guy will have something to remember after the police turn him free, the drugged up little shit.

The guy's screaming had wound down to a plaintive mewing by the time the patrol car arrived. The cops got out, Bram stepped aside.

"He's in here, officer."

The police officer looked into the car. "Come on, out!"

The fellow didn't move, so the officer grabbed hold of an arm and pulled. The guy sank to the ground, howling. Together, one on each side, the cops lifted the man up and tried to put him on his feet. With a scream the fellow sank back down again. *"My legs!"*

Letting go of him, one of the policemen directed a flashlight at his legs. There were small red spots on his blue jeans where they had been stuck between the door and the bodywork. The other cop grabbed the man's shoulder again. "Come on. Up. We haven't got all night!"

"Hold it, the position of the feet is funny—look."

Now, Bram saw it, too. The man looked like a rag doll.

"Officer Klaas, call an ambulance. I'm not dragging this one to the station." Then he turned his flashlight into Bram's face. "Seems to me you have broken his legs. That doesn't look good, sir. I'm afraid you'll have to come with us to the station. You two together?" he asked.

Thijs nodded, not at all happy with the situation. He could foresee the item in the local paper: ALDERMAN AND FRIEND BREAK DRUG ADDICT'S LEGS. However, he couldn't possibly just walk away. There was nothing he could do but ride it out.

The policeman inspected the interior of the car. "Loose wires, damaged dashboard. Door lock damaged. Forced open with a screwdriver, as usual."

He was talking aloud as he made his observations. Bram and Thijs both stood watching the cop, glancing every now and again at the trembling figure on the ground. The man was mewing softly.

Gradually, Bram had the awful realization that he had damaged another pair of legs. He hardened himself against it. This bastard had it coming. Justly so. You can't just go around demolishing cars and stealing things belonging to other people. And if you did, you could run into some hard luck. That was what you were asking for. This had nothing to do with Dick.

An ambulance came around the corner and moved up the street at a slow pace, searching for the victim.

After the guy had been loaded into the ambulance, Thijs and Bram were invited to get into the patrol car.

Thijs said, "Is that necessary, officer? I only phoned you at his request. I did not touch the car door, nor the young man."

"You are a key witness. Breaking someone's legs is a serious offense under the criminal law."

"He was stealing my radio," Bram said, "and I have the right to hand over to the police anybody who is committing a crime. So, I have done my duty as a good citizen. I can give you my name and address and that is all there is to it. I won't claim any damages. You can't pluck feathers from a frog."

"That's all good and fine, sir, but when somebody is seriously injured I prefer that somebody higher up makes the decision whether you applied justifiable force in the course of the arrest or whether you applied unnecessary force and thus caused unnecessary harm in the execution of your lawful right to stop a person committing a crime. So if you'll be so kind?"

"No, I won't be so kind. This is *nonsense!*"

"You have the option to go to the station in handcuffs or without them." And turning to Thijs, "What about you, sir?"

"I don't like it but I see your point. I'll come along."

"And you, *sir?*"

"I understand that as a simple policeman you cannot see the difference between a criminal and a decent citizen, so we have to leave that distinction to your superiors, who, I hope, have more intelligence than you."

The officer shone the torch in his face and held it there. "I always like to remember the face of a customer. Now get in the car . . . please."

"Let me close my car door before somebody else finishes the job he started and before the rain spoils the leather."

"Don't touch it, sir. Fingerprints, you know. Get in the patrol car," he said, and grabbing Bram by the shoulder, he pushed him toward the vehicle in which Thijs already sat.

The moment Bram bent over to step into the car, he was pushed in the back and bumped his head against the side of the roof.

"Been drinking too much, sir? A car door is lower than the door of your house. Never forget that."

"Fuck."

The cops got in and they drove off.

Thijs pulled Bram's sleeve. "Don't provoke them. I'll get us out of this."

At the station they were ordered to sit on a bench. The sergeant in charge asked what was the matter.

"These two broke the legs of a youngster who was taking the car radio of the tall guy. The boy is on his way to the hospital. Shall I lock'm up, sarge, till we have the medical results?"

The sergeant looked in their direction, concentrating on Thijs. After a while he got up from his seat and walked over to them, scrutinizing Thijs's face further.

"You're familiar to me. Can it be that I know you from some official function?"

"I'm Alderman Van der Berg, sir."

"Right! That's it. I'm Sergeant van Willigen. What's going on, Mr. Van der Berg?"

Thijs told him what had happened. He was almost finished, when the door opened. Inspector Blokland came in and recognized Thijs.

"Hello, Thijs! What are you doing here?"

"We've been helping you to do your job, Hans. We arrested a car burglar. At least my friend here did, and I phoned the police. Now we'd like to go home, if that's all right with you."

"What are you keeping them for, Sergeant van Willigen?"

"Well, Inspector, the case is not as simple as that. The attendants of the ambulance believe that the thief sustained two broken legs, and he has been taken to hospital. My men thought it wise to bring these gentlemen in and take their statements here. It is quite a lot of injury in the light of the crime committed."

It was after twelve by time their statements had been taken. Thijs had gotten the assurance of his friend, the Inspector, that he would keep his name out of the daily news release the police gave to the press, so he felt quite relieved. He had also phoned Marjet. When he asked Bram if Marjet should call Francien, Bram had said no. It would only make her anxious for nothing.

The same two cops brought them back, first dropping Thijs, who had parked elsewhere, and then proceeding to Bram's car. The door of his car stood wide open, and as it had started to rain heavily, the driver's seat and the floor beneath it were soaked.

"The bastards! Fingerprints, my ass." Banging the door shut, he angrily turned around to the cops. "You will hear more about this fingerprint bullshit! I hold you responsible for the damage."

"That's fine with me, sir," said the one who had given him the push.

"We'll meet again, then." And saluting, he turned around, got into his patrol car and drove off.

When Bram tried to open the car door, it stuck. "Damn it to hell!" Suppressing a strong desire to smash the window, the door or the whole car, he inserted the key in the lock and turned. The key stuck in the damaged lock. Trying to force it out, it broke.

"God damn it!" he shouted and banged the roof of the car with all his might.

11

The kids were finally asleep and Marjet was watching the late movie and tidying up for the night when she heard the key in the front door. She went to the kitchen to make coffee, because she knew Thijs would want a cup.

"Hello there." Approaching her from behind, his fingers circled her neck, followed the line of her cheeks and then softly touched her lips while pressing his pelvis against her buttocks with slow, soft thrusts.

"Well, well, we are in a good mood. You got a raise?"

Thijs chuckled. "Just pleased to have you."

"You stayed away long enough to make me doubt that. Coffee, I presume?"

"Yes, please. You didn't wait up so late for me, did you?"

"Of course I did. The whole evening I sat at the window, my heart jumping for joy with every car that turned into the street. The life of a housewife is a lonely one, you know."

While the coffee filtered through, Marjet turned around in his arms.

"And you? You also had a lonely evening, being confined to male company?"

"Lonely, but not alone."

"I can imagine that . . . at a police station. Although they do have women there nowadays."

"Sure, but not for that purpose."

Bending forward a little, he touched her forehead with his and smelled her and the coffee, a heady mixture of domesticity and romance.

Thijs told the story of the car radio.

"It was quite a relief to me that Hans came in and promised to keep the story out of the press."

She took down cups from the cupboard. "Did Bram also promise not to let Francien know that you told him about her suicide attempt?"

Blushing, he looked into the gray eyes, the gray of steel at the moment, at other times the gray of soft clouds carrying salutary water. There was no smile of triumph around her lips, no playful sparks in her eyes. She just waited for a simple answer to a simple question. Before Thijs answered, the coffee was ready. Marjet loosened herself from his embrace, placed the pot with the cups and the sugar bowl on the tray, picked it up and walked out of the kitchen. Thijs followed slowly, refusing to buckle under, but knowing that it wouldn't be easy.

"A brandy, darling?"

"Yes, please."

Marjet lit a cigarette, blew the smoke to the ceiling and waited for his answer.

Thijs realized that by waiting so long before answering her question he couldn't deny anything anymore.

"No, he didn't promise it. But he's not going to tell her."

"I have urged Francien never to tell Bram. So it'll be very embarrassing if she finds out you told him."

"I had to tell him."

"Can you explain why? You wouldn't do that out of an uncontrollable desire to gossip, because then you would have phoned him Monday morning."

"I had given it considerable thought. I had two reasons: I had to tell him, and *he* ought to know it. Although we're not exactly blood brothers, through the two of you we have become sort of friends. Now let's assume that Francien loses control and tries it again. Bram finds her, saves her, narrow escape, and then she tells him she has tried it before, where and when. Would Bram have a reason to be mad at me for not telling him what had happened?"

Marjet remained silent.

"That's why I had to tell him. Now, why he had to know: Suppose Bram has had a light heart attack and the doctor tells him to take it easy. You and I know, but Bram has managed to hide it from Francien, because Francien would be all over him with 'you shouldn't do that,' 'let me do this,' 'I'll drive,' and so on, all the more since she's an ex-nurse. Now what would you do? Suppose she, unaware of his weak heart, tempts him into an orgasm that carries him straight into heaven . . . for good. What would she think of you if she found out later that you had known about his heart condition all the time?"

"That's quite obvious, and rightly so, but I would insist she never let Bram notice she knows."

"Don't worry, he won't tell her he knows. He agreed."

"Let's hope he'll stick to that. What do you think? Is he deeply in love?"

"Difficult to judge. He's not exactly a guy with his heart on his sleeve, but if you ask me, he's further gone than he realizes."

Thijs reached over and filled the cups again.

"Francien will have to brace herself," said Marjet.

"Don't you think it's Bram who should do something about it?"

"What can he do? Fall out of love? You know, Thijs, a husband cannot help his wife when she has a problem and he himself is the cause."

"This sounds utterly selfish. Pushing your wife nearly around the bend and then claiming it's *her* problem. You don't think *he* should do something about it?"

"Thijs, believe me, if a husband brings his wife to the brink, then puts her back on her feet again, he has lost a wife, because he won't respect her anymore."

"Heavens!" Thijs exclaimed. "In politics I have heard a lot of people twist things around, but this beats everything. *She* loses *his* respect, while *he* is the one who is unfaithful?!"

She shrugged. "Bourgeois standards seldom survive battles like this. What about his respect for her if she scrambles back onto her feet all by herself?"

Thijs thought about that. "I must admit, in that case he would have more respect for her."

"Weakness never demands it. On the contrary, it commands only pity."

"But isn't it the meaning of wedlock that we help each other?"

"Sure, as far as it concerns me and the lid of a jar, or you and the tie you can never knot properly, or me and a rapist, or you and your political party or the press. But when it's between you and me, it's everybody for himself and herself."

"With the Lord's assistance we'll manage," said Thijs, rising to pull Marjet out of her chair. "And with the assistance of these we'll both manage," he said, taking hold of her buttocks, and pulled down the zipper of her dress.

"Mr. Alderman, are you aware that we are Dutch?"

"Yeee-sss," he said, making his voice as throaty as he could, "and that means that we have long cocks and the women have beautiful asses."

"That's right, Mr. Alderman, but it also means that we are renown for leaving the curtains open."

Bram sat in his dark living room. He poured a glass of whiskey and thought about how complicated his life had become of late.

Pauline—her smell, her color, her warmth and her softness. The fact that he had left her behind on the side of the road bothered him despite the fact that it had only been a dream.

The trail of destruction he'd left behind. He had smashed Dick's legs, got one fellow killed and had blinded another in Italy, driven Francien close to the edge and now, to top it off, he had broken the legs of that junkie car thief. He had seen more policemen in a season than he had in his whole previous life.

He should have left Milan earlier, like he had intended to, and *not* have given in to Lantini, who had invited them for supper. He shouldn't have thrown his full weight against the car door. Half would have kept the guy where he was.

What was wrong with him. He was losing control.

And why had Pauline still not accepted his invitation to come to Antwerp? Did she have another friend? A flame of jealousy soared up inside him. No, she could have all kinds of reasons, but why didn't she tell him? Why didn't she level with him?

The fact that she didn't think it necessary to give an explanation piqued him. He wanted to know what was going on inside that head of hers. He *had* to know, otherwise he couldn't handle her. Otherwise he couldn't make her feel what he wanted her to feel. But you couldn't take a human being apart like an engine and find out how it worked. Why couldn't he accept her the way she was? Intriguing and quixotic.

Francien he knew like the back of his hand. Her suicide attempt, just emotional lousy blackmail. Of course, he wouldn't let her know that he knew. It was much easier if you could pretend not to know. Now he could ignore it without insulting her.

And the cold shoulder he'd given Dick. Thank heaven he hadn't boxed his ears. Then he would have had to agree with the Italian inspector who had shouted at him, "Violenza terminato!" But he hadn't killed the Italian guy; Francien had. Good girl. She had saved his life, that was for sure. How many women would have done the same. Very few. Of course, the hoodlums had asked for it. Just like the guy stealing his radio. Got what they asked for. Anyway, what's a broken leg nowadays? And two heal in the same time as one. That he drove Francien to the verge of breakdown was not true, either. That was just her way of trying to bully him away from Pauline. Same as throwing the ashtray.

And Dick's was just a very stupid, very sad accident. He was trying to undo the damage as much as possible. He was *not* a man of violence. He loved peace and having everybody happy. At heart he was a friendly guy, no matter what others thought.

He poured another finger of whiskey, and wondered how Dick could bridge the gap between being an invalid in a wheelchair and a professional Formula One racer. Thijs might be right. If there were no drastic changes, he might have the boy on his hands for the next decade. Not that he would mind, but if he was to be involved, he had to make a plan. You couldn't just wait and let things develop on their own. That would involve Pauline, too, for the next five or ten years. Again, he wouldn't mind, but . . . He closed his eyes, feeling very tired, and very burdened. He had to get back on top of the situation.

He shrugged, finished his drink and went to the bedroom. He un-dressed in the dark and slid carefully between the sheets in order not to wake up Francien. After a few moments he had a strange feeling. He had often come to bed when Francien was already asleep, but this time he felt no warmth. Inching a little closer to her side, the sheets remained cold. His hand searched. Nothing. The bed was empty.

He sat up and switched on the light. Francien wasn't in bed at all. He stared at the empty spot. For thirteen years she had been there and now she was not. Where could she be?

He looked at his watch. Nearly three o'clock. She had said nothing about going anywhere, so he had no idea whom to call. Marjet? Yes, Marjet might know where she would be, but phoning at three o'clock in the morning . . . The cinemas and the theaters had closed hours ago. A lot of things could have happened between midnight and three in the morning. The police? If she had had an accident, they would know.

Sitting on the edge of the bed he explained his problem over the phone to the officer at the emergency number.

"Give me the name and a description, and then I will see if we have something on her."

"Aardsen. A-A-R-D-S-E-N."

"Wait a minute. Are you the guy that was here tonight for breaking that young man's legs?"

"I was at the station because somebody was stealing my car radio, if that's what you mean."

"Are you so aggressive at home as well? Maybe you better try the Battered Women Shelter first. You know, that institution where women go when their husbands beat them up. Let me see, I've got the number somewhere."

"I don't need that number!" He was too loud, he knew.

"How come, are you gay? Maybe your wife has found herself a real man who has more spunk than someone who breaks a sickly junkie's legs. Anyway, if she pops up we'll give you a ring. That is, if she has no objection. We can't force her back, can we?"

In anger Bram flung down the receiver. The inspector, that friend of Thijs . . . Fuck, what was his name? He dialed Thijs. It rang three times and then someone answered, "Hello."

"Marjet, Francien is gone. Have you any idea where she went tonight?"

"What do you mean, 'gone'? For good?"

"No . . . at least . . . I don't know. She isn't home. I thought maybe you'd know where she went tonight."

"No, Bram, I haven't talked to her since Monday. What time is it? Three. Dear me. Did you phone the police?"

"Yes, I did, but I got nowhere. Can you give me Thijs, please?"

"Sure . . . Thijs, Bram wants you." The phone was passed.

"What's the problem?"

"Francien is gone. I phoned the police, but I got that same bastard on the line that pushed me into the car. What's the name of that inspector? That friend of yours?"

"Blokland, you mean?"

"Is that his name? I'll try him, because that stinking cop didn't want to take it seriously and Francien hasn't been one night away in all the thirteen years that we've been married."

"You know what, Bram, let me call him."

"Would you? Sorry for waking you up in the middle of the night."

"I'll call you back."

Bram put on his robe and padded barefoot into the hall. He switched on the light in the living room. It was then that he saw the note Francien had left.

I am out with a friend.
   See you late or tomorrow morning.
                    Francie

Bram stared at the small piece of paper and read the message a few times, not knowing what to think of it. Then he realized that there was no use anymore in phoning the inspector.

Thijs's number was busy, so he put the receiver down for a couple of minutes and then tried again. Busy. After a short time he tried again and then he figured Thijs might be trying to call him. Thijs had said he would. He had to wait. Otherwise, they could go on endlessly trying each other.

It was ten minutes before the phone rang.

"I spoke with Blokland. Nothing. Did you find anything out? Your line was busy."

"Sorry, Thijs, but I was calling to tell you she left a note. She is out with a friend and she will be back tomorrow morning."

"You didn't see the note earlier? Are you sleeping apart?"

"I didn't go straight to bed. Thanks for your trouble and sorry I woke you up. Good night."

"It's nothing. Good night."

After Thijs hung up, Marjet came in from the kitchen with two cups of tea.

"Well?"

"He found a note saying Francien would be home late or tomorrow morning. Out with a friend or something. Didn't know she had any, did you?"

"No one close that I know of, but it may have been somebody from the hospital where she worked before she met Bram."

"He's a strange guy. He comes home, and sits in the dark thinking. I never thought of him as a thinker."

"He isn't, but he uses his brains once in a while. Just enough, I would say. Francien couldn't stand a thinker. That's a primitive girl if there ever was one. We saw that in Italy, didn't we?"

"You can say that again. You know what intrigues me? That the whole incident is never mentioned anymore. Just as if we had agreed to keep quiet about it, which we had not."

"That struck me, too, but what else can one do? Heroism that saves a life is a better topic than heroism that takes a life. One doesn't say 'serves him right' when that *him* is dead. It is sad enough that somebody comes to meet his end in this way. You can't celebrate a funeral, can you?"

"The Italians did, awarding her that crazy prize."

"Mentalities harden towards the equator, that's why there are no bull-fights in Amsterdam."

Thijs nodded slowly. "Do you think Francien might have taken a boyfriend?"

"Like one takes a taxi?"

"Sorry?"

"Oh, nothing. Let's go back to sleep, because Wanda will be around at eight and by then she has already been awake for more than an hour. It beats me where she get's the energy. Turn off the light, please."

In moments Marjet was off to sleep again, but Thijs was intrigued by the question of whether Francien was in bed with another man at that very moment. Bram must have been wondering too, he realized.

———

Dick rolled his chair to the table. His mother sat opposite. He buttered a slice of bread and loaded it with peanut butter.

"You really like it that thick?" she said.

Dick nodded, took a bite, and washed it down.

"You don't really believe it'll make you world champion like that cyclist, what's his name?

Dick concentrated on his plate.

"The ad on television with the boy at the bus stop, eating bread with peanut butter. You know who I mean?"

Dick remained silent, kept staring at his plate.

"Dick?"

"Bram is mad at me."

"Bram? You're kidding."

"No, I'm not. I can't go to the cart track next Wednesday and he won't come and pick me up anymore."

"Are you sure? Are you sure you understood him right?"

Dick nodded.

"What happened?"

"I drove the *Jiffy* from the track to the garage while Lazy Willem was talking to the track manager."

"And Bram didn't want you to?"

"No. And Lazy Willem said I should tell Bram, because he would find out anyway and then it would be worse. And Lazy Willem said he might lose his job. And that it would be best if I told him myself. So I did, and then he said that there would be no training next week."

"And that he won't pick you up anymore?"

"No, that was later. In the car, when I asked him if he had really meant it about the training. He said he meant it. And that it was very dangerous because I could be overlooked in the traffic. And then I said not much more could happen to me as I had already lost my feet."

Pauline stopped cutting her bread. Casually she put down her knife and fork. "And what did he say then?"

"Nothing."

"Nothing at all?"

"No, he didn't say a thing all the way. He was mad at me. But I didn't say anything wrong."

"You think so?"

Dick lowered his eyes and shrugged.

"Didn't you tell him it didn't matter anymore because you had already lost your feet?"

"Uh-huh."

"And who did that to your feet with his car?"

"But I didn't mean that. That was my own fault!"

"What *did* you mean, then? That it doesn't matter if you are crushed under the wheels of a truck, because your feet are already gone? Is that what you meant?"

Dick shrugged and looked at his plate again.

"Look at me, Dick. You are twelve. You're always bragging that you use your brains. Use them now."

Mother and son sat looking at each other.

"Dick?!"

His chin sank a little lower, the white curls flattened from the way he had slept.

He should comb his hair before he comes to the table, Pauline thought. Most likely he hasn't washed his face, either.

"Did you mean that it doesn't matter anymore if you are damaged further or killed, but that it *would* matter if you still had your feet. Is that it?"

Dick shook his head.

"You were mad that he canceled your next training?"

Dick nodded.

"And so you said something nasty. Bram hit you with his car, didn't he?"

Dick nodded, his head bowed.

"Don't you think it's nasty what you said?"

She couldn't see his face, but his ears were reddening. She watched the bowed head, the narrowed shoulders and his hands beside the plate, the long fingers scratching the tablecloth. A tear fell on his plate and disappeared into the bread crumbs. Then his hands gripped the wheels, and he rolled around the table to Pauline, who stretched out her arms to embrace him. However, the awkwardness of the chair hindered their bodily contact. For two days he had bottled up the fear that he had lost Bram. He let himself topple out of the chair, and landed on Pauline's soft lap, sending the wheelchair back till it bumped to a standstill against the sideboard.

His knees on the floor and his arms around her waist, he quieted under her soothing hands. She stroked the back of his head.

Looking up, his eyes wet, he asked, "Do you think Bram is still mad at me?"

"Did he say that you can't go next Wednesday?"

"No, but he's not coming to fetch me."

"It's time he stops it. He has other things to do than act as your chauffeur. Other boys don't have private chauffeurs, either." She bent over and kissed him. He put his arms around her neck and hung there till her back warned her that she had to let him go.

"My back," she whispered.

When he let go of her and she of him, he slid to the floor and landed on his bottom. When Pauline rose to stretch, Dick grabbed her skirt to pull himself onto his knees.

Although he was a frail boy, his weight was too much for the button on her waistband. It flew off, and Dick fell back again, pulling the skirt with him. Astounded, they both looked at her slender legs.

"Gosh, that goes easy." Surprise was on Dick's face when he looked up at his mother. Pauline stepped out of the skirt, squatted, her face level with his, and ruffled his hair.

"You have to learn other ways, young man. Now, do me a favor and find the button. I have to go shopping. Are you coming along?"

Relieved that his world looked so much better than before, a warm feeling made him pull her toward him to give her a big kiss. It was too much for Pauline's equilibrium. They toppled over together, which sent Dick off in a jubilant laughing fit.

After Pauline had put on another skirt and Dick had climbed back into his chair, she fetched her coat and his windbreaker from the hallway.

When he stuck out his hands to take it, she held it back.

"Have you made a promise?"

He looked at her seriously. "I think I have, but what was it exactly?"

"That you will never bring up your missing feet when you have an argument."

He nodded. "All right. Without feet."

Bram had a nail in his head. Too much whiskey and too many cigarettes. When he remembered the night before, he looked beside him. No Francien. Where in the hell could she have gone? After what he had heard from Thijs, she wouldn't be in the mood to start something with another guy. She had had other men before she met him, yet he couldn't believe it of her. Still, it was an odd note she had left him.

The phone rang. It was Thijs. Bram said, "No, she hasn't come back yet. . . . No, I have no clue. . . . No, I don't know of any guy she fancies except you, but you have an alibi."

Bram hung up, went into the bathroom, stuck out his tongue to the mirror, scratched his head and took an aspirin. He showered and shaved, and felt a lot better.

In the living room, dressed in easy weekend clothes, he stared at the table he found set for breakfast. He also smelled fresh coffee. Francien?

He looked around the room and, seeing nobody, he went to the kitchen, where Francien was in the process of placing coffee things on a tray. Not knowing what to say and not wanting to ask the obvious question, he remained in the doorway, looking at the shapely back, the narrow waist and the apple-shaped buttocks gracefully covered by the material of the dress. He had never seen that dress before.

"Hungry?" She asked, picking up the tray and turning around.

The simplicity of the straight-to-the-point question, and the matter-of-fact way she'd asked it, made it really impossible for him to ask her where she had been.

"Nice dress," he said, stepping aside to let her pass. He followed her to the living room.

"You think so?"

Hesitantly, he seated himself, and not knowing how to start small talk, he followed Francien's example and started buttering a slice of bread.

"How was it last night? Did Thijs have something special?"

"No, not really." Bram told her the story about the junkie and the police, that his car was still in town, and that he would phone a cab later on to pick it up.

"If I had *my* car I could bring you."

"You'll get your car, but it will take a bit longer."

"What does it look like?"

"That's a surprise. You will see."

When he rose from the table, he couldn't get himself to kiss her on her hair and hold her breasts from behind, as was his habit when the mood was there. Instead, he put his hand on her shoulder for a moment, and then turned away to phone a cab.

He went to the hall and picked up the morning paper. Walking back to the living room, glancing over the front page, he froze in his tracks.

ALDERMAN BREAKS ADDICT'S LEGS

Haarlem alderman T. van der Berg and garage owner A. Aardsen caught 20-year-old F. S. red-handed attempting to steal Aardsen's car radio. With Aardsen's help, he managed to jam the junkie's legs between the door and the bodywork until the police arrived. The addict was taken to the hospital, where it was found that both his legs were broken. He has declared he will file a complaint for maltreatment and sue for damages.

Thijs' telephone was busy. By the time the taxi arrived, Bram had cooled off a bit. He took his spare key from the desk drawer, stuck *De Telegraaf* into his pocket and gave the driver Thijs' address.

Marjet answered the door. Thijs was on the phone.

"Have you read this?"

"No. We have an early evening edition, but Thijs has been on the phone for the last half hour. He's quite worried about it. You know him, he's allergic to adverse publicity."

"Don't worry, he had nothing to do with it. He didn't even see what was happening, let alone participate in it, and it's even more ridiculous that *he* did it with my help. We'll sue this goddamn newspaper, the fucking journalist or the bastard cop who informed the paper, or all three of them at the same time."

He walked into the living room to Thijs who was still on the phone. Without hesitation Bram pressed the button, cutting the connection.

"What the hell you think you are doing?! Haven't you done enough damage as it is? This was the mayor I was talking to, *you . . . elephant!*"

"Okay. So you call him back, but Marjet tells me you have been on the phone for half an hour, giving instant reactions to every curious asshole who cares to dial your number. Why didn't you phone me in the first place? I'm your key witness. Now, you call the mayor back, give him the story and then don't answer the phone anymore. Marjet can answer it and tell them that you are out for the day. If you happen to be called by a journalist, you'll have had it. You know how those bastards work. They can make you say anything." Bram released the button of the phone and stood looking outside while Thijs dialed and told the mayor what had happened. The instant he hung up, the phone rang again.

"Don't pick it up! Let Marjet do that."

The ringing stopped, so Marjet had apparently taken the call upstairs. She had escorted the children to their rooms, not wanting them to peer at their nervous daddy.

Bram gestured for Thijs to sit.

"Have you got a cigarette?" Thijs said.

"Sure," Bram said. Thijs's hand was shaking when he took one from the package Bram offered. "I thought you stopped smoking? Maybe you better have a drink as well. I can use one, too."

"You think I should?"

"Why not? No harm done. You'll stay out of sight today anyway.

Here, read the article first, otherwise you won't know what you're talking about."

The paper shook in Thijs's hands. Bram went to the cupboard where Thijs kept his stock of liqueur. He poured them both a Jonge Jenever.

"Listen, Thijs, I know it's my fault. I knew already last night that you disapproved, but I'll see to it that I bear the consequences and not you."

"Nice talk, but the consequences are already on my plate. You know nothing about politics, man!"

"Maybe, but I do know that if you don't play it cool, you will hang yourself. And I know enough about politics to know that there are no friends there, only mutual interest, and when the other guy doesn't see the mutuality anymore, he turns his back on you, regardless of what there ever was between the two of you. Right?"

Thijs nodded and deeply inhaled his cigarette.

Marjet entered with a tray. "Coffee, boys?" And pointing at the glasses she said, "If you two go on with *that,* you'll be flat out by noon. The phone is off the hook."

"So now what?" Thijs asked.

"What about your friend, Mr. Blokland? Didn't he say that he would keep your name out of the police news release?"

"He did, but apparently he didn't."

"I think that lousy cop phoned some journalist friend," Bram said. "You think so?"

"Absolutely. By the way, what did the mayor say?"

"He didn't like the story, but if my version was right, it would be a different cup of tea . . . *if* I could prove it."

"The bugger. But let's see what we'll do now. First thing is, stay out of sight till Monday. Let it cool down a bit. Who did you talk to so far and what was said?"

"Let me see. Bastens was the first one. He's a slimeball, and he hates my guts. He took me completely by surprise. Started off with something like, 'Good work if an alderman starts fighting petty crime with his own hands.' I asked him what he meant.

"'The car robbery last night.'

"And I tried to make light of it, wondering where he got my name, and I said something like 'One does what one can.'

"And then he retorted, 'That's quite a lot, Alderman. Breaking the poor fellow's legs. You will hear more about that.' And then he hung up."

"You *didn't* deny it? Damn. Anyway, that just proves you better make yourself scarce till Monday. By that time the story will have died down and you will know what to say and what steps we are going to take."

"Steps *we* are going to take? Please, Bram, spare me that: *We* are going to take?!"

"Later. Were the rest of the conversations in the same tone?"

"Not all of them. Verscheer complimented me, but he's a radical fire-eating rightist, whom I'm better not being seen with. And then there were two members of the opposition who despise my method of handling the drug problem. By that time I grasped that the blame was on me, and I told them I had nothing to do with it. I doubt whether they believed me. They wanted to know if I was there, and I had to admit I was."

Bram sat drumming the table. "It's a mess. We got to do something, but what? Where do people go with kids on the weekend? Isn't there something yours have been nagging you about?"

"The Efterling, Daddy." Wanda was standing in the door opening, her little face radiant with expectation.

"There you are," said Bram. "Good idea. What about you, Marjet?"

"Fine with me. Killing two birds with one stone. But, Wanda, you should have stayed in your room as I told you. Now go and clean it up a bit. Otherwise you can't come."

The little girl got the message and and rushed upstairs. "Jeroen, we are going to the Efterling! Hurry!"

"You know what, Thijs? To make it more fun, you take the minibus. It'll make it special for the kids. I'll pick up my car on the way to the garage. You can leave your car there and take the bus. In the meantime I'll think the whole thing over and you do the same. Call me tonight and we'll see where we'll go from there."

Seeing his children's joy at the prospect of going to the Efterling tamped down Thijs's ominous feeling. He straightened, patted Marjet on the shoulder and poured Bram and himself another Jonge while Jeroen was telling Wanda there was a giant with such a long neck that he could see the whole country, and that you could see Hans and Gretel, roasting in the oven because they had eaten from the roof of the witch's house, and that there was a man flying on a carpet.

"Replugged the phone?" Bram asked, when Thijs was on the verge of closing the front door behind him.

"Yes."

In Thijs' car, Bram between the children on the backseat, Jeroen pulled his sleeve.

"Uncle Bram, is Dick coming, too?"

"No, Dick is not coming," Thijs answered.

Bram thought about it. He might like it. "Would you mind Thijs, taking him along if he should like to come?"

"Of course we wouldn't mind," Marjet answered. "It's not far out of the way, is it?"

"Not really, but you'll have to leave the highway for a short while. What do *you* say, Thijs?"

"If that's what Jeroen wants, it's fine with me, but can he come?"

"I'll phone him from the garage."

Lazy Willem was working on the *Jiffy* when the group arrived. Bram told Pauline what had happened and what the plan was. Dick would love to come. Bram told Thijs how to find him, filled a plastic bag with Cokes from the machine, filled up the tank of the minibus and waved them off with a thumbs-up to Thijs, who only just managed to reciprocate the gesture. Walking back into the garage, he realized that Pauline might be at home alone the whole day.

"Hey, Bram, nice story in the paper."

Lazy Willem was the only employee who dared call him by his first name.

"I'm not so sure."

"Serves him right, the bugger. Now he has plenty of time to get off drugs."

"I bet they'll give him drugs in the hospital. What can you expect in a country where there are drug-addicted and drug-free sections in prisons?"

The telephone rang. It was Francien. She had tried to call Marjet, but at first the number had been engaged and now they didn't answer. Bram told her what they had decided, that he still had to fix his car, that he didn't know how long it would take, but that he would be back for dinner, anyway.

"Oh . . . I see . . . Bye then." She hung up.

Guilt crept into Bram's chest, but he hardened himself against it. Checking the telex, he found a message from Milan. They referred to his order for the convertible. Due to a cancellation he could have his next week. That would mean Francien could have her car four weeks sooner, and that took care of his guilt. Humming, he went back to the workshop. After he'd changed the lock and readjusted the radio wiring, he looked at his watch and figured that Thijs had already picked up Dick. So he phoned Pauline.

"Hello?"

"Pauline, I'm still at the garage. I'll be with you in forty-five minutes."

"I won't be here then."

"Why? There are no fashion shows at this hour of the day, are there?"

"No, there are not, but still I won't be here."

"But can't you arrange something?"

"No, I won't do that, Bram."

"Why not?"

"Your friends might think that you had arranged for them to take Dick so that you could come and see me."

"But I didn't arrange it."

"I know. Your friend, Thijs, told me."

"So you won't be there when when I come," Bram repeated, dejectedly. "What about next Friday?"

"I don't know yet. That depends on whether I can arrange something for Dick."

"You just said that we couldn't see each other now because it might look as if I had arranged it. And now you are trying to arrange something yourself."

"That's a different thing. Your friends would not like the idea that you walk in here the moment they have left with Dick, would they?"

Bram hesitated. "I guess not."

"You know what you should do? You should go and see that guy in the hospital. Bring him a bunch of flowers and apologize for breaking his legs."

"Whaaat?!"

"You didn't mean to break his legs, did you?"

"No, but—" His whole being revolted against the vision of himself in the hospital, apologizing.

"I've read the morning paper. It would do your friend a lot of good if you came into the open, out of your own free will, and before that journalist gets on to you. Leave your aggression home and you can do it. What is a car door to you? Meet the guy and make sure you leave your name and address on a card with the flowers, just in case he wants to sue you. Bram, I have to go. I'll let you know about Friday as soon as possible." He heard her kiss, and then she hung up.

Dumfounded, Bram sat staring until Lazy Willem came in to say he was going home.

"Problems?"

"To be solved. Have you slowed the cart a bit?"

"Yeah, I put a screw under the throttle so that I can control how far it can come down. It will take him a while before he discovers that. However, I don't think I'll need it for the time being. The other kids have more experience and both their feet. I'm leaving, have a good weekend. See you Monday."

"Same to you."

Alone, Bram sat for a while with the feeling that he had received one cold shoulder and one warm shoulder. *No* now, but possibly *yes* on Friday. He didn't realize the full merit of her advice. Nevertheless, he phoned home and told Francien that he was going to the hospital to bring that junky a bunch of flowers and tell him he was sorry for the unnecessary injury he had caused.

"I'd like you to come with me. You are good at these things and the ground is familiar for you."

"But Bram, this bastard—"

"I'll explain it to you later. I'll be home in half an hour. I have to find out where they parked the guy and what his name is. See you."

Francien was pacing up and down the room. He had asked her to come along. It had been a long time since he had needed her for something. It had been hell, the whole week. But she had managed not to phone Marjet. She had clung to the fact that she also managed to make Bram promise to give her a car of her own. That, and cycling fifty kilometers a day, had kept her from drinking herself to pieces. It had been tough. Fifty kilometers was a long stretch when you were completely out of condition, but she had forced herself. Pedal stroke after pedal stroke, she pushed herself forward along the empty cycle path through the dunes, angrily fighting the wind that blew tears from her eyes. She got on the bike at times she was dying for a drink. When she came back she took three fingers of whiskey. The drinks waiting at the end of the fifty kilometers kept her going. She found she deserved them.

It also gave her satisfaction that she went faster every time. Her body did feel better. The only thing that still rankled her was that woman. But apart from Friday, Bram had come home every night that week. They ate, watched TV and made love in a matter-of-fact way. He would make love differently in Gouda, she was sure of that. Thinking of him and *her* still hurt. She was afraid; sure she was afraid. Other women were so compact, so sure that the world would treat them nicely. But, of course, they had produced children, they had done their job, and she had not. Even that woman had a child, although she surely could not give him a decent upbringing. Models! With the shows and the traveling and the screwing with the men that flocked around them. Why didn't she have children? Then she wouldn't have the problems she had. That would tie up Bram for good and then she could have her peace, having done her duty. But not she and now that slut . . .

She stopped pacing and slammed a hand against her forehead. Not *again!!* Bram would be here any minute and he wanted her to come along, and he was giving her a car. She brushed her teeth, checked her makeup, inspected her handbag and then remembered the purpose of the visit they were going to make. He had talked about flowers and apologizing. She could not really believe it—Bram and apologizing?

Bram had already bought the flowers when he came to pick her up.

"But, Bram, why are you doing this? That means that you are admitting you are guilty and then he will sue you for sure."

"I did do it. I did break his legs, didn't I? I meant to hurt him for sure, but I did not intend to *break* them and certainly not both of them."

"But apologizing to a creep like that. They should be grateful that you got him off the street for a while."

"It was me who got him off the street and not Thijs, and Thijs is afraid this whole story will be damaging to his career. I got him into trouble, so I'll get him out of it. By the way, the junky's name is Frans Stokkenhout."

When they entered the room Bram was shocked by the sight of the mound over the legs and the pale face in the pillow. It reminded him of the first time he had seen Dick. For a moment, he wanted to turn and run.

Francien didn't have that problem. She had already taken the flowers from Bram. Stupid, a man giving flowers to a man, she thought. She walked over to the side of the bed. "You are Frans Stokkenhout?"

"Yes."

"This is my husband," she said, pointing at Bram, who had followed her to the side of the bed. "You broke into his car last night."

The eyes in the pale face moved to Bram and stared at him without comprehending.

"I'm sorry, but I didn't mean to break your legs." It was easier than Bram had expected. The bed, the pale face, the unhealthy skin, the skinny arms—this was not the enemy, who needed to be beaten up. The guy looked back at Francien, who put the flowers on the bed and went away to get a vase. Bram stood watching the pitiable face and finding it impossible to make small talk. What could he ask? Of course, he was jobless. Of course, he used drugs. Of course, he had been caught before. Or not? He was curious to know what the guy would have done with the radio and where he would have sold it, but that would make him sound like a policeman.

The door opened again and Bram turned around. It was not Francien but a young man with a tanned face, long hair and a camera around his neck. He walked straight up to Stokkenhout. "Hello, I'm back."—and then pointing at Bram—"Who is he?"

"I'm the one who got in the clinch with him last night."

The newcomer looked Bram over.

"You are not Alderman van der Berg, so you must be the other one."

"Yes, my name is Aardsen." And extending his hand to the man, he said, "Pleased to meet you."

Hesitantly, the other one took it, and when Bram held it and waited, he said, "De Wolf, journalist."

Francien came back with a vase she had found in the nurses' quarters and looked questioningly from Bram to the newcomer. Bram introduced them and when Francien realized who she was shaking hands with, she put the vase on the floor, planted both her fists on her hips, her solid legs apart. "So, you are the one who wrote the lies about Thijs van der Berg."

The reporter wanted to say something, but he didn't get a chance, as Francien launched into him: "And *you* must be the one who came up with the idea of suing the alderman. But let me tell you something, snotnose, if you want to sue, you have to sue him . . . and me," she added, tapping her breast with her forefinger.

"I don't—"

"Shut up. You don't want me to believe that this guy, whose only problem is where he can get his next shot, has come up with the idea of suing anybody. But let me tell you something else, Mr. De Wolf, there is somebody going to be sued and that somebody is going to be *you*," she declared and tapped his breast with her forefinger.

De Wolf tried to back up a bit but was cornered. Stokkenhout kept looking from one to the other, failing to understand what it was all about. Bram feared that Francien might go too far. Picking up the flowers from the blanket and holding them towards Francien, he said, "Did you bring a vase, my dear?"

Francien took the flowers and shouted at de Wolf, "Get out of my way!" She held the bouquet up as if to whack him in the face with it.

De Wolf, back against the wall, slipped past Francien and walked backward to the door.

"Frans, I will come back on Monday with a solicitor. Don't you worry. We will get them!" Lifting the camera to his eye, the flash went off and then he was gone.

"The scum," Francien said, while arranging the flowers in the vase. She looked at the face on the pillow.

"Are you all right, young man?"

He nodded, but he looked far from all right. Once in the hospital Francien did not see him as part of the riffraff that made the town unsafe, but as a miserable looking patient. On an impulse she kissed him on the forehead. Before she could withdraw, Stokkenhout put his arms around her neck and held her. Embarrassed by the gesture, she looked at his closed eyelids and the unhealthy pallor of his skin, wondering how much his body had been eroded by drugs. Then she loosened herself from his grip and lowered his arms onto the bed.

Leaving the hospital, Bram looked at Francien. "The guy liked you."

"He's sick. That happens."

"I don't know. To me it seemed personal."

Francien remained silent, but she felt good at that moment.

On the way home, more to himself than to Francien, Bram said, "That was a good idea. Now we know the name of that journalist as well."

He was glad he had gone, and so was Thijs when Bram told him the story later that evening. "I'll be darned" was his reaction. "Where did you get that idea of going to see that guy?"

A complacent smile was Bram's only answer.

On Monday Bram and Thijs went to the newspaper together. The editor promised them a correction and agreed that it was not Mr. De Wolf's task to incite people to initiate law suits. He would call Mr. De Wolf to task.

Once outside, they grinned at each other with satisfaction, like men who knew how to handle things.

Marjet invited herself to coffee with Francien, dying to know where she had spent Friday night.

"Where were you Friday night?"

"In the guest room."

"What?"

"In the guest room."

"And the note?"

"I had to do *something.*"

"So you were sleeping in the next room all the time he was phoning high and low at three in the morning, worried stiff that his precious Francien was gone!?"

Francien put her hand on Marjet's arm. "You're kidding?"

"No, I'm *not!*"

"He really phoned around to find out where I was?"

"He hadn't found the note because he'd left the lights out. So he phoned the police, phoned us . . . Thijs phoned the police, too, and all the time you . . ." And then they burst out laughing and laughed till their cheeks hurt.

What a joke! Every time they looked at each other and imagined Bram phoning around desperately and her asleep in the other room, they were in stitches. In years they hadn't laughed like that—makeup ruined, tears running down their cheeks and unable to control themselves whenever they looked at each other.

When Francien walked back into the house after seeing Marjet out, her muscles were tired. She ached. But deep in her bones she felt all right.

On Tuesday, Bram got word from Milan that he could expect the convertible on Friday. On Wednesday, Dick had his first lesson on the combustion engine from Lazy Willem. On Thursday Pauline phoned Bram to ask what time he would pick her up.

That evening he told Francien that he was going to the Bugatti reunion the next day, that he would be back on Saturday and that she would have her car the following week, refusing to tell her what it looked like.

On Friday he made an appointment with Mrs. Hildebrink to deliver her new car the next Tuesday. He bought a golden leather shoulder bag, and at four-thirty he nosed his Alfa into the dense traffic on the A-9, with butterflies in his stomach, yet feeling right about doing something wrong.

12

Bram was surprised at the ease with which Pauline circulated through the crowd of men during cocktails.

At dinner they sat next to each other, but the man on the other side of Pauline was all over her with his platitudes, his jokes, his excellent career, his castle and his two Bugattis in which she should ride one day.

They had agreed that Bram should go up first. No need to have somebody notice they shared a room. When the first guests started leaving, he caught Pauline's eye, winked and went to their room, where he kicked off his shoes, took off his tie and lay down on the bed. After filling the room with cigarette smoke, he opened the window, letting in too much cold autumn air. He started walking from the door to the TV, and from the TV to the door, wondering what was taking her so long. The idea of all those horny males closing in around her became unbearable. He sat down on the bed and picked up his shoes. With his left foot halfway in, he limped to the bathroom in search of a shoehorn. Coming back, he picked up his other shoe and turned to sit down on the bed. With the shoe in one hand and the horn in the other, he saw Pauline standing with her back against the door—tall, slender and smiling, showing immaculate teeth, white as polar ice.

"Well, well, here is an impatient man."

She walked up to him, held the back of his head in her hands and kissed him while her fingernails roved through his hair, sending shivers down his spine. He felt awkward with one shoe in his hand and one shoe on his foot. Pauline closed her body in on his, pressing breasts against breast, pelvis against pelvis, till the back of his knees touched the edge of the bed. Trying to hold his balance, he dropped the shoe and the horn and clung to her in a fruitless attempt not to fall bachward onto the bed. She landed on top of him.

Their heads touching, her hair in his face and his head resting in her hands, they felt each other's heartbeat, wishing their clothes would disappear and the light fade. They remained like that for some time, the outer world gone, tensions being pushed away by the bliss of having and holding each other. Bram's fingers were intoxicated as they made tiny, uncertain movements over the fabric of her dress, gradually covering larger areas, until they found the zipper and inched it down, and further down, over her buttocks.

Pauline moaned softly when her bra came loose. Having the feeling that they had all the time in the world, they lay like that for a while, his hands moving softly over her bare back. When Pauline pushed herself up, the dress slipped off her shoulders. Her small, firm breasts and hard nipples showed themselves proudly to Bram's eager eyes. Her black hair loosely framed her face, giving it a wild femininity. Bram touched her nipples with the palms of his hands, making small circles, and then his hands slid around her narrow waist and over her arching hips, grasping her buttocks, pressing them down for closer contact with his body.

Leaning on one elbow she freed an arm from the sleeve of her dress and caressed his face. He closed his eyes, the subtle touch of her fingers neutralizing the growing desire for violent penetration. He felt her hands wander over his chest, loosening the buttons of his shirt with such a slow, soft confidence, as if she owned him. Bending over, she kissed him lightly on the lips, whispered, "Come," and rose slowly, the dress slipping down as she stretched, catlike. She smiled at his astonished face when he noticed that from the waist down she had been completely nude underneath it.

"I am thirsty." She stepped out of the dress and walked into the bathroom, while he admired her back, narrowing down from the shoulders to her hips.

When she came back he was naked and standing in front of the minibar, filling two glasses with white wine, his prick stretched out full-length and hard. Turning around, a glass in each hand, he looked down at himself and then grinned at her a bit sheepishly.

Touching glasses, they stood looking into each other's eyes, underarms resting on each other's shoulders, his penis touching her pubic hair. Not able to control himself any longer, he took the glass from her hand, put both glasses on the bedstand and lifted the covers. When she lay down he lowered himself on top of her and slowly entered between her moist lips.

The third time that night, Pauline came twice before Bram. In between they had dozed off, but the newness of their bodies woke them up again, reviving their appetite.

Pauline woke him at eleven with a kiss. She was already dressed in tight, dark green slacks, beige cashmere sweater and a silk scarf loosely around her neck disappearing inside the collar.

"My friend will bring Dick back around two. Presuming that you are starving after this performance *grandioso,* I take it that you'd like to have breakfast before we leave." Bram pulled her down and held her till she softly loosened herself from his grip.

In the bathroom he smelled his hands and his arms. It was Pauline all over. The female way to take possession of a man, he thought, and smiled.

After a shower, shave and the familiar smell of Savanne applied in abundance, he had his own body back.

They were too late for breakfast in the hotel, so they stopped at a restaurant along the highway for orange juice, coffee and rolls.

"Pauline, I have been pondering Dick's future. What do you think? Does he really want to go into the racing business?"

"Don't you think you are a better judge of that than me?"

"You are his mother."

"The only thing I can say is that he has been fond of anything that has wheels from the time he was a toddler."

"You know, I'm not sure whether it'll do Dick a lot of good for me to keep his racing dream alive. If his handicap can't be overcome, the disappointment may be devastating."

"Is it technically possible?"

"With a computerized gearbox, maybe."

"Now, suppose you drop racing. What else would there be left that you both would be interested in? Dick talking with you about his homework? He adores you. I think that if you told him now that you wouldn't have that racing nonsense any longer, you would hurt him more than he could ever be hurt by failing his own expectations. You think the decision is still in your hands?"

Bram remained silent, chewing his bread and drinking his coffee. After a while he said, "Maybe you are right. Maybe the decision is not in my hands anymore. But then where do we go from here?"

"Back to Gouda, I would say."

"Sure, back to Gouda, but you know what I mean."

"What *do* you mean, Bram?"

"He's twelve years old. It will take at least five years before he'll ever see a racetrack through a windscreen. I'm not an experienced coach, but someone has to . . . you know, guide him. Tell him things, wipe his nose and slap his back."

"I think you are extremely good at wiping noses and slapping backs."

"But what about us?" he said.

"I don't know. If you know it, you may say it. I have the feeling Dick's adoration for you might be contagious, whether I like it or not."

"Why wouldn't you like it?"

"I'm not even going to try and explain that to you now. You have a tower of an ego at the moment. If you were a cock, you would fly to the top of the roof of this restaurant and crow for the whole world to hear, batting you chest with your wings."

"I would not!!"

Pauline smiled, took his hand, kissed it and rose. "Let's go. I don't want to be late."

When Pauline had left the car, Bram saw his present was still on the backseat. He called her back to his open window and handed her the parcel. "Not matching the occasion, but the best I could think up."

While Pauline looked at the parcel, he lifted his foot from the clutch and accelerated sharply, as if he feared that without the help of the 192 horsepower he would not be able to pull himself loose from the frail silhouette he saw in the rear mirror.

On the way to Haarlem it started to rain, low gray clouds shedding rain onto empty meadows that didn't need it. He remembered Pauline's remark about the contagiousness of the adoration: "Whether I like it or not." Why wouldn't she? She liked him well enough, that was clear. She had meant something important with that remark, but what?

After a while he decided it was meant to tease him. What else could it be? Afraid? Of him?! Impossible.

Lord, what a great girl, but her own person. Aloof as a queen. She hadn't opened up to him, not shared the secrets of her heart with him. He regretted that.

He had no clue where they would go from there. Pauline didn't know the answer and neither did he, but the glow of the night lingered.

Turning onto the street where he lived, he overtook a soaking wet Francien on her bike, two shopping bags hanging from the handlebars. Parking the car beside the house, he walked back to the pavement, feeling tender towards her there in the rain.

"Here, let me take those. I'll be glad when you have your own car. Why didn't you take a cab?"

"With my bike on the backseat? It wasn't raining when I left."

He carried the bags into the kitchen. Francien entered from the yard after she had put her bike away. "Before I forget, Bram, Dick called last night. His wheelchair broke down."

It gave Bram a fright, but he controlled himself. "Okay, I'll give him a call and see what can be done. Can't be something I can't fix."

"His number is near the phone!"

It wasn't Pauline's number, either. He dialed.

"Hello." A woman's voice.

"Is Dick Verwal there?"

"I'm sorry, he's just left."

"I'm told there was something wrong with his wheelchair."

"Are you Bram?"

"Yes, I am. How did he get home? Has it been fixed in the meantime?"

"No, but Pauline phoned and told him to take a cab. I suggested to Dick that we could find somebody here to repair it, but he wouldn't hear of it. 'Bram will fix it,' he said."

"A taxi? Where do you live then?"

"Waddinxveen, that's not too far."

"Well, thanks. Good-bye."

"Wasn't that his home number?" Francien asked.

"No, somebody in Waddinxveen, but he isn't there anymore. I'll see what the problem is. He'll be home by now."

Pauline answered the phone.

"Can I have Dick, please?

Dick told Bram what was the matter.

"Okay, I'll come and pick you up and fix it."

After he hung up, Bram said to Francien, "Since it has to be fixed anyway, I can just as well do it now. I'll be back at six."

"Shall I come?"

Flabbergasted, Bram stared at Francien. "Why?"

"Well, I talked to him quite a while last night. He sounds like a pleasant kid, and he thinks the world of you. The first time I saw him I hardly talked to him . . . but maybe this is not such a good idea after all."

You can say that again, Bram thought, but remained silent.

"You know what you can do? After you fix the chair, why not bring him along for dinner. What about it?"

Bram was speechless. For a moment he had imagined, with horror, arriving at Pauline's with Francien at his side. In comparison the alternative looked much better, but he was still confused. The glorious night with Pauline, his flash of tender feelings toward Francien, the fear of discovery, the picture of her coming along and now a dinner invitation as if it were the most normal thing in the world.

What was she up to? What had she learned from Dick? At any rate, that Pauline hadn't spent the night at home. Francien's behavior was so out of character that he could not help staring at her with a mixture of suspicion and disbelief. Francien saw it as surprise.

"Well, what do you think? Dick has never seen where you live, has he? I'll make something simple: french fries with applesauce. All the kids like that."

Something in the whole situation was familiar, but he couldn't put his finger on it.

"I've got ice cream for dessert," she said.

"He'll like that, but let me see. Four-thirty at the garage. Depending on the repairs, an hour, maybe a bit longer." He felt trapped and saw no way out. "I'll ask him. I'll phone you from the garage. He may have something else planned with his mother."

"With a broken wheelchair?"

"You are right. Okay, if he wants to come, I will bring him along. If not, I'll take him right back and we'll have dinner in town."

On the way to Gouda he barely paid attention to the road. Something fishy was going on and why didn't he want Dick to come to his house? Why did he have that déjà vu feeling? Francien could do stupid things sometimes, but she was not retarded. She couldn't believe it was coincidence that both he and Pauline had spent the night away from home. Yet she had not made a row, thrown vases and shouted at him. Instead, she asked him to bring Dick back for dinner. It had been his secret wish, but why didn't he want it now? Something was going on that he didn't understand and he didn't like that.

Pauline said, "This is quicker than I expected. The peace at home in shambles?"

"On the contrary. She asked me to bring Dick along for dinner."

"Not to eat him, I presume."

Bram smiled in spite of himself. "Do you think he would like that?"

"No doubt, but do you? You don't look it."

"I . . . uh . . . of course, I'd like him to come, but how about you?"

"I see no problem at all. It had to come to that sooner or later. What's your worry, that the decision was not made by you?"

"BRAAAM!" Dick shouted from the living room, getting impatient.

"Macho," Pauline whispered when she stepped aside to let him pass. He raised his eyebrows. She smiled.

Dick liked it. The chair was no problem and while Bram was working on it Dick explained how it had happened and that he had phoned and talked with . . . Francien. He used her first name a bit hesitantly. While Dick chatted away easily, Bram was still puzzled by the whole thing. It had been his own idea to go to the Chinese restaurant together a fortnight ago where Dick had met Francien. He must have wanted the two to meet.

Dick interrupted his train of thought. "Where were you last night?"

"At a meeting of the Bugatti Club." It was out before he knew it. What had Pauline told him? You should have asked her, you fool.

"That's much nicer than where Mom was."

"Is it?"

"The parents of my dad. They live in Groningen. I've been there. Dull! They treat you like you're a baby. 'Wouldn't my little Dicky like to have a cookie?' And when you're bored they give you a coloring book. Imagine, a coloring book!"

"Does your mother go there often?"

"No, once a year or something, and they tell her what they have heard from my dad. Why did you go to the Bugatti Club?"

"For fun, for business. They are such lovely machines. In their time they won all the races, with Ettore Bugatti in the grandstand, smoking big cigars. That was before Alpha Romeo, under Enzo Ferrari, took over."

"But Ferrari had his own Ferrari cars, didn't he?"

"That was later when he broke up with the Alpha owners and went on his own. Okay, that's it, young man," Bram said, moving the welding glasses up his forehead.

Ten minutes later Dick hobbled over the threshold into the living room, where Francien had already set the table. They greeted each other in a kind of formal way with handshakes. Francien had changed into dark brown slacks and a high-collared autumn sweater that complimented her green eyes and red hair perfectly.

"Find yourself a place, Dick, while I get you something to drink. Coke?"

"Yes, please."

While Francien went into the kitchen and Bram to the bar for their drinks, Dick slowly wheeled around, his eyes wandering over the furniture, the overloaded bookcase, the drawing of an antique racecar, a landscape, the radio, the record player and tape deck, each a different make. In a corner was a tiny cupboard with a curved glass door and a Chinese tea set with feather-light lacquered cups, painted with prim-faced ladies in long-sleeved dresses.

"What are you looking for?" Bram asked when he saw Dick surveying everything carefully.

"Where have you got the model of the Grand Tourissimo?"

"I haven't."

"You mean you haven't got a model like I have?"

"No, and I tried hard, I can assure you. I told you, it was something very special when you got it."

When they were seated at the table it was a good thing they were having dinner. Filling their mouths regularly, they were excused from saying much. The silence was only punctuated by pro forma questions: What school are you going to? . . . What class are you in? . . . You like it at school?

After a long interval, Dick touched Francien's arm. When Francien looked at him, he smiled and his eyes lit up playfully. "It's yellow, sits in a tree and is dangerous. You know what that is?"

Francien tried to make an associative connection the way they had when she was a child.

"It's yellow and stands on one leg. Glass of eggnog. But this one? Yellow, in a tree and dangerous?" She pursed her lips. "A snake?"

"No."

"Yellow, sits in a tree and dangerous?" she repeated.

Dick nodded.

"I give up."

"A canary with a machine gun. And what about this one: It's white and it walks in the meadow."

"White, . . . and it walks in the meadow?"

"Yeah. You know it?"

"A white cow?"

"Nope, it's bigger."

"Okay, a white elephant then?"

"A herd of yoghurt. This one is easy. It's white and comes from two sides."

"No idea."

"Stereo yoghurt."

Dick howled, Bram chuckled. The boy was really enjoying himself. When he ran out of riddles, Bram asked him which tire wore down the least in a curve. Dick tried to figure it out. The tires at the outside surely took the brunt. It had to be one at the inner curve, front or rear.

"Front-wheel drive?"

"Doesn't matter."

"The front wheel at the inner side of the curve."

"Nope," said Bram, "the spare tire."

"You got me!" Dick grinned.

Francien said, "You know what happened one day back when I still worked in the hospital?"

"No."

"In those days they had those wards with ten or twelve people in one room. One of the walking patients saw a doctor's coat hanging on a peg in the corridor. A joke, he thought, and put the coat on, entered the ward, went to the first bed and barked to the patient named Johnsen, 'Turn around, Johnsen. We need to take your temperature. Pull your pants down and now wait till I come back.'

"He left the ward, and after a couple of minutes the intern on his rounds comes in, walks up to that patient and exclaims, 'Hey, Johnsen, what are *you* doing?!'

" 'Taking my temperature, Doctor.'

" 'With a tulip?!' "

Dick laughed so heartily that Francien and Bram couldn't help joining in, although they had heard the joke several times before. After Dick quieted down, he enjoyed his ice, grinning occasionally when he imagined the man with the tulip again.

After dinner Bram drove Dick home and on the way back it suddenly dawned on him why he had had that sense of "déjà vu." Marjet! She had told him she would have invited Dick home if she were in Francien's shoes. She must have told Francien. He stopped at the first phone booth. Marjet answered. Had she told Francien to invite Dick.

"Definitely not. Last Monday I told her to solve her own problems, and I haven't given her any advice since. Nor would I ever tell her to do a thing like that. If she doesn't think it up herself, it doesn't work anyway. But I'm very pleased to hear she did. What about you, did you enjoy it?"

"Well, I had mixed feelings. I'm not sure why."

"I do. You just can't stand it that somebody else can come up with something of value, especially Francien. Only if she kills the man who's about to kill you, can you admire her. But outside of that, you act like you're her camp counselor."

"Come on, you're kidding. I'm not like that. You don't mean that."

"You bet your life I do, Mr. Aardsen. I must admit that you are the nicest dictator I know, but a despot you are. And being nice is what makes it so bad. You can't revolt against a benign dictator, can you? By the way, where are you now?"

"In a phone booth along the A-9. I had to know whether you had whispered that into her ear."

"Well, now you know, and don't you dare doubt my word or you will insult me."

"I wouldn't dare. How's Thijs? Recovered from the shock, I hope?"

"He sure is, but you have me puzzled. Where did you get the idea of going to see the guy in the hospital?"

"That's for me to know and for you to find out. Bye, sweetheart, and give my regards to your old man."

The rest of the way home he thought about what Marjet had said to him. That's twice in one day I've been told that I am overbearing. 'I'll be dammed if this isn't the most unfair accusation I've heard in years. You arrange things. You look after somebody. You provide food and shelter, as

Thijs would say, and then all of a sudden you're a bully. This is too ridiculous for words, and only because *you* decide what's good food and what's a proper shelter. She wants a car, you provide a car. But what will happen?

I will be a dictator again, because I picked the type *and* the color. Apparently, I should have had the decency to let her choose the color. Stupid females, being satisfied with a minor detail like the color. Not the horsepower, the road contact, the braking system, the rust resistance— vital things. No, they don't bother about that. Too complicated for them. The color. That they can handle. No wonder a has to man look after them and decide what's good for them. Dames.

By the time he got home his temper had cooled down. Of course, it was all nonsense. Francien would be ever so pleased with the car and the more so when she got the feel of it.

Francien was watching television—the umpteenth episode of *Dynasty*. He poured them both a drink and sat down. After the program was finished, Francien switched off the set.

"Funny sense of humor these kids have nowadays. Don't you think so?" she said.

"You can say that again. In our day we only had something like, 'It hangs on the wall and ticks,' and then it wasn't a terrorist with a time bomb in his pocket. No, just a clock."

"Well. Shall we call it a day?"

Bram yawned. He could do with some sleep.

They made love. After Pauline he noticed a difference. It fascinated him. It took him a long time to come, but it was a delicious pain when he did.

He was asleep seconds later, but Francien was wondering whether they were crazy or wise. Bram believed she had spent the whole of a Friday night somewhere else and hadn't asked a single question. A week later Bram spends Friday night in Antwerp, and that woman is away, for the night, too.

Francien did not ask questions, either. What was left of a marriage when everybody could go and come as he or she pleased and nobody was interested enough to ask where he or she had been? That she herself hadn't asked was because she had somewhere read a story about a married woman in love with somebody else. She had tried to imagine what she would do in a situation like that. She couldn't. Anyway, not a situation to look forward to. Now she was getting a car of her own, next week he'd said. A farewell present or a gift from a man caring to please his wife?

The fact that she had invited Dick for dinner pleased her. Sitting there at the dinner table, the three of them together. It was clear that Bram and Dick were buddies, like a man and his son, with their mutual understanding that they were the ones who held the power in life. She felt excluded from that confidence.

———

On Monday Bram phoned Pauline and told her how dinner had been, wanting to hear from her what Dick had said about it.

"He liked it well enough," Pauline said. "Enjoyed the food, and especially Francien's joke. Tells it to everybody."

Bram rubbed his hands with satisfaction. Having had Dick over for dinner, Pauline's mentioning Francien's name in the casual way she did, sleeping with both of them, and looking after the child of the one and the car of the other made him feel important. It felt like a kind of family.

On Tuesday he went to deliver the new car to Mrs. Hildebrink and take back her old one.

"Oh, please, *do* call me Suzanne. It's Bram, isn't it?" she said after she let him in. "Sit down, please. This calls for a celebration, don't you think so? Let me see." She walked to a solid oak cupboard, opened it and studied the bottles, wondering which choice would fit her mood.

In the meantime Bram sat watching her body. He also liked the way she had matched the color of her blouse with that of the pants.

Turning around, she caught him studying her. "What would you like? I am hesitating between a Chateau Saint André 1970 or a Chateau Saintout La Grange, a Bordeaux from 1975. What do you think . . . about the wine, I mean?"

He saw the sparkle in her eyes, which he knew wouldn't have been there had she caught him reading one of the magazines from the side table.

"I was thinking that you dress well. You understand more about colors than I know about wine. When I have to order wine, I always choose on the basis of the sound."

"The sound?"

"The sound of the name. Chateau Saintout La Grange sounds very nice to me—style, grandeur, nobility, everything I associate with wine."

"You're kidding. A man with your experience?"

She turned and picked the bottle, two glasses and a corkscrew from the cupboard. She walked slowly toward him and lowered herself close to him on the leather couch. She smelled like roses. She offered him the bottle and the corkscrew.

"A man's job, isn't it?" she said, teasing.

He turned his attention to the bottle: unwound the lead cap and pushed the screw into the soft cork. He felt her hand lightly on his thigh.

"Excuse me." He rose from the bench. "I better uncork it over the table. You would never be able to remove wine stains from a carpet like that. It's wool, isn't it?"

"As a matter of fact it is. Is that relevant?"

"Mmmm. Wool threads are hollow. They suck up the wine— capillarity. Artificial threads are solid, so the liquid stays on the outside. Shall I?" He held the bottle toward the glasses.

"Yes, please."

He walked to the other side of the low table, poured the wine, handed her a glass, took his and raised it toward her.

"Here is to your new car, Suzanne. I hope you enjoy it."

Then he took the easy chair opposite her.

"I always like to sit facing a beautiful woman. Otherwise I can't see her well."

Suzanne scrutinized his face from behind her glass, then she drank a little, put the glass down on the table and leaned back, her hands in her lap and a slightly mocking smile on her face.

Bram handed her the papers over the table. "Your license plate certificate. Green card. The handbook. The warantee and the invoice. You preferred to pay cash, you said?"

"I do." She rose, strode to the rolltop desk near the window, turned the key in the lock and pushed the slatted cover up. Coming back, she seated herself on the table and handed him an envelope.

Bram counted the money. Suzanne picked up her glass and sipped, watching his hands.

"You gave me too much."

She accepted the change and stashed it inside her blouse with the same ease that men put business cards into breast pockets.

Bram got up. "I think I better show you now how everything works in your new car." He handed her the keys and led the way to the door.

She drove smoothly while he demonstrated the working of the various buttons. Twenty minutes and they were back. Standing in front of the house, Bram looked around and then questioningly at Suzanne.

"She is in the garage. But come on in first. I have to get the papers and we still have the Saintout La Grange to finish, or didn't you like it?"

"Oh, yes. It's really delicious."

He followed her. Seated as before, she asked him whether he had been married a long time; whether he had kids; whether he would like to have them or if running his business was the only thing he cared for. "Like my husband. He works from morning till night, and he doesn't care what I do, as long as I enjoy myself."

When the Saintout was finished Bram rose and so did she, taking the car papers and the keys from her handbag and giving them to Bram.

At the front door he turned around and embraced her. After they had stood there for a few moments, both feeling the newness of the other's body, he released her and, holding her shoulders, smiled apologetically. "I'm sorry, but I think I have recently fallen in love with someone else."

It brought a smile to her face.

"Let's go and get my car for your friend."

They trekked to her distant garage. He took possession of the auto and got in. She refused his offer to bring her back. It was only 300 yards, she insisted. Standing beside his open window, she bent down.

"You don't fit at all in a car like this." She touched his cheek softly with the back of her hand. "Lucky bastard." Then she walked away.

On the way back from Leiden to Haarlem the traffic was so heavy that he couldn't really try her out. Lazy Willem was still there when he arrived at the garage.

"Are you busy tonight, Willem?"

"Nothing worthwhile. What's up?"

"I would like you to take the convertible and test it for an hour or so. Can you do that?"

"Sure."

"Fine. Bring her in tomorrow and give me a complete list of all the improvements you can think of. Don't forget the radio, and if it doesn't rain tonight, take her to the car wash to see if the roof leaks. New bumpers, dazzle lamps and whatever you can think of. Check the leather and have it repaired if need be. The paint is still good, but I want it to look like new, so touch it up where needed and give it an undercoating."

"Sure. Who is it for, Bram? Dick's mother?"

"Why?"

"Well, she would be worth the trouble, wouldn't she?"

"How do you know?"

"Last week we missed the train so I thought, what the hell, and brought him home. He wanted to show me his Grand Tourissimo model, so I met her."

"Shit. Why can't you just do what you are told!" His voice sounded loud in the empty workshop. He lowered it, but he couldn't lower his temper: "You let him drive back from the track. You bring him home when I have told him to travel by himself, and you come and go when it pleases you."

"That's why I'm here now, boss. Making up the time."

Bram turned on his heel, stalked to his car and left, with engine roaring and tires screaming. Lazy Willem smiled. He sauntered up to the convertible and patted the roof. He got in.

"Now, lady, let's see how much spunk you've got left after three years of nail polish."

———

A quarter past ten the next morning Lazy Willem knocked on the door of Bram's office, stuck his head in and said, "Can you spare a moment, boss?"

Bram waved him in and pointed at the chair facing the desk. "Coffee?" he said.

"Please."

"Belinda, two coffees, please. Now, what have you got?"

"On the whole she's fine. The engine is amazingly pliant for a woman's car. Usually they get lazy as hell. No leakage. The clutch is a bit slack. New tires, with white sides, I would suggest. The upholstery is undamaged. A bit of wax and it'll smell like new. A routine check will do the rest. What kinda radio you want in it?"

"A sledge. If they cut up the roof to pinch the radio, it's going to cost a lot of money. Put two extra speakers in the doors. When will it be ready?"

"Thursday, I guess. By the way, shall we keep it out of sight. I'm sure it'll catch Dick's eye."

"Do that." Bram was unwilling to make Willem any wiser. Let him gossip and then let them find out how wrong he had been.

"By the way, if you drop him off at the station, drop him off at the station. He has to learn to stand on his own two feet."

"You can say that again."

"Damn it, Willem, you know what I mean!"

"I do, but it may take him longer than the other boys."

"Or shorter."

"Shorter?"

"His handicap may force him into maturity."

"Let's hope so. I'll keep you posted on the progress with the convertible."

Wednesday afternoon Dick arrived at the garage. Bram had decided to go with him to the track. It would be Dick's first experience with competition. Van den Bosch had charted three racers and told them what was on; they should take it easy and not forget that the boy lacked foot control. He introduced them—Jaap, Wim, Henk and Dick—and gave them each a different color helmet from the club's stock. Jaap got a white one, Wim a blue one, Henk yellow and Dick a red one.

After they had circled around to warm up the engines, van den Bosch collected the four of them at the starting line. Standing in front of them, he told them that there would be four races of ten rounds each. The one he saw pushing somebody aside would be disqualified and excluded from the next race. The winner would get three points, the second two and the third one. If somebody was disqualified, it would be two for the first and one for the second.

"Understood?!"

The four helmets bobbed.

Next, Van den Bosch walked to the side of the track, held the flag high and then moved it down sharply, sending them off, the tiny engines screaming.

Dick reached the first curve two yards ahead of the others. For a split second he looked around to see where they were, drifted to the outside of the curve, oversteered, spun around and saw the other three pass by in a flash, never to see them again at close range in this first race.

Bram remained where he was while the boys idled, waiting for the next race. The fastest lap was 38 seconds. Lazy Willem had been right. No need to slow him down. He lacked experience.

The next race, Dick was second at the first curve and followed so closely in the slipstream of the blue helmet that Bram feared he might touch him. Dick never tried to pass, just followed the blue helmet's line over the track. Smart, Bram thought, he's learning to steer the most efficient line.

The white and the yellow were following at close range, changing places at almost every round, but never trying to overtake Dick. Coming out of the last curve, Dick steered away from behind the blue, but was short by half a meter when they crossed the finish line. He got two points.

When he came round back to the finish line, he stopped in front of Bram. The others did another circuit at a slow pace.

"I need more power. I can't get the throttle down far enough," he shouted at Bram over the stuttering of his idling engine.

Bram smiled. "Sure you need more power, but first more experience."

From the corner of his eye Bram saw the other three moving over the track side by side, and from the movements of their helmets he figured that they were talking together. He had the feeling they were up to something, but there was nothing he could do. They knew that Dick was crippled. Their slow start in the first race made it obvious that they had wanted to make it easy for Dick. He looked at the screw under the throttle.

"Cool it, man," he said more to himself than to Dick. Looking at the grim, pale face, smaller than normal under the large helmet, he could not help hugging the narrow shoulders, and then looking into the gray eyes and patting a shoulder, he said, "You do the best you can and that's all there is to do for today. Got it?"

Dick stuck up his thumb and steered to the starting line for the third race.

This time Dick reached the first curve last and tried desperately to get out of last place. A couple of times he passed the number three, the yellow helmet, by taking the curve full throttle, but then he drifted far to the side of the track in order to avoid spinning, and the yellow helmet retook his place by steering the much shorter inner curve. On the last curve Dick didn't fully floor the throttle, but held back a little so that he didn't swing out so widely. They were side by side approaching the finish line and Dick earned his third point by only centimeters.

Bram had been looking at the gathering clouds, hoping it would start raining. It would be an experience that Dick needed. Feeling a few drops, he walked up to Dick at the starting line for the last race. Squatting down and looking into the tiny white face of the little man who was fighting for his dream in spite of his handicap, he swallowed his emotion and said, "If you don't spin, you win. It's going to rain."

The moment the flag went down, the rain started. In torrents. Dick entered the first curve as number four, but the blue spun, taking the white one with him.

"Easy now, boy! Easy!"

Van den Bosch looked at Bram with raised eyebrows, but Bram saw only the yellow helmet and a vague red one following in the spray of water thrown up by the wheels. The blue and the white were half a track behind and presented no danger anymore.

When the first two passed the finish line for the last lap, Dick moved out of the slipstream and Bram felt his heart sink.

"Not yet!" he shouted. Dick moved back behind the yellow helmet when they turned into the curve.

Approaching the last curve, Dick steered out of the slipstream again and came abreast of the yellow.

"My God, not on the outside—if he spins he takes you along with him! Get back!"

As if Dick had heard him, he released the throttle just before entering the curve. The yellow helmet had seen Dick at his side and was afraid that he couldn't hold him on pure speed. He held the throttle down a fraction of a second too long, spun off the track and landed in the wet, soft earth.

Van den Bosch flagged Dick down as number one. Elated, Bram jumped up like a soccer fan when his team scores. Just as quickly he felt foolish standing in the rain, his coat open, his suit getting wet, waiting for Dick, who braked, turned back and headed straight for Bram. Skidding to a standstill, he took his helmet off and stretched out his arms for Bram to lift him from the *Jiffy*. It was the only moment when Bram was glad the boy had no feet, otherwise he could never have taken the boy in his arms and walked around with him. It was Dick, who kissed him on both cheeks, and pointed to his wheelchair standing empty in the pouring rain.

Bram lowered him onto the wet seat. He was wet anyway. Opening the minibus, he lifted Dick into it, chair and all, and then walked up to van den Bosch. He squeezing the man's hand till it hurt and thanked him for his assistance. "If you ever have a problem with your car, call me—anytime and *do* it."

Van der Bosch looked him over. "Sure, I'll do it. That's not your son, is it?"

"No, it's not."

"Well, I have seen a lot of crazy fathers, but you beat them all. I have to go now. Dry him off before he catches a cold. I'll call you one of these days and then we'll have a drink and a bite. Okay?"

"Anytime."

Back in the garage Lazy Willem sauntered toward them. Bram met him halfway down the floor, grinning.

"He's soaking wet, has a sore back from the tension and is catching a cold. Get him under the shower, chair and all. He can help himself as long as he can reach the taps. Then put him in overalls and bring him home, will you?"

"Bring him home?"

"You heard me. To the door. He deserves it."

After Willem had unloaded the *Jiffy*, Dick rolled toward him shivering, his teeth chattering.

"I"—he took a deep breath to control his voice—"won!"

"Congratulations. If you were older I would give you a brandy, but let's get you under a real hot shower."

He turned on the taps and got the water temperature right, then pushed Dick into the stream. "I want sweating like hell. We'll talk later." He left overalls and a towel. "As hot as possible and at least ten minutes, you hear me?"

Dick nodded and Willem closed the door.

Sitting under the delicious stream of warm water, he gradually filled out his skin again and color returned to his cheeks and hands. The tension ebbed and a deep joy took hold.

I did it! I did it! I can do it, feet or no feet!

Naked in his wheelchair, his stumps still showing where they had sewn the flesh together, he stretched his arms up into the stream of water. "I did it."

Lazy Willem saw that the light in Bram's office was still on, and that the convertible was back from the undercoating company.

He rolled down the big garage door, went to the canteen, took two cans of Heineken from the fridge and walked into Bram's office without knocking, sat down opposite Bram and shoved a can over the desk.

"I'd liked to have seen it. He's proud as hell. Is it true that in the last round he tried to make the other bloke nervous by pretending he would overtake him?"

Bram stared at Willem. "Damn, and I was thinking that he really tried.

He fooled me as well. By the way, I have to talk to van den Bosch. I have an inkling that he instructed his guys to take it easy. The first race they just *gave* him the lead and if Dick hadn't spoiled it by spinning in the first curve, they might have let him have it for the entire race. The last race was different. They wanted to win."

"You warned Dick about the rain, didn't you?"

"Yes, but, my God, he was fooling me, too. I was shouting like a madman when he pulled out of the slipstream.

"That little fellow will keep us busy. Did you know, for instance, that he found out about the screw under the throttle? That he turned it down before the last race?"

"But you told me you hadn't stopped the throttle with it because you didn't think it necessary since the other boys had more experience and more supple engines."

"That's true, but I phoned van den Bosch and asked for the fastest lap on record. When he said thirty-seven seconds, I thought Dick was too close to it, so I turned it up a bit, making it just tight enough so that I still could adjust it by hand in between runs, if need be."

"Why didn't you tell me?"

Willem grinned sheepishly, and hesitated.

"Well, why didn't you tell me?!"

"Okay, to be frank, I thought I would be taking him to the track, and I was a little pissed off when you decided to go yourself, so I thought, Figure it out yourself. That's why."

"Talk about nuts. Okay, we'll take turns. That is *if* you strictly stick to the plan you and I agree on. And in case we cannot agree, I decide. Not because I know better, but because . . . just because. Agreed?"

Willem stuck out his hand and Bram shook it. After Willem fetched more beer, they sat around like boys, planning and scheming how they could make the *Jiffy* faster.

On Thursday Willem entered Bram's office by noon.

"The car is ready. Want to come and have a look?"

"In a minute."

He looked out the window. Clouds, clouds and more clouds, and rain coming down from them steadily. He was *not* going to present a convertible on a rainy day. A sunny day in spring was ideal, but in the rain in November it was pure shit. She'd have to wait. He picked up the phone and dialed the weather forecast.

The front would drift into Germany by the end of the day. The forecast for tomorrow was an occasional shower with lots of sunny patches in the afternoon along the coast. So tomorrow it was, he decided, and went down to the workshop.

She was a beauty. Maybe the white sidewall tires were a bit old-fashioned, but Francien would like them. It looked expensive, anyway. The black leather upholstery looked chic and the dazzle lamps gave it a sporty style. A small golden vase was stuck with a sucker to the black dashboard, still empty.

Willem walked up to him. "What d'you say? If it were a woman I'd kiss her feet." He looked at the car with satisfaction. "When is the big moment?"

"As soon as it stops raining."

"Well, then, she may well sit here till next spring."

"I don't think so. We'll get some sunshine tomorrow. Put her in the showroom with SOLD on it. Nice piece of work, Willem. Thank you."

"You can bank on me when you need me, Bram, if you don't mind me not being here when you don't need me."

"I do . . . at times . . . but you must have put in quite a lot of extra hours of late, with the *Jiffy* and this one. How's your wife taking that? Doesn't she grumble?"

"Not anymore. She's gone."

Bram was dumbstruck for a moment. "I'm sorry to hear that."

"I'm not. Not that she was a lousy woman, certainly not. Solid chassis with a good body on it. Maybe I'm not fit for marriage, not the romantic type. Liked to fondle her headlights, get my piston into her cylinder, slap her rear bumper once in while—but she didn't like me talking like that. She wanted the candlelight stuff."

"You *talked* to her that way?"

"Yeah, maybe that was the problem. I can't help it. I see a woman the same as a horse or a car. You feed a horse, you brush it, and you ride it under your butt and between your legs. Legs are more important than reins, you know. Car is the same. You fill 'er up, you polish her and you drive around, and you know the feel in your ass and the touch of your feet are more important than your hands at the wheel.

"So, I fed her, dressed her and rode her, but that's not good enough nowadays, is it? They want to talk. Okay, fine with me, let them talk, if they can find somebody who cares to listen, but that's not it. It's you they want to talk to. Tell you that you are wrong and that they are equal. Now figure, your horse feeling equal to you and discussing with you who is riding on whose back. And you know, Bram, it's all caused by the fucking TV. It started with Ed the Talking Horse, and now you have a talking frog, a piano-playing bear, and even a talking sow. The Muttons or something, speaking animals. No wonder women want to talk, too. Can't really blame them. My father always said: 'Can't have two cocks in one yard, my boy. The Lord knew that, so in His wisdom He made a difference, one is the boss and the other is not.' Not our fault, Bram, that we are made that way, is it?"

"If you say so."

"It's easy for them. They drop a child or two, cook an egg, fry a sausage and that's all there is to it. We have to get a house for them, clothes, food, and take 'em out once in a while. You know, we even got to do the fucking fucking. It's unfairly divided in the world, if you ask me."

"Willem, what about your kids? You have two girls, don't you?"

"Yeah, eight and nine. I see them mostly every other week. As I said, Brenda—that's her name—Brenda is not a bad woman, but she wants to talk and talk. She wants to be equal. Now she's shacked up with a teacher who says she's equal."

"A teacher?"

"Not much of a teacher. For retarded children. You haven't got to know much, have you? Most of them kids will never count to ten. No wonder she can be his equal."

"Must be lonely when you come home and there's nobody."

"Kind of. Yeah. But you know, Bram, where I live there are a lot of run-down cars owned by people who can't afford repairs. The guys buy me a beer and the women cook me a meal, and when they can't cook they pay me in kind, if we speak the same language. So I'm not all that lonely. That's why I'm late once in a while. Some times they pay me in the evening, but sometimes they pay me in the morning. See?"

"I see. . . . Okay, into the showroom she goes."

Willem put a plastic cover over the seat, got in and started the engine, and slowly the convertible rolled through the big sliding door.

The engine sounds good, Bram thought, walking back to his office. Mustn't forget the flowers. I'll take her out for lunch. Think up something so she hasn't a clue.

Back in his office he dialed Pauline's number. Ha, she was home!

"Pauline, can you have a late visitor tonight?"

"How late, Bram?"

"Say ten, ten-thirty."

"That's possible. I presume that you are the late visitor?"

"Yes. How's Dick? Did he catch a cold?"

"No, he didn't. He is tickled pink. I'd like to hear your version of the race. By the way, Bram, what a marvelous handbag. I forgot to thank you Saturday. I am *very* pleased with it. I have to go now. I have to be in Amsterdam at one-thirty."

Next he phoned van den Bosch and invited him for dinner. After that he phoned home.

"Hi, it's me. Have you got something special tomorrow?"

"Not really," Francien said.

"Lantini and his wife are flying in tomorrow. I would like you to join us for lunch. Would you mind?"

"If you want me to, I'll be there. Any idea what I should wear?"

"Whatever pleases you. Something sporty, perhaps? By the way, I'll be late tonight, got to take a guy out for dinner. So don't wait up for me."

"I won't," she said and hung up.

Over dinner Bram told van den Bosch what his connection with Dick was and asked whether he thought Dick had it in him.

"It's hard to tell. I must admit, however, the way he drove his maiden race, I was impressed. He's a fast learner. The way he pushed that other kid over the limit in the last lap impressed me."

"You knew what he was doing at that very moment?"

"Sure. It was clear he had no intention to pass him that early."

"I thought he was just being stupid."

"No, he wasn't. He has the spirit all right. But, Bram, it's still such a long way before he can even get near a pit."

"Tell me, did you ask the other racers to let Dick win?"

Van den Bosch grinned. "Not exactly, but I told them to take it easy and not wipe him off the track completely. They picked up the idea nicely, didn't they?"

"Yes, I saw them discussing something in between the second and the third race, so I had a hunch."

"But in the last race Henkie felt free to win and did his utmost, I can assure you. They were quite surprised. We talked afterward, when you were gone. They couldn't figure out how Dickie could handle the pedals with no feet at all. You must have done a hell of a job on that cart."

"My mechanic did most of it. My problem is, where do we go from here?"

Van den Bosch pondered it for a while. Then he said, "The track record is thirty-seven seconds. I would not let him meet competition before he comes within a second of that record. He had quite a bit of luck and they underestimated him, but if Halsma really goes at it, he is quite a nasty bastard. You know these boys can be cocky.

"All right, yesterday was for love only, with a fortunate ending for Dickie. I'm sure he feels great now and that's good, but he still has to learn a lot. To get near the record will keep him busy for two or three months. Get a good stopwatch. Swiss. You'll see that he'll gain only by hundredths of seconds as he gets nearer to it. Within two weeks he'll blame your stopwatch."

———

Pauline wore a white cotton duster that reached her ankles and had wide sleeves. They kissed, they necked and then they went to bed. When their storm subsided, they went back to the living room where Bram told her about the race.

"He was marvelous and I must tell you it does something to you to have your own guy in a race. Something like betting on a horse. It becomes *yours* for that race and if it wins you love it."

"So he's justly walking with his head in the clouds?"

"For a day or two, but then he has to come back with his feet on the ground. I'm sorry, I keep forgetting."

"That's all right. I wish more people did."

"I've been thinking about where we go from here. First, he needs better clothing, better protection from the weather. Would that be a problem for you?"

"I shouldn't think so."

"I have no idea what a model makes these days. I could chip in."

"No need for that."

"Fine, then there's something else. The *Jiffy* remains my property. In that way I can spend on it whatever I like. I don't know yet how to tell him that. How's he doing at school?"

"So-so. He's not really interested at the moment."

"If he does his best, what grades can he get?"

"Sevens, eights, sometimes a nine."

"What if I told him that he has to average seven at the end of each semester and that I'll lock up the *Jiffy* for three months if he doesn't?"

"Would you really do that?"

"Sure, because I don't want to spoil his education. How would he react to that?"

"He'll have less problems with that than with you telling him that the *Jiffy* isn't his."

"You think I can't get away with that anymore?"

"If you have the right reasons, he might swallow it. If not, he will take it badly."

"I'll think up something."

"You intend to take him home with you more often?"

"Would you mind?"

"Wouldn't your wife mind?"

"It was her idea, and from what I have seen, they don't get along so badly. I still think it's out of character for her to invite him, but I like it. Last Saturday I was taken by surprise, and maybe you were right that I wasn't all that enthusiastic just because I had not thought of it. Still, I can hardly believe I'm like that."

"I can," said Pauline, and smiled.

Bram looked at her: the smile, the poise.

Pauline got up to bring him another beer. Bram followed her into the kitchen. When she bent over to take a can from the fridge, he put his hands on her hips. She straightened and turned. He pulled her to him. His eyes closed, his heart yearned.

"Your beer is getting warm and my hand is getting cold," she whispered.

Seated again, facing, he looked at her, cast his eyes down and then looked at her again, all the time holding the can over his glass but not pouring. He put the can back on the table.

"Pauline, I think that I have fallen in love with you."

She smiled.

"No, this is serious. Last Tuesday I had to deliver a car to a good-looking lady in Leiden. She made a stylish pass at me and I turned her down. This is unusual for me, to say the least."

Pauline's smile broadened. "It's nice to know that I have the right influence on you. You are a married man, who should not succumb to passes by strange ladies."

He shook his head. "You are an original if there ever was one."

He picked up his beer, walked around the table and sat down next to her. "You do love me, too, don't you?"

"Would you be here if I didn't? I certainly do not belong to the black-stockings legion, but making love . . . There aren't many you can do it with."

Bram gazed at her. She put her arms around his neck, pulled him close to her and whispered, "You are a darling, Bram," then softly kissed his lips.

It was way after twelve when he drove along the River Gouwe. The full moon cast a silver sheen over the countryside. He drove leisurely. Dark farmhouses. Black, naked trees bending in the wind; the waves on the river sparkling silverly—winter was approaching. Why hadn't he stayed? His heart yearned, and yet he'd gotten into his car and gone. What drove him away from where he loved to be most? He couldn't find the answer.

Only mechanically paying attention to the road, his mind remained focused on her. Of course, she loved him. That was not the question, but *how* she loved him. The distance she kept, the aloofness—in an odd way she made *him* feel taken care of. She did give him the feeling of safety. Yet, he wanted her to surrender to him. What was in her heart, behind those blue eyes? What made her tick? Could she love in another way, or was this her way of loving? Like the moonlight, beautiful but cool. He couldn't imagine her ever losing her temper, shouting at the top of her voice. She would have no need to. But she loved him, of that he was sure, be it in her own way.

She was so different from Francien. With Francien he sometimes had the feeling that he was in bed with his daughter. Pauline had brought back the excitement. She had made him desire like when he was young, but what to do with his prey now? He couldn't drag her into his cave. As a matter of fact, he wasn't sure who was the prey and who the hunter. A woman with a soft voice, soft hands and a will of steel—he wondered what it would be like living with her. He wondered so much that he missed the N-11 and only realized it when he saw the sign TER AAR, a small sleepy village. It took half an hour on narrow country roads before he was heading home again.

CHAPTER

13

That was one thing the bike-riding did to you. You slept like a log. And Marjet had been right, the wild panic and the anger were less. That week she had succumbed to only a single whiskey.

Seeing his wrinkled pillow, she wondered what time he had come home. Irritating bastard, that's what he is. Comes and goes as he likes. He must have been screwing *her,* the fucking bitch.

Why did she have to put up with it? And for how long? How would it end? For her or for that slut?

Sweat started prickling on her skull. Her stomach tightened. Marjet? No, she had to help herself. Out! She wanted out! Away from it! She jumped out of bed, rushed into her training suit and combed her hair with her fingers. She hesitated at the kitchen door, but her stomach didn't feel like eating. So she rushed to the shed, got her bike and headed into the biting wind for the beach, using all the strength her strong legs could muster.

She reached the esplanade of the Zandvoort beach. The angry breakers, whipped up by the wind, tired themselves out on the smooth sand; the white clouds, hurried on from over the sea in the strong wind; and the sun, used every available opening to brighten up the autumn gray. The doom in her thoughts faded away somewhat. At the end of the esplanade, where a cycle path led into the dunes, she halted and let the sea wind pull at her hair and her training suit until it blew her body warmth away. Chilled but with her worries cooled down, she got on her bike again, switched into third gear and let the sea wind blow her home, where she arrived by eleven, hungry and not in panic anymore. A glass of milk and a slice of bread would help her along till lunch with the Lantini's.

She didn't dare take a bath. Floating in the warm water might bring back thoughts she couldn't cope with. She took a shower. Drying herself in front of the mirror, she wasn't unhappy with what she saw. She had lost three kilos without even trying.

As she was pulling the waist of her dress over her breasts and shaking the skirt loose around her legs, the telephone rang.

"It's me. I'll pick you up for lunch at twelve-thirty. Is that okay with you?"

"Yes, that's fine."

"Okay, see you. Wear a raincoat and a scarf. I have a visitor just now, bye."

Puzzled, she walked to her dressing table. "A raincoat and a scarf?" Why had he said that? He didn't think she would come without a coat in November, did he?

When she walked up to the car, Bram couldn't help being impressed: black, open raincoat with a wide collar and epaulets, white dress, black high-heeled boots and a white scarf. She looked a lot better than she had for weeks and her attitude had changed.

"Where is Lantini?"

"They missed their plane, so it will be just the two of us. I have to go back to the garage for a moment and then we'll have lunch somewhere."

She felt warmth creeping into her heart but also fear that this would drive her crazy. One moment she was already a divorced woman, carelessly thrown away into shameful loneliness, prey for every hunter who liked to take her for a ride; and the next she was the wife of a middle-aged charmer, who apparently enjoyed taking her out for lunch.

"Sorry, Bram, I wasn't listening. What was it you said?"

"I said that in the furor over the newspaper article, I forgot to ask whether you enjoyed yourself last Friday evening."

The question came so unexpectedly that it left her shocked and speechless.

A ball rolled from between two cars onto the road. Expecting a child to follow, he braked sharply, but the boy stood between the cars and waited for him to pass.

"Thank God," he said. "I think I couldn't stand another kid under the wheels. You know it happens everyday and you don't pay attention to it. I had always thought that I was able to imagine what a driver who hit a child feels. But with Dick it affected me more than I'd ever expected. There's such a difference between hearing about it and being involved in it."

"What is the difference?"

He hesitated, ably easing the car through the traffic. Francien waited patiently, still not knowing how she should answer his earlier question about last Friday.

"It's difficult to explain. As a nurse, you have patients who once in a while express their gratitude in a touching way. When you tell that to somebody, he understands that. He probably is pleased to hear it. When you are the one who is touched, it makes your day. Imagination can never produce that. If your favorite racer wins a grand prix, it makes you happy, but your happiness gets nowhere near that of the winner. Nor does your sadness get anywhere near that of the loser. If it could, you would go crazy because you would live all the misery in the world. Maybe it's better the way it is. Everybody suffering his own grief, and the rest of us happily chasing whatever we are after till our turn comes."

"Don't you think that's damned selfish?"

"Maybe, but what if I take my turn when it comes and don't bother others? Anyway, here we are."

He parked the car in front of the showroom.

"Shall I wait, or shall I come in?"

"I won't be long, but come in all the same."

When they entered the showroom, Francien walked straight up to the convertible and stood looking at it like a tot at a Christmas tree. Then she touched the door and the leather upholstery and looked at the white freesias in the tiny vase. When she saw the SOLD sign, she turned around.

"What a beauty, Bram! Who did you sell it to? To one of the fancy ladies in Wassenaar?"

"I haven't sold it and I don't mean to."

"You don't mean to?"

"It's a present."

"A car like that, a present? You're kidding."

"No, I'm not. It's yours."

"What did you say?"

"I said, it's yours."

Francien's mouth fell open. She wanted to say something, but couldn't. She looked at the car, then at Bram, back at the car and again at Bram. "You are teas—"

He shook his head. "I told you, I would see to it."

Trying to catch her breath, tears welling up in her eyes, she cried, "Oh, Bram." And then she jumped around his neck and clung to him with a strength that surprised and at the same time embarrassed him.

She needed a car, he thought, and a bit of a showpiece was good for business, and so it had to be a car that fitted, but that was all there was to it.

"It's not a new one," he said, abashed by the emotion it had provoked.

The inner door of the showroom opened and Lazy Willem looked at them, raised his eyebrows, shook his head and then closed the door again.

"Come on, you must try it." He removed her arms from around his neck, held her back and saw tears on her cheeks.

"There, there," he said, handing her his handkerchief.

"Is it really mine?"

"Sure, the papers are in your name. You can crash it, sell it, go on holidays in it, do with it whatever you like. It's yours."

She looked back over her shoulder at the car and then she hung around his neck again, kissing him all over his face, leaving smudges of lipstick everywhere.

"Well, that's enough," he said roughly. "You know what you should do? You should sit in it while I deal with what I came here for, and then you take us out to lunch in it."

"Oh, dear. On the street?"

"It may look fast, but it doesn't fly." A smile broke over his face. He took her by the arm, turned her to the car, opened the door and gestured to the driving seat, like he had done so many times before.

"Enjoy it, Madam, it's a fine vehicle."

When she was seated behind the wheel, he closed the door with a solid thud and left the showroom.

Crossing the workshop, Lazy Willem called after him. "A Mrs. Hildebrink has called. She had a crash, only dents, but she wondered if she could have her old car back while this one will be in repair."

"Sorry, I have just given it to my wife. But we'll help her out in the usual way."

"To your wife?"

"We are going to have lunch at Bouwes in Zandvoort, in case you need me."

"Then I suggest that you first check yourself in a mirror, Bram."

Grinning, Lazy Willem went back to the car he had been working on, leaving Bram rubbing his fingers over his cheek and finding them red.

He washed his face clean in the washroom and went to his office. Belinda had nothing further. He instructed her to phone Mrs. Hildebrink back and tell her that her old car had been delivered, but that they would help her out.

When he came back into the showroom, Francien was still behind the wheel, with mascara and a big smile all over her face. He slid the big door open and gestured for her to drive out. She shook her head. Shrugging he walked back up to her.

"Aren't you hungry?"

"No, or maybe yes, but I want you to take it outside. I can't drive it at the moment."

He studied her face with the makeup ruined and the green eyes wide with emotion. Maybe she was right.

"Okay. Move over."

Leaving the showroom door for his staff to close, he drove straight to the parking lot next to the soccer stadium and stopped there.

"Now, I think you better touch up your face again because it hasn't survived your gratitude."

While Francien started to work on it, he pulled a sport cap from his inner pocket and fitted it on, examining the results in the mirror of the sunshade.

Stashing her makeup things back into her overloaded handbag, she looked at him.

"Now you really look like one of the smart set," she giggled.

"Well, it's cold and I am hungry, so get out, look her over and try her out till you get the feel of her a bit."

He slipped out the driver's side and walked away. From a distance he watched Francien get out, walk around the car and then get behind the wheel. She started the engine and drove straight up to him.

"Take a lap." He made a large circle with his hand. She complied. She drove onto the track and took off.

When she came back he looked up from his watch. "Forty-five seconds, you can do better than that."

The third time around she made it in thirty-six. "That's better, and now to Bouwes in Zandvoort where I have reserved a table."

Over lunch he told her the ins and outs of the car and the pros and cons of it being a convertible, and she gradually quieted down to a happy bliss, feeling at peace with the world.

"You are so generous, Bram. And so selfless to give up your garage to my poor vulnerable beauty. I couldn't bear the thought of her sitting outside, day and night, exposed to wind and weather."

"Damn, that's what comes from emancipation. Give women a finger and they take your whole hand. First they want to eat as much as you, so you have to get more food. Next they want to eat at the dinner table, so you need another chair. Once they learned to write, they wanted a section in the paper. Then they started smoking, too, so you needed more cigarettes, and then drinks. Now they want to go places and need a car of their own, and now I need another garage. Emancipation is more expensive than one would think. And all this because we so necessarily must be in their good graces to get them into our beds, and after that we want to parade them around to show the other fellows how well we are doing. One day we will kill ourselves in our zeal to please the dames. A good thing that women nowadays think they are entitled to have a job. We should let them have it all, so that *we* can stay home, drink with the other fellows, play tennis, look after the kids, grow old and be the ones who benefit from the pension. My God, that would be the day. Now this—parking in my garage?"

She kissed him and put her arms around his neck. "Bram, she's so delicate. Yours is big and strong. He can stand being out in the cold, and moreover, you're the early riser. And she needs pampering. She is no VW Beetle."

"Incomparable. The Beetle is a workhorse, but this is a thoroughbred. Can you even imagine what 5,000 piston cycles per minute means. Not per hour, per minute."

"That's a lot, isn't it?"

"A lot? It's unimaginable. A plain miracle. I calculated it once. With a stroke of 72 millimeters, that means that the piston twice covers 7.2 centimeters, 5,000 times in one minute. So 10,000 times in one minute, the piston starts from a standstill and covers that 7.2 centimeters with an average speed of 80 kilometers per hour. So in 3.6 centimeters, the piston's speed increases from zero to 160 kilometers per hour and comes down to zero in the next 3.6 millimeters.

"It's my trade, but it still beats me how you can fling a piece of metal up and down from zero to 160 and back to zero 10,000 times in one minute and have it stay in one piece. Not to mention driving to Italy and back, or driving 100,000 kilometers without engine trouble. It goes zero–160–zero, I don't know, some 500 million times or more. I also have that feeling when I see a 747 taking off. Something like, no matter what's wrong with us all, those are the things we made."

Francien shook her head. "A miracle," she said. "Maybe we could build a grotto for her instead of keeping her in the garage."

"I'm going to get you for that," Bram said, smiling.

"I hope so," she said, licking the cafe latte froth from her spoon.

———

Willem picked up Dick from the railway station and, on instructions from Bram, took him to van Delden's sportswear where he let Dick buy the best stopwatch they had. With it, they went to the track where it took Dick an hour before he managed a go around in 38.6 seconds. He was far from satisfied. He had expected to go up against the other competitors again. When Willem told him he had to make a lap below 38 seconds before he would meet the competition again, Dick threw himself into it with the intention of achieving that level in the next ten minutes. When he hadn't reached it after an hour, he even doubted the quality of the stopwatch.

"You heard the man, boy. It's the best there is."

"You fiddled with the engine."

"One more remark like that, sonny, and I will dust your pants."

"But you retarded the throttle the first time."

"Yeah, and I'm ever so sorry you found out. If you hadn't, you wouldn't be in the filthy mood you're in now. You think you're the king, don't you? These guys last week didn't take you serious, don't you see that?"

Dick was silent for a moment. "You mean they went easy on me?"

Willem could hear the pain in the youngster's voice. "Not the last race, although two of them were sloppy in the first curve. The last race was genuinely yours. But when you meet them again, it will be different, take my word for it. There will be no surprising them. If you can't get around in less than thirty-eight seconds, you won't stand a chance, and even then it's an open game."

"When can I race them?"

"You better ask Bram. He wants to have a word with you, anyway. So let's call it a day."

"What does Bram want to see me about?"

Willem shrugged.

When they arrived back at the garage, Bram was in a meeting with his accountant and Dick had to wait for half an hour. The waiting increased his irritation about the disappointing results on the track. Finally he was summoned. He turned down the Coke offered.

"How did it go?"

"Shit."

"What was your best?"

"Thirty-eight point six."

"Stopwatch all right?"

Dick's expression hardened and he didn't answer.

"Well?"

"You know very well. You told Lazy Willem to have me pick it out. I wouldn't be surprised if the shopkeeper was in on it, too."

"In on what?"

"Why couldn't I race the other guys one more time? I can lick 'em."

"Dick, my boy, if ever you enter a race completely sure you can win, you'll lose."

"Did van den Bosch tell the other boys to let me win?"

"What would you do if you had to swim against a fellow with one arm?"

"That would be unfair."

"I didn't ask what it would be. I asked what you would *do.*"

"Okay, but the last race?"

"You were better than that boy with the yellow helmet."

"Henk."

"Yes, but the other two were not concentrating. You don't know whether you were the best of the four of you. Got it?"

"When can I race them again?"

"Depends on you, but I think it's time to lay down some rules. You sure you don't want a Coke?"

"No thanks."

"Fine." Bram took a piece of paper from a drawer and put it down in front of him. "I have made up a contract to keep things straight for the future." And he read from the paper: "One, the *Jiffy* is, and remains, property of Bram Aardsen who is responsible for spare parts, the fuel and the transport. Two, Bram Aardsen undertakes to go with Dick Verwal to the races. Three, Dick Verwal's school grades are to average seven. If not, he shall not have access to the *Jiffy* for the following semester. Four, for the next school year Dick Verwal has to get an average grade of eight. If not, it will have the same consequences as under point three. Five, Bram Aardsen shall decide the races Dick Verwal will participate in.

"Six, the technical condition of the *Jiffy* is the responsibility of Dick Verwal and Mr. W. ter Duin. I have had the deal written down. Read it carefully and tell me if they're all clear and whether you will abide by the contract."

He offered Dick the sheet of paper, but Dick didn't take it. He sat in his chair, looking at his hands, the slight shoulders bent. Bram leaned forward, rested his elbow on the desk and kept the paper stuck out toward Dick, waiting for him to take it. Will against will—the boy, devoid of any economic power, and the man, vulnerable by sentiment—both unwilling to budge.

"The *Jiffy* is mine," Dick finally said, and as if gathering courage from hearing his own voice, he looked up, hostile gray eyes in a pale face. "You gave it to me."

"When?"

"The first time. You said you had a surprise for me."

He glared at Bram, who needed all his self-control.

"I did have a surprise, didn't I? So we disagree on point one; let's see how we fare on the other five. Look them over, will you?"

Reluctantly, Dick took the paper and glanced over it.

"Point two, agreed?"

Dick nodded.

"Do me a favor Dick, just say yes or no. This is your first *contract* on your way to racecar driving. We will both sign it once we agree."

He pressed the button of the intercom. "Belinda, one coffee please." He looked questioningly at Dick, who shook his head no.

To give the boy time to get over the shock of point one, he lit a cigarette, and when Belinda brought in the coffee, he stirred it thoroughly. When he had drunk it, he continued.

"Point three?"

"What has school got to do with the *Jiffy*?"

"Nothing, and I want to keep it that way."

"Well, why then all this about grades?"

"I don't want the *Jiffy* to lower your performance at school. You can easily make a seven average. If you don't, you are daydreaming about being the one who brings the checkered flag down first. Can you or can you not make the average?"

"I don't know," Dick retorted, looking away and shrugging nonchalantly.

"Okay, then I better make an appointment with your teacher. Let me see. Wednesday afternoon, I think. Let's go there next Wednesday afternoon. Have you got the phone number?"

"No need to. I can make sevens."

"Point three agreed then?"

"It's Christmas in four weeks. I have only two weeks left to improve my average. Had I known this from the start, it would have been no problem."

"Bram nodded. You got a point there. Six and three quarters?"

"Six and a half."

"All right"—and handing him a ballpoint—"change that.

"Point four: Next year you'll have to average eight. There is no arguing about this. You reach the entry level for the university in six years. You'll be eighteen then and we will decide whether you'll be a pro or a professor."

"Okay."

"Point five?"

"Why can't I say where I want to race?"

Bram smiled. "No, Dick. Look, that would mean that you decide where and when I have to take you. That's point two. I can't have you decide about my time."

"All right, you decide."

"Point six: maintenance by you and Mr. ter Duin."

"Who is Mr. ter Duin?"

"Lazy Willem."

"Does that mean that Lazy Willem and I can tune up the engine?"

"If you stay within the limits of the rules *and* within the limits of your skill—yes, you can."

"Can't we use other fuel?"

"Dick, we are dealing with a contract here and not with technical tricks. Point six agreed?"

"Yes."

"Okay. Back to point one. I can see that you thought the machine was yours, but you can understand that I would have been very surprised if you had sent somebody to the garage the next day who would have said to me, 'I've come to pick up Dick Verwal's go-cart.'"

A trace of a smile appeared on the boy's face.

"Furthermore, who do you think owns the Formula One cars, the drivers?"

"The factories."

"Right. They build them, they maintain them. That costs millions, which a driver couldn't possibly afford. Compared to you, I am as rich as a factory.

"Drivers are paid," Dick said.

"When they have the skills, not before. The surprise I had for you was to enable you to get a taste of car racing. I never intended to give the *Jiffy* to you as, for example, a birthday present. I gave you—and this contract reaffirms it—the possibility of driving something with an engine. I think that is far bigger than an assembly of nuts and bolts, which is what the *Jiffy* is in fact."

Bram stepped out of the office. Dick looked over the paper. It was then that he saw the word "Contract" at the top and the three dotted lines with their names typed

Bram returned with Lazy Willem. When they were seated, Dick looked from one to the other, his eyebrows slightly raised.

"Well, Mr. Verwal, are you prepared to sign this contract? Mr. ter Duin will cosign."

It took Dick a moment to catch on.

"Yes, Mr. Aardsen, I am."

"Well, well," Willem said. "If this isn't high level, I don't know what is."

Bram took the top off his Scheaffer fountain pen and offered it to Dick. Dick didn't take it, but held up his hand in a halt sign. "After you, sir."

Bram signed all three copies, turned the papers around and slid them over the desk to Dick. Then he offered him the Scheaffer.

Dick looked at the contract and then looked back at them. "I don't have a signature."

The other two laughed. "Your name will do. You'll get one later."

He scribbled "Dick." That would be his signature.

When Lazy Willem had cosigned, he handed the paper back to Bram, who asked Belinda to make extra copies.

Willem said. "I'm not sure, Bram, but seeing how this is an official occasion, don't you think that this young man and we should celebrate it with a glass of champagne?"

"Don't you think Mr. Verwal is still a bit too young for champagne?"

"Since he isn't too young to sign a contract, he can't be too young for what comes along with it, I would say."

Bram went to the small fridge, hesitated between a Chandon and a sparkling wine, and choose the latter.

They touched glasses and toasted. Dick told them Coke was nicer. Bram pulled open a drawer of his desk, produced a plastic bag and threw it in Dick's lap.

"What is it?"

"Look."

Dick took a piece of stark red fabric from the bag. Unfolding it, he held it up. It was a T-shirt, and on the glaring red was written in big black capitals:

AARDSEN

FOR

ALFA

"I am your sponsor, so you advertise for me. Try it on."

It hung a bit baggy around the frail body.

"He'll fill it up in time. Eat more bacon," Willem said.

Dick felt touched and embarrassed, a prisoner in his chair. Then he stuck out both his hands over the desk to Bram, who met him halfway. Dick squeezed the large hands, his eyes blinking.

"No problem, just fun," Bram said, rising. "Well, we got work to do and you're off to do your homework. Will you drop him at the station, Willem? Pick up a copy of the contract for him from Belinda."

Bram sighed with relief. It had been close, but he'd always known that if you treated them above their age, children liked to live up to it. They did like to play house and cowboys and war.

With a happy grin Bram raised his thumb to Dick, who did the same. Men didn't embrace.

———

Friday night. It was near six. The workshop was empty. It was drizzling outside. Bram sat in the gloomy twilight, staring into nothingness with a feeling of having gotten stuck. Had he achieved his goal too early? Having his own car company had been his wish since he was a youngster. Now he had it. Why did he feel imprisoned? Was this all there was? Running it for twenty more years, selling it and then going shopping with Francien in the supermarket every day, discussing with her every jar, can or carton she picked from the shelf? The wives painted their faces with too-juvenile colors, their silvery "permanent waves" touched up with a gloss of blue or pink. He had seen them those parched men dressed in the same expensive suits that had girded them years earlier—the former managers, book-keepers and department heads. They looked so out of place belaboring decisions about which jar of peanut butter had the most value for the money.

Why didn't those guys do something they had always wanted to do, or something they had never done before—play the guitar in the shopping center, buy drinks for everyone in the nearest pub, and go home feeling high and in love with their sober women, and try to screw them before dinner?

They didn't. They washed the windows of their oversized houses, vacuum-cleaned their excess rooms and looked like monuments to a glorious past.

The telephone shocked him out of his musings.

"Bram?" It was Pauline.

"Yes."

"I have to work a show next week in Paris, Monday and Tuesday. Would you like to come?"

He held his breath for a second, while his heart skipped a beat.

"What was it you said?"

"I think you heard me all right. Would you like to come?"

He was already leafing through his diary.

"Let me see. I have a meeting in Milan on Monday morning. I could take an afternoon plane to Paris. You know where you are staying?"

"The Holiday Inn."

"Can you make it a double room?"

"I never have a single. The show is in the afternoon. Shall we have dinner?"

"Marvelous. I'll let you know in case something comes up."

"By the way, you did a hell of a job on Dick. He will be smoking cigars before long. He sleeps in that T-shirt, otherwise I wouldn't recognize him."

Bram chuckled. "Yeah, we had a bit of a tough session, but he handled it well, I must say."

There was a noise on her end of the line. "He's coming in. Till Monday, looking forward to it."

Before he could say any more, she had hung up, leaving him dazed, his blood rushing through his veins.

It had suited Lantini better that he could come as early as possible, and Francien had understood that a conference of the major dealers from various countries took more than one day.

Pauline was not in her room when Bram phoned from the lobby. He handed his suitcase to the bell captain and went to the bar to get a drink. Pauline was sitting on a stool, having an animated conversation with a gentleman whose face was vaguely familiar. He hesitated, wondering where he had seen that face before, but he could not place it. The moment he decided to walk up to her, the man rose, kissed her hand and took his leave.

Silently standing behind her, he suppressed the urge to cup her breasts.

"Hello, Bram," she said without turning her head.

"Can you feel me approach?"

"Yes, I can, but only when I look straight ahead."

He looked at her face in the mirror behind the bar.

"Is that the way the famous female sixth sense works?"

She smiled and squeezed his hand. "Sometimes."

"Who was that guy you were with?"

"Have you been watching?" she said, head tilting.

"Only from the moment he kissed your hand."

"He's the man who sat next to us at the Bugatti Club dinner. Von Steltenburcht is his name."

"What's he do for a living?"

"I don't know. I'm not the cross-examining type. I listen."

"And what did you hear, listening to him?"

"Don't quote me, but I heard a bachelor with blue blood and black money."

"That's an unusual combination. What did he want?"

"Do I hear in your voice the authority of a boss questioning his secretary or that of a married man questioning his wife?"

"I'm sorry, how did the show go?"

"Splendid, how was your business in Milan?'

"The same. Come on, let's go and eat."

It was about one in the morning. They lay face to face, pelvis to pelvis, looking at each other in the amber light of the dimmed bed lamps. The soft warmth of her silken skin was a luxury.

"Marry me," he said.

Her fingers stopped roving. Moving her head a little backward on the pillow, his face came into better focus. She smiled.

"I mean it," he said.

"Of course."

"You mean you will?"

"Of course, you mean it."

"You're teasing. I mean it. Marry me!"

"Is that a request or a command?"

"Will . . . you . . . marry . . . me, Pauline?"

For moments she just lay there and looked at his face. Then she rose on one elbow, bent over, kissed his temple, his ear and his cheek, her left hand caressing the back of his head. Then she slowly withdrew and lay on her back, looking long and slender.

"That is not a yes," Bram said, encircling her waist to pull her to him.

A tear, sparkling like a diamond in the corner of her eye, stopped him.

"Are you crying?"

She did not respond.

"Pauline? I only asked you to marry me."

Suddenly she sat up, swung her legs over the side of the bed, rose and slipped into the bathroom, closing the door behind her.

Startled, Bram sat up. What had he done that was so wrong? Not knowing whether he should go after her, he stayed where he was. He heard a tap running and the sound of glass on glass. After a while he heard the light switched off.

He was on the verge of going to see what was happening, when the door opened and Pauline came back, her hair brushed and lipstick renewed. The sight of her female beauty and the mane of wild black hair framing her face took his breath away. He reached out to her with both hands.

She took them, but when he tried to pull her toward him she sat down upright on the side of the bed.

"Bram, come back to earth. You don't know what you are asking. I would love to live with you, but it cannot be."

"Why not, because I'm married?"

"Let's forget about marriages for a moment. I am a model, not just by profession, but by desire. I was born that way. It's my whole being. I create the image of a dream woman, wearing clothes no normal person can wear. I *am* that fantasy woman."

"Well, what's wrong with that? I'm a car freak and there is nothing wrong with that, either."

"Bram, I'm not only for the show. I *am* the show. I can't be a housewife. I couldn't live for washing dishes, making beds, dusting furniture, cooking meals and waiting for *him* to come home. Why do you think my husband is in the States and I'm here?"

"Because he's a jerk to leave you behind on your own."

She shook her head. "You don't understand. There are men—good men, men I could love—but those men want a wife, to serve them, to play second fiddle to them. It is my fate that I fall in love with men like that. I like their ambitious mentality, their manliness. But there is something in me that prevents me from serving them, from protecting them like your wife did in Italy. She knocks a man out cold. In spite of her servile role, she feels she owns you. You are her property and she fights to protect it. The twist is that she protects you just to be able to continue serving you. I could never do that. I can't even fight. Yes, I can stab somebody with my eyelashes, but scream, scratch and pull hair—I haven't got it in me. And fighting to protect my man would degrade him in my eyes. You protect your children, not your man.

"Don't you see that you would have to walk on your toes all the time, otherwise I would turn as cold as ice. There would be no snapping at me, no bickering. Look, I wear men down, and afterward I have the guilty feeling that it's me who ruins the relationship by not having any desire for domesticity. I miss wedlock. Yet if we were to live together, that would be the end of us as friends, unless we broke up in time. Like my husband and I did."

"Pauline, this is nonsense. You wouldn't need to wash dishes and the lot. We could have somebody doing all the domestic tasks. You are wrong, very wrong. You couldn't wear me down even if you tried. I understand you love me, too; what else do we need?"

She closed her eyes and sat for a while. Then she reached over to the nightstand and took the package of cigarettes. She lit two and gave one to Bram.

"I'm thirsty. Can I have a Perrier?"

Bram padded to the minibar and poured her a Perrier and himself a whiskey. She joined him, took her glass and sat down in one of the easy chairs. Bram took the other and sat down, too.

He had a strong urge to take her in his arms and just hold her so everything would be all right. Only he couldn't. She was too tall; no, not too tall, too . . . the way she sat there, naked and yet like a queen. She was looking at him with a soft smile on her face. He felt protective, but he couldn't act on that. He couldn't just take her in his arms, pat her softly on the shoulder and tell her, "There, there." She just wasn't the type.

"Pauline, this . . . what you were saying is not true. Not true for *us*. Okay, you tried it and it didn't work, but that was with another man. I'm different. Why don't you give us a try?"

"You remember the breakfast after the Bugatti dinner, when I told you that Dick's admiration for you seemed to be contagious, whether I liked it or not?"

"Yes. Why *did* you ask me here if you knew beforehand that nothing could ever come of it?"

"You asked me, twice, 'Where do we go from here?' I wanted an answer too. You think I could tell you what I have about myself over the phone? And suppose I'd done that. You would certainly have considered it a lure.

He thought about that. "You may be right, but you can't convince me that it won't work out between us. You have *your* idea about it, I have *mine*. You know I am a modest man, but—"

Pauline's sudden laugh made him look up, astounded.

"Yes I *am* a modest man," he said stubbornly, "but I do think that I'm an important party in this. I can certainly influence the way it will develop between us."

Pauline was shaking her head with a smile on her face. "You are as modest as I am homely. We are stuck with our natures."

Bram rose and walked to the minibar to pour himself another drink.

"Will you join me or do you prefer to stick to the Perrier?"

"One finger, to celebrate this wonderful night."

"You just turned me down and you think it a wonderful night?"

"To have it off my chest, to have said what I had to say, makes me feel good about myself. I deserve that drink and it was wonderful to experience this with you. You don't know, Bram, but I have been scared to death that I would have let myself be led into temptation. That I would lack the guts to tell you the truth. I am a great lover of fairy tales, too. I would love so much to believe we had a future together, but I can't. And I love you, and myself, too much to see what is between us end up in sullen hostility or bruised egos. Either way, the qualities that I think we both have would fade away."

This was somewhat beyond Bram, but he wasn't a man to take no for an answer once he had set his mind on something. He had not planned to ask her to marry him, but now that he'd said it, he hung on to the objective.

He finished his drink, stabbed out his cigarette and held out his hands to her. She rose, put her arms around him and made their foreheads touch.

He said, "Will you marry me . . . till noon tomorrow? My plane leaves at two."

"Yes, I will."

He swooped her up, lowered her on the bed, switched off the lights and made love to her with abandon, as if to compensate for his lack of arguments.

She kissed him good-bye in front of the hotel at two minutes to twelve like a wife and returned to to the room to pack her things. On the table was a huge vase of roses, with a small envelope attached. The little card read: WILL YOU MARRY ME? BRAM

She stood for a while, smelling the fragrance, and then she left, taking the roses with her.

———

Dick got his lap times down to 38.3 seconds, and he started to understand that progress would be slow. After their return from the track, Dick went straight to Lazy Willem.

"Well, young man, how did it go?"

"A little better, but can't we make it lighter? The extras for my feet are made of iron. Can't we use aluminum? That'll make it lighter."

Lazy Willem nodded. "Indeed. I'll see if I can find the time. We're rather busy. With the beginning of the winter season, all the defects that went unnoticed in the summer weather come out now."

"Can you do it before next week, please? Maybe Sunday? I'll come and help you."

"Hey, what are you, some kind of slave driver? Even the Lord was tired after six days of work. On principle I do nothing on Sundays—go to the soccer match when Haarlem plays at home, and watch television in the evening."

Dick was looking at the man's big hands deftly applying tools to an engine. They were laid out precisely around the open hood like instruments in an operating room.

"And Saturday? I can come on Saturday as well."

"Was it point three of your contract that was about your schoolwork? I should not take that lightly. Why don't we fix it up during the Christmas holidays? Then I'll have plenty of time, and then we'll know whether or not you're allowed to touch the cart during the next quarter. By the way, how many times did you skid off the road?"

"Only in the first race," Dick answered proudly.

"Then you stay too much on the safe side. You can only learn where your limits are by going over them once in a while. The knack for a race driver is to be exactly *on* his limit from start to finish, otherwise he disappoints his mechanics. When I am convinced that you ride the limit all the time and still don't win, then I'll know the ball is in my court. But if I have the idea that you stay on the safe side of the line, why should I try to improve an engine that runs like a jaguar? That's the teamwork between the pit and the driver, and there's trouble when the driver thinks the boys in the pit don't know nothing about engines, and the pit boys think the driver is too chicken to get everything out of the machine it's got. Think that over when you can't sleep. Now let me drop you at the station, otherwise your mother'll get angry, and when she gets angry, the boss gets angry."

"My mother doesn't get angry very quickly."

"Would that the same were true of my boss."

——

On Thursday Bram found a personal letter in the mail, the envelope of expensive, silver gray paper. The handwriting was elegant and beyond doubt female. Inside he found a small note: FOR A DAY OR TWO, YES. P.

On Friday morning Bram came in late, and stopped at the reception desk just to see what was going on. Before he could inquire, the receptionist informed him Belinda was looking for him because there was a visitor who had been already waiting for him for twenty minutes—an odd-looking guy, a baron or something.

In the small waiting room Bram recognized the man as the same one

Pauline had been talking to at the bar in the Holiday Inn, the one from the Bugatti dinner.

"Aardsen. How do you do? Sorry to have kept you waiting."

"No problem, sir. I'm not in a hurry and I've no appointment. Von Steltenburcht is my name. I had some business in town, so I took the liberty to see if you could spare me a minute."

"Sure, come in, please?"

Bram led the way into his office and read the card his visitor had given him: *Baron H.J.F.K. von Steltenburcht, Rue de la Victoire 375, Brussels. Trade Enterprise.*

After the generalities and coffee, Steltenburcht came to the point. "I'm crazy about cars, old as well as new, but professionally I am an investor. I happen to have some capital and I would like to get involved in the car business. I like the ambience, and I would like dealing with car manufacturers and meeting the test and racecar drivers. So . . . I want to buy your company. I'm not like a lot of business people who start discussing all the details and, in the end, come up with a price that would have precluded the deal from the beginning. I have in mind a price between one and one-and-a-half million."

"Belgian francs?"

Steltenburcht smiled and shook his head. "Guilders."

Bram was flabbergasted and didn't know what to say. "Another coffee?"

"Yes, please." The baron smiled.

He asked Belinda to bring in more coffee, lit a cigarette and studied Steltenburcht's face through the smoke.

"So, you are serious."

"A tentative price, not a firm bid yet. I have made some inquiries, and I understand that the value of your business is somewhere at that level—lock, stock and barrel."

"Does that include me?"

"Not necessarily. I can understand that it may be difficult to change from owner to manager. What has to be in the deal, of course, is your dealership for Alfa Romeo. It's my fancy for the Alfas that brought me here."

"Who put you on to me? There are many other Alfa dealers in Europe."

"If you don't mind, I would rather not disclose that. All that matters is whether you are prepared to transfer the real estate, the movables, the know how and the good will for cash, which you can receive anywhere you like—Switzerland, Liechtenstein, the States, you name it."

"I didn't ask who put you on to me because I want to know the name. I was just wondering whether somebody had told you I wanted to sell."

"Mr. Aardsen, you can rest assured those few I mentioned my intention to immediately said you would never sell."

"To be frank, Mr. Steltenburcht, I think those few are right."

"Mr. Aardsen, I should like to explain to you why I didn't follow that advice. Nine years ago you bought this place, run down as it was, for one hundred twenty-five thousand guilders—that is, twenty-five thousand guilders of your own money and one hundred thousand guilders from the AMRO-bank. You managed to become the sole importer of Alfas in the Netherlands. You are forty years old. In my opinion you are a builder, not a keeper. It's the same with soccer trainers. Some pick up a third grade team and in a couple of years make it champion. Then that trainer has to leave, because he can't keep it at the top. He gets bored." The baron arched an eyebrow.

"In my opinion, it's not unlikely, once you start thinking about it, that we may come to an agreement that will enable you to collect your profit and provide you with enough means to start something new somewhere else."

Steltenburcht waited for him to say something but Bram did not volunteer anything. After a while he resumed. "I have come without an appointment and I have certainly surprised you with my proposal. I'll go now, but I would like to contact you in a week or so to learn whether you are willing to have another discussion about this matter. If your reply is positive, I expect that we'll reach the dotted line or a deadlock somewhere in January."

"As long as it's no promise, you may call me the second week of December, but if for some reason or another you shouldn't feel like it, don't bother. Just forget it."

"I won't, and here's a letter that enables you to get information from my bank, the Credit Suisse at Brussels. That's only one of the banks that I avail myself of, but, I trust, their information alone will satisfy you."

Steltenburcht left. Bram sat for a long time at his desk, staring.

I'll be darned. One million guilders. A lot of money; one and a half, even more. One and a half million! Hold it, man, don't get carried away. Let's say one and a quarter. No, for the purpose of getting the feel of it, one million is sufficient. What was it Pauline had said about this guy? "Bachelor with blue blood and black money."

Of course it was she who had given Steltenburcht the idea, or at least his name. He picked up the phone and called her.

"Pauline, I love you. Will you marry me and have you got a moment?"

"Hi, Bram, what's the good news? You sound happy."

"You remember that bachelor from the bar in Paris, the one you figured as having blue blood and laundered money?"

"Yes."

"Did you tell him or suggest to him that I might be willing to sell my company?"

"No, why do you ask?"

"Well, he just left after telling me that he is interested in my company."

"I see. No, Bram, I didn't even mention your name. Nor did he. People don't approach me to talk about cars?"

"Well, it was a thought."

"Tell me, he just dropped in and said he wanted your business?"

"Yeah, but he had done his homework and the price looks terrific to me . . . but I don't think . . . I don't know. It's nice to hear that you have built up something. Can I see you? Now, I mean?"

"I'm sorry, Bram, but I have a show in Enschede and I have to leave in half an hour. What about tonight?"

"Impossible—visiting friends, long overdue. The weekend is a problem. There's not much left of a man's freedom, is there?"

"The less you possess, the more freedom you have."

"I thought it was just the other way round."

"Well, then, here is your chance to find out, thanks to that baron, or don't you want to sell?"

"Of course not. I think . . . I want . . . you know what I want? I want a white beach, green palm trees, a blue sky with one little white cloud, and you and I naked on the golden beach, drinking Baccardi Rum, eating Bounties and smoking Stuyvesants. That's what I want for the rest of my life. No more hard-to-please customers, haggling buyers and grumbling mechanics who unfix more than they fix."

Pauline chuckled. "You would last on that beach for two weeks and then you would want an ax."

"An ax, what for?"

"To chop a tree and make wheels. It would be a work beach in no time, that is if you didn't kiss me good-bye after a week because you wanted to see what was going on in the world."

"Me? Never! We would make love in the afternoon, when it was blazing hot, and in the cool of the night. In between I would fish a bit, open a coconut and sit on a rock, thinking about life and why it's so difficult."

"You mean, why you can't have everything and all of it at the same time."

"Pauline! I'm not like that! I am a modest man, why can't you see that? I just want tranquility. Doesn't that alone make me a modest man?"

"Not particularly. Peace is the hardest thing in life to come by. Now I've got to go."

"Wait a minute! When am I going to see you? What about Monday night? Let me see what I can arrange and phone you in the morning. See what you can do. Please, Pauline."

"I will try, but no sulking if I can't make it."

"My disappointment will be terrible yet I would only sulk for a day or two, proving that I am a modest man. I will phone you. Take care of yourself."

"You, too."

———

As Francien was loading her shopping bags into the backseat of her car, a woman's voice said, "Good morning, Mrs. Aardsen."

Looking around she saw Mrs. Wasserdam who lived farther down the street. Surprised, she said, "Oh, hello."

They had never exchanged more than a nod. The Wasserdams' house was bigger, with a double garage. He had a Mercedes, she a BMW. They had no children.

"What a lovely car you have."

"Yes, it's nice, isn't it."

"The light green and the black leather—perfect."

"My husband chose it for me."

"By the way, was it your husband who was involved with the drug addict stealing his car radio? I read about it in the paper. He was with Alderman Van der Berg, wasn't he?"

"Yes, that's right."

"Awful, isn't it? All these people stealing things. If we don't protect ourselves, who will? Not the police, I daresay. A good thing people like your husband know how to administer quick justice. Did he get in trouble afterward? Something was said about a suit for damages."

"No, we never heard any more about it. My husband and Thijs, the alderman I mean, talked to the management of *De Telegraaf,* and that was the end of it."

"Nice to hear that. By the way, why don't you drop in for a glass of sherry one day? We're off to the Canary Islands next week, but I'll give you a ring when we come back. Let's say, after the holidays, beginning of January, if that's all right with you?"

"Uh, yes, of course." Francien could hardly believe her ears.

"Well, don't let me keep you any longer. You'll hear from me. Good-bye."

And then Mrs Wasserdam proceeded to her BMW, her straight back in an expensive fur coat. Francien stood staring after her. Invited by Madam Wasserdam?! She shook her head in disbelief.

She was still surprised about it when she came home and told Bram. He was much less impressed. "Maybe they want to buy an Alpha," he said.

"He has a Mercedes, and she a BMW."

"You mix with classy people then."

Francien stuck her tongue out at him.

———

Pauline phoned him before he got around to dialing her, and said she could make it for the evening only.

"Not for the night? I just reserved a room!"

"Sorry, no. Cancel it."

"But why not. It has been ages already. I can't go—"

"Come on, Bram! I thought you were Mr. Modest. Where?"

"You're right, I am. In the Posthoorn?"

"What time?"

"Make it as early as possible. Seven?"

"If I'm not there by eight I won't be coming at all."

"Why is that? I'll wait."

"Then you'll wait for nothing."

"Can't you phone if you'll be later than eight?"

"Of course I can, but I don't like to have to. Moreover, I like to have ample time when I'm with you. We can also meet tomorrow night, if that's okay with you."

"Okay, tonight, before eight."

She appeared at 7:45 and Bram was very glad to see her. Once they were seated at a quiet table in a corner of the restaurant, had an aperitif and ordered their meal, Bram asked Pauline what she thought about the offer from Baron Steltenburcht.

"How many zeros?"

"Six."

Pauline smiled. "A millionaire. How does that feel?"

"It's nothing definite. Maybe just talk. But what do you think about it?"

"It's more important what you think about it."

"Well, eventually it'll be my decision, I know, but I'd like to have your opinion. It's a lot of money and I'm very tempted. But it would change my entire life."

"What would you do with the money? Have you already given it some thought?"

"Plenty of thought. I could go to another country, buy another run-down garage and rebuild it, or go to the States, for that matter. What country would you like to live in?"

"The States. I like the American business mentality. If you're good, you're in. If not, you're out. Would you like to live there? Or are you too Dutch?"

"What do you mean, too Dutch?"

"Nothing negative, but I think an American would react differently if he got a bid like you have. He wouldn't buy another run-down shop."

"What would he do, then?"

"If he's for real, he would go to the bank, borrow ten times as much, buy an entire garage chain and make himself president. Then he would buy a big house with a big mortgage to make clear to everybody that he had made the American dream come true."

"And worry himself to death about how he would pay all the interest."

"See, you are too Dutch. Of course he wouldn't. He would hire a man to do the worrying for him. If he finds the right man, they both won't have to worry, and if he doesn't, he'll start from scratch again."

"How come you know so much about Americans?"

"It's not much and, don't forget, my husband lives in Atlanta. When he moved there, I seriously studied the possibility of going along, but our relationship at that time didn't justify it. To be on my own out there with a boy of eight on my hands didn't appeal to me. But with capital like you'll have, if the deal goes through, that would be different. For an enterprising American male this would be the first stone of an avalanche rolling uphill."

"Uphill?"

"The increasing amount of money brings you to the top of the mountain."

"Well, I'm not in a hurry. And maybe I'll never hear from him again. I haven't spoken with anyone else about this. Don't like to make a fool of myself if it turns out to be a flop."

Pauline finished the last bit of her entree, lit a cigarette, leaned back and smiled.

He said, "Are you enjoying yourself because of my problem?"

She shook her head. "No. But the coincidence is remarkable. In Paris after the show, an American, a Mr. Valentine, came up to me. He's in the fashion business and wondered whether I would like to work for him."

"Where? In Paris?"

"That, too, but also in the States. Los Angeles."

Bram put his fork down and pushed his dish away.

"And?"

"I said no."

"Just like that?"

"Of course not. That's not my style. I explained the situation with Dick and I thought that would put him off."

"And it didn't, did it?"

"He said he would discuss it with his people and give me a call if he could get his partner on the same line. He was going to telephone me today. That's why I was a bit uncertain whether I could see you."

"Well?"

"He wants me to fly over and meet his partner."

"Are you going?"

"Yes. I also wish to terminate the last official link that I still have with my husband."

"You mean divorce?"

"Yes."

"What kind of guy is this Mr. Valentine?"

"Not my type, but he seems a nice man—gentle, serious, and crazy about clothes . . . designing and all that. He seems to have a wife and two sons. They are in manufacturing, at least his partner is, and he is in charge of the selling. He thinks I am the type of model they need."

"And what about Dick? What does he think about it?"

"I haven't told him. But that's where I would like to ask you a favor. Could Dick stay with you while I'm in the States? Say, during the Christmas holidays?"

"Jesus Christ, Pauline! Now you are asking something! What can I say to that? Dick would like it, and Francien wouldn't mind if I tell her that you are going to America for an interview. And I can sweat all the while whether you will come back divorced or not at all."

"I can't help that. I could send Dick to my in-laws in Groningen, which he'd loath. He's looking forward to the holidays, intending to spend most of the time on the *Jiffy* with his friend, Willem. I'm almost sure he'll ask Willem if he can't stay with him."

"Lazy Willem would like to have him. He lives alone. But it would be odd if he stayed there and not with me. When will you be leaving?"

"The nineteenth of December. Do you think Francien will agree to have him? It would mean a lot of extra work for her."

Again Bram noticed the ease with which she used Francien's name, as if she were just another friend. The independent woman—he knew they existed but he had never experienced one. He was awed by her ego and he didn't know what he admired more, her beauty or her independent mind. Living with her would indeed be different from living with Francien—more difficult, more challenging. Also more rewarding.

"Well," she said, "what do you think. Will your wife agree? If it's difficult, don't worry. I can also take him along. He might like that as well, but I think it would be better for him to make a trip like that when he is out of his chair."

"I will ask her. If she says no, that'll be it. I can't force Dick on her if she doesn't like it, can I?"

He kissed Pauline good-bye at her doorstep and drove home. When he opened the garage doors he saw the convertible and remembered that before long he would be scraping ice from his car's windshield in the mornings. He shrugged, locked his car and went inside.

Francien switched off the television and offered to make him coffee. When he turned it down, she joined him for a whiskey.

"By the way," he began, "did you have any plans for the holidays?"

"No, not really, and I think, with all the money you spent on my car, we better stay at home this time."

Bram nodded. "The reason why I ask is that Dick's mother phoned today and asked if Dick could spend the holidays with us."

"Dick's mother! Using me as a nursemaid?! Never! And what for, going with you to Acapulco or something? Who does she think she is? Her Majesty the Queen? Forget it! I'm not going to take any orders from her. This is . . . that woman is absolutely *mad*. Me, taking orders from a call girl, and a fine—"

"Model."

"Okay, a model. So what! Shows off in somebody else's clothes, gets all the attention in the world and shifts her brat onto somebody else's lap. If madam wants to screw away with some married guy with a lot of money and an overcharged libido, who . . ."

"I'm not that guy."

"What?"

"I said, 'I'm not that guy.'"

"No, of course you're not. I will see to that. Landing me with that brat and you running away screwing his mother, you . . . you . . ." The thought alone insulted her so much that words failed her.

"As I said, I'm not that guy."

"What guy?!"

"The married guy with a lot of money and an overcharged libido."

He rose and walked into the kitchen, took a tray of ice from the fridge and returned to the living room with it. He broke the ice from the tray and grabbed a handful of cubes, clinking them into their glasses and filling the spaces with whiskey, Francien was trying to get hold of herself. She thought about what Marjet had said: "If you don't know what to say, say nothing. You've said too much already."

Bram moved a glass towards her. Francien looked at it and remained silent.

He took the cigarettes from the table, offered her one and, when she took it, fished his Dupont from his pocket and lit it. When she inhaled, he resumed:

"Pauline has been invited by an American fashion company to come and talk about working for them in the States. Since we have no plans, I couldn't see any reason why we couldn't have Dick here during his school holidays, unless you can't stand him."

"That's not it. I like him well enough . . ."

"You know, he told me a while ago, when he was in the garage, that he usually goes to his grandparents in Groningen, but they treat him like he is eight and he's bored stiff out there. I think Lazy Willem would like to have him as well, but since you invited him for dinner, and the two of you got along so well, I had to ask you. It's extra work for you, of course. I understand that. It's up to you."

"I wouldn't mind the work and you know that." She desperately tried to grasp the situation.

Bram waited. After a while he took the empty ice tray from the table, went to the kitchen, filled it with water and put it back in the fridge. Then he went to the toilet, although he had no need to. Next, he went to the guest room where he puttered around a bit.

When he came back into the living room Francien looked up.

"But if he comes we have to have a Christmas tree as well, and presents. Maybe we could ask Marjet and Thijs over with the kids for dinner on Christmas day."

"That seems like a good idea. Will you discuss that with Marjet?"

———

Dick was ever so pleased with the prospect of spending the Christmas holidays with Bram and working on the *Jiffy* with Willem.

Francien was very busy with what the Christmas dinner should look like and the presents and the decorations. Marjet had liked the idea of celebrating together.

"Are you keeping up the regimen?" she asked.

"What?"

"The exercise. Be careful. Don't believe it's over."

"If she goes to work in the States, she's gone."

"That's right, *if*. But I have the feeling this isn't over yet. Too much Christmas illusion and not enough reality. So you better stay off the booze and on the bike. Strong body, strong mind. You'll need it."

"Marjet, what are you talking about? Just when I'm beginning to see the light again. You are the optimist, remember?"

"Maybe Thijs' reformed pessimism is catching, I don't know, but keep up the biking, will you?"

"I will. I'm kind of getting to like it."

Bram still didn't know whether he wanted to sell or not. The Credit Suisse in Brussels had told him that Steltenburcht could easily handle a deal like that. They had also told him that they had known Steltenburcht from the time he had stepped into his father's shoes and that if they agreed about the price there would be no reason to expect any problems about the payment.

Steltenburcht reappeared on schedule and asked whether he had contacted the Credit Suisse.

"I have and I must say they think highly of you."

"They are good people. I can recommend them to you in case we do business. Does the fact that you did not call me to cancel this meeting mean that we *are* in business?"

Bram shook his head. "It only means that I haven't decided to call it off. I asked my accountants to make an estimate of the value of my company, which I will get next week. There is, however, one decision I have made. *If* I sell, I will go. I don't want to be an employee in my own garage."

"That I can understand, and as I told you before, I would have liked you to stay on, but it will not be a condition. Would you mind telling me what other obstacles there are? Maybe I can take them away."

"I don't think, Mr. Steltenburcht, you can help me there. This company is my baby. You don't sell babies easily."

"That's true, but it is done, and most of the time for peanuts. This is only an exchange from one commodity into another. Is Pauline Verwal a good friend of yours?"

The sudden change of subject surprised Bram. "I know her," he said.

"She was with you at the Bugatti Club, wasn't she?"

"She sat next to me at the table, but she also sat next to you."

"That's right, but weren't you in Paris together two weeks ago?"

"You were kissing her at the bar in the Holiday Inn, if I remember well."

Steltenburcht smiled. "Only her hand. I just thought that she might be a factor in our deal. I hope for you that you know her better than I do."

"I hope the same for you."

"No chance." He made a helpless gesture. "Women like her don't fall for me. You know I'm still a bachelor. I am thirty-eight, I am rich, I have a title, but I have no woman. Of course I can get them by the dozens—good-looking, poor-thinking, money-eager creatures. But someone with class like Pauline Verwal, who could receive my guests, be my companion wherever I go, a partner—that's hard to come by. Maybe I'll give it another try," he said, more to himself than to Bram. "Well, that's my problem. Can I assume that I will hear from you when you have received your accountants' report? You let me know whether my idea of price is somewhere near theirs. I suggest that once we agree on the value I give you a firm bid valid till the end of the day on the first Friday in January. If we are both pleased with the price, we'll have the motivation to settle the details."

"Make it the second week."

The Baron paused. "The second it is."

"We are not in a hurry, are we?"

"Not really."

After Steltenburcht left, Bram sat for a while reviewing the conversation. A strange approach, telling your price first. If he sold the whole operation, there wouldn't be many details to work out. Maybe for Steltenburcht it was just routine. Eager he is. Let's first see what Pauline has to say when she comes back from the States. Anyway, he'd better start thinking about buying some presents. According to the girls, he had drawn Thijs as the one to buy a present for. Apart from that, he wanted to get something for Dick and for Francien, but first he had to find something for Pauline, for she would be leaving for America on the nineteenth.

———

The nineteenth was a Friday. He took the whole day off. Pauline had arranged for Dick to be picked up from school by her friend in Waddinxveen, where Bram would come for him in the course of the evening. Her plane was scheduled for seven. Bram had booked a room in the Hilton at Schiphol, where they arrived the morning of her flight.

After lunch they went to bed. Bram closed the heavy curtains. Their ardor was intensified by their upcoming separation. She would be far away and the fear of losing her made him take her with a possessive drive that exhausted them both. They fell asleep and did not wake up until five-thirty.

Rushing into their clothes, out of the hotel, and into the airport check-in counter left him no time for all the things he had wanted to ask. Still glowing with rapture and not quite recovered from the unusual midday sleep, they hugged each other in front of Passport Control.

"Do come back, please?"

"I will."

And then she was gone, leaving him standing there unaware of the people who rushed past him.

After a while it dawned on him where he was and that he was very thirsty. He went to Refreshments, sat on a stool at the bar and ordered a beer. Putting his hand in his coat pocket for his cigarettes, he felt the tiny box with the ring he had bought for her.

He had even put a little note in it.

> Don't go away,
> Stay,
> Every day,
> Every hour,
> My desert flower.
>
> Bram

He had heard it on the midnight soft-soul radio program "Candlelight."

14

Francien, Dick and his car were gone. Yawning, he scratched his bottom and the back of his head. He put on his bathrobe, made himself a cup of tea and sank into his chair with the fat Saturday edition of *De Telegraaf*.

Half an hour later, Francien and Dick blew in with a lot of energy and crisp air, maneuvering an oversized Christmas tree through the corridor into the living room, where they discussed where the tree would fit best. They agreed on the corner in front of the veranda door that led to the garden.

"Bram, we have got to go and buy decorations. Would you be so kind and put the tree up over there?"

"We never had it there. It always—"

"I know, but we need more space for presents this year. Come on, Dick, let's go before it gets too crowded and the nicest stuff is gone." And off they went, leaving him behind, amidst the resin esters of the tree the two of them had abandoned in the middle of the room.

He picked up his newspaper again and continued where the two had interrupted, but with the tree in the center of the living room, he couldn't concentrate anymore. After a while he folded the paper, took a deep breath, showered, put on some old clothes and went to the shed for tools and a pair of gloves. There was no job he hated more than putting up the Christmas tree. The needles stung, the stem was either too thick or too thin and the top seldom suitable to hold the top decoration upright.

The last Wednesday before Christmas Dick came around the course in under 38 seconds.

Willem twice clocked him at 37.8. Shining with pride, Dick went through the garage, telling every mechanic that he had made it. Later, alone with Lazy Willem, Bram looked at the mechanic with furrowed brow.

"How come, Willem?"

Willem smiled. "Christmas present. Special gasoline."

"Are you crazy? You know it's not permitted."

"I know. But next week I'll replace the extras for his feet with aluminum ones. That'll lighten it, and then he will make it with normal stuff."

"Next week you tell him the truth, will you? I don't like these tricks. That boy will lead us by the nose before we know it. No need to teach him anything."

"I'm sorry. Just wanted the bugger to feel all right over Christmas."

Willem turned to go, but Bram caught him by the sleeve of his overalls. "Normal people don't think of giving a boy high octane gasoline for Christmas. Anyway . . . what about your daughters? Are you seeing them over Christmas?"

"Yes. Their mother will be in London."

"Good for you. Have fun."

"The same."

On Christmas morning Bram woke up at his usual seven o'clock and went to take his usual leak. Then he went into the living room and stood by the window where the tree was, with soft, tiny sparkles in the glass balls.

There was no snow. The street looked wet in the shine of the streetlights.

Bram walked around the tree, found the plug for the tree lights and stuck it into the socket. The tree sprang to life, making circles of light in the angel's hair around the candles. The subtlety of the circles fascinated him, like soap bubbles once had done. The plain glass balls reflected all the candles. The top of the tree stood straight. He walked back to the spot from which he had checked the top and did it again. Satisfied, he went to the table, picked up his cigarettes and lit one. After putting the package back on the table, he walked up to the window again, unaware of the picture he made, nude, next to the tree that threw soft, rimming light along his body.

Using a flowerpot on the window sill as an ashtray, he stood there with his arms crossed, smoking and thinking about the old days, when they rose at four on Christmas morning. How the snow crackled underfoot when they walked from the empty streets of the outskirts of town toward the church in the center, with more and more dark figures gradually joining in the same direction.

The huge church with the tall pillars and the roaring organ, the carol singing during the third mass, and the candlelight breakfast at six in the morning—he could still smell the frying scrapple. But that was in the east of the country. Here, in the west, they didn't know what scrapple was. Maybe they didn't know it in the east anymore, either. Things changed. The night mass was at midnight nowadays, he had heard, and it was in Dutch. No Latin anymore. Last time he had been in his hometown the entire church was gone. It had shocked him. It had been a real Catholic church, not one of those Protestant churches that looked like a school building. Wide arches had supported the high slate roof, which looked so distinguished with its purple-blue color. It had been a real church with a slender tower that narrowed at 250 feet high at the top into one leg of a golden weathercock that had stood there in the sunlight, unafraid, safeguarded by the lightning rod that reached even higher. He wondered what they had done with the cock. Had they just knocked it off and dropped it through the slated roof because it didn't matter anymore? Or had they lowered it down carefully?

After extinguishing his cigarette in the earth of the flowerpot, he went to switch on the stereo system. He had already put "Silent Night" sung by Mahalia Jackson on the turntable the evening before.

At two o'clock that afternoon Thijs, Marjet, Jeroen and Wanda arrived, everybody wishing everybody else a Merry Christmas. Parcels of all shapes with ribbons and paper of all different colors were stacked under the tree. Drinks were poured, snacks offered, and gradually everybody found a place—Thijs and Marjet on the couch, Bram in his chair, Francien in hers near to the kitchen so that she could take care of fresh supplies. Dick, Jeroen and Wanda sat around the dinner table, drinking Coke and talking in low voices like conspirators. After a couple of minutes Wanda got up and came to Bram, who was discussing the latest terrorism with Thijs. (Six Muslim bombs at the French and American embassies in Kuwait, a bomb at Harrods, and a sacked employee setting fire to a sex-and-gambling club in Amsterdam, killing thirteen.)

"Uncle Bram?" Wanda was pulling his sleeve.

"What is it?" Thijs asked, but Wanda didn't look at him. Instead, she moved around a bit so that Thijs saw more of her back and kept looking up at Bram, who smiled at her.

"Uncle Bram, when are we going to open up the packages?"

Marjet's hand on Thijs's arm stopped his reprimand. He only shook his head in disapproval. The boys at the table were watching anxiously to see whether Wanda would complete her mission successfully. Bram shot a glance at the boys, lifted Wanda up and put her on his lap so that her back was toward her father.

"Do you think there will be presents for you, too?"

"Of course. All the other rooms in the house were locked, so that I should not see them."

"But don't you think that Jeroen and Dick would like to wait a little longer?"

A big smile came on her face, confident as she was that Bram was completely wrong there.

"Of course not. Even Mama said she was curious to know what she was getting, isn't that so, Mama?"

"That's true, but I also said that we all should wait nicely till the time came."

Wanda turned her head back to Bram. "And now is the time, isn't it, Uncle Bram? Dick said so, too."

Bram looked at Dick, whose face appeared very innocent.

"Well, I think the best thing is to vote. Who is in favor of opening them now?"

Four arms shot up: the kids' and Francien's.

Bram looked at Thijs apologetically. "The drawback of democracy, my friend, is dictatorship by the majority."

"It's more the drawback of lowering the voting age if you ask me. But why not."

Jeroen had already jumped off his chair and Dick wheeled along with him toward the tree. Bram rose with Wanda on his arm. "I wonder, young lady, how long it takes before you have them running errands for you. You might as well hand out the parcels. You are growing fast, young one. It won't be long before you are grown up."

"And then I am going to marry you," Wanda replied. Her kiss landed on Bram's chin, as he lowered her to the floor.

"Then I'll be your father-in-law," remarked Thijs dryly. "And the wedding has to be in church. I'll see to that."

"Well," said Bram, looking at him with a big grin on his face, "we can always elope, can't we?"

They grouped around the tree, bringing along glasses, cigarettes and ashtrays, and slowly the avalanche of torn paper and discarded boxes ensued, with Marjet and Francien saving the ribbons for reuse. With a lot of *ah*'s and *oh*'s and knowing glances to the suspected giver, a collection of objects grew around each of the children. Thijs was most pleased with a fat volume about religion and politics since the Middle Ages, and Francien looked gratefully at Bram when she unpacked a pair of black openwork-leather car gloves with the fastening on the back of the hand.

"This one I know," Wanda said, and walked straight to Dick. She held in her hand a parcel with a drawing on the outside. Handing it to Dick, she stood next to him and pointed at the drawing. "I made it for you."

In the drawing was a wheelchair with two little figures in it.

"Who are they?" Dick asked.

"That is you," she said, pointing at the taller one, "and that's me."

"Why are we together in one wheelchair?"

"Because we are married and that's cozier, then you haven't got to look back at me all the time when you tell me something."

"Hey," Bram said with indignation, "what's this? I thought you were going to marry *me*?"

Wanda looked at him, a little embarrassed now that all eyes were focused on her. When nobody came to her rescue, she nodded to herself and then said to Bram in a reassuring tone, "I made the drawing yesterday."

During the laughter that followed she returned to the tree to proceed with her task, while Dick unpacked a toy telescope and was surprised at the magnification when he looked through it to the other side of the street.

Bram had collected a new agenda book, a car calender and an expensive pair of sunglasses with leather-covered frames. He had thrown an appreciative glance at Francien, who acknowledged it. When all the parcels were opened, Bram rose and asked for everybody's attention.

"I'm sorry, but I feel that for this once I have the right to break the rule that our presents be anonymous."

Walking to the sideboard he opened a drawer and produced a plain square box. Returning to his place in the circle, he said, while opening the box, "This summer, Dick, you and I met on a very unfortunate occasion, which landed you in a wheelchair. I have here a miniature of your wheelchair and this miniature is made of gold. The choice of the metal is not accidental. Neither is the fact that it has been built on a pedestal. I have watched you taking the blow that has been delivered to you, Dick, and I must say, you took it like a man. As I'm convinced that you will leave your wheelchair behind you before long, I want you to have the miniature, so that if ever in your life you have another blow delivered to you, I want you to see this chair and remember how you overcame this one. I'm convinced you can overcome any further setback that you might encounter, and rest assured, there will be many more to come before you will be where you wish to go.

"I had thought about a miniature *Jiffy,* but in the *Jiffy* you still have to prove yourself. In the wheelchair you have done it."

After that, he heaved a sigh, squatted down beside the wheelchair, handed Dick the present and pulled the boy's head against his shoulder. Dick put an arm around Bram's neck.

Marjet's applause, joined by the others, broke the tension. While Francien started gathering the rubbish, Marjet picked up Wanda, who had stood staring at Bram and Dick.

Thijs occupied himself inspecting the presents Jeroen had gotten, leaving Bram and Dick to untangle themselves, Bram rubbing his face hard with both hands and Dick looking at the tiny wheelchair on the dark wooden pedestal, his head bent to hide his eyes.

"Anybody care for another drink?" Not waiting for the answers, Bram picked up a couple of glasses and went to the bar.

"That was most probably the longest speech you ever made," Marjet said when he handed her a refill.

"You can say that again. Francien, listen. I have been thinking. It's not good having all seven of us at the dinner table. The kids want to play with their toys and they play on the floor. Why don't you set the big table for the four of us and let the children eat at the low table. Dick can sit on the floor as well. Just put down a few plates and some food, and then we can eat in peace and so can they."

"You think Dick . . ."

"Sure, otherwise he is too high for them."

"Okay, if you think so."

Turning around, she saw that Dick had already lowered himself onto the floor and was explaining to Wanda how to play tiddlywinks.

The kids loved to be out from under the control of the adults, and to eat and play at the same time.

During dinner Bram told about Dick's progress, his contract, and his friendship with Lazy Willem. When Marjet asked what kind of man Lazy Willem was, Bram told them the reason for his divorce and Willem's opinion of it. They all laughed except Thijs, who was appalled.

"By the way, Bram, did a Mr. Steltenburcht ever contact you?" Thijs asked.

Thijs's question startled him. "The baron?"

"Yes, that's him."

"I met him some time ago in Antwerp. Why do you ask?"

"He came to see me about a month ago. He wanted to know everything about the economic situation in Haarlem—investment possibilities, building regulations and so on. I helped him as best I could with brochures and the like. In the end, he told me that he was interested in investing in the automobile business, so I gave him your address and told him how well you were doing, your expansion. You would have had tears of gratitude if you had heard me. Did he ever contact you?"

"He did. He wants to buy my place lock, stock and barrel, including me."

"Oh no!" Francien sighed.

"He doesn't want to buy it without you?" Thijs wanted to know.

"I can have it as I like it, but I have already decided that I would never again be an employee, and definitely not in what had once been my own company. But sold or not, Francien, I would never part with the chair you gave me when I started up. Although I am not a believer, I am superstitious in a certain way."

"That's what happens when you have no true religion," Thijs couldn't help saying. And he also couldn't help yelping, "Ouch!" when the point of Marjet's shoe hit his shin. "That's *unfair*. We agreed that if somebody was out of line and the other wanted to stop it, we should only touch the other one's leg, not break it. Now I'll need an ambulance to get home, I'm sure."

"Daddy, maybe you can borrow Dick's wheelchair," Wanda suggested happily.

"Little pitchers have long ears," Thijs said under his breath.

Marjet apologized. "But, you see, we had agreed that religion would be left alone today. Thijs has had the opportunity to say grace and that should be it. Sometimes I could kick that man."

"You do!" said Thijs, rubbing his shin.

"You should have become a missionary or maybe that would have been worse. You would consider every convert a trophy, like a scalp. Why can't you leave men be? Men will always be men. No matter whether they are gangsters, politicians, priests, pastors, business tycoons or captains of industry, they are all after power. It's only the method that differs—guns, words, promises, sentiment, even pity. Deep down they are all after one thing and that's power over other people. They often remind me of the small man with the huge dog or the small man in his big car."

Thijs grinned. "Isn't it pathetic to be a man?"

"Now listen"—Francien rose—"extinguish all the lights."

She went to the kitchen and the party waited tensely in the dark living room.

"I'm a ghost." It was Jeroen forcing his voice as low as possible.

"Bang."

"Ow."

"You are not a ghost. Ghosts don't feel pain." Wanda remarked with satisfaction in her voice.

"You hit me."

"Jeroen, stop it." Thijs ordered.

"Francien," Bram yelled, "you better hurry, otherwise we will have a war on our hands."

"Bram, come in here, please?"

"What's the problem?"

In a hush-hush voice Francien said, "I have made a real English Christmas pudding. You have to pour rum over it and bring it in aflame, but it won't catch fire."

Bram looked at the label. "The alcohol percentage is too low."

"Shit, I even told the guy in the shop what I needed it for. The jerk. What shall I do, stick a candle on it?"

"Wait a minute. Have we still got fluid left that we used for the fondue?"

"But that's denatured alcohol. Then you can't eat it anymore."

"You got enough here. Where is the bread knife?"

Francien fished it out of the dishwasher and handed it to Bram who shouted, "*Hang in there,*" and cut an inch off the bottom of the Christmas pudding. Putting the top back, he poured the fuel over it and placed the plate on a metal tray. He whispered, "Light it, and give it a few seconds to burn. We'll eat the piece that I cut off. Okay, have your show, you'll have the best illuminated Christmas pudding in the country."

The pudding ignited. Flames shot up and then settled. The kids rewarded Francien with enthusiastic *ooh*'s and *ah*'s.

It was after ten when Dick was asleep and the dishwasher running. Francien came from the kitchen. Bram had poured them a brandy and was swirling it in his glass.

During the rest of the evening Francien had realized what had been going on behind her back. Given the presence of her friends and the kids, she had managed to control herself. Having held her temper till they had left, she held her tongue a little longer while cleaning up and getting Dick to bed.

"What's he willing to pay?" she said.

"That's what I call 'cut the bullshit.' He has something like a million guilders in mind."

"When did he visit you?"

"Hey, what's this, an interrogation or something?"

Francien had to summon all her self-control not to fling the hot coffee in his face. She put the cup back on the table, rose, left the room and went to the bathroom. She locked the door behind her, took the Valium from the cupboard and washed two tablets down. Then she stood for a while, holding her head high, her eyes closed, fists clenched.

She was almost collected when Bram tried to come in and asked through the closed door whether she was all right.

"I am. I'll be with you in a minute."

She came out, bringing a glass of water with her. She sat down and lit a cigarette.

"Bram, would you please tell me all about this Mr. Steltenbug, or whatever his name is."

Bram told her the whole story, including that his accountants had estimated the shop's value at 900,000 guilders and that he had received a firm bid at 1,150,000 guilders to be replied to in January.

"Why didn't you tell me?"

Bram shrugged. "I don't know."

Francien was dying for a whiskey but she took a swig of water.

"You told *her*."

"I only discussed the matter seriously with my accountants, because they are the only ones I know who understand things like that."

"I am your wife, you should have told me." She kept her voice down in order not to wake up Dick.

"I would have told you once I had sorted it out myself."

"I am your wife, you should have told me," she repeated stubbornly.

"Maybe I should have, but I didn't. I'm sorry. Maybe I didn't want to burden you given all the things you had on your mind with Dick and the presents and the dinner. There's plenty of time. What good would it do to stir up a lot of uncertainty just because an odd Belgian baron passes by, showing off that he can buy my life's work like somebody else buys a package of cigarettes?"

"But you say that you have a firm bid till next year of over a million guilders."

"I received that only three days ago. Before that I never thought he was serious."

"But why didn't you tell him right away that he could go to hell?"

"Can't you imagine that I would be curious to know whether someone was really willing to pay such an amount for my business?"

The Valium was gradually taking effect.

Bram poured himself another brandy. "You're not drinking."

"What will you do if you sell the garage?"

"I don't know. I haven't thought about it. I don't know whether I want to sell at all."

"Have I got a say in the matter?"

"You mean to say no when I say yes and to say yes when I say no?"

Francien hesitated.

He rubbed his eyes and pinched his nose. "Let's sleep on all that. There's time. I'll let you know beforehand, when I have made up my mind, and then we can discuss it again. Meanwhile you can think about it as well. All right?"

Francien nodded. She needed to talk about it with Marjet.

"I must say, that was a wonderful dinner, and I like the sun glasses. Did you enjoy the party, too?"

"It was fun arranging it. Marjet has asked us back for dinner tomorrow. I said you would like that."

"Two days with Thijs in a row? Although I must admit that he's not all that bad, in his own way. You know, for a long time I have wondered what a free-thinking girl like Marjet saw in a God-fearer like Thijs. Maybe the free-thinker needs the security religion and party provide. So, you have accepted the invitation. Well, Dick will like it, anyway."

"He is a nice kid, isn't he? Where did you get that speech? You've always said you hated speaking."

"I still do, but I had to." Bram finished his brandy. "Let's hit the sack."

It wasn't so much the alcohol in that one brandy as the alcohol that had been in the aperitifs and the table wine, mixed with the valium, that gave Francien the feeling of being overpowered by Bram's huge body, towering over her and shielding her from whatever danger life might have in store. She never reached anything but a feeling of peace under that over-whelming body that tried to be closer to her with every thrust. When he moved off her she felt exposed for a moment but, snuggling up against him, she sank into a deep dreamless sleep, too exhausted to worry anymore.

Eleven o'clock, the evening of the twenty-sixth of December. Francien was already in the bathroom. She had just dropped her panties into the hamper and was inspecting her breasts for cysts when the telephone rang.

Bram picked it up.

"Aardsen."

"Hello, Bram, it's me, Pauline."

Bram threw a uneasy glance in the direction of the bathroom but didn't say anything.

"Listen Bram, I know what I'm doing. Just listen. I have a proposal from Mr. Valentine and his partner, in writing. They would like to take me on for a year. They had already arranged with their agent in Paris to have a show on the twenty-eighth and they want me to be their leading model. I want to discuss my future with you. Can you come to Paris on the twenty-eighth so that we can talk after the show? That's the day after tomorrow. If I didn't think it was important, I wouldn't have called you. I have to fly back to the States on the twenty-ninth for a meeting with my husband's attorney. I take it Dick is all right."

She waited a second for him to say something and when he didn't, she said, "I have to see you. Holiday Inn, the twenty-eighth."

He heard a kiss and then the bleep-bleep of the disconnected line. He cradled the receiver and, turning around, saw Francien.

"Who was that at this hour?" She was nude and oblivious to the open curtains.

Bram was at a loss for words. With Dick in the house he didn't think it wise to tell her. Lazy Willem could take Dick to his house tomorrow night.

"Let's discuss that tomorrow night," he said, and went to the bedroom. Francien switched off the light and followed him.

"Why can't you tell me? Why must you always be so secretive? What man wouldn't tell his wife if he got a funny call at odd hours?"

"Maybe I am not 'what man.' I'm me, and I am going to bed now, and I promise you I will tell you tomorrow."

"Why is it up to you to decide whether tomorrow is the proper time for it and not tonight?"

"Because it was I who took the call."

He walked into the bathroom and when she followed him, he stepped under the shower and opened it up full blast, barring further discussion.

When he returned to the bedroom, the main light was off and she was standing in front of the bed, spread-legged, hands on hips, breasts jutting out and apparently not prepared to take no for an answer.

The glow of the bed lamps illuminated the sides of her body, outlining its femininity. He could not see her eyes but he could very well guess their expression.

"You are a stubborn bitch if there ever was one."

She remained silent. He walked up to her. He would be damned if he would let her force him. "Dear Francien, are—"

"Well, that's a long time since you called me 'Dear Francien.'"

"Isn't that a matter of your inciting me to do so, or are you entitled by law to fifty *dear Francien*'s a month?"

"Fifty? In your best days you didn't even make five."

"But I made up for it by making love to you between five and seven times a week."

"Not so loud, you left the door open. Dick might hear you."

"Well, let's talk without words, then." In a flash he bent forward, and with one hand between her legs, he grabbed her bottom and lifted her from the floor. His face close to hers he said, "Dear Francien—that's twice in one day, mind you. Dear Francien, will you offer me the pleasure of your delicious body, or will I have to phone my solicitor to sue you for denying me my matrimonial rights?"

Her rigid body told him his forced banter didn't work. He lowered her on the bed and lay down on his own half. "Let's go to sleep—I promise, tomorrow."

Francien remained silent for a long time, struggling hard to swallow his decision. "All right, but I am too awake to sleep. I'll go and read a little."

After she had left, Bram had the bed all to himself to toss and turn in. What could it be? Was she willing to marry him? Had she found something that he could invest the money in? Or wasn't she coming back at all? But then why the hurry?

Bram was home by seven, as he had said he would be. Upon Bram's suggestion, Dick was spending the night with Lazy Willem.

They ate at the low table while watching television. After the eight o'clock news, Francien switched off the set.

"Well?"

"The phone call was from Pauline."

"I knew it!"

"Francien, please hear me out first. Pauline has asked me to meet her in Paris tomorrow. She is there for one day. She has been offered a job for one year, and she wants to discuss something with me. She said she knew what she was doing and if it hadn't been important she wouldn't have phoned me at home. That's all I know, and I have decided to go and see what she has to say."

"Of course. Her majesty phones and you come running. Don't you think she is pushing her luck too far?"

"What do you mean by that?"

"She comes when she likes, she goes when she likes, she can order you around like an obedient dog. How I hate that woman!"

"Why? Now, be honest. What has she actually done to harm you?"

"She is trying to take you away from me."

"How do you know? Suppose I was the one who did the trying? Why are you so sure about what she is up to, or do you believe she threw Dick in front of my car to get in contact with me?"

"Don't be ridiculous." Francien remained silent and Bram too.

"Are you in love with her?"

Bram hesitated.

"At least give me an honest answer. I have been imagining for weeks what it would be like if it was me who was in love with somebody else and married to you. So . . . are you in love with?"

"I think so."

"I *knew* it. I *knew* it from the first time I saw her."

"Francien, falling in love with somebody is not an act of free will. It happens. No human being can, by an act of will, decide to fall in love with somebody."

"You have been to bed with her."

"What's more important? Whether I love her or whether I go to bed with her?"

Francien didn't reply.

"You wanted me to tell you," Bram said. "You insisted we talk. We are talking. Now you must answer my question, otherwise we are *not* talking but just flinging accusations around. Please answer *my* question."

"Being in love is more threatening. You know that and I know that, but what good does it do?"

Bram shrugged.

"Now *you* answer. Do you want my benediction?"

"I don't think that would have any impact one way or the other. If I stay with you, it has to be by my own decision and not because you force me to. What kind of man would you have if you could just make me knuckle under, if your threatening, your violent outbursts, scared me off? If I let you away with that, you would use it again the moment I so much as looked askance at someone. You would immediately start bullying me again."

"I—"

"Hear me out, please. You may consider me a dominant man, but you fell for that dominant person. What would become of me if you were to put on *my* pants? What would you end up holding onto? A jerk, Francien, nothing but a jerk. One of those men you despised, because they have no balls. Those are your very words."

Bram rose from the armchair.

"Where are you going?"

"To make coffee while you think over whether there is something wrong with my point of view."

Bram waited in the kitchen till the coffee was ready and then came back with everything on a tray. When he had poured the coffee, he asked her whether she cared for a brandy with it. She turned it down and he poured himself one.

"Well?" he said.

"I'm scared."

"I understand. Anyone in her right mind would be scared in this situation. Can't you imagine that I'm scared, too, at times?"

"You?"

"Yes, me. Don't you see? I am tempted to abandon my business, my house, my wife, which is exactly *all* I have in life. Suppose I make a wrong decision in a moment of exaltation and live the rest of my life regretting it?"

"So just stay put and make no decision at all. That's not so difficult, is it?"

"Doing nothing is also making a decision. Let's assume Pauline would agree to marry me—"

"Of course she would!"

"Not every woman is the same, but for argument's sake, suppose she wants to marry me and I do nothing and she goes away. Isn't it possible that I would later regret not having seized the opportunity?"

Francien nodded.

"Right, and suppose I then started constantly comparing you with her, that I imagined all the time how she would have done better, said nicer things, looked nicer? I wouldn't even adjust the picture I had in my mind to the fact that she grew older, too. In my mind she would always look like she looks now. Suppose you had to compete with that? Wouldn't that be a battle lost beforehand?

"Now, suppose I don't sell my company. Lantini dies. For one reason or other people don't like Alfas anymore. The new president, who is responsible for the poor designs he has authorized, would, of course, blame me for the loss of sales. How long do you think that I would be their representative in Holland? And if that happened, how often would I pull the hair out of my head, regretting I hadn't sold when I could? Taking these possibilities into account, would you like to decide whether or not to sell?"

Francien was biting her underlip, but held her tongue. Bram refilled the cups and his glass. He held the bottle out to her.

"Okay, a drop."

They sat for a while drinking coffee and sipping brandy.

"So there is nothing that I can do but sit tight?" Francien said quietly.

"I can't see it otherwise, but sitting tight in this situation is certainly not easy."

"Will you come back from Paris?"

"I will come back from Paris," he said.

Francien shook her head several times. All this was so bizarre, she thought, like a dream, a bad dream, likely to turn into a nightmare. Would she wake up before she went mad? It couldn't be happening to her. She couldn't believe it. This bizarre discussion, like about a business trip. Would other women have agreed that it was unreal, that it couldn't be happening to them? Hatred and jealousy were understandable, but this? Was she crazy or wise? When was the last time that she asked herself that question? Yes, the night she had slept in the guest room.

"Would you do me a favor, Bram?"

"What?"

"Would you mind sleeping in the guest room tonight?"

It took him a moment to process the question. It's easier to sleep with a man when he's come back than before he goes.

"Yes," he said.

They ate breakfast in silence.

"Will you pick up Dick in the afternoon? Being there the whole day yesterday and part of today will have been enough. The trouble is, he cannot do all that much, mainly watch what Lazy Willem does."

Francien didn't say anything but nodded.

When Bram was gone, she poured herself another cup of coffee and sat staring at the table: two slices of ham; the butter dish with butter smeared over the side, his empty plate, which looked like he hadn't used it. He had the dirty habit of wetting the top of his index finger with his tongue and removing all the crumbs. Only the knife showed it had been used. He always wiped it clean on the edge of a slice of bread, but it didn't shine like it did coming straight from the dishwasher. She took the coffeepot, shook it and poured the rest into her cup.

Taking the cup with her, she sat on the couch and lit a cigarette. Her mind was with their conversation of the night before. She knew it sounded all very reasonable, but she had trouble remembering how it had exactly fit together. She felt like she had felt so often during her nursing course. When things were explained, it was all crystal clear, but when she had to do her homework later on, it was hard to understand. Still, she had passed her exams, so she had mastered enough to answer the questions and work as a nurse for twelve years. Maybe it was the Valium, she thought, although it had only been one tablet this morning. To be able to manage without was a slow process, but she would manage.

I think so, he had said when she had asked him if he was in love with her. She thought about him meeting her. Where? In bed of course. She forced herself to think about the two of them in bed and control her anger at the same time. Was it really what Bram always said, "only a pencil-length penetration for a couple of minutes, after which you took it back out"? If it was only *that,* she wouldn't mind so much. Like Marjet had once told her when it seemed as if Thijs was up for a change: "So what, he can only bang her, but he can't love her."

But Bram and Pauline would also eat together, which he would pay for, of course, from their money. And, of course, they would go to a nice place. For her nothing would be good enough. And *then* he wouldn't drink beer. Oh no, an expensive wine for sure. And the coffee would be accompanied by an expensive brandy, nothing less than a Remy. And all the time they would look into each other's eyes and talk. About what? About her? Having fun? About how they were taking her for a ride? She wasn't sure. Would Bram do that? Bram would walk away if he was fed up and would forget you. Bram had no need to poke fun at losers.

He had promised he would be back. All of a sudden she realized that he would not be back that same day but tomorrow, so he would spend the whole night with her. When she reached for another cigarette she saw that her hand was shaking.

Here we go again. Don't *do* it, girl. What did you conclude last night—there was nothing you could do but sit tight—so *sit* tight for God's sake, and for your own good.

She got up and decided to take the bike for a tour in the cold wind. Then she remembered that she had to pick up Dick. She would be alone with him the whole evening. What should she cook? She had to do some shopping. It stung her that Bram would be going to the finest restaurants with that woman, while she had to . . . But why? He wouldn't mind if she took Dick out for dinner. She had a car now. She could go anyplace she wanted. She could take Dick to Amsterdam, or The Hague, or Rotterdam. Even to Brussels if she wanted.

She left the table as it was, climbed into a jogging suit, fetched the bike from the shed and rode to Zandvoort, the southwesterly wind hitting her hard on the left arm, and she hitting back at the pedals as hard as she could.

At the boulevard, she turned left toward the cycle path that ran through the dunes to Noordwijk aan Zee. There she was alone with the sand reeds, and rabbits, the sea gulls, the fast-moving clouds. The wind strong on her right arm now, she had to stand on the pedals where the path ran uphill. She had figured out that she could make it to Noordwijk aan Zee but when she reached the golf club she had done 22.5 kilometers in an hour and a quarter. She decided to forget about the last two kilometers to Noordwijk aan Zee and turned around. Shifting into the highest gear, she pushed the pedals hard. Helped by the strong wind, she felt the power of her leg muscles, she heard the whizzing of the tires and she gave it all she had, making over forty kilometers an hour coming downhill, trying to race the clouds and the sea gulls that drifted on the wind.

It was clouding over when she put her bike back into the shed. Breathing hard and sweating a lot, she entered the house and ran the bath while she cleared the breakfast things from the table.

The hot water added heat to her already hot body. After she had dozed off a couple of times, she washed herself and got out. For a full fifteen minutes she kept sweating. Losing moisture and weight made her feel lithe. When she had cooled down a bit, she showered, standing under the icy water as long as she could bear it.

Opening the closet she pondered what to wear. The best of course, but chic or sporty? She decided for chic. His mother was chic, but she had a fur coat, too. Or should she . . . yeah, what? Maybe the great dame wasn't such a good idea. A skirt or jeans? A skirt. She didn't know why, but of that she was sure. She picked a tartan skirt from the rack and matched the overtone of tree-bark green with a spring-leaf blouse. She chose the boots she had bought in Milan three years ago, high heeled and amber colored. Putting on her beige raincoat with the epaulets and the wide collar, she inspected herself in the mirror and was rather satisfied with the impression of well-to-do sportiness.

Dick was surprised to see her enter the garage at a quarter past two. Bram had told him that he was going to Paris and that Willem would drop him off at the end of the day.

Everyone stopped what they were doing when Francien click-clacked to where Dick was working on the *Jiffy*. To her surprise, Francien saw that he was really dirtying his hands. The cart had been placed on a shelf supported by trestles. It enabled Dick to get his hands on the machine. His face had black smears, too.

"Hello."

"Hi."

"Good afternoon, madam," said Lazy Willem.

"Hello, Willem. I came to fetch your assistant for an afternoon at the Automobile Museum in Rosmalen. Can you spare him?"

"Francien, can't we go tomorrow? I'm very busy. Willem and I are just now taking the engine apart. Please?"

Dammit, she thought, Bram said he just hung around.

"Madam, don't listen to him. I wouldn't mind if you took him off my hands for half a day."

"Hey, Willem, come off it, will you?"

"Dick, you see that car over there, the blue 164? It has starting problems. It's being picked up today. We'll do more tomorrow. Go and wash your hands."

Dick dropped the wrench onto the shelf, rubbed his nose with the back of his hand and turned to Francien, looking skinnier then ever in the oversized overalls he had been given.

"Where did you say we were going?"

"The Automobile Museum, and we'll eat somewhere afterward."

"You mean the Autotron. I'll wash my hands." He turned his chair around and wheeled off to the washroom.

"And your face!" Francien shouted after him.

"A nice kid, wouldn't you say so, madam?"

"Yes."

"How is the beauty, madam?"

"I don't know." She just swallowed "you better ask my husband."

"How is that? You don't know? The engine ran like a twitter when I was finished with her. Do bring her in, then I can have a look."

She realized that he had meant her car and not Dick's mother. "Sorry," she smiled, "I misunderstood. She is fine. I love her."

"Don't let her get lazy. Step on it whenever you can. That's the way to keep her lithe."

"I will, thank you. And thank you for taking care of Dick last night."

"My pleasure."

The museum was a good choice. Dick did the talking and she did the listening. On the way back she picked the roadside restaurant west of

Utrecht along the A-2. No use going into town with the wheelchair and all that.

After Dick's enthusiasm about the automobile exhibition had run its course, Francien asked him about his father—where he was and when he had left.

"He is in the States and he left some time ago."

"Don't you miss him?"

"I don't know. He came in late and he left early. He never said much."

"Have you always lived where you are living now?"

"Yep. And you?"

"I was born in Rotterdam. My father was a sea captain. I never saw much of him, either. He drowned when I was young. I can't really remember him."

"So that makes us two of a kind, doesn't it? Can I have ice cream for dessert?"

Francien understood that Dick wanted to change the subject. They finished the meal talking about her car, his *Jiffy,* Lazy Willem and what Bram had arranged with Kees of the carting club. School was a topic that didn't last long. They were eating their dessert in silence when Dick suddenly looked up to Francien.

"Why did you take me out to the museum?"

"Because I thought you would like it."

"You didn't like me at first."

Francien was shocked. She looked into the steel gray eyes.

"What makes you think so?"

He shrugged. "Did you?"

"I didn't know you then."

"Can I stay up late till Bram comes back?"

"Bram isn't coming back tonight. He'll be back tomorrow."

"Oh."

"Are you missing your mother?"

"She's all right. She'll be back."

"Do you want her to be back soon?"

"Willem and I have to rebuild the *Jiffy* first because it's too heavy now. We are going to dismount the . . ." And on he rattled about how they would lighten it and that he had to practice more.

Apparently his instinct told him it was better not to discuss Bram's lover with Bram's wife. Children are very sensitive to matters concerning people they depend on.

Francien decided to leave him be and paid the bill. On the way back she stepped on it and overtook everybody, apart from a Porsche and a couple of Mercedes. Dick said nothing all that time.

When they were home she ran the tub and added a shot of bubble bath.

"Can you get into the bath by yourself or shall I lend a hand?"

"I don't need a bath."

"Yes, you do. You can't go back home stinking like a pig, can you?"

She walked into the bathroom, checked the temperature of the water, laid out a fresh towel and came back into the living room.

"Well, alone or together?"

"I have never been in a bath in all my life. We only have a shower. Mama puts the temperature right and I can sit on the floor."

"I checked the water. It's nice and warm. Dick, listen. I was a nurse for many, many years. I undressed young people, old people, boys, girls, men and women, so I know what you look like naked. No need to be embarrassed."

"They had feet."

"You're wrong there. I have seen them without legs, with arms missing, even with their prickies missing. You know what? You go into the bathroom and I'll give you five minutes to get into the bath. Put your clothes on the floor and try to get in. I've made a very special bath. Now get going."

She switched on the television and when Dick saw her watching the screen, he slowly wheeled to the bathroom and closed the door behind him. Francien turned the sound low but stayed where she was. After a while she heard a big splash and a bump like from somebody thumping the side of the bathtub. She jumped up and hurried to the bathroom, where she found Dick emerging from the layer of bubbles that covered the water. He had two inches of foam on his head.

"My eyes sting."

Francien filled a glass with water and threw it in his face.

"Wow, that's cold." Then he opened his eyes and looked at her triumphantly. "I made it, but it wasn't easy."

"You will learn, but I think I better lift you out, because if you slip onto the floor it's a much harder surface than the bath water."

She went to the kitchen to fetch a rag to mop up the water from the floor.

When she came back Dick was playing with the soapsuds, trying to blow bubbles.

"How do you make all this soap?"

She handed him the bottle. "Bubble bath. You can buy that."

"Now you can't see my feet."

"The trouble is, Dick, that I couldn't see your feet even if the water was crystal clear. However, it's not your feet that are important. It's your heart that counts. I'll leave the door ajar. You call me when you want to get out. All right?"

"Yep."

She went to the bedroom, took off her clothes and put on a white coat that did up at the back, which she still had from the time she wore them daily.

After a while Dick called. Francien came and lifted him from the water with one arm around his back and one under his knees. He had one arm around her neck. She lowered him onto the towel she had spread on the floor, and covered him up with the rest of it. Next, she picked him up again, towel and all, and carried him to the guest room, where she lowered him onto the bed.

"Just a minute."

Dick was shivering when she returned with a towel she had warmed on the radiator.

"Cold?"

He nodded.

She rubbed his hair dry, his back, his chest, his belly and legs, as far as they went. She inspected the sewn-up ends carefully and then looked at him. "That's a nice piece of work this surgeon did. Who did it?"

"Van Wouw or Van't Woud, I'm not sure."

"Dr. Verwouw. I know him, one of the best. You were lucky to have him. Now lie straight with your arms along your body."

With one jerk she pulled the towel from under him, turning him on his belly in the process, and started to rub his back dry with experienced hands that made his skin glow.

"Well, that's it, young fellow," she said, and when he turned on his back she tucked him in, kissed his forehead and patted his cheek. "Sleep well."

When she reached the door she heard his "Thanks."

After winking an eye at him and getting one back, she closed the door and went to clean up the bathroom and throw the white coat in the hamper: Waste not, want not.

While Francien was settling down with a cup of coffee in front of the television set, Bram was sitting looking at Pauline over the last glass of wine.

He said, "From what you tell me the job looks good. Earning twice as much isn't bad, but what will you do with Dick?"

"That's what I wanted to discuss with you. Will you take care of him?"

It took Bram quite a while before the full import of her question dawned on him. "You mean have him stay with us for that year?"

"Yes. If I take him along the consequences for him will be the following: a new language, a new school, a new house, alone when I am working, no friends, a new hospital. No more racing dream, no more Lazy Willem and no more Bram. I can't do that to him. I will turn this offer down if you can't have him. I know that I've got a lot of nerve asking you, after I turned you down when you proposed to me"—a shadow of a smile passed over her face—"but, Bram, from the beginning, I have said that what's between you and me shouldn't interfere with what is between you and Dick. I trust you agree with that."

Bram ordered coffee and two brandies and waited until the waiter had left.

"You should have become a solicitor. You certainly have a way of presenting your case."

"Please, Bram, try to see it my way. I would like to continue our relationship, but marrying . . . I haven't the nerve, because I don't think I'm cut out for it. My profession is the only thing I am good at. When my looks go, can you see me as a librarian, working in stuffy surroundings with worn-out books that have passed through more hands than a prostitute and then retiring when I'm sixty? Or marrying a rich oaf like, for example, that Steltenburcht?"

"But what do you want then?"

"I want to get some capital and then I want to buy myself a place in the fashion industry in a position where the decisions are made."

"Fair enough. And you think you can scrape together the starting capital in the States?"

"I have already saved up something. I think that I can save some twenty-five thousand dollars in one year. That's about fifty thousand guilders. I can borrow from the bank if I pay in that much myself, can't I?"

"If the bank believes in your business, yes."

"After one year I'll see. Either I come back, or Dick comes to the States, or he continues living with you. That will depend on you and him. Not on me. You know, Bram, he has lived with a woman for twelve years. His father never showed much interest in him. I think it'll do him a lot of good to live with a man for a while, before he matures. Can you understand now why I wanted to talk about a decision like this before I make it? Am I making the right decision? It may have far reaching consequences. You are the only one who cares for both of us. You can't find answers to questions like this with neighbors, colleagues or priests. That is why I had to see you, and I'm pleased you could make it."

"I see." Bram was holding his chin in his hand, elbow on the table. "I have been wondering since your call what it was that you had to talk about. But this! How do you imagine I tell that to Francien? No, don't answer that. Let's first talk about Dick. You pointed out the disadvantages for him of going with you to the States. What will be the disadvantages when you leave him behind? He'll lose contact with his mother, after already having lost his father. Aren't you afraid he may get the feeling that you are abandoning him? That you are trading him for a better job?"

"Bram, I understand what you mean, but listen. Who came into his life as the big guy who opens the door to the fulfillment of his boy's dream at the very moment all his chances of ever making it come true were blown to bits? You did. You gave him hope and a lot of it. Who do you think would betray him more? You by forcing me to take him with me to the States like a good mother should, or me leaving him in your hands?"

"I'm not forcing you to take him to the States. I'd rather force you to stay here."

"It's because of you, Bram, that I can't take him with me to the States. I may be able to find a friend who could keep an eye on him while I work. They have prostheses in the States as well, maybe even better ones. But where do I find a guy with a garage who is fond of him, and a Lazy Willem on top of it?"

"I swam into my own net? Is that what you mean?"

Pauline nodded and smiled. "But you trapped Dick and me as well."

"What if I sell the garage and we all go to the States? Then the whole thing would be solved."

"That's fine with me, as long as you don't see it as a dowry. The bride brings the dowry, not the groom. Have you already made up your mind about selling?"

"I can decide any moment."

Pauline lit another cigarette.

"How is Dick getting on with Francien?"

Again he noticed the ease with which she used his wife's name.

"They get along pretty well. I even think Francien would not really object to his staying with us, especially not when it means that you're clearing off. However, it might cause a problem if he would leave after a year the moment you wish it."

"I'm not going to wrench him away, Bram. It will be what Dick wants. He will be thirteen by then. Kids at that age are granted opinions of their own nowadays."

"Suppose Dick agrees. Suppose Francien agrees, and let's say I agree. Where do you go from there?"

"Let's walk back to the hotel and have a drink before we go to bed. I want you to hold me and I want to hold you. When is your flight tomorrow?"

"At three."

"Fine, mine is at two. We will have the entire morning together. Let's sleep on it."

They walked to the hotel, hand in hand, both with their own thoughts. They made love. Not desperately as at Schiphol, but with the tenderness of the bond that had hesitantly started to grow between them.

When they woke up they held each other once more and were just in time for breakfast. It was Bram who started on the subject again.

"So, I'm tied up on all sides. Will you break the news to Dick when you come back; I'll discuss it at home. When *will* you come back?"

"The third of January. He'll still have two days off from school. I will call you at the office. If Dick agrees, and of course if Francien agrees, you can come and pick him up after I have made some arrangements about my things—something like that."

"There is one right that I want to reserve. I want the authority to call the whole thing off after I have met Dick. I want to see for myself how he takes it. And if he loves you half as much as I do, I think he'll take it badly."

"The love of a child and the love of a man are two different things. But it's okay with me. I will keep myself tentatively committed until you have decided."

"Just to keep things completely clear, Pauline. What if one of us—Francien, Dick or me—doesn't like your idea?"

"Then I won't take the job. In a year or so Dick will be a different boy."

They went to the airport together, and when they kissed good-bye he slipped the small parcel with the ring and the poem into her handbag.

When he had passed the customs at Schiphol and walked into the hall, he was jolted into another world as he heard Dick yelling, "Bram! Bram!" and saw him wheeling toward him, Francien following a couple of meters behind. He dreaded the moment he would have to tell her about what he and Pauline had discussed in Paris.

Dick went in the car with Bram. Francien overtook them the moment they entered the highway. Dick waved when she honked and watched her speed away. "She is a swell driver," he remarked.

"Yeah, she's not bad."

"Can't you go faster?"

"Sure, but I don't see the use of risking a speeding ticket. I have already gotten two this year. Francien is still a *tabula rasa*."

"A what?"

"A clean slate. You don't lose your license the first time."

That evening Francien waited till she thought Dick was asleep.

"What was it all about in Paris?"

"She can get a job in America as a model. She did a show for the Americans in Paris. They want to break into the export market and have the idea that they need a European model—not just for her style, but also for her knowledge of the way shows are done here. She can get a contract for a year."

"Is she going to do it?"

"It's not as simple as that."

"Why not, if the price is right?"

"She doesn't want to take Dick to the States."

"Well, that's what I would call a lousy mother."

Bram exhaled.

"What real mother would leave her son behind if she got a job somewhere else?"

"Doesn't that also depend on what's best for the child?"

"So, she doesn't take the job."

"That depends."

"On what, for God's sake. You are beating around the bush, aren't you?"

"Not really, but I admit it looks like it. Okay, imagine Dick goes to the States. Any idea whether he would like that? What will he find there and what will he leave behind?"

"You don't want him to go, do you? And you do not want her to go, either."

Bram feared the conversation was heading in the wrong direction. He leaned forward and lowered his voice. "Listen, girl. Let's cut the crap about me wanting her to do this or that. There are four people involved: Pauline, Dick, you and me."

"Me?! What have I got to do with it?"

"Look here, the situation is as follows: Pauline refuses to take Dick to the States because she doesn't want to destroy his dream about becoming a racecar driver. I have kept that dream alive with the *Jiffy* and by promising him he can participate in go-cart racing. I made a contract with him, and he takes that very seriously. Willem has joined in and is his mechanic, so to speak. Pauline feels that his dream will be shattered if she takes him with her. Over there he will only be an invalid boy. On the other hand, she would like to take the job and she has asked whether we would look after Dick for that year. That's the story and believe me, I haven't been looking forward to telling you."

Francien opened her mouth and closed it a couple of times. Then she threw her hands in the air, shook her head and still couldn't find the words to express . . . she didn't even know what . . . such an absurd proposal! She was really flabbergasted.

Bram went to the bar and brought back two glasses of whiskey. Next he went to the kitchen to fetch some ice. When he came back Francien was still speechless. It surprised him that she hadn't yet burst into a barrage of abuse. He refrained from touching glasses with her, sipped his whiskey and then continued: "I can understand that you can't say anything straight away. I did spring this whole thing upon you. I can tell you that I feel trapped myself by this whole situation. Really trapped, I mean."

"Are you nuts, Bram?"

"Well, if I am, I would be the last to know, so you tell me, am I nuts?"

"But who does she think she is, dumping Dick with us and then dashing off to America?"

"Well, it's up to you. You can decide about the future of the other three involved."

"Me, how do you mean?"

"If you agree, Dick comes and she goes. If you say no, she stays and Dick stays with her."

"What about you?"

"I have already discovered that I have no say in the matter. So you can count me out."

"But Jesus, this is the bloody limit. When is she going to America?"

"That depends, but I have insisted that she talk with Dick first, and then I want to see him to find out how he feels about it. Then it will be up to you. For me it does not matter so much. If you say no, nothing much changes, does it? Anyway, I have told you. You can think about it. Pauline comes back the third of January, either to stay or to pack. And that's up to you. For the time being I suggest that we don't mention this to Dick. It's a matter between him and his mother right now."

Francien took her glass, needing a swig badly. Then they just sat for quite a while. They couldn't go anywhere.

15

It was the start of January in no time. With Dick really being able to assist Lazy Willem with the overall check of the *Jiffy,* he spent those few days on the work floor.

New Year's Eve was celebrated together with the Van der Bergs. Bram enjoyed buying and setting off the fireworks with Jeroen and Dick. Francien and Marjet had fun frying the *oliebollen* and the *appel-flappen.* Neither of them had made them before. It was only the home cooking freaks who still did. Most people bought them from the baker or from stalls that were put up in the streets when Christmas neared.

Together in the kitchen, accompanied by a bottle of sherry, they giggled a lot, but in the end managed to mix the 1,000 grams of flour, four eggs, 50 grams of yeast, 20 grams of salt and the 100-gram mixture of currents, raisins, candied orange and citron peel into a liter of lukewarm milk for the *oliebollen.* They had to stop Wanda from looking into the pan to see whether the dough had risen. She was afraid that there would not be enough for all of them.

The frying was fun, and standing on the kitchen stool, held tightly by Francien, Wanda was allowed to scoop up a spoonful of the risen dough and let it slowly glide into the oil. When it got a bit crowded in the pan, she was told to stop. Watching the swelling balls become brown, she discovered that one looked like a goat. "Look, that one looks like Uncle Bram!"

"He behaves like one, too, sometimes," Francien said to Marjet under her breath.

"Mine is more like an *appel-flap,* weaker inside, you know."

"Here's to them," said Francien, lifting her glass. "At times it's hard to remember why you chose them, don't you think?"

"That's not because our memory is so bad. It's because they change so much."

"Although the way I got my car, I don't know."

"You *are* a lucky dog, aren't you? When I want to buy as much as a salt shaker I get a complete course on economizing, alternative application, warnings against becoming a purchase addict—the whole lot."

"You are kidding. For a salt shaker?"

"You're right, I was kidding. I would never mention—"

"Now they all look like Negroes, Mama."

"Oh dear, the skimmer, quick!"

"We won't have enough, Mama."

"I won't throw them away, dear. We'll put them underneath the others. Maybe somebody likes them well-done."

Francien had put Wanda on the floor, and when Marjet put the next light brown load on top of the burnt ones, Francien watched with a sad face and shook her head.

Ladling new spoonfuls into the oil, Marjet glanced sideways. "Hey, what's the matter? There are more where they came from. I've bought enough stuff to supply an orphanage."

Francien shook her head. "That's not it. Why is it that the black ones always go underneath?"

"Simple. Because we hold the skimmer," and poking her elbow into Francien's side, she said, "Knock it off, will you? You are not going to cry! You know you look awful when you cry. It's bad enough that your hair smells like cooking oil. A good thing the whole house smells like it, too. That's what creates the real atmosphere of New Year's Eve."

After another cigarette and another glass of sherry, they started on the *appel-flappen.* They dipped the apple rings into the dough and then dropped them into the oil.

Half an hour later they entered the living room, each carrying a full plate, the soft sugar giving the pastry a wintry look.

Wanda, her elbows on the armrest of Bram's chair, leaned over, and told him in confidence, "The Negroes are underneath."

. . .

The day before his mother was to return, Dick said he would like to be at the airport when she arrived. Bram suggested that he should bring his things at the same time so that he could cart them both to Gouda in one trip.

Since planes from America arrived early in the morning, Francien had set the alarm for 5:30 A.M. so that they would have ample time for breakfast. Dick was still fast asleep. She sat on the side of his bed and watched his face—pale and regular, the eyelashes long against the white cheeks. He would undoubtedly become a handsome man.

She looked around the room, surprised at how quickly the boy had taken possession of it—a mess of dinky toys, comic books, Wanda's drawing stuck to the wall with a thumbtack, and two library books on the small desk. The *History of the Combustion Engine* lay open and next to it a sheet of paper with something scribbled on it and a sketch of a go-cart passing the finish line at full speed. At the back were more carts, but they were still a long way off from the man with the checkered flag.

Boys, she thought, out to win, at that age already. No wonder males ruled. They started fighting earlier than girls and for other purposes. Their life was, as a matter of fact, simpler than that of women. They just fought the other males and fucked the females. Nowadays women had to fight the male of the species and sleep with him, too.

After shaking Dick several times, he came to life.

"Up, my boy. You have to be at Schiphol Airport at seven."

Dick yawned, stretched and studied her.

"I'll have breakfast ready in twenty minutes," she said.

"Are you coming with us?"

She shook her head, rose from the edge of the bed and turned toward the closet. "Do you know what you are going to wear?"

He didn't, so she went through the little pile of clothes and picked a shirt, a sweater and trousers.

Apart from "Pass me the butter, please," "Can I have the salt?" and "It's a soft winter so far," they ate breakfast in silence. When they were getting into their coats and scarves, she had the feeling of them being two men on a mission and she wondered if they felt that way, too.

It was still dark outside, apart from the circle thrown by the outdoor lamp. They loaded the car and took off. When the taillights disappeared around the corner, she shivered and went inside.

Coming into the living room, the silence and the used breakfast table depressed her. She had always hated after-meal tables. They were so demolished; *raped* was a better word: pieces of food on the tablecloth, smeared knives and forks, dried-up drops on the cups, crumpled-up napkins with the smears on them, the tacky yellow bottom of the orange-juice jar, the sticky glasses.

She shook the coffee pot. There was still some left. She cleared the table and went back to bed with *De Telegraaf* and the rest of the coffee. She could not sleep anymore. She leafed through the paper, but wasn't interested in cars crashing, trains crashing, planes crashing, politicians crashing. The only thing at that moment was whether her marriage would crash.

Her confidence had been restored a bit with Dick around. His careless chatter, their meals together and at regular hours. Now that he was gone, she had a feeling of emptiness. She tried to imagine what it would be like if he would be there for a whole year. It seemed a long time when it was ahead of you, but afterward, she knew, she would wonder where the time had gone. Not that she had decided yet. She just couldn't make up her mind.

What should she do? What would happen if after a year his mother wanted him back? Wouldn't she grow very attached to him and wouldn't Bram? But would Dick want to go when this racing thing—whatever they were dreaming of—developed? What chance would there be that he would want to leave?

What if the adoption came through in the meantime? A year, Mrs. Jas had said in their last interview. That could be the coming summer. Where would they put a little baby if Dick was in the guest room? A stone fell on her stomach as she wondered whether Mrs. Jas had read about her killing the robber in Italy. A little baby with a woman who smashed skulls. The small statue of the Goddess of Peace had wandered from the living room to the bedroom to the guest room and was now in the storage loft, gathering dust. So was her pride about that encounter.

The morning paper slid from the bed. She let it be. Why couldn't they live like other people? Like Marjet. She looked at her watch. Eight-thirty, too early to phone. Having a hunch that Marjet couldn't help her, either, she tried to make her decision alone.

At nine she did phone and at ten Marjet arrived.

"My goodness" was Marjet's reaction when Francien finished recounting events. "When did you say you have to make up your mind?"

"Tomorrow, or the day after. Something like that."

"Any idea what you are going to decide?"

"No. I can't seem to think it all through. I feel like somebody is forcing me into something that I might not have objected to if it had been my own doing. I get so fed up with that woman messing around with my life. I don't call her a slut anymore. I discuss things with Bram, and when he mentions her name in my house, I don't throw things. Even when I know that he is going to see her in Paris and I am convinced that he is going to sleep with her, I sit tight. But, my God, how long will she be prowling around my marriage like a tiger around a village? And what can I do? Nothing. I can't go out and shoot her. To sit and wait is not my style. I'm an attacker. I want to blow her to bits."

"And have Bram collecting the bits and pieces and putting them in a shrine?"

"I know, but what if Dick wants to stay? I already miss him this morning, and that's after only a little over a week. What about a year in which he also has to learn to walk on prostheses?"

"Well, Francien, if Dick hates you after a year and you him, then it's simple. Just good riddance. But suppose you become very fond of each other and all the ties get stronger—with Bram, with Lazy So-and-so, the cars, and you. What will happen then? Will he jump when his mother decrees?"

"Perhaps not, but how am I to know?"

"You aren't. We all run risks. What if you have a baby of your own? How are you to know it won't be born blind, deaf or dead? How are you to know it won't die from crib death? You can lose Bram, me or your own life. You don't even need a year for that. What do you think I feel about the certainty of having Jeroen and Wanda? You read the papers, too."

"I know, but that's different. You are not facing the situation that by the end of this year somebody will come and tell you whether Jeroen can stay or not. And what if she comes back to Holland and wants Dick to live with her again? Who can refuse that? Suppose she comes and lives in Haarlem? So that he can easily stay in touch with the garage? Then there's not a single reason that he shouldn't go back and live with his mother."

"If you say no, she won't go?"

"Yes, that's what Bram says."

"Would you be worse off then than you are now?"

Francien pondered the question. Would she be worse off if Pauline stayed in Holland? It struck her as crucial. When she knew the answer to that, she would know what to do.

"Darling," Marjet continued, "we are housewives and they are always looking down their noses at us as without profession. It took twenty years to make the cops accept *housewife* as a profession when they gave you a ticket, and still there are those die-hard judges in court who can't say 'Your profession is housewife?' They just say 'You are a housewife?' Every workman is entitled to a canteen where he can eat in peace and where somebody cleans up after him. Not you. All the guys can go home and forget about their jobs. We can't. We eat on the job, sleep on the job. We have to clean the sheets we are laid on."

Francien sat looking at Marjet with a worried face.

Marjet frowned. "I'm sorry, dear. I got carried away. You are facing a tough decision, and you are on your own in this. When you see all the marriages that hit the shoals, wedlock looks like a kind of roulette. Thirty percent in our country, fifty percent in the States. So let's hope you have a lucky hand. Keep me posted. If I think of something, I'll let you know. Yes, there's one thing: Taking care of the boy for a year will enhance your adoption chances."

"You think so?"

"Yes."

Bram carried Pauline's suitcases inside her house. He kissed her good-bye while Dick was inspecting his room after his ten days absence.

"Dick! I am leaving! Tomorrow is Wednesday, so I'll see you tomorrow afternoon."

"Why!? I'm still off from school. Why can't I come now?" He glanced at his mother. "Or tomorrow morning?"

"You better sort that out with your mother. I'll see you some time tomorrow. You two have a lot to talk about."

He ruffled Dick's hair and left.

Dick watched as he closed the door and then spun his chair around to his mother.

"Did I do something wrong?" he said.

Pauline shook her head. "No, you didn't. Tell me all about your stay. After that, I'll tell you all about my visit to the States."

"You like him, don't you?"

It took her a second to understand what he was asking. "He is a very nice man. Now tell me, how was it? How was the Christmas party? Did you get nice presents?"

So, Dick told and Pauline sat listening. She enjoyed his enthusiastic stories about the garage, the museum, the Christmas party and the fireworks at New Year's Eve. He left out the miniature.

When he finished, Pauline said she had to do some shopping since there was nothing in the house. In the meantime he could unpack the presents she had brought him. She put them on the table and told him to wait till she was gone.

He didn't even notice her going or coming back. Flat on the floor, he was trying to steer the Porsche and the Thunderbird at the same time. It wasn't easy. His left hand was very clumsy.

"Hey, you fool, can't you drive?" he shouted at the Thunderbird. "Don't they have drivers' licenses in the States?!"

When he saw Pauline's feet he looked up, a broad smile all over his face. Pushing himself onto his knees, he stretched out his arms, but as he was too heavy Pauline sank to her knees and received his gratitude sitting on her heels.

"You like it?"

"Sure, but it's difficult to keep the steering apart."

"You didn't even unwrap the rest."

Dick walked on his knees to the table, scrambled onto a chair and opened the other two parcels.

One was a book about the history of the Ford motor company and the other a watch with so many buttons that it took him a long time to deduce their functions. The more he tried it out, the more he liked it. The stopwatch included the time per lap and the total elapsed time.

She sat down next to him at the table. He put his arms around her and leaned his head against her shoulder. She stroked his hair. They sat in silence. After a while he straightened himself up.

"What is it like in the States?"

"I don't know, I was there for only ten days and America is so very big. It's two hundred, thirty times bigger than Holland. There are about two hundred twenty-six million Americans and there are only fourteen million in Holland. The only thing I can say is that they are friendly people, that it is a huge country, that they have a lot of space and that they have a job for me."

"You mean work?"

"Yes."

"In the States?"

"Yes."

"For how long?"

"A year."

"I *can't* go away that long! I have to race next month. Can't you postpone it?"

"Maybe I could, for a week or so."

"Yes, but . . ."

He couldn't grasp all the consequences right away. "Why do you want to work in America, anyway?"

"Because it's a better job, a much better job."

Dick sat in silence, fiddling with his new watch.

"Let me make something to eat," Pauline said, and went to the kitchen.

While she was busy, Dick mulled the consequences of going to America: saying good-bye to Bram and Lazy Willem and *Jiffy* and the go-cart races and the contract.

Pauline came back from the kitchen with two plates. "Milk or Coke?"

"Coke, please."

As they sat and ate, he looked up at her. "You are teasing me, aren't you?"

Pauline shook her head.

Dick bowed his head and concentrated on his sandwich. He had lost his appetite.

"Can I take the *Jiffy?*"

"That might be possible," she said.

"But I don't know anybody there. Is Bram coming with us?"

"Why would he?"

"Anyway, he won't like it, I'm sure."

"Not like what?"

"That I'm going away."

"That's not a factor."

He nibbled some more at his sandwich, drank from his Coke, and avoided his mother's eyes. He said, "You like him a lot, don't you?"

"Yes. I do like him a lot."

"Then why go away?"

"Because I would like to take that job, if it can be arranged."

"Arranged?"

"It seems to me that you would rather stay here. Is that so?"

"I don't know anybody in the States. And I have a contract with Bram."

"Well, what do we do? I would like to go and work and you would like to stay."

"Can't you go and I stay?"

"Just like that?"

Dick remained silent, and looked at his plate. Then his face lit up. "I can stay with Bram, till you come back."

"Are you sure?"

Without answering her question, he dropped what was left of the sandwich onto his plate, nose-dived to the floor and crawled like a baby to the desk where the telephone was.

"Hey, wait a minute. What are you going to do?"

"Call Bram and ask him."

She rose, walked up to the desk, took the receiver from his hand and cradled it. Dick sat on the floor. Pauline also lowered herself to the carpet and smiled at him.

He did not return it, but looked at her with reproach.

"Why don't you ask him tomorrow? Then you'll have more time. Isn't that better than bluntly putting it before him over the telephone?"

His face softened. "Does that . . . does that mean that you wouldn't mind me not coming with you?"

"I *do* mind. I mind very much. But I also understand that you don't know anyone there. But living with Bram and Francien for a year is way different from living here. You will have to go to another school to start with. And what about Bram's wife?"

"She's all right. She's a swell driver, and she said that my feet had been sown up nicely. I had a bath."

"Really! And could you manage?"

He grinned somewhat sheepishly. "Not so well. I nose-dived into it and it took a while before I surfaced. The water was all covered with bubbles. Funny, just like sitting in warm snow. You know you can buy bubbles?"

"Yes, my dear, I know. There are a lot of things you can buy when you have the money. That's why I want to take that job."

"Will we be rich then, and are you then going to buy a convertible like Francien's?"

The following morning he was up at seven and at eight-thirty he was wheeling into the workshop, disappointed that Bram and Lazy Willem weren't in yet. He wheeled toward the *Jiffy* and was surprised to find it looked so new. The new aluminum adjustments for his feet shone silvery. It had new tires. On the back of the seat was an ALFA ROMEO sticker.

He was burning to get into it, to feel the engine's vibration in his butt and the road in his hands. It would go fast; he was sure he could beat the others now. He would be the fastest. And later he would drive real cars, with engines that roared when you stepped on it.

"Winning races again?"

Bram's voice startled him from his reveries. Dick blushed.

"What brings you here so early, young man?"

"Can I stay with you, when Mama goes to the States?"

"When what?"

"When Mama goes to the States. She can get a job. Otherwise I can't race the boys, and I can go to school here. Francien wouldn't mind, would she?"

"That's a lot of questions. Why don't you come to my office and explain what this is all about."

Seated opposite each other, Bram heard him out.

"Mama doesn't mind if I'm not coming."

"She doesn't?"

"Sure, she does, but she doesn't . . . I mean it's okay with her, and when she's rich, maybe I can be with her in the summer holidays, when I can walk again. What do you think?"

"I think a son should be with his mother and not with strangers."

Taken aback Dick stared at him. "What strangers?"

Bram didn't answer. He only thought, This boy will be a tough nut to crack if he continues this way.

"Where are we? Your mother wants to go to the States and you want to stay with us. That's it?"

Dick nodded.

"You say your mother agrees with your staying behind with me . . . with us?"

Again Dick nodded.

"I think I would like to hear that from her. Any objection?"

"You don't belie—. Okay. You ask her." He pointed at the phone.

"Later. Next, there is the question of whether Francien is eager to have another man to look after—to wash his clothes, to cook his meals, to buy his Coke, to sew buttons on his shirts."

"She won't have to mend my socks or polish my shoes," he joked.

"You know what? As far as I know, Francien is at home, and if you really have spunk, go and see her and talk her into it yourself. It's okay with me. You never doubted that, did you?"

"You mean I must ask her?" Dick looked from Bram to the phone and back.

"Why not? Ask her if she can see you. One of the boys can drop you off. I have work to do. Good luck."

Patting the boy's shoulder, he left the office and told Belinda that he was off to Brussels and would be back by the end of the afternoon.

Dick sat staring at Bram's phone. He couldn't possibly have put into words why, but asking Francien was way different from asking Bram.

He looked at his new and complicated watch. Too early yet.

Belinda came in, said hello to Dick and put the mail on the desk. Could she help him one way or another? She went around nipping yellow leaves from plants here and there. "Are you sure there is nothing I can do for you?"

"No . . . I just have to make a phone call."

"Don't you know the number?"

"It's too early yet."

"It's after nine. It's not Sunday. Who is it you have to call?"

"Mrs. Aardsen."

"The boss's wife? She's in the automatic dialer, here." And before Dick realized what Belinda was doing, she had pushed a button on a kind of box and handed him the receiver as she left.

"Mrs. Aardsen speaking."

"Hello, Francien? It's me, Dick."

Francien sat with the phone in her hand until she noticed and cradled it.

"The fucking bastard."

She spoke the words out loud and from the bottom of her heart.

"Sending the boy straight to me. He *is* a coward. Hiding behind a child."

But this means, she realized, no further postponement. He is coming to see me. So he's in favor. Bram doesn't object, even though it means *she* will be gone.

What bugged her most was the fact that it was *that* woman who had thought the whole thing up. Her hatred hardened. No way, that she was going to look after *her* brat, and for free on top of it. They had again worked it out nicely between the two of them. Send the boy and she cannot possibly refuse.

But I can refuse everything! Crippled or not, doesn't make a difference. Bram's very words were "treat them like normal people," and so I will. My nursing days are over and I don't intend to start a private clinic for the offspring of his mistresses, the motherfucker.

Here she stopped herself. Dick was on his way. They could all go and soak their heads.

The sound of a horn made her look up. The minibus was there and one of the guys from the garage was lifting Dick out. He held the garden gate open for Dick to wheel through. The wind was tugging at Dick's white hair. His face had the same color. A bag of bones, she thought, and went to open the door and help him up the steps.

Once inside, he took off his windbreaker and Francien moved a chair away from the dinner table, so that there was space for the wheelchair.

"I haven't had coffee yet. You care for a Coke?" she said.

"Rather, coffee."

"Coffee?"

Dick nodded.

"Okay, coffee it is. I have to make it but I won't be long."

In the meantime Dick was trying to formulate his request. Gradually, he realized it wasn't so easy to ask somebody to look after you for a year, the more so with the handicap he had. Once he had his prostheses it would be easier. Then he could walk and sit on any chair he liked.

Francien came back with the coffee. He still did not know how to start.

"Sugar and milk?"

"Yes, please."

Sitting opposite each other, she controlled her aggression toward Bram and he smiled faintly when he looked at her.

"Well, Dick, you wanted to see me."

"Mama is going to the States and I don't want to go. I asked Bram if I could stay with him. Here, I mean. And then he said I should ask you."

He was visibly relieved he had said it.

"Well, you can't. It's nothing personal but I don't feel like it. Also, a son belongs with his mother."

"What is *personal?*" He was fidgeting with his fingers.

"Well . . . uh . . . I mean . . . it's not that I don't like you."

"It's only for a year."

"That's quite a long time."

"When I have my feet back, I won't be a problem. Then I can take a bath all by myself." He was breathing rapidly.

"With prostheses? It will take months before you can walk properly. You think that they are just like a pair of new shoes? They are not. You'll have to learn to walk like a baby. A few steps a time. It'll be a long period of trial and error."

He hadn't realized that. Nobody had told him. He did realize, however, that he'd brought up the wrong thing. He felt very small and hadn't touched his coffee. Forcing himself, he tried it, but Francien saw from his face that he didn't like it.

"Wouldn't you really rather have a Coke?"

"When people talk business they drink coffee, not Coke." He didn't look at her when he said it, and he drank some more.

"So you want to talk business with me?"

He nodded, uncertain whether he was making things worse or not.

"Okay, let's talk business. What about the costs?"

He looked up at her. "The costs?"

"Yes, you would need food and clothes and pocket money, wouldn't you? Who is going to pay for all that?"

His first thought was Bram, but he swallowed that. "Mama is going to be rich in America. Can I ask her?" He looked in the direction of the phone.

"No need to just now. What about your school? You can't be commuting up and down to Gouda every day."

"They have schools here. I can go to school here, can't I?" He recovered himself a bit now that he could answer her questions.

"And who will be looking after you, when you have to learn to walk again?"

"I can learn it by myself."

"You can't. That would take ages. You will need somebody to help you. To push you. To stimulate you. Somebody who knows what it takes."

His hopes sank. It had all seemed so simple. He fought his tears looking into his cup.

"But I don't know anybody at all over there!" The desperation rang through his voice.

"No, I guess not."

Francien rose and went to the kitchen, leaving Dick with the feeling that the discussion was over and that he had failed.

When she came back, she put a glass of Coca-Cola in front of him and moved his cup of coffee aside.

"People *do* talk business over Coke as well."

When he looked up at her, she saw that he was trying desperately not to cry.

"Oh damn it. To hell with the lot of them. I'm going to get you back on your feet again, come hell or high water. I'm the only one who can handle that properly, but don't give me anymore of that business-talk crap. And I'm not in for that contract business that you have with Bram. You do as I say, there and then, and only what *I* say. Is that clear?"

Completely taken aback by her sudden outburst, he stared at her, trying to understand what she had blurted out and wondering whether he should say that it was clear or not.

"Does that mean that I can come?"

"Only *if* you will promise to do exactly as I say when you have to learn to walk again. And don't agree to it lightly. It will be a rough time, but I will get you back on your feet again. Yes, you can come."

With a sigh of relief he lost control over his tears and stretched out a hand to Francien, whom he only saw in a blur.

She took his hand, squeezed it hard and then went into the kitchen to fetch another cup of coffee. When she came back he looked at her, and there was still a trace of disbelief in his eyes.

"It's all right, don't worry. But don't forget about the costs. You're her son, not mine. So let's keep that straight. Will you take care of that?"

"Sure," he nodded. He leaned back in his chair, happy but very tired.

When she dropped him off at the garage, she went to the office and asked Belinda if Bram was in.

"He's in Brussels, he'll be back later in the afternoon. Shall I ask him to call you when he comes in?"

"No, never mind." It was better this way. It wouldn't do to give him a piece of her mind in his office. The bastard, sending the kid to do the dirty work.

Brussels, my ass—Gouda for sure. Anyway, I am sending that bitch off to another continent. The moon would have been even better.

When she crossed over the work floor, Dick called her.

"Look," he said, pointing at the *Jiffy*. "Beautiful, isn't it? New tires."

"I like my car better."

He grinned. "Of course, but you wouldn't fit into this one, anyway."

She lightly pulled his hair and left for Marjet's.

When Bram came home that evening, her anger was gone. Marjet had convinced her that it was far better this way. Now it was between her and the boy and not some decree handed down to her by Bram.

"I heard from Dick," he began as he put his coat away. "He was quite pleased. You apparently had a nice chat."

She looked at his face, expecting him to be cynical, but he went on in the same casual way.

"He said you would help him get back on his feet again, but that he had to talk with his mother about the costs."

"Naturally, I'm not going to fork out all that money while she is getting rich in America."

He realized he shouldn't forget she still hated Pauline.

"When will he be coming?" she said.

"I don't know. Do we still have time for a drink or have you got dinner ready?"

"We can still have one."

———

The day of Pauline's departure Bram left early in the morning. When he pulled the front door closed behind him, Francien woke up. Through a slit in the curtains she saw how he put his flight bag and a suitcase in the trunk, got in and drove off. She did not pay much attention to it. With all his traveling it was a familiar scene to her. Snuggling back underneath the blankets, she thought about preparing the guest room for Dick, and how she could make it more like a boy's room. Then she fell asleep again.

At nine o'clock Bram told Belinda that he wouldn't be back and left for Gouda.

The front door of the flat was ajar, so he entered. There was nobody in the living room.

"Dick!"

No answer.

He waited in the middle of the living room. Somebody had pushed the button of the hall door lock, so somebody had to be in. He walked toward Dick's room, opened the door and looked in. He saw only a suitcase and some plastic bags grouped in the middle of the room, waiting to be taken away.

Pauline's room? He hesitated. Then he sat down and lit a cigarette, but he felt ill at ease. He rose again, went outside and looked up and down the street to see whether Dick might have gone down to wait for him or maybe Pauline had gone down to buy a last item.

When he returned to the flat, Pauline was standing in the living room, an expectant smile on her face. Bram stopped dead in his tracks and stared at her.

"Well, what do you think?"

Bram stared at her hair—platinum blond! It was Pauline, all right, but . . .

"What have you done with your hair?"

"Nothing, this *is* my hair. Don't you like it?"

"Uh, yes, but . . ." He kept looking at her. "It isn't black!"

"No. This is my natural color. So, you don't like it?"

"I do. It's nice, but . . . you look like a different woman."

"And you are not going to kiss this different woman?"

Bram smiled sheepishly, walked up to her, put his arms around her, but kept looking at her hair. Pauline put her arms around his neck, pulled him toward her and kissed his lips.

Close up, the impact of the platinum hair was even stronger. He closed his eyes and kissed her back.

Pauline released him and held him at arm's length. With an amused smile on her face, she slowly shook her head.

"You are a monogamous man, Bram. Many a man would get a kick out of his woman suddenly looking like someone else."

"It is very becoming. You look like a Teutonic goddess. You had dyed your hair black?"

"Yes, but in America I want to be my real self, the way I was born, and I wanted you to see me like that. The black-hair-and-blue-eyes combination was effective for modeling but fake. There's too much of it in my life. My marriage was a fake, so my name is a fake. My profession—the show of a gracious, queenlike, very rich, lovely young woman who feels at home among the smart set, like a fish in water—all a fake. I sometimes even wonder if my motherhood is not a fake—leaving my child in your hands."

"You know better than that. By the way, where is Dick?"

"At school, saying farewell to his teachers and his friends."

"You have already packed all your things?"

"All done."

They stood holding each other when the front door opened and Dick wheeled in, a full plastic bag on his lap.

"Mama! Hi, Bram. Mama, look what I've got!" He held up the plastic bag. "A book from the headmaster, an English dictionary, and dinky toys from the boys and a kiss from Yolanda. It's all in here," he said, pointing at the bag.

"The kiss, too?" Bram asked.

"It's here," he said, pointing brazenly at his cheek, but he did blush a little.

"Okay," said Bram, "let's get moving."

Sitting at the dinner table having her breakfast, Francien thought with satisfaction that she had handled things well of late. A few more hours and *she* would be gone.

She wondered whether Bram would come straight home from the airport or still go to the garage. She walked to the phone and dialed the office. Belinda told her Bram was gone.

"Sorry, Mrs. Aardsen, he's gone and he won't be coming back."

Of course he would be coming back. Then she remembered him throwing things into the trunk. What things? A suitcase . . . What for? And a flight bag . . . What for? Verwal? In Gouda?

She did not have the number. She phoned information and got it. However, when she called, an impersonal female voice told her, "This number is not in use. Please check the phone book or ask information."

An alarm bell rang in her mind. Then she remembered that, two days earlier, Belinda had said he'd gone to Brussels. She hadn't believed it; Gouda, she had thought. But that Steltenburcht, he was a Belgian. Brussels? She wasn't quite sure of that, but Bram had a firm offer. He had said that he could just accept it, collect the money and walk out. But leave Dick, with his racing? She shook her head. Of course, with that much money he could buy a garage in America and ten go-carts. God knows, maybe the money was already in America. Maybe the money had been in America all along. But the garage—Belinda was still there, and Lazy

Willem, and all his men. He couldn't just walk away from it. But if he could walk away from her, why not from his staff?

Panic crept into her heart. She paced up and down the room, looking for something—something that would tell her it wasn't true. The house— *their* house—the furniture, his chair. But, of course, *she* wouldn't want his old furniture, what with a million guilders . . . ?! What a sucker she had been. What a miserable sucker.

Perplexed by her own naiveté she sank onto the couch, and looked at the bar. Off the booze and on the bike—She reached for the phone, but didn't pick it up. What good could Marjet do? Marjet would ask when Bram was expected back. She didn't know, she hadn't asked. Later, if at all.

She rose, walked to the bar, opened it and stared at the brown liquor in the decanter, her self-pity fighting hard with her survival instinct. If she drank now, she would drink herself to pieces. She shut the bar with a bang, put on trousers and a windbreaker, and hurried to the shed. The bike was there. She hesitated. All those times she hadn't minded getting on it. She had even started to enjoy it. But now . . . She felt she was being pushed and she didn't like being pushed. She didn't want to be pushed around anymore! Dammit! She was nearly forty. Why could they all manipulate her as they pleased? That filthy Italian, Lanjoni, that woman, Bram, Dick . . . She remembered the gray eyes brimming with tears, afraid that he would be rejected. Afraid, afraid—it was always fear that did you in.

She stood at the entrance to the shed, one hand on the knob, looking at her bike and feeling very much alone. She closed the door slowly and went back into the house.

So she was alone. So what? She'd been alone before. The mantel clock struck when she entered the living room. Eleven. She would know in a couple of hours.

If he's gone, I've lost. If he comes back, I win. She repeated to herself: If he comes back, I win.

The ugly fear and the panic slowly moved over for the tension, to sweat it out. Hadn't she sweated many times before? After exams, after their first meeting, when he'd promised to phone?

If he comes back, I've won, she told herself again. The realization she still had a chance lifted the deadly gloom. She had fought back, mostly against herself but she had fought, protected her interests.

She walked into the bedroom, threw the windbreaker on a chair and kicked the trousers after it.

I'll goddamn cycle, when it suits *me*.

Under the shower, the hot water needling her skin full blast, she realized the woman would still be there—far away, but there. Smile about it? She couldn't. She had understood what Marjet had meant, how it could reduce a great love to an immature whim. Yet she couldn't smile about it. At best she could . . . ignore it. That was it. Ignore her. Ignore that she was anything more than Dick's mother. Ignore that Pauline was his lover.

Since she couldn't handle it, anyway, what else could she do? Ignore was as near as she could get to "smile about it."

If he comes back, I've won.

She closed the taps, dried and dressed. She felt better. She had found an attitude toward what had nearly done her in. However, the tension remained. It made her restless. She had to move. She would do what she had intended to: turn the guest room into Dick's room.

With her coat on, her car keys in her hand, she glanced over the living room. Then she went to the bar, took a big swig from the decanter, and wiped her mouth with the back of her hand. She felt she had deserved it— earned it. The welcome shock of the liquid.

In the car she restored her lips in the mirror. If he comes back, I've won, she repeated to herself, and started the car.

On the way to the airport not much was said. The approaching separation quieted them. Dick's bags had been left behind. The wheelchair took up too much space.

Unloading the luggage, Bram saw the flight bag with the camera in it. He had intended to take a picture of Pauline, but he left the bag and camera where it was.

After Pauline had checked in, she came back into the visitors' area. "I nearly forgot. Here are the keys to the apartment. Can you drop them at the address on the label? That's the company that will store my furniture. It's in Moordrecht. You can also mail it, if it's too far or inconvenient."

"No problem," Bram said, putting the keys in his pocket.

Then they stood together awkwardly. Dick's presence precluded what was left to say between the two of them. Dick, paler than normal, looked at the people milling around, without really seeing them. Every time Bram looked at Pauline, he had the feeling that he had already lost her before she had really left. It was only the hair color, he realized that. But there was no time anymore to get used to it.

She said, "I'll write to your home address and I'll keep it cool."

"That shouldn't be too difficult for you," said Bram, but his smile softened the words. "I have never met anyone as cool as you. I mean your head, not your heart."

"Maybe you're not used to that," she said, and then, "I think I better go before I get bitchy. I really do appreciate what Francien is prepared to do. A pity you can't give her my love."

They hugged, clung and kissed, and then she squatted beside the wheelchair and the two of them also hugged, clung to one another and kissed. To his surprise Bram saw tears on Dick's closed eyelids. Pauline had to free herself from the boy's grip. After kissing him once more on the forehead, she picked up her handbag and her beauty case and walked toward Passport Control. She disappeared inside without once looking back.

The man and the boy stood staring at where she had vanished but she didn't reappear.

Without a word Bram, turned around, gripped the handles of the wheelchair and started pushing Dick to the exit. It took Dick a few seconds before he realized what was happening. Then he grasped the wheels, halting the chair, and shouted, "I can do that myself."

Shocked, Bram let go of the handles and followed the boy through the automatic doors and to the parking lot.

On his way to the storing company in Moordrecht, Bram realized that he had forgotten the metal sheets to slope the thresholds for the wheelchair. Swallowing some curses, he turned back. Dick did not bother to ask where he was going. He just sat and stared ahead of him. Not a single word had been spoken between them since they had left the airport. It was the first time Bram felt the full load of responsibility for this child. Their feeling of loss was the same, but they could not share it. Nor could he take away the boy's unexpected but evident misery. He felt too miserable himself.

After he had picked up the metal sheets and handed over the key in Moordrecht, he took the freeway to The Hague and from there sped on to Haarlem, disregarding the speed limits. In spite of the fact that he needed all his attention on the road, he saw the boy sitting big as life beside him, yet he couldn't touch him. The fury with which Dick had shouted, *I can do that myself!* had created an emotional chasm he could not bridge.

When they arrived, Francien wasn't there. They both hid their disappointment. The burden of the silence between them grew heavier. When

Bram asked Dick if he wanted something to drink, the boy shook his head. At a loss, Bram switched on the television.

In the 747 Pauline rested her head against the back of her seat, closed her eyes and felt the pain of the farewell. If it hadn't been a plane but a train that was taking her away from the two men she loved, she might well have descended at the next stop to take the first train back. Now she refused to let her emotions run away with her, and kept repeating the arguments that had led to her decision.

She would only know whether his love was genuine, and not a mixture of guilt and admiration, if it survived that year. They would all be terribly hurt if it didn't work out, all four of them. A senseless divorce for Francien and Bram, a dying love ending in a broken relationship, and Dick in the midst of it growing up. She shuddered.

He would have to sort out his relationship with Dick first, rid himself of his feelings of guilt and bring his fatherly feelings down to normal proportions once the newness wore off. He would not sell the garage. She was sure of that. He might have done it a year ago. Too many strings held him now.

For Dick it would be a godsend to be in a man's world for a while. Something she could never have provided. They would have their fights and learn from them. Dick could try out his dream of racing. She hoped it would wear off.

It was all so clear, but still the yearning remained. When the stewardess came, she turned down the lunch. She didn't feel like eating.

Turning into their street, Francien saw Bram's car. An enormous relief surged up inside her. Her gas foot went down of its own accord. She honked loudly as she halted her car, tires screaming. When she saw Bram rise, she waved, grabbed a couple of plastic bags from the backseat and hurried up the path.

Bram opened the front door. "Where have you been?"

It took her a few seconds to realize he'd said his farewell. It tempered her enthusiasm but didn't affect her satisfaction.

"How is he?"

"Miserable."

"Hello, Dick, how is it? Why are you sitting with your coat on?" She put the bags on the table and turned to him to unbutton his coat.

"I can—"

"'. . . do that myself,'" she cut him off, and smiling at him she proceeded to pull the coat off and throw it on a chair near the table. Combing his hair with her fingers she said, "Now have a look at what I got for you."

She unrolled a sheet of paper and held it up. It showed small boys in go-carts flashing by, the colored helmets blurred by the speed, the front wheels of the leader of the pack off the tarmac, as if the cart were going to take off. Dick's face brightened as Francien handed it to him.

"And what about this?" She unrolled a second poster, showing a Formula One Ferrari in a neck and neck race with a Porsche. "You think you can stand them in your room? Now come and tell me where you want them. Can you pour us something to drink, Bram, and a Coke for Dick?"

Not waiting for Bram's confirmation, she proceeded to the guest room with Dick following her, but he had trouble with the threshold. That reminded Bram of the metal sheets, so he fetched them from the car and fitted them over the thresholds to the living room, the kitchen, the bathroom, the guest room. Francien was following Dick's directions for hanging the posters and arranging his drawers.

When he brought a whiskey for her and a Coke for the boy, Dick had a gold-colored racing helmet on his head and was unwrapping a parcel. He put the glasses on the small desk and went to retrieve from the car Dick's suitcase and the one he'd taken that morning to put loose things in.

Back in the living room, he sat down, sipped his drink and watched a children's program on the television. Pauline would be well on her way by now.

All through dinner Francien and Dick kept up an easy banter, barely paying any attention to him.

When Francien had put the boy to bed, she came back into the living room. "He's all right now. Go and say good night to him."

Sitting on the side of the bed, he took the young boy by the shoulders, pulled him up and held him close. After lowering him back onto the pillow, he touched the boy's cheek with his open hand. "See you tomorrow. Good night."

"Good night."

Before he switched off the light he noticed the golden wheelchair in an open space on the bookshelf.

Bram was glad that there was a soccer match on TV, and when it was over he suggested they call it a day. There was nothing to talk about. When

Francien came out of the bathroom Bram was already in bed, flat on his back, his hands behind his head, staring at the ceiling, a forlorn look on his face. Francien got in on her side, dimmed the lights far down and turned on her side towards him.

After a while her eyes got used to the near darkness.

"Bram?"

"Mmm."

"You remember the night in Italy when we had dinner together?"

"This year?"

"Yes, but it's already last year. The very neat restaurant, the night before we were arrested?"

"Yes."

"You remember how we talked about all the places where we could go on holiday next year?"

"Yes."

"That is settled now."

He was not in the mood at all to talk about vacations, so he remained silent.

"This summer we'll go to America. Then you and Dick can go and see his mother, while I'll tour the country by train. He should be walking by then."

They both held their breath. Then he reached up and turned off the light, because he did not want her to see that he was fighting tears. He didn't know what to say, but he knew that if he were to speak, he would fall apart.